WARRIOR'S HEART

COLLEEN HALL

To my good and long-time friend, Cindy Jantz, who read my childish scribblings and every manuscript since then. She's been one of my most loyal supporters who tells me she always knew that one day I'd be a published author.

ACKNOWLEDGMENTS

Many thanks to my long-suffering husband, who put up with long evenings and late nights while I closeted myself in my workspace with my laptop, who cheerfully ate sandwiches for supper, cleaned up the kitchen, and folded the laundry so I could work on my latest manuscript. He accompanied me on endless research trips and visits to museums. I tell him that it's a good thing he enjoys history!

Thanks also to my very techy sons and my artistic daughters-in-law. My sons help me when technology gets the better of me, and my daughters-in-law lend their artistic talents to creating swag and helping with my newsletter. My writing journey has become a family affair.

Thanks to Andrea Eliasson, my friend from church who critiques my manuscripts and gives me invaluable feedback. She's one of my biggest supporters, and I depend on her for sound suggestions.

And my acknowledgements wouldn't be complete without mentioning my editor, Eden Plantz, who kindly points out things that makes my manuscript a better book and guides it all the way through the editing process. Thank you very much, Eden.

ABOUT THE AUTHOR

Colleen Hall wrote her first story in third grade and continued writing as a hobby all during her growing-up years. Writing her Frontier Hearts Saga has allowed her to combine her love of writing with her love of history and the West. In her spare time, she enjoys spending time with her husband and family, working with Monty, her Morgan/Paint gelding, reading, and browsing antique stores. She lives in South Carolina with her husband and family, one horse, and two very spoiled cats.

You can follow Colleen at colleenhallromance.com.

ALSO BY COLLEEN HALL

The Frontier Hearts Saga

Her Traitor's Heart

Wounded Heart

Warrior's Heart

Northeastern Colorado Territory
Spring, 1876

CHAPTER 1

The rider halted his mount on the bluff's crest and remained poised for a moment, silhouetted against the blue Colorado sky. Della Hunter rose to her feet. She shaded her eyes with her hand and frowned. Something familiar about the man nagged at her memory.

The spring bunch grass rustled in the restless wind and made Della's split riding skirt play about her boot tops. The blue silk bandana tied about her neck flapped, and the chocolate-colored curls that had loosened from her French braid danced about her face. The breeze teased her nostrils with the scents of ripening earth and wildflowers. She ignored the distractions while she studied the horseman atop the ridge.

The High Plain's greening swells spread out on both sides of the rider, creating a stage with the sky as a backdrop. He and his mount appeared to be carved from ebony, motionless except for the horse's billowing tail. Though some distance separated them, the man's stare touched her. An uneasy *frisson* shivered down Della's spine.

The rider on his piebald mount eased off the rim and angled down the slope. They reached the bottom of the bluff and approached her at an easy walk.

Without seeming to hurry, Della left the grave where she'd been kneeling and paced to the cemetery gate. The spiked iron barrier squealed when she pushed it open. She stepped toward her gray grulla gelding, ground-hitched just outside the fence. While the horseman drew near, she stood at the gelding's shoulder, within easy reach of her Winchester.

The rider halted mere yards from her. Recognition punched Della in the chest. She hadn't seen this man in almost seven years, yet she knew him. *Wild Wind.* Shane's Cheyenne half-brother sat his mount almost within touching distance.

For silent moments, Wild Wind stared down at her. An eagle feather fluttered from a lock of his long, dark hair. A fringed buckskin shirt and leather leggings molded to his muscular frame. A rifle slung over his shoulder hung from a leather strap.

The years they'd spent apart hadn't tempered his arrogance. He sat tall and erect upon his mount, head unbowed, his lean features expressionless. At last, he spoke. "Lona."

Hearing him utter the name he'd given her years ago took her back to the weeks she'd spent in his Cheyenne village. Weeks when she'd thought she would marry him, if Shane didn't rescue her first. Remembering the more recent tales she'd heard of Wild Wind and his Dog Soldiers fighting the army in bloody raids during the last six years reminded her this man had a reputation as a fearsome warrior. "Wild Wind. Do you come in peace?"

He nodded. "I have laid down my rifle and no longer wage war against the pony soldiers, or your people."

"We have no cause to fear you?"

His unblinking regard held her gaze. "I did not raise my hand against your uncle or his people in all my years of fighting. I will not do so now."

"That is good. And how is Yellow Wolf?"

"My father lives on the Cheyenne reservation in Montana."

Della nodded. She'd heard that Congress had designated a large portion of land in southern Montana to be a Cheyenne reservation. "Is he well?"

"He is well, but we have no buffalo to hunt. There is little food, and there is sickness among our people."

Della reached out to him, then dropped her hand to her side. "I'm sorry, Wild Wind. Truly, I'm sorry. Uncle Clint is raising beef cattle to sell to the army for your people, so that should help."

"The cattle do not always reach the reservation."

She suspected corruption in the Bureau of Indian Affairs might have something to do with the cattle not reaching the reservation. "I'll have Uncle Clint look into it. He has contacts with the army."

Wild Wind shifted on his mount. "Your uncle, the general, is an honest man. I believe he may help us." He glanced about. "And where is my brother, Little Wolf?"

His words pierced Della's heart, reminding her of why she'd come to the cemetery. Gathering her composure, she closed her eyes and breathed through her nose. Tears pricked behind her lids, but she willed them away. She opened her eyes and motioned toward the new grave inside the railed iron fence. "Little Wolf... Shane... your brother is there."

Wild Wind's nostrils flared, though he gave no other sign the news touched him. "What made my brother travel the Road of the Departed?"

Della stared at him, struck mute. To reply would be to experience again her bereavement, yet Wild Wind deserved to know how his brother had died. She made an attempt to detach herself from her painful loss and recite the details as though Shane's death had happened to someone else and not herself. "A terrible blizzard hit us in late February. Shane and some of the men rode out to bring the horses in off the range. The snow cut them off before they could get home. His mustang brought him back, but it was too late. He froze to death."

Wild Wind seemed to contemplate the news for several moments before he motioned toward Shane's grulla gelding. "You ride his mustang."

"Somehow, riding his horse makes me feel closer to him." Della stroked the grulla's neck. Silence fell between them while they eyed each other. "And what of you?"

"I have been on the reservation for many moons." He paused. "I married Little Fawn."

Della tried to smile at him. "I'm glad you found someone to love."

Wild Wind lifted his head and stared down his straight nose at her, all male arrogance. "I married Little Fawn because her brothers died fighting the pony soldiers, and she had no one to care for her. She did not bring the sunshine to my heart."

Della covered her mouth with one hand, unsure of what to say. She couldn't look away from Wild Wind's savage face. Lowering her hand, she said, "Did you leave her in your village?"

He shook his head. "Little Fawn and our babe died from the illness that takes many of my people on the reservation."

Della caught her breath and stepped closer. "I'm so sorry. I know Little Fawn loved you very much."

With fluid grace, Wild Wind slipped from his mount and strode toward Della, halting before her. Though his chiseled features remained a stony mask, his blue eyes, a legacy from his blond-haired mother, blazed down at her. "A cold wind has blown through my heart since you left. My heart is frozen, as the ice in winter."

Della quailed at his fierceness. Though she'd seen his gentle side, in many ways he remained wild and untamed. His primal spirit, obviously untempered by the intervening years, reached out to her. She wanted to step away, to put more distance between them, but to do so would be to admit he intimidated her. Instead, she jutted her chin and met his relentless stare. "A marriage between us wasn't meant to be."

"You married Little Wolf. The news came to me on the wind. To think of you married to my brother made my heart howl like the wolf grieving for its dead mate."

"I loved him very much. I love him still."

"Was there sunshine in your lodge? Did Little Wolf make your heart soar as the eagle?"

Della squeezed her eyes closed and shut out the warrior standing before her. Her throat clenched, and she had to swallow before she could speak. She opened her eyes. "Yes. Shane and I were very happy."

Wild Wind moved closer, crowding her. The fringe on his buckskin tunic fluttered against her short sheepskin jacket. Though his nearness made her palms sweat, Della refused to back away. Their stares locked, while his essence nearly overwhelmed her. She couldn't breathe.

"Is there no room in your heart for me?"

"My husband is recently buried. I cannot think of love for another man."

Wild Wind nodded, then said, "It is fitting that you mourn my brother. He was a good man. I can wait. I have the patience of the hunter."

Della thought it time to change the conversation. "Why are you here?"

"I cannot live on the reservation. The army wanted to take my horse. I will not give up my horse. I am not a man without my horse." Fierceness tightened Wild Wind's face. "They wanted me to give up my rifle. I will no longer kill your people, but I will not give up my rifle."

He paused while he swept the prairie's billowing knolls with a penetrating stare. "My spirit dies on the reservation. I thought to come to my brother and ask if he has a place for me on the ranch. I can work the horses."

What would Uncle Clint's reaction be to Wild Wind working on the Slash L? Della wondered. Would he trust Wild Wind? Still, since Shane's death had left them without a trainer, they needed someone to gentle the four-year old Morgans purchased by the army. "Come along with me. I must discuss this with my uncle, but you can stay until I've talked to him."

They mounted their horses. Della cast a final glance at the scar of earth that covered her husband. Tender spring grasses made a pale verdant carpet over the mound of his grave. The resting place of their two-year old daughter lay beside him. The loss of her daughter and that of her husband left a wound she thought might never heal. Feeling Wild Wind's burning scrutiny, she glanced at him. Sitting astride his gelding, Shane's brother watched her with the unblinking intensity of a predator, yet she trusted him.

"Lona, one day you will look at me with sunshine in your eyes. Your heart will heal."

"I cannot think of it now. I mourn your brother."

"I will give you time to mourn him. Then I will court you. You will melt the ice in my spirit, and I will bring sunshine into your life. Our hearts will beat as one, and we will marry."

Della couldn't reply. Recalling Wild Wind's determination to marry her when she'd been a captive in his village, she didn't doubt his intentions. She decided to deal with him later. At the moment, she felt too raw to challenge him on the topic.

Turning Shane's grulla gelding about, she headed in the direction of the ranch. Without speaking, Wild Wind rode beside her. His presence filled her with a tumult of emotion, battering her from within and threatening to destroy her hard-won control.

CHAPTER 2

Della eased her mustang down the slope toward the ranch. Wild Wind straddled his bareback gelding as though he were an extension of the horse. Never could she have foreseen this moment, when a Dog Soldier of fearsome reputation would accompany her home.

The track from the cemetery meandered down a gentle knoll toward the high adobe wall that enclosed the ranch courtyard and buildings. Since Clint Logan had expanded his business to include raising cattle, his holdings had increased by several thousand acres, spilling over into the Wyoming territory. The headquarters for the cattle side of the business had sprung up along one outside wall of the enclosure that surrounded the house and original buildings. A large horse barn had been built at the edge of the prairie, with smaller buildings and housing for the men and their families clustering closer to the headquarters gate. The compound resembled a small town.

Della and Wild Wind rode through the arched gate into the Slash L headquarters. The imposing two-story, black-shuttered white frame house Clint Logan had built for his family reigned along the back of the adobe wall's right flank. To their left, the corrals and a weathered wooden horse barn took up most of the compound's area. Between the barn and the family dwelling rose a blacksmith shop and the bunkhouse for the horse wranglers. Tucked into the space next to the bunkhouse and the family's spacious dwelling squatted a small adobe house where Emory Dyer, who kept the books for the Slash L, lived.

Della halted Shane's gelding in the middle of the courtyard and glanced at Wild Wind.

"Are you sure you want to stay?"

Wild Wind lifted his head and scanned the compound, then swung his blue stare back to Della's face. "You are here. I wish to be no place else."

"Very well. Let's put our horses in the corral. Then I'll show you where you can sleep. Before we married, Shane lived in a stall in the horse barn. It still has a cot and some furniture. You can stay there. I think you'd prefer that to living with the other men in the bunkhouse."

Leading their mounts, they crossed to the corral. An urchin who appeared to be about five years old erupted from the horse barn. He charged toward them. Spurts of dust rose around his booted feet at each step. The denim-clad youngster flung himself at Della's legs. "Mama! Where have you been? I looked everywhere for you."

Della knelt and gathered the boy in her arms, hugging his sturdy frame. She tousled his hair with her fingers, hair the same dusty blond color that Shane's had been. Peering into his face, she said, "I visited your papa's grave. I told you I'd be back."

The worried expression that had filled his blue eyes eased. "You did come back."

Della nodded. Her glance trailed upward to rest on the looming titan who had followed her son from the barn. Scipio, the head wrangler entrusted with the responsibility of her uncle's horses, came to a halt behind her son.

"Jake, he worried when you were gone a long time. He thought he might lose his mama, too." Scipio propped both fists on his hips and frowned down at Della.

She caught the mild reproach in Scipio's tone. Since Shane's death, Jake had clung to her. She rose to her feet. "I'm sorry, Jake. I lost track of the time." Della placed both hands on her son's shoulders and turned him to face Wild Wind. "Here's someone I'd like you to meet. This is Wild Wind, your uncle. He's your papa's brother."

Jake caught sight of Wild Wind. His blue eyes, identical to his uncle's and testimony of their shared lineage, grew round. Della wondered what her inquisitive son might say, but he remained mute.

Wild Wind crouched, bringing his height down to the boy's level. For a few moments, the two regarded each other before Wild Wind addressed his nephew. "I see my brother's son is a small warrior. You will grow to be a brave man."

Jake stared at his uncle, taking in his dark hair and burnished skin. "You don't look like my papa."

"I am your papa's brother. You will see we are not so very different."

With lithe grace, Wild Wind rose to his feet. His gaze snagged Della's, and wordless communication pulsed between them. When she'd lived in his village, he'd told her she would give him brave sons. The unspoken memory hung in the air.

Della cleared her throat and nodded toward Scipio. "Wild Wind, let me introduce you to Scipio. He has the responsibility of our breeding stock and is the personal groom for Uncle Clint's private horses. Scipio, this is Wild Wind, Shane's brother."

The two men, equal in height, took each other's measure. Finally, they acknowledged each other with stiff nods.

"Wild Wind will be staying in Shane's old room in the barn," Della continued. "He may be training the four-year-olds."

"Does your uncle know this?"

"Not yet, but I'll send him a message."

Scipio shrugged but didn't comment. "Me, I've got work to do." He turned on his heel and crossed the yard, disappearing through the barn's wide double doors.

When Wild Wind had been settled in his quarters, Della trudged to the house, Jake's small hand tucked into hers. Coral, her uncle's Southern wife, met her on the veranda. A blue shawl tossed about her shoulders provided protection against the spring breeze. Della climbed the steps, with Jake skipping along beside her. At the top, Della loosened her hand from her son's.

"Why don't you find Flossie? Then the two of you may go to the kitchen and ask Silvie for a piece of gingerbread."

At the promise of gingerbread, Jake scampered into the house. The door banged shut behind him.

Coral observed her husband's niece in silence.

Della returned the perusal, reflecting that no matter how hot or cold the day, Coral always presented a picture of refined elegance. Not a hair strayed out of place in her upswept, curled coiffure. From the top of her sorghum-colored hair to the hem of her blue and white striped dress, Coral embodied the ideal of stylish Victorian womanhood. Her slender figure showed to advantage in the current fashion of straight lines at the skirt's front and masses of fabric gathered over a bustle in the back.

Coral nodded toward the barn, indicating the newcomer who now stood in the doorway. "Who is that?"

Della glanced across the yard at the imperious figure who stood proud and erect, looking out across the ranch compound. He turned his head in her direction, and his stare touched her once again. "That's Wild Wind, Shane's brother."

Coral's eyes widened. Everyone in the family knew the story of Shane's and his mother's capture by a band of Cheyenne warriors when Shane had been a child not much older than Jake. The Cheyenne chief had loved and married Shane's blond-haired mother and had adopted Shane as his own son. Wild Wind was a product of that marriage. Coral caught her breath. "Isn't he dangerous? The stories I've heard..."

"He told me he no longer fights the army and has been living on the reservation. I believe him. And we have to admit that Wild Wind and his Dog Soldiers never attacked our people or stole Uncle Clint's horses in all the years they fought the army. Wild Wind promised me he wouldn't, and he kept that promise."

"I suppose... but what brought him here?"

"He wants a job. He thought to ask Shane if he could help with the horses."

Coral studied her niece, sympathy softening her features. "We do need a trainer."

"I know. I'll send a message to Uncle Clint and ask what he wants me to do."

"He'll trust your judgment. You and Shane have been handling the training side of the horse ranch ever since you married. My husband will defer to your decision."

"Still, I should ask." Della laid a hand on Coral's arm. "Aunt Coral, you needn't stay here at the ranch with me any longer. Uncle Clint needs you in Denver. I can manage by myself now."

Coral lifted her head. "I'll stay here as long as you need me. Don't chase me back to Denver before you're sure you're ready to handle everything by yourself. Clint doesn't expect me any time soon."

Obeying a sudden impulse, Della bent and hugged her diminutive aunt. "I know, and I appreciate the sacrifice you and Uncle Clint made for me after Shane died. But it's time for me to pick up my life and move on. Uncle Clint needs you with him in Denver."

"Right now, he and the other delegates are too busy drafting the Colorado state constitution to think about their wives. I'm sure he doesn't even miss me. I'll stay here for a bit longer. The ranch is a much better place for the children than Denver."

The spring winds gusted about the corners of the house and danced along the veranda. Afternoon sun slanted across the yard. Blue shadows streaked the ground.

Della glanced at the barn. Wild Wind had vanished.

Later, after the children had been tucked into bed and the house had settled for the night, Della retired to her room, shutting the door behind her with a soft *snick*. Moonlight's silvered glow spilled into the chamber. Her glance swept the empty room, a room bereft of Shane's presence, and a chill froze her heart. Her head drooped. At last, in the privacy of her bedchamber, she could stop pretending to be brave. No one could see the loneliness she hid or the fears she tamped down. Here, in her room's privacy, she could wallow in her grief.

She pushed off the door and crossed the room. Nights were always the worst. Lying alone in the wide bed, without the comfort of Shane's loving arms, sleep refused to grant her relief from her sorrow. She lay awake into the wee hours, missing Shane's warmth beside her and remembering shared laughter, shared dreams, and shared love in that very bed.

    Halting near the four poster, Della plucked Shane's worn black cowboy hat from the lamp table beside the bed. Her fingers trailed along the hat's brim. Memories of Shane wearing this hat flashed through her mind. Images of him smiling at her beneath the brim battered her without mercy. With the headgear clutched to her bosom, she collapsed onto the mattress, falling sideways onto the crocheted white coverlet. She tucked herself into a ball. The fingers of one hand curled into the counterpane while scalding tears seeped from her eyes.

CHAPTER 3

Della squeezed her eyes closed against the morning sunlight filtering through the lacy drapes at the windows on either side of her bed. She groaned and rolled over. Couldn't she indulge herself for once and stay in bed? Must she get up and drag herself through the day, pretending to be strong, hiding the grief that smothered her spirit with its black mists?

Wild Wind... The memory of the warrior's reappearance into her life brought her upright. She must arise and face the day. Jake, whose young life had been devastated by Shane's death, looked to her for security. The men who worked the horse ranch needed her direction. To think of herself now and to neglect her responsibilities would be the height of selfishness.

With a heart-weary sigh, Della thrust back the covers and swung her feet to the floor. She pushed aside the chocolate curls that tangled about her shoulders and dangled across her eyes. The early morning chill nipped at her skin, raising goosebumps along her arms. Reaching down to the foot of the bed, she grabbed the robe she'd left lying across the coverlet and shrugged into its warmth. When she'd toed her feet into her slippers, she rose and drifted across the room to the marble-topped walnut vanity located near the fireplace.

Leaning over the vanity, she peered into the mirror. A tall, slender girl with haggard features stared back at her. The morning light embellished half of her face with merciless clarity. Lines of exhaustion from too many sleepless nights etched both sides of her mouth and framed her eyes. Perhaps a little powder would conceal the ravages.

Curls tumbled about her back in a chocolate cloud. Since her marriage, she'd fallen into the habit of leaving her hair loose at night instead of braiding it into respectable order. Shane had loved her hair and preferred her to leave it loose in the privacy of their bedchamber. She closed her eyes in an effort to block out the memories of the countless times he'd tangled his fingers in her tresses and buried his face in the chocolate mane.

She could almost hear his Western drawl calling her "Della, darlin'."

Pinching the bridge of her nose between a thumb and forefinger, Della dragged in a deep breath and opened her eyes. Her reflection stared back at her. Curls danced about an oval face. Sooty lashes framed exotic, almond-shaped violet eyes. "Pansy eyes," Shane had called them, due to their color. Her gaze dropped to her mouth, full and lush. Shane had so loved kissing her.

Each feature brought memories of Shane's adoration, recollections of whispered love words in the dark while he worshipped her beauty.

A sepia tintype in an ornate oval frame rested on the vanity's marble top. Shane stared back at her from the photograph, his expression grave. His hat, worn low over his brow, shaded his eyes. Seeing his image in the frame clenched her heart, searing her with pain so intense she staggered and grasped the vanity's edge to steady herself. "Shane," she whispered. "How can I live without you?"

She whirled, turning her back on the mirror and the tintype. Her gaze fell to the worn leather Bible lying on the lamp table. Shane's Bible, which they'd read together in the evenings. The patterned Aubusson carpet muffled her footsteps as she crossed the room. Della lifted the Bible from the table and dropped onto the bed. Opening the book, she turned to a favorite passage where the Lord promised never to leave or forsake His people. She needed the Lord's presence now, when she felt so alone and helpless. After meditating on God's promise and offering a heartfelt prayer for strength, Della returned Shane's Bible to the lamp table and rose.

Responsibilities awaited her. People needed her. She could shirk her duties no longer. Squaring her shoulders and lifting her chin, Della hurried across the room to the mahogany wardrobe and opened the door. She pulled her clothes from their hooks and flung on a split riding skirt and a blouse. With nimble fingers, she styled her hair in a French braid and tied a piece of rawhide about the tail. After stomping her feet into her riding boots, she left the room and went downstairs to the kitchen.

∼

Della balanced in both hands a plate heaped high with fried potatoes, steak, and two biscuits dripping with honey. A white napkin draped over one wrist. She crossed the yard with careful steps, wending her way to the horse barn. Her shadow danced before her across the packed dirt.

She failed to see the figure leaning against the corral fence, but she heard her name when he called.

"Lona!"

Della halted and turned. Wild Wind straightened his long length away from the rails and, with ground-eating strides, approached her. When he stopped before her, she tipped back her head to look into his face. His blue eyes settled on her with a gladness and warmth he didn't attempt to conceal. For long moments, they stared at each other. The force of his presence reached out to her, surrounding her, taking her back to the days she'd spent in his village when his claim on her had protected her from harm. She almost felt like that girl again.

Her gaze roamed over his face. Wild Wind really was a most impressive specimen of manhood, Della mused. His hard features melded both sides of his heritage. From his Cheyenne father, he'd inherited his light bronze skin and glossy dark hair. From his blond mother, he'd inherited his blue eyes and his refined cheeks and square jaw. His patrician nose could have graced a Greek coin. Wide shoulders filling out his fringed deerskin shirt were heavy with muscle. The long, supple limbs beneath his deerskin trousers belonged to a warrior. Years spent beneath the hot sun and buffeting winds had scoured any softness from him.

Recalling that Shane had told her the tribes considered the Cheyenne to be the nobility of the plains, Della thought Wild Wind seemed every inch a regal chieftain.

She trembled, remembering the time she'd seen him dressed for battle, wearing only a breech cloth, war paint, and moccasins. He'd captured her that day, taken her captive to his village, and set about wooing her with a gentleness she'd not expected from so fearsome a fighter.

"Lona."

Wild Wind's husky voice recalled her to the present. She indicated the plate of food in her hands. "I brought you breakfast."

He nodded with grave appreciation. "Thank you for seeing to my needs." His chest rose and fell as he exhaled a deep breath. "Only now, I cannot fulfill a husband's duty to provide for his wife. I can give you nothing that others have not already provided for you."

"Our ways are different from those of The People, but white men also provide for their families. If we marry, you will do as others in my culture do. And just so you know, I didn't cook this." Della nodded toward the plate. "Cooking isn't one of my talents."

"Yet you brought it to me."

"You must eat. Until we decide what to do with you, I'll bring you your meals."

His eyes glittered down at her.

"And you promised to give me time to grieve. I'm not your wife, and you aren't my husband. You shouldn't speak so."

Wild Wind's nostrils flared, and he pinned her with a fierce stare. One large fist pressed against his chest. "Here, in my heart, you are my wife. You belong to me. Little Fawn did not take your place in my heart."

Della sighed. "Enough. Let's go into the barn. You can eat in there."

He nodded. "I will eat. And I will wait, but in the end, you will be my wife."

Della shook her head at him. "This time, I have a choice. I'm not a captive in your village."

His lips firmed before he replied, and his eyes grew flinty. He crossed his arms over his chest. "I could carry you away to the mountains, where no one would find us. We would live together as husband and wife."

She lifted her chin, and her eyes challenged him. "You could, but you won't. Would you take me from my son? You have more honor than that. I will come to you willingly, or not at all."

A trio of wranglers interrupted them, crossing the yard from the cook shack to the corrals. The men's curiosity turned hostile when they saw Wild Wind. One of the men spat on the ground as they passed, giving Wild Wind a belligerent glare.

Della shot a quick glance at her companion. His face remained an impassive mask. Not by so much as the flicker of an eyelid did he acknowledge the insult.

When the wranglers had passed them, Della said, "Come, you must eat. Then I'll show you around."

Inside the barn, the scents of horses, hay, and leather greeted her. Della led the way to the tack room. Setting the plate on a flat-topped trunk, she dragged a stool close. She laid the napkin beside the plate and pulled a fork and a knife from a pocket in her riding skirt. Placing the utensils on the napkin, she stepped back and motioned toward the makeshift table. "Eat."

While she prepared the table, Wild Wind had watched her without speaking. Now he stepped to the trunk but didn't sit. "I would have you join me."

Della stared at him. It had been her experience while living in his village that the women served the men and ate after the men had finished. For Wild Wind to invite her to join him was a breach of custom. "You want me to sit with you while you eat?"

"It is the habit of your people for men and women to eat together, is it not? I am here, among your people. I would do as your people do."

Della scrounged the tack room. In place of a stool, she found an empty wooden bucket which she tipped upside down opposite Wild Wind. When she had seated herself on the bucket, he lowered himself to the stool.

Della watched him reach for the silverware. His long fingers handled the utensils as deftly as though he'd used them every day of his life, though she doubted he'd touched a fork since he'd run away from the army fort after he'd been taken there with his mother when she'd been rescued. Staring at his hands, strong and beautiful, Della's imagination conjured the violent things those hands had done to her own people. The tales of his brutality toward his enemies abounded. What had she been thinking, to invite him to work at the Slash L?

She shivered.

Wild Wind paused and laid down the silverware. He frowned across the trunk at her. "Lona? You are troubled?"

She caught her breath and attempted to distract him. "Why do you ask?"

"You are the heart of my heart. I would know what troubles you."

Della met his gaze, deciding only complete honesty would serve. "Wild Wind, are you sure you want to work here? The men won't take kindly to you being at the ranch. There may be trouble."

"I have met trouble before. It is nothing new."

"Yes, but the men may be angry and afraid of you. Some of them have families. They've heard stories of your raids. Can I trust you not to hurt anyone?"

Wild Wind rose from the stool with lithe grace and crouched beside Della. One hand cupped her cheek with a gentle tenderness at odds with the strength so evident in his powerful frame. The fingers of his other hand wrapped about her own hand where it lay on her lap. He squeezed. "I told you I have laid down my rifle against the pony soldiers and your people. I will not go back on my word. I would do nothing to hurt you or those about you."

Della stared down into his face, a hard face stamped by a life of battle. Lines grooved furrows around both sides of his mouth, lines that hadn't been there when she'd known him as a younger warrior. Yet she saw determination there, as well, and honesty in his promise to her. In the tack room's dusky dimness, he seemed earnest. She couldn't insult him by offering distrust in return for his pledge. "Very well. I believe you. But we must expect trouble. It will come. All the men know about you is what they've heard."

Wild Wind nodded. Knowledge of the unspeakable atrocities committed by the tribesmen upon white settlers hung unspoken between them.

"And another thing. Here, at the ranch, you should call me Della."

His expression firmed in denial. He shook his head. "You are Lona. I cannot call you Della." His thumb stroked once across her cheek before his hand dropped. Pushing to his feet, he returned to his seat.

Of their own volition, Della's fingers touched the cheek he had just caressed. In spite of herself, his tenderness moved her. Perhaps Wild Wind's presence presented more of a danger to her heart than to anyone else at the ranch.

CHAPTER 4

With Wild Wind at her side, Della stepped from the barn's shadowed interior into the morning sunlight. Together, they crossed to the larger of the two corrals, where the Morgan horses purchased by the army had been penned. Della and Shane's brother reached the corral bars. Della rested her forearms on the top rail. Wild Wind stood at her shoulder, considering the horses inside the pen.

The wranglers had forked hay into the enclosure, and the Morgans gathered around the feed, keeping a wary eye on the two humans outside the fence.

Wild Wind seemed content to stand at her side, and Della felt no compulsion to break the silence. She relaxed against the rail and savored the moment. Lifting her head to the sun, she closed her eyes and relished spring's warmth. The constant breeze feathered about her face, pulling errant strands of hair loose from her braid and tugging at the brim of her black cowboy hat. Feeling herself watched, she opened her eyes and cut a glance at Wild Wind.

Her companion had turned sideways and propped an elbow on the top rail. Once again, the force of his presence, so close to her, nearly overwhelmed her. He leaned against the fence post, staring at her with unnerving intensity.

Della pivoted, dropping her arms to her side. "What? What is it? Why are you staring at me? Do I have dirt on my face?"

An expression she couldn't interpret flashed in Wild Wind's eyes before a corner of his mouth lifted in a lopsided smile. He stroked a finger down her cheek. "No dirt on your face." He lowered his hand to his side. "I am getting used to looking at you. For long years, your memory has been as smoke in the wind, yet my heart remained true to you. Now I stand beside you, close to you, and you fill my senses. We are together again."

His fervor held Della captive. She couldn't wrench her gaze from his face. The sounds of the ranch—the horses chewing hay, men calling to one another, the clang of metal ringing on metal from the blacksmith's shop—all faded from her consciousness. His determination to wed her battered the defenses she'd erected. "It's not as simple as you believe. And you promised to give me time to grieve."

"You will grieve, and I will wait. You haven't realized it yet, but our destiny is written in the stars. We shall be one."

"I don't believe in signs, not like that."

"Believe what you will. It won't change what will be."

Della glanced across the corral, a part of her mind aware of the Morgans bunched against the fence on the paddock's far side. She tucked an errant curl behind her ear. "Wild Wind... I don't know what to say. You've knocked my whole world out from beneath me."

Standing motionless while his attention ranged over her face, Della submitted to his perusal.

"When I heard that you had married my brother, I had no hope. My life was as ashes in the wind. I cared not whether I lived or died. My warrior brothers and I fought the Crow and the Kiowa. I counted coup many times on my enemies. Bullets buzzed about me as angry bees when we fought the pony soldiers, but their bullets wouldn't touch me. My medicine must have been very strong. Death wouldn't come to me no matter what I did. I lived, and your memory stayed with me."

"Perhaps God protected you from the soldiers' bullets. He must have a plan for you."

Wild Wind shrugged. "My life is what it is. Now we are together again, and life is precious to me." He made a closed fist and raised his hand high, then opened his fingers and thrust his palm beneath Della's nose. "I hold your heart in my hand. I will keep it safe until you give me your heart, freely. As you hold my heart in your palm."

"I don't want to hear this."

"You must hear this." Wild Wind straightened away from the corral post and looked down his aristocratic nose at her. "When I chose to leave the reservation to come here, I thought to look on you as a sister, since you were Little Wolf's wife. But now, having seen you again, I know it would not have been possible. You could never have been as a sister to me. I could not have stayed here if Little Wolf were still alive."

Though her grieving heart protested, his words held her spellbound.

"Now you are free to marry me. Sunshine has filled my heart once more. Many summers have passed since we knew each other in my village. Now, we are not the same people as we were then. We have much to learn about each other. We will learn while I wait for you."

"You must remember also that I would marry a man of my own faith. We will talk about that while you wait."

Wild Wind nodded. "You may talk to me of my mother's God, who is your God."

"We can have many discussions of my God. Now, what do you think of the horses?" Della turned toward the corral.

Wild Wind allowed her to change the subject. Turning toward the corral, he propped his elbows on the top rail. For long moments, he scrutinized the Morgans. "Your uncle, the general, knows how to breed good horseflesh. The pony soldiers will have better mounts than many of the war horses our warriors ride." He made a dismissive gesture. "But the pony soldiers are like sacks of grain. They cannot ride."

Della hid a smile with her hand. Wild Wind had a point. The tribesmen showed superior horsemanship over the American cavalry. Compared to the Cheyenne warriors, who rode bareback from young childhood, many of the army's mounted soldiers appeared awkward in the saddle. "I'm afraid you're right."

Dropping his arms from the corral railing, Wild Wind slipped through the bars. He stood without moving, allowing the Morgans to become accustomed to his presence. In soft tones, he crooned to them in his own language.

The front door of the house banged. Jake erupted across the porch and leaped down the steps. His schoolbooks dangled from a leather strap. Legs pumping, he charged across the yard to the corral and skidded to a stop beside his mother.

Della turned toward her son, her mother's critical glance sweeping over him. "Did you eat breakfast? Are you ready for school?"

Jake's head bobbed in a vigorous nod. "Flossie and Aaron and I ate in the kitchen with Silvie. I even washed my face."

Della noted his sandy curls looked sleep tousled. "Did you comb your hair?"

A wash of guilty color stained his face, and his gaze slid away toward the corral. "What is Uncle Wild Wind doing with the horses?" he asked in an obvious attempt to distract his mother.

"He may be taking over your papa's job of training them." Della's fingers gripped her son's shoulder with a tight grasp and turned him to face her again. "You didn't answer my question. Did you comb your hair?"

"Aww... why do I need to comb my hair? The wind will just blow it to smithereens."

"You comb your hair because we're civilized humans."

Jake shrugged and scuffed the toe of his worn leather shoe in the dirt. "I don't care if I'm civilized. And why do I have to go to school? I don't need to learn to read and write and cipher."

During their conversation, Wild Wind had returned to the fence and leaned against the top rail. He listened without commenting.

Della cast him a frustrated glance and returned her attention to her son. "When you grow up, you'll need be able to read and cipher, so you can help Uncle Clint with the ranch books. An education helps a man get ahead in life. Maybe you'll be a lawyer like your Uncle Clint."

Jake set his jaw in mulish defiance. "I don't want to be a lawyer. I want to break horses like my papa."

"Your papa went to school. He got an education. He only trained horses because he wanted to."

Jake shrugged his mother's hand off his shoulder and stepped closer to the corral railing. He stared up at his uncle. "Uncle Wild Wind, I'll bet you never had to go to school, and you know plenty of important stuff."

Wild Wind ducked through the bars and stood beside his nephew, looking down into the youngster's upturned face. "I did go to school while I lived at the fort. I hated school, but I learned to read and write." Reaching out, Wild Wind gave Jake's shoulder a gentle shake. "Your mother is right. In your world, an education opens doors that would be closed to you otherwise. Listen to her. She is a wise woman."

Wild Wind turned his head, and his blue gaze fastened on Della. Wordless communication shimmered between them, making her insides quiver. The house door banging shut again broke the tension holding them captive. Both Della and Wild Wind glanced toward the house.

Coral and her children stood on the veranda. With the toddler, Jessie, propped on one hip, Coral gave each of her older children a one-armed hug. Eight-year old Flossie and six-year old Aaron broke away from their parent to dash down the porch steps and across the yard.

Della gave Jake a little shove. "Go on, now. Go with your cousins to school."

Jake flung a mutinous look at his uncle before he joined Coral's children in the middle of the yard. Della watched the three youngsters scamper beneath the arched entrance gate and turn right toward the ranch's cattle headquarters and the adobe schoolhouse.

Coral strolled toward them, still holding her youngest. A pink dimity morning gown graced her figure.

Della touched Wild Wind's arm. "Aunt Coral wants to meet you."

Coral halted when she reached them and smiled up at Wild Wind. "Della tells me you're Shane's brother."

Wild Wind nodded, and Della stepped into the breach. "Wild Wind, may I present Aunt Coral? She's Uncle Clint's wife. Aunt Coral, this is Wild Wind, my husband's brother."

Della held her breath, wondering how Wild Wind would handle his first social encounter in the white man's world. He ducked his head in acknowledgment of the introduction and, after a slight hesitation he thrust out a hand, offering a handshake in the manner of his mother's people. Coral placed her own hand in his without a moment's misgiving.

"Mrs. Logan. I am honored that you should be pleased to meet me."

Coral's hazel eyes crinkled at the corners, and her cheeks dimpled. "Della told me about you when Shane brought her back from your village. Now, I'm happy to have the opportunity to meet you in person. She was very grateful for your care while she was under your protection. I hope we can repay you for the hospitality you showed her then."

Wild Wind tossed Della a glance as Coral reclaimed her hand. "Lona is showing good care for me."

Della met her aunt's questioning look at his reference to her as Lona. "Wild Wind named me Lona when I lived in his village. He still uses that name instead of my English name."

"I know of no woman named Della." Wild Wind's hand made a slashing, dismissive gesture that sliced the air. "Lona is the woman who stands beside me, who brings sunshine to my heart."

"I see," Coral said without blinking, her plantation hostess manners on full display. "When you're a bit more settled, you'll have to come to dinner one evening."

"Thank you, Mrs. Logan. You are very kind." Wild Wind turned his attention to the chubby toddler in her arms. "This is your baby?"

Coral laid her cheek on the baby's dark head. "Yes, this is Jesse, our youngest. He looks like his papa."

Wild Wind reached out a hand. Jesse gripped his forefinger and gurgled.

"He likes you." Coral smiled again, while Jesse crowed.

Wild Wind smiled down at them. "Children are as arrows in a warrior's quiver. They are a sign of strength."

"Do you like children?"

"Children are treasured among The People. One day, my lodge will be filled with the laughter of children."

Though Wild Wind didn't look her way, his words hit their mark. Della's heart stuttered, and she couldn't breathe. He shouldn't be speaking so. She couldn't think of bringing children into the world with Wild Wind. Not yet, not while she still grieved for Shane.

"I must get back to my duties." Coral's voice returned Della to the conversation. "I'm sure Della will show you around the ranch."

At Coral's departure, Della pivoted toward Wild Wind. "That went well, I think."

"When will I meet your uncle, the general?"

Della tipped up her chin to better peruse her companion's face. A grave expression firmed his features and tightened his mouth. "Uncle Clint is in Denver right now. He's one of the delegates who is crafting Colorado's state constitution. I'm not sure when he'll get back to the ranch."

"You will let him know I am here?"

She nodded. "This morning I sent a letter to Uncle Clint by messenger explaining the situation. It's two day's ride to Denver from here, so it may be a week or so before I get a reply."

"I will work with the horses until we hear from your uncle. I must have something to do."

"Work with them as you see fit. Your method of training probably isn't much different from Shane's." Della glanced away at the mention of her husband, then brought her gaze back to Wild Wind's face. "These four-year olds haven't had much handling. We have a couple dozen more in another paddock who are green broke and will need finishing. The army will pick them up during the summer. We'll look at those horses later."

"What of the other men? I have seen several men here."

"Well, you've met Scipio. He's responsible for the care of the horses, but he doesn't train them. Shane had three or four other men working under him who started the Morgans' training by halter-breaking them, teaching them to stand tied, and getting the horses used to a saddle. After that, Shane broke them to ride and finished them, at least to the army's standards. If you take Shane's place, the men will continue to work for you as they did for Shane."

Wild Wind's shoulders lifted and dropped. "White men will not work for a thievin', savage Injun."

Della caught her breath at his self-deprecating reference, a term she knew many white men reserved for the tribesmen. She shook her head at him and gripped his arm. "Don't refer to yourself in that way! I never want to hear you call yourself a thieving, savage Indian again."

A fierce light blazed in Wild Wind's eyes. "It is what the men will call me. You will not be able to find a man who will work with me."

Della reflected that he probably spoke the truth, yet she didn't want to admit defeat before she'd even asked the men to help him.

Wild Wind thrust out both hands, his expression ferocious. "These hands have killed many white men. Some pony soldiers, some ranchers and their women. I have burned white men's homes. Do you think your uncle's men will work with me?"

Della stumbled back a pace, frightened a bit in spite of her trust in him. He stepped toward her, breaching the distance between them so that the fringe on his deerskin shirt brushed her blouse. She felt the heat from his body, coupled with the force of his being, envelope her. Both of his hands flashed out and gripped her upper arms. She pressed her fingers against the hard muscles of his chest.

"Lona, I cannot change what I have been or what I have done." His fingers squeezed. "Your uncle's men will see only the savage warrior. You yourself told me this was so. It is as true as the sun's journey across the sky each day. I have brought you much trouble."

Della's head tipped back. As civilized as Wild Wind could be, she glimpsed once again the untamed side of him, the combatant that lurked beneath the veneer of decorum, and she quivered. This man had many faces, she reminded herself. Could she ever live with the whole man, the savage warrior as well as the tender suitor and the brave champion? She wet her lips and cleared her throat before she spoke. "You protected me when I lived in your village. I can do no less for you while you live here at the ranch. We'll face the trouble together."

Scipio's voice cut through their preoccupation. So caught up in their private drama, neither had heard Scipio approach. "Miz Della, do you need help?"

Della glanced at her uncle's head groom. Concern etched his dark face. She tried to smile. "Thank you, Scipio, but I'm fine. There's no need for you to worry."

Scipio shrugged and sent a warning look toward Wild Wind.

Ignoring Scipio, Wild Wind didn't move. He still held Della by the arms.

"Miz Della, you holler if you need me. I'll be just inside the barn."

"I appreciate your concern, Scipio, but I'm fine. Don't let me keep you from your work."

Wild Wind dismissed Scipio's retreat. His hands stole from her arms up to her shoulders, and then his long fingers framed her face. His velvet voice shivered along her nerve ends. "Lona, my brave woman. You have the heart of the eagle as you stand at my side, facing trouble with me. Yet I feel you tremble. Do not fear me. You have nothing to fear from me."

Of their own accord, Della's hands crept up to curl about Wild Wind's muscular forearms. "I'm not afraid of you, not the way you think. I'm afraid of what you can do to my life, and to my heart." Unable to stop herself, she shivered again. The heat from his calloused fingers clasping her face scorched her.

Wild Wind's eyes narrowed, and a tiny smile quirked the corners of his mouth. "As the hunter stalks the elk and slays it, you have captured this warrior. I am helpless in the face of your charms. You can turn my will to please yourself."

Della smiled at the ridiculous image his words evoked. "I very much doubt I can make you do anything you don't wish to do."

"Cheyenne wives are esteemed by their husbands. We are as clay in our women's hands."

Her experience in his village had taught her that, though Cheyenne wives were indeed esteemed, and women had standing in the tribe, she suspected that he teased her. "Not you. I can't see any woman turning you into clay."

Della stepped back, breaking the contact with Wild Wind. His hands dropped to his sides, and she breathed deeply to regain a measure of composure. "I must meet with Uncle Clint's business manager now. Study over the horses and do what you will with them. After lunch, we'll ride out, and you can have a look at the ranch."

She left him standing beside the corral and hurried across the yard to Emory Dyer's house, where her uncle's business manager had his office. She felt Wild Wind's stare sizzling at her back all the way. Outside the door, she halted and closed her eyes, pressing a hand to her thumping heart.

Her insides jangled, as though her reflection stared back at her from a shattered looking glass, her image distorted by the broken pieces. Wild Wind had disrupted her very existence, and she drifted in a churning sea of emotion. Taking another deep breath, she stuffed down her unruly feelings and forced herself to acquire at least the appearance of composure. It wouldn't do for Uncle Emory to guess what Wild Wind could do to her.

CHAPTER 5

After rapping on the paneled wooden door, Della entered the small front room that served as an office. She closed the portal behind her and leaned against it.

Her Uncle Clint's long-time military adjunct-turned-business manager stood at one window looking out into the ranch yard, both hands stuffed in his trouser pockets. He glanced toward her. "I hope you know what you're doing."

Straightening away from the door, Della stepped into the room and pivoted to face the man she fondly called "uncle." "Uncle Emory, Shane's brother couldn't stay on the reservation any longer, and he came to me looking for a job. I couldn't turn him away."

"It appears that he came for more than a job."

"He didn't know that Shane had died until he arrived yesterday." Stepping closer to the grizzled lieutenant, Della touched his shoulder. "You might as well know. Wild Wind wants to marry me."

Disapproval tightened Emory Dyer's pleasant, but plain, face. He pierced her with a stare. "I remember that your husband once fought him over you. Now that he knows you're a widow, he's not wasting any time."

Della sighed. "He told me he never got over losing me, and I believe him."

Her companion regarded her with solemn gray eyes and curled his weathered hands about her own. "Missy, right now isn't the wisest time to be taking up with a Cheyenne brave. And with your husband only two months in the grave."

"I'm not taking up with Wild Wind!" Della's chin went up, and her eyes flashed.

A rap on the door interrupted them. Della stepped away from the lieutenant.

Hugh Donovan, the lanky, gray-haired ramrod of the Slash L cattle enterprise, slipped into the room and shut the door behind him. He swept his low-crowned hat from his head and nodded at the two occupants already in the office. "Didn't mean to keep you. I hope I haven't held you up."

"We haven't started yet." Emory Dyer crossed the room and rounded the large oak desk at the back wall. He glanced at the open ledger spread out on the green leather blotter on the desk's scarred surface. "If you're ready, we'll begin now."

Della and Hugh Donovan trailed along behind him and seated themselves in slat-backed wooden chairs placed before the desk. The foreman laid his hat, brim up, on the desk.

"Della, why don't you begin?" Emory Dyer seated himself and leaned back in his chair, elbows resting on the chair arms.

"As you know, the men have brought the four-year olds in off the range and have put them in the large corral. Without Shane to break them, the men are just handling them and reminding them of what a saddle is."

"And how many four-year olds do you have?"

"We lost a few in the blizzard, so we're down to about three dozen. I know the army contracted for more, but we won't be able to fulfill the order." Della paused, reluctant to deliver more bad news. "We also lost six of last year's foals and a couple of yearlings."

Emory Dyer leaned toward the desk and picked up a pen. Without comment, he recorded some figures in the ledger. When he finished, he pointed the pen at Hugh Donovan. "And what about the cattle?"

The ramrod shifted in his chair. Many years spent on the range had leathered his skin, and squint lines fanned out from each side of his eyes. A serious expression warned his news wasn't good. "The storm took a total of about forty head of cattle. Some were steers and some were cows who were with calf."

Della's shoulders drooped, and she sagged against the back of her chair. Every rancher expected some losses each year, but with Uncle Clint's operation in its early stages, the death of each horse and the livestock represented a higher risk of failure. The loss of forty head of Shorthorn cattle would severely limit his profits. Enough loss in the early years, before he could become established, could doom his enterprise.

"Also, the men have reported seeing bands of Sioux and Cheyenne warriors, so there'll be greater risk taking the herd to the summer range after the branding is done. We could lose more cattle to the Indians," Hugh said.

Emory Dyer's pen scratched across the page while an uneasy silence settled over the office. The army's war with the tribes over the incursion of prospectors into the Black Hills had heated up during the past year. The discovery of gold had brought men into the Sioux's sacred territory. Equally ferociously defended was the Cheyenne Powder River area. Americans, lured by the promise of free land, had begun to settle on Cheyenne hunting grounds.

Della sighed. Having lived in Wild Wind's village and being married to Shane had given her insight into both sides of the issue of who controlled the vast High Plains prairie.

"Blood will be spilled this summer," Donovan predicted, his tone grim. "I hope to provide enough firepower for the cowboys, so they can defend themselves and the cattle from the hostiles."

"You can't really blame the tribesmen for protecting their homeland. Still, civilians see this land as theirs for the taking and expect the army to protect them." Emory Dyer tossed down his pen and leaned back in his chair.

When the meeting concluded, Della and Hugh Donavan left the office. They paused outside in the warming April sun. Donavan settled his low-crowned hat on his head and squinted across the yard. After a moment, he nodded toward Wild Wind, who stood in the corral with the horses.

"What do you plan to do with that breed?"

Della glanced at him, catching the sharp tone in his voice. She bristled. "I assume you're referring to Shane's brother?"

"You know exactly whom I mean." The foreman shot her a level look, his hazel eyes steady. He propped his lanky height on one leg.

She met his stare and refused to back down. "Wild Wind came here asking for a job. He didn't know Shane was dead." She faltered over the words before she continued, still not able to speak of her husband's death with composure. "I couldn't turn him away."

"I'm sure it's crossed your mind that, given the state of Indian hostilities right now, the men will see him as a threat. They've all heard of his reputation. If he stays, we may have a mutiny on our hands, and I need every man to ride herd this summer. I can't afford to have any of them walk out."

"I told him as much, and he's aware of the possibility."

"Is he a straight shooter?"

For an instant, Della hesitated. Did she really trust Wild Wind? What did she know of him, after seven years of separation? Still, her heart cried out that he was trustworthy. She nodded. "Yes. Yes, I trust him. I don't believe he'd lie to me."

Donovan hung his fists off his gun belt, elbows akimbo. "Well, then, ask him why he quit fighting when so many of his fellow Dog Soldiers are still making war." He shrugged. "Myself, I don't care if he works here, as long as he keeps the peace, but some of the men will feel differently."

Della had no reply.

The foreman's stare bored into her. "Ask him." Then, touching his fingers to his hat brim and dipping his head, he strode off toward the compound's gate. The soft jingle of his spurs and the thud of his footsteps faded while the distance between them lengthened.

Switching her attention to Wild Wind, she watched the chieftain tract Donovan's progress toward the gate. Wild Wind stood motionless, his face unreadable. What was he thinking? Della wondered. As if he felt her stare, he turned his head toward her. Their gazes collided. Even from across the yard the impact of his regard impaled her. She caught her breath, struggling against the force of his will, which commanded her to come to him. Breaking free of the spell he'd cast over her, Della fled to the house.

People stopped to stare. The few women they encountered watched with apprehensive expressions. Beneath the brims of their cowboy hats, the men's cold faces betrayed their hostility.

Della and Wild Wind rode their mounts at an easy walk through the cattle ranch's headquarters. On their left, they passed the cabins of the married cowhands, then the school, the commissary, a blacksmith shop, and the barn. Across the dirt road, against the outside wall of the horse ranch's adobe enclosure, nestled the cook shack and the bunkhouse which quartered the single cowhands. A complex of large corrals flanked both sides of the lane just beyond the barn.

She knew the people who lived here. Della greeted each one they met. One woman sat on her porch, a butter churn between her knees. Another struggled against the wind to hang flapping sheets on a clothesline strung between two houses. They scarcely responded to her overtures.

They met a third woman strolling toward them from the commissary, a basket over one arm. Her other arm cradled a sleeping infant.

"Good afternoon, Molly." Della halted her mustang beside the woman. "How is little Sarah doing? Is she over the croup?"

Molly's glance darted past Della to Wild Wind, who had drawn his mount to a stop nearby. Beneath the rounded brim of her calico poke bonnet, Molly's face paled. She wet her lips and swung her attention back to Della. "Sarah is doing fine now, Mrs. Hunter. The herbal remedy you sent fixed her right up."

"I'm glad to hear it. She's looking much better." The bittersweet memory of her own dear Fanny pierced Della's heart. Fanny, a lively toddler, had succumbed to the croup the year before Shane's death. No herbal remedy had cured her. Their struggle to save her had been futile. Della forced a smile to her lips. "Well, I won't keep you. I know you have much to do before Sarah's brothers get out of school."

Heeling the grulla into motion, Della rode on. Wild Wind's gelding kept pace with hers. Outside the commissary, a cowboy leaning against a porch post turned his back on them when they rode by. He strode into the store without returning Della's greeting. She waved at the blacksmith when they passed. Standing motionless beside his forge in front of the shop, one gloved hand gripping short-handled maul, the blacksmith ducked his head without responding. He lifted the hammer, and the mallet fell. The clear *pang pang* of his hammer striking metal rang through the afternoon air.

Della clamped her lips shut and stole a surreptitious glance at Wild Wind. His impassive face concealed any reaction to the snubs they'd received.

Just beyond the ranch compound, mottled red, white, and roan Shorthorn cattle dotted the grasslands. Some of the cows had spring calves by their sides. Others would calve within the next month. Cowboys riding the fringes of the herd kept the cattle from straying.

When they'd left the ranch headquarters behind and the solitude of the prairie surrounded them, Della said, "I must apologize for my people's rudeness. I'm sure once they get to know you, things will be different."

Wild Wind remained stoical, though he shrugged. "I am not a child who is hurt by words or actions." He glanced at her. "Do not fret, Lona, though your concern for me is balm to my heart."

Their horses sliced through the buffalo grass. Profusions of spring flowers painted the billowing range with a patchwork of color. Golden ragwort spread over the land in a yellow carpet. Spikes of lavender gayfeather thrust upward through the grass, and prairie smoke flowers added bursts of vivid pink. A sky of softest blue arced overhead. Della breathed in the sweet spring air. The scent of greening grass and flowers teased her nostrils.

Wild Wind remained silent, while his alert gaze scanned the plain. Both of them had rifles thrust into their scabbards. They rode with caution, keeping off the ridgelines and concealing themselves in the creases made by the prairie's slopes. Content to let silence lay between them, Della accompanied him in mute satisfaction. Miles passed beneath the hooves of their mounts.

After a time. she glanced at him and indicated the bay Morgan gelding he rode. "What do think? Do you like him?"

"He is a fine horse." Wild Wind shifted in the saddle.

"Why don't we try a gallop so you can see what he can do?"

In reply, Wild Wind's muscled legs squeezed his mount, and the bay leaped forward. At Della's cue, Shane's grulla mustang flung himself into a run, and the two horses thundered across the plain, shoulder to shoulder. The wind snatched Della's hat from her head so it hung from its strap and bounced against her back. Exhilaration filled her. When they finally reined in their mounts, Della laughed with sheer joy, forgetting her sorrow in the moment's pleasure.

Wild Wind's eyes crinkled at the corners, and the creases on either side of his mouth deepened in a smile while he studied her glowing face. "Your laughter is like the music of the brook."

"I do so enjoy a good gallop."

"Your spirit is one with the horse."

"Yes, I think so." She tipped her head toward his bay. "And what do you think of that fellow now?"

"I think I will like these Morgan horses of yours. Your uncle, the general, knows how to breed a fine mount." Wild Wind looked her way before returning his attention to the horizon. A couple of antelope does bounded away at their approach and disappeared over a hillock.

Della settled her hat on her head once again.

A beat of silence fell. Della hesitated to bring up the question that Hugh Donovan had challenged her to ask Wild Wind, so she launched into another topic instead. She brought the grulla to a halt and swung him to face Wild Wind. "If you stay here, your life will be very different from what it was in your village. You'll have to adapt to our ways."

Wild Wind walked the bay toward her until their mounts stood alongside each other, head to tail, and his knee bumped Della's. Awareness jolted her at the contact.

"I stayed with my mother at the fort for two years before I left. I know what kind of life the white man lives."

"Shane told me you weren't happy at the fort, and you ran away to your village."

Wild Wind shrugged again and leaned toward her, curling one hand about her saddle horn. "I was a boy, with a boy's thoughts. I am no longer a boy. I am a man who knows what he must do. Sometimes, the way of a man is hard, but a man must do what he must do."

His words, simple in their logic, touched Della to her core. She laid her hand over his and squeezed. "I admire you for that."

"And you are here. I would do anything to be with you."

"A marriage between us isn't guaranteed. I don't know what the future holds."

An expression she couldn't interpret passed over his face. "It is settled."

Unsure of what his comment meant and loathe to shatter the moment, Della nevertheless knew the time to question Wild Wind had come. She drew a deep breath. "I must ask you something." Her eyes met his, and he stared back at her with a steady regard. The memory of the time she'd looked into his eyes when he'd captured her, ferocious blue eyes above the black and red war paint smeared across his face, flashed into her thoughts. Now, his eyes revealed a curiosity tinged with wariness. "I've been wondering... you never said... why exactly did you stop fighting the soldiers and join your band on the reservation?"

His gaze never wavered, meeting her own with forthrightness.

"After much fighting, I began to realize that my father was right. Our villages were attacked, our men were killed, and the pony soldiers kept coming no matter how many of them we killed. The white men kept coming. The buffalo are almost gone, white men live on our hunting grounds, and we are pushed further and further onto land that can't sustain us. What wisdom is there to keep fighting an enemy that will never stop? I am a chieftain. My people needed me. My father needed me, so I put down my rifle and joined my people on the reservation."

His words held the ring of truth. In that moment, her doubts fled. A curious lightness filled her. His strong, beautiful, deadly hand still lay beneath hers. She squeezed again. "I believe you. I'll explain that to Uncle Clint if I must."

"Your uncle. He seems to be a good man. A man who might see both the way of The People and the white man's way."

"He is. Uncle Clint is a wise man and a man who will listen. He's not one of those who wants to exterminate the tribes."

"Would he help my people? I must do what I can for them. The way of the tribesmen is changing, and I must change, too. Perhaps your uncle, the general, can help. My people are starving and sick on the reservation. I think it will be better for them if I can live with one foot in your world and one foot with my people. Your uncle would be a powerful ally."

"I can make no promises on his behalf, but I think you're right. I'm not sure when I'll see him, but I know he'll at least listen to you. He has the ear of the military, for what that's worth."

Wild Wind nodded. "For now, that will be enough." His hand turned beneath hers, and he laced their fingers together. "Lona, I am eager for your time of mourning to end. I will try to be patient, but my heart cries out for us to be one."

Her smile wobbled. "I still grieve for Little Wolf. I don't know how long I'll grieve, but you must wait."

Wild Wind didn't reply. His knee bumped hers again when their mounts shifted, and she shivered. His stare roved over her face, and where it touched, she burned.

CHAPTER 6

One week after the messenger Della had sent to Denver left, a cavalcade of riders swept into the ranch compound. Della and Coral had just finished the noon meal and still sat at the table when the pounding of hooves sounded in the yard. The women exchanged a glance of apprehension.

"Who could that be?" Coral wondered.

Della shrugged. "Let's see."

They pushed back their chairs and hurried from the dining room. Coral reached the foyer first.

Stained glass insets on either side of the wide mahogany door cast rainbow prisms onto the plank floor. Through the oval etched-glass window in the door, they glimpsed horses clustered in the yard. Men's voices could be heard from outside. Coral reached for the crystal knob and pulled open the portal. She halted on the threshold.

A tall, dark-haired man with a lean Yankee face stood at the bottom of the veranda steps, one foot on the first tread. His handsome features brightened when he caught sight of the woman poised in the doorway.

"Clint!" Coral shrieked. She darted across the porch, and her husband bounded up the stairs. They met at the top step. Bending down to embrace his petite wife, his arms locked about Coral's back. He nuzzled her neck while her arms clutched him close.

Standing just outside the door, Della swallowed around the tightness in her throat and glanced away to give them privacy. The love her uncle felt for his Southern wife always moved her. They'd overcome the differences in their Northern and Southern backgrounds and had forged a stronger bond because of it. The visible evidence of their love reminded Della of her own loss. In that moment, grief over Shane's death struck her as a blow so raw she nearly staggered.

She stared past them to the riders grouped in the yard below. The messenger she'd sent to Denver held the reins of her uncle's mount, but the other riders were strangers. Half a dozen men wearing cowboy garb fanned out behind Clint's gelding. She noted that a Winchester rifle was thrust into the scabbard attached to each rider's rig, and a six-shooter hung from the gun belt on every man's waist. Their faces carried the stamp of seasoned fighters.

Della looked back at her uncle. A gun belt encircled his waist, as well. The situation with the Sioux must be worse than she'd heard if he felt the necessity to travel with an armed escort.

A feeling of being watched overcame her. She glanced toward the barn. Wild Wind stood outside the corral bars, his face turned in her direction. His stare seized hers and held her captive. The force of his essence affected her as strongly as though he stood beside her and touched her physically. The seconds hung suspended while emotion arced between them.

"Della." Uncle Clint's voice broke through her preoccupation. She closed her eyes to free herself of Wild Wind's grip, then turned toward her uncle and flung herself into his outstretched arms.

"It's so good to see you." She burrowed into his embrace, feeling safe and loved. "What brings you back to the ranch?"

With a forefinger beneath her chin, he tipped up her face and smiled down at her. "When I get a message from my favorite niece asking if we should hire a former Cheyenne Dog Soldier, I thought it best to come discuss things in person. Also, I need to consult with Hugh about some details of the ranch."

"I'm glad you're here," she said, relieved that the decision of hiring Wild Wind didn't rest on her alone. "I'm not quite sure what to do."

"I'll meet Shane's brother. Then we can decide how to best handle this situation."

Coral tugged on her husband's arm. "Are you hungry? We just finished eating, but Sadie can bring the food back to the dining room if you haven't eaten."

"A meal would be much appreciated. We rode hard to make it here by early afternoon." Turning away from the women, he jogged down the steps and consulted with the men waiting below.

After a brief conversation, Della's uncle rejoined the women on the porch. "I sent them to the cook shack. Toby can feed them."

With an arm about each woman, he ushered them into the house, passing through the foyer and hall to the dining room. Coral hurried to the kitchen to put together a plate of food, while Della and her uncle seated themselves at the table. He leaned back in his chair at the table's head and stretched out his long legs. He scrubbed a hand over his face and sighed.

"It's good to be home. The task of writing a state constitution that would be best for both the state and its citizens is wearying."

"Aunt Coral doesn't complain, but she misses you. I tried to get her to go to Denver, but she wouldn't hear of it. She says the ranch is best for the children. I know that's just an excuse to stay here with me."

"I might convince her join me after school lets out for the summer."

Della scrutinized her uncle's dear face. Lines of exhaustion grooved his cheeks. More silver gleamed in the dark hair about his temples than when she'd last seen him.

At the moment, concern for her etched his features. "How are you holding up, Della?"

She squeezed his hand where it rested on his knee. "I'm doing well. I'm much too busy during the day to brood."

"That's not what I asked you."

Sighing, Della glanced away, then looked back at her uncle. "I still grieve for Shane. Sometimes now, I can get through an entire morning without thinking about him. Then I feel guilty for forgetting him." She thought it prudent not to mention that Wild Wind's presence had been the cause of her forgetting Shane for hours at a time.

"It's natural for those of us left behind to move on after a loved one passes. I know. I've been there myself. You mustn't feel guilty for not thinking about Shane all the time. It's part of the healing process."

Years had passed since Della had thought of her uncle's first wife, who'd died before the Civil War began. She'd been a child when his first wife had died, so her memories were hazy, but now, she recalled that he'd been a widower when he met Coral. He knew from experience what she now lived through. "I suppose you're right, but I feel it's somehow wrong for me to be happy when my husband lies cold in the ground."

"Shane wouldn't want you to stop living your life just because he's no longer a part of it. He'd want you to heal, and be happy, and move on. He'd want you to one day love again."

"I'm not ready for that yet," Della replied in a small voice.

"I'm sure you're not, but don't shut out the possibility. You're still young, and when you're ready, you may find someone else to love. Look what the Lord did for Coral and me after we'd both lost someone. Now, I can't imagine my life without her."

"But how will I ever find a man who can match Shane? I can never settle for less than what he was."

"If the Lord has someone else for you, He'll give you someone who will be just as suited to you as Shane was."

She tried not to think of Wild Wind, a man who was Shane's equal but whose religion was animism. Tears gathered in her eyes, and she blinked them away. "Uncle Clint, I'm so afraid I'll forget his face, that I won't remember what he looked like."

"You have a photograph or two to help you remember. When his face fades away from you, look at those. Perhaps one day, it won't matter."

Della slipped from her chair and knelt beside her uncle. She buried her face in his chest and curled her arms about his neck. "Uncle Clint, you're so wise." She sniffled while he stroked her hair.

"I've lived a lot, that's all." She heard the smile in his voice as he spoke above her head. "Just live one hour at a time. After a while, you'll get through a whole day without thinking about Shane, and you won't feel guilty for doing it."

Coral interrupted them, then, when she entered with a plate heaped with food. Della sat back on her heels and looked up at her uncle's wife.

"Aunt Coral, do you know you're married to the wisest man in the world?"

Coral laid the plate, a fork, and a glass of lemonade on the table before her husband. She rested a loving hand on his shoulder. "Yes, I know. I'm very fortunate."

Rising to her feet, Della returned to her chair while Coral sat near Clint. They watched in silence while he devoured his meal. When he'd finished, he emptied his glass of lemonade and wiped his mouth with a snowy cloth napkin. "I suppose the children are still in school?" he asked his wife.

She nodded. "You won't see them for at least another hour. And Jesse is down for his nap."

"Well, then, tell me all about Wild Wind." Turning toward Della, he settled against the carved chair back to listen to her tale.

The story tumbled out. When Della had finished, she said, "I think he'd be just the person to take Shane's place with the horses, and he could help with the calf branding and haying. The only problem is the men. I'm sure you know what they think about working with a Cheyenne."

"Let me meet him now. I have time to talk to him before the children get home."

They found Wild Wind in the corral working with a sorrel gelding. Clint leaned against the rails and watched. Della stood beside her uncle and rested both hands on the top bar. Wild Wind gave no indication that he noticed them. When he finished with the gelding, he turned toward the herd. He moved with calm confidence amongst the wary horses, getting them used to his presence and touch.

Apparently satisfied that he'd done enough for the time being, Wild Wind eased through the herd and approached the fence. He slipped between the bars. Standing beside Della, he waited for her to speak.

She dropped her hands from the rails and faced him. "Uncle Clint needed to discuss some ranching affairs with our foreman, so he decided to leave Denver and come home for a few days. That way he can meet you, too." With one outstretched hand, she indicated her uncle. "Wild Wind, I'd like to present General Clint Logan, my uncle." She reached her other hand toward her brother-in-law. "Uncle Clint, Wild Wind, Shane's brother."

For a brief moment, the two men eyed each other in wary silence before Clint stepped forward and extended his hand. Wild Wind accepted the general's overture of friendship, and the men shook hands to seal their fledgling relationship.

"Coral tells me you'd like to break the Morgans for the army."

"I would do what my brother did."

"I can see that. Shane's methods of training the horses seem similar to yours, but the army is always in a hurry for their mounts. We don't have time to ease them into riding, so in the end, you'll probably have to climb aboard and let them buck it out."

"I can do that, if I must, but I have been letting them get used to my touch."

Clint touched his niece on the elbow. "Della, could you give Wild Wind and me some privacy? I'd like to talk to him, man to man."

She'd been dismissed in as polite a manner as she could wish, yet her uncle had dismissed her, nonetheless. His tone brooked no argument. "Certainly. I'll be in the house if you need me."

With her back erect, Della crossed the dirt-packed yard. Ignoring the rose bushes Coral had planted on either side of the steps, she climbed the veranda stairs. Shadowed by the porch roof, she turned and watched her uncle and Wild Wind. As Shane had, Wild Wind matched the general for height. The two men stood eye to eye, apparently taking stock of each other. Clint was talking, and Wild Wind listened with the self-assured arrogance inherent in the Cheyenne male, his head held high, his arms crossed at his chest, moccasined feet planted wide. Wild Wind responded when her uncle finished speaking.

What were they saying? Della wondered. What would she do if Uncle Clint decided hiring her brother-in-law posed too great a risk to the ranch? She hated to admit that she'd miss him, that she'd grown accustomed to his presence, and that he brightened her days, yet honesty forced her to concede the truth. If he left, she'd be dealt another loss. Coming so soon after Shane's death, she wasn't sure she could survive another such blow.

CHAPTER 7

Uncle Clint entered the parlor holding two paper-wrapped parcels. The evening meal had been cleared from the table, and the protesting children had been sent to bed. Now, the adults had the parlor to themselves. Both Coral and Della came to their feet when the general stepped across the threshold, a conspiratorial smile twitching his lips.

"Clint, what do you have?" Coral demanded. "I see you've been keeping something from me."

Her husband halted before her, his face grave, though his eyes twinkled. "Wife, would I dare keep anything from you? Somehow, you always manage to uncover my secrets." Lowering his head, he dropped a light kiss on her mouth. When the kiss ended, the two shared a lover's intimate look before Clint offered one of the parcels to his wife. "This is for you."

Turning toward his niece, he held the other out to Della. "And this is for you."

Della snatched the package from her uncle. "What is it? Why are you bringing us presents?"

"Open it and see."

Della and her aunt exchanged puzzled glances before they untied the ribbon holding their parcels closed. Della tore the paper apart, excitement bubbling. The wrapping fell to the floor, and yards of slick black satin and lace spilled into her palms. She looked up at her uncle, but he was watching Coral open her package.

Coral's packet contained enough satin, tulle, and lace for an evening gown. The satin's mulberry color gleamed with a rich patina in the lamplight's warm golden glow. Coral caught her breath, then flung her arms about her husband's neck, her face alight with pleasure. Uncle Clint caught her up in his arms.

Watching, Della thought Coral looked no older than when she'd married the Yankee cavalry General, Clint Logan, eleven years before. She still retained the sylph-like slenderness she'd possessed when they'd wed. The spun-sorghum color of her hair showed no trace of silver, and her face looked youthful. Della tried not to envy her aunt the charmed life she seemed to lead, where not even time seemed to touch her.

"What is the occasion for all this fabric?" Coral asked, leaning against her husband's encircling embrace. "We certainly don't need new evening gowns here on the ranch."

"Plans are afoot in Denver for a big July 4th celebration to commemorate Colorado's statehood and the nation's Centennial. I thought you ladies would like to attend the festivities. There will be dinners, balls, the theater, and a July 4th parade. You'll each need at least one new ball gown."

Coral hugged her husband again, and Della laid a hand on his arm.

"Thank you, Uncle Clint. I'm sure Denver will be entertaining, but I think I'd rather stay here."

He freed one arm from his wife and pulled Della into a shared three-way embrace.

"Nonsense, Della. You certainly won't stay here. It will do you good to go to Denver and attend the festivities. I won't hear of you staying at the ranch."

"But..."

"No buts." He shook his head at her. "It will do you a world of good to get away."

Della paused, excitement warring with her reluctance to enter society without Shane. She laid her head on her uncle's shoulder for a moment before she looked up into his sympathetic blue eyes.

"You need to do this, Della. It will be another milestone in getting used to life without your husband. You can't hide at the Slash L forever."

"I know." She took a deep breath and put aside her misgivings. "Very well. I'll go to Denver. Thank you for the fabric."

"I'm sorry I had to get you black, but at formal events, you'll be expected to wear mourning. Here at the ranch, it doesn't matter, but as you recall, Denver society will have different expectations of you."

Della hadn't forgotten the strict rules governing the lives of society's gilded members. Denver certainly wasn't Boston, but even there, she'd have to conform to certain social mores.

"I brought some material for Silvie, too, so you ladies can make up your dresses together."

Della laid the satin fabric on a nearby medallion-backed parlor chair and turned once again to her uncle.

"Uncle Clint, we haven't had a chance to discuss Wild Wind. What did you think of him?"

Her uncle released his wife and gave Della his full attention, his expression thoughtful. The lamplight gleamed on the silver threaded through his dark hair.

"I think he's very capable of training our horses."

"But what else? Should we hire him?"

"I think he's sincere when he says he's done fighting, and he wants to do his best to prepare his people for a new way of life. Any fears on the part of the men are unfounded, although I don't know if they'll believe that."

"But should we hire him?" Della held her breath, impatient to hear her uncle's opinion.

"Hiring him will be a risk. I could lose men over it, but I say to go ahead. He'll get the job done, and having him here at the ranch might actually help protect us from attack by the other tribes."

She let out her breath in relief. Wild Wind needn't leave the ranch after all. "Thank you, Uncle Clint."

"The quartermaster from Fort Bridger will pick up the horses in July," her uncle said.

A beat of silence fell. After a moment, Della brought the conversation back to Shane's brother. "Did Wild Wind mention the situation with his band on the Tongue River?"

"Yes, we discussed that. He's concerned about the woeful conditions on the reservation. I told him I'd look into it. The Bureau of Indian Affairs agent over the Cheyenne territory should be investigated. I suspect he's been selling many of the supplies intended for the reservation and pocketing the money."

"That's what I told Wild Wind."

"Unfortunately, the system is rife with corruption. It's hard to find an honest man who's willing to work with the tribes."

"I told Wild Wind I thought you'd help."

Uncle Clint's sudden grin lightened the moment. "Did you, now? And what else did you promise him?"

"Nothing," Della protested. "I didn't promise him anything."

He pecked Della on the forehead. "Niece, I know you and your soft heart for those in need. If I'm not careful, I'll find you've committed me to supplying Wild Wind's band with enough beef and medicine for the entire year."

A wash of guilty color stained Della's cheeks. She'd toyed with the idea of doing something of the sort. From her weeks living in Wild Wind's village, she'd come to know and care for his people. The thought of their suffering plucked at her heart.

Her uncle gave her a discerning look. "See, I can tell from your expression that I'm right. Please don't beggar me with your philanthropic efforts."

"You know me too well, Uncle."

"That, I do. Now, Coral and I will bid you good night. I've had a long two days of traveling and am ready to sleep in my own bed."

Her uncle and aunt left the parlor, their arms linked. When they'd vanished into the foyer, Della stood unmoving, staring after them through the empty doorway. The night's silence enveloped her. The sense of aloneness that crept through her crushed her. Its awful weight smothered her, making her struggle to catch a breath. She turned in a slow circle, taking in the expensive furnishings that had been shipped by train from her uncle's home in Boston. The familiar medallion-backed sofa before the windows, the mahogany lamp tables covered by frilly doilies, the piano against the wall by the door, a rocking chair before the wood stove, and the cream and burgundy Aubusson carpet covering the floor all should have offered comfort by their familiarity. Instead, she felt only loneliness.

She had no one waiting for her upstairs in her bedroom, no one to hold her during the night. With a bone-deep feeling of solitariness, her slow steps took her across the room to the oil lamp burning on the carved lamp table beside the sofa. The flame blossomed and died when she turned down the wick. A thin ribbon of smoke curled upward from the lamp's chimney, bringing with it the pungent scent of kerosene. She did the same for the remaining two lamps, and blackness devoured the light.

Standing alone in the dark, Della refused to let despair overtake her. By the grace of God, she'd find her way out of the darkness back into the light and relearn her place in the world. Shane's death wouldn't defeat her.

CHAPTER 8

The next morning after she'd sent Jake to school with his cousins, Della joined her uncle and Emory Dyer in the business manager's office. Hugh Donovan arrived behind her.

Uncle Clint greeted his foreman with a hearty handshake. "Thanks for coming, Hugh. I must return to Denver tomorrow, and I want to discuss a few things with you before I go."

"Sure thing, Boss."

Clint gestured to the straight-backed wooden chairs arranged before Dyer's oak desk. "Have a seat, and we'll start talking."

Hugh and Della seated themselves in the chairs before the desk. Della twitched her black split riding skirt into decorous folds about her tooled leather riding boots and laid her black leather gloves on the desk. Emory Dyer took his seat behind the desk, while Clint remained standing off to one side.

"I've called this meeting because I wanted to apprise you of the situation that we'll be facing this summer." Clint planted his feet wide apart and clasped his hands behind his back, adopting the military stance that previously had been so much a part of his life. He favored each person before him with a slow perusal. "The Indian situation is coming to a head. Now that the weather is warming, many tribesmen have left their reservations and are moving about in bands of half a dozen or more warriors. Red Cloud, Crazy Horse, and Sitting Bull are on the prod, stirring up their men. A stagecoach on its way to Denver was attacked last week. A ranch house north of here was burned to the ground and the family murdered. Raiding parties are attacking homesteads. So far, we've never had trouble with the tribes, but we can't rely on past good will to protect us."

Della listened with mounting dread. She'd hoped for a more peaceful resolution to the problems created by the two cultures clashing.

Her uncle turned to his foreman. "Hugh, if the married men would prefer for their families to sleep inside the compound, we'll find places for them. We should consider placing guards about the ranch headquarters day and night. It will be a hardship for the men, I know, but we need to be prepared."

Donovan nodded. "I'll see to it."

"That brings me to another point. We'll must keep a closer eye on the cattle this summer. That will mean a lot more riding for everyone. Send out patrols, and I don't want anyone riding alone. We'll need to travel in groups, heavily armed. The horse herd will need to be protected, as well."

He stepped closer to the desk. "I could sell every head of cattle I own to the army. To try to bring the tribes under control, the army is moving hundreds of soldiers West and building a string of forts along the edges of the Sioux reservation and the unceded Cheyenne territory. Those soldiers need to eat. The army would buy every steer I have to feed its enlisted men, but I've promised what beef I can spare to the tribes on the Tongue reservation. I have a feeling my niece will hold me to that commitment." He smiled in Della's direction.

Della frowned at her uncle. "The army will have to get its beef from another rancher. The reservation Indians need to eat, and we've promised to help them."

"The condition of the Cheyenne on the reservation is of great concern to my niece, and I support her in that." Uncle Clint took a turn around the office and halted once again beside the desk. He leaned forward and braced both arms on the table, his palms flat on its scarred surface. "This brings me to my final point. As you're both aware, Shane's half-brother has come to us looking for work. I told Della to hire him. I know the men will object, but it will be to our advantage to have him here. Hugh, if too many men quit, I'll hire more in Denver."

When the meeting had concluded, Della left while the men discussed protecting the ranch and its people from the expected hostilities. She stepped into the yard. On her way to the barn, a lanky cowboy with a horseman's loose gait intercepted her. She halted and gave him a quizzical glance.

"Mornin', Miz Hunter." He whipped off his tan felt cowboy hat and ran his fingers through his mink-colored curls, giving his hair a wind-blown look.

"Good morning, Grady." Della looked up into his engaging features. His dark eyes twinkled down at her.

Holding his hat alongside his leg, he flashed her a winsome smile. "You're lookin' fine this mornin', Miz Hunter. It must be pleasant having the boss back at the ranch."

Feeling a bit wary of his warm greeting, Della replied in a neutral tone. "Aunt Coral and I are very pleased to have him here. We were surprised when he arrived yesterday."

For a moment longer, his gaze roamed her face before his expression sobered. "There's talk among the men, ma'am. They don't like havin' that breed on the place. Some say they'll quit if he stays."

Della brought herself up to her full height, her back as rigid as if a fireplace poker had been thrust between her shoulder blades. "Indeed."

Grady nodded. "I just want you to know that whatever happens, I'll stick by you. I won't run out on you. I reckon if you trust that breed, he must be a straight arrow."

Della flung up her head and froze him with her stare. "Please don't refer to Shane's brother as a *breed*. He has a name. *Wild Wind*. Use it."

Grady settled his hat back on his head and flung up both hands, palms out, in a conciliatory gesture. "My apologies, Miz Hunter. I meant no offense."

Mollified by his seemingly sincere apology, Della gave a stiff nod in acknowledgment and didn't demur when he fell into step beside her as she resumed her stroll toward the barn.

Grady appeared to have recovered his good humor. "If there's ever anythin' I can do to help you, just ask. I mean, now that your husband's gone and you're runnin' the horse ranch by yourself, you might want a man's advice now and again."

Torn between amusement and offense at his brass, Della tossed him a veiled glance. "Thank you. I'll remember that."

Matching his stride to her shorter steps, Grady pressed his offer. "I've had experience with breakin' hosses. Worked some down in Texas. After that, a pardner of mine and I captured some mustangs and broke them to sell. I could do for you what Mr. Hunter did."

"I'll admit you've been an asset since my husband's death, but it's always been our intention to hire someone to finish the horses. Wild Wind uses the same techniques as Mr. Hunter did." Della knew well the cowboy method of breaking horses, and she didn't want that approach used on the high-bred Morgans.

"Well, don't forget my offer. When you need a man at your side, I'll come runnin'."

"Thank you again, but Uncle Clint should be all the man I'll need." Della struggled to keep her irritation from showing. That Grady should presume she couldn't manage the ranch without a man's advice made her determined to prove him wrong.

They reached the barn's open sliding double doors. The cowboy showed no inclination to leave her side. He passed with her through the aperture and into the stable's shadowy interior. The wide corridor between a double row of box stalls stretched the length of the building. A breeze sifted through the open doors at the barn's far end. Bars of afternoon sunshine falling through the wall boards striped the puncheon floor and gilded the dust motes hanging in the air. The *witt witt* call of barn swallows swooping about in the rafters above their heads mingled with the more muted sounds of horses chewing.

A man carrying a currycomb emerged from a stall halfway down the aisle and secured the latch on the stall's half door. A tall man, with flowing dark hair and clad in buckskin. Wild Wind turned toward them and flicked a brief look at Della. Waiting for them to approach, he erased any expression from his face.

Della and Grady halted before him. Della waggled her fingers in the cowboy's direction. "Wild Wind, this is Grady O'Brien. He's agreed to work with you doing the basics with the horses. Grady, may I introduce Wild Wind, Mr. Hunter's brother."

After a slight hesitation, Wild Wind extended his hand and gave a curt nod. "We will see how we work together."

Grady shook the proffered hand. "I'd do anythin' to help Miz Hunter. I will work with you."

Della expelled a breath she didn't realize she'd been holding. She hadn't been sure how Wild Wind would react to being introduced to the cowboy. Meeting one of the men who was willing to work with him had been the first hurdle, one of many more.

After a bit of conversation, Grady departed.

Wild Wind stared after him for a brief moment before he swung his gaze to Della.

"I guess from that conversation you know Uncle Clint has agreed for you to stay and work here."

Wild Wind nodded. "So, one of the men isn't afraid to work with me. We shall see if we can work together, or if he will have a problem with that."

"He'll cooperate, or he won't continue to be employed here."

Wild Wind laid the currycomb on a wooden shelf beside the stall door and turned his attention to Della. Silence fell between them. Della felt Wild Wind's intent regard as a physical touch, though he kept his hands at his sides. Her gaze clung to his face. The air between them tautened, seeming to pull tight and draw them together. When she thought one of them must either move, or burst, she plunged into speech with a breathless gasp.

"Since you'll be working here, we should go to the commissary and get you whatever you need. You brought nothing with you, so we must purchase several things. Everyone who works here has an account at the store, and the tab for purchases is totaled each month and deducted from each person's pay."

He nodded. "If I am to stay in the white man's world, I must dress as one."

Della eyed Wild Wind. He so closely resembled his brother in size that she thought Shane's clothing would fit him. The notion of giving Shane's clothing to Wild Wind made her stomach clench. Would she be able to see Wild Wind clad in Shane's shirts and jeans and not feel as though her heart was being ripped from her chest? Once she gave away Shane's clothes, that link to her husband would be forever severed. Still, to keep his things when Wild Wind had need of them seemed selfish. She plunged ahead before she could change her mind. "Shane's clothing should fit you if you don't mind wearing it. You won't have to buy so much at the commissary if you take Shane's things."

Wild Wind's blue stare perused her face with an intensity that made her want to fidget. "You did not bury Little Wolf's belongings with him?"

Della shook her head. "It's not our way. He was buried only in the clothes he was wearing."

"It is the Cheyenne custom when a man dies to give away his possessions to those outside of his family. You did not give away Little Wolf's belongings when he traveled the Road of the Departed?"

Della swallowed. "No. I couldn't bear to part with them."

Wild Wind stared at her a moment longer, then gave a nod. "I will take them, although The People do not give a man's possessions to his relatives."

"If accepting Shane's clothing makes you feel that you're violating your customs, then please don't take them."

All expression vanished from Wild Wind's face. "I will take them, as long as you do not see Little Wolf in me."

Della searched his blank features, trying to guess what he thought. His perception of her emotional ties to Shane's clothing made her squirm. "I must admit that seeing you wearing Shane's things will remind me of him, but I'll get over it. And I'm not trying to make you over into him."

"Then I will take Little Wolf's clothing."

"I'll get them from the house after we go to the commissary." Della turned toward the tack room. "Since you'll be gentling the Morgans, you'll need Shane's tack. His saddle and rig are in the tack room. I'll show you which gear is his."

After Della had pointed out Shane's gear, they left the barn together. Wild Wind paced beside her with his loose, graceful stride. They crossed the yard and passed beneath the arched compound gate. Turning to the right, they continued past the married men's quarters. They neared the schoolhouse.

"It must be recess," Della commented, her gaze on the grassy area fronting the building.

Several children ranging in age from elementary grades through early teens gathered outside. The younger girls chased each other, and the boys knelt in the dirt before the steps, shooting marbles. The older girls huddled at the corner of the building and gossiped. Their teacher, Hugh Donovan's wife, sat on the steps and supervised her charges.

Jake, catching sight of his mother and his uncle, raced toward them. The other students froze and goggled at the sight of the tall, long-haired warrior wearing buckskin and moccasins. Mrs. Donovan clutched the step's wooden railing and rose to her feet, apprehension plain on her face. Flossie left her playmates and skipped along behind her cousin. Her gingham pinafore tangled about her legs as she ran, and her honeyed curls bounced.

Jake skidded to a stop before his mother, tipping up his freckled face. "What are you doing here with Uncle Wild Wind?"

"Uncle Wild Wind will be training the horses, so we're going to the commissary to get him a few things."

Jake's eyes rounded at the news.

Flossie's face brightened. "Truly? And will you scalp us?" She sparkled at the gruesome prospect.

At Flossie's question, Della hissed, "No, Flossie. Wild Wind won't scalp anyone."

"My friends say that he'll scalp us all in our sleep."

Della knelt before her niece and took her hand. "You can tell your friends Wild Wind won't scalp anyone. We're all perfectly safe with him."

Surprising her, Wild Wind stepped closer. He squatted before the children and laid his hands on their shoulders, one on Jake's and the other on Flossie's. Peering into their eyes, he said in a gentle voice, "Jake, your father was my brother. That makes you my family, and your mother is my family. Cheyenne warriors protect their families and everyone they love."

The children stared into Wild Wind's face. Jake spoke first. "I'm glad you're staying, Uncle Wild Wind."

"Me, too," Flossie echoed.

"You must tell your friends not to be afraid," Della said. "Now, I think recess is over and Mrs. Donovan wants you to go back inside. Go on, now."

Turning the children about, she gave them each a little push. With a final glance over their shoulders at Wild Wind, they darted to the schoolhouse, where Mrs. Donovan waited for them on the steps.

Della rose to her feet with a sigh. Wild Wind shoved to his full height and stared at the closing schoolhouse door.

"The children are only repeating what their parents say," Della said to him.

He looked down at her. "It will take much time for your people to lose their fear of me."

"I hope this will be a good start. We'll just take things one day at a time."

They strolled the rest of the way to the commissary and mounted the steps. As mannerly as if he'd been reared in genteel society, Wild Wind halted at the open door and placed his hand at the small of Della's back, indicating she should precede him.

Della stepped over the threshold into the cool dimness of the mercantile. Wild Wind entered behind her. She took two strides and came to a standstill as an abrupt silence descended.

Behind the counter at the back of the room, Mr. Smith, the clerk, froze. His bespectacled eyes rounded, and his mouth dropped open. One of the cowboy's wives, standing on the near side of the counter with a basket in her hand, turned. The skirt of her gingham cotton dress began to shake when she sighted Wild Wind. Off to one side, two men wearing cowboy garb reached for their six-shooters.

CHAPTER 9

Wild Wind exploded. With his palms on her shoulders, he shoved Della away from him and leaped to one side to keep her out of the line of possible gunfire. He crouched and bunched his fists as if preparing to spring at the two men.

Della steadied herself from Wild Wind's push. "Stop!" she cried. "Put away your guns! Wild Wind won't harm you."

When the men balked, she employed the tone of voice she used on Jake when he resisted taking his Saturday night bath. Her fists propped on her hips, arms akimbo. "There will be no shooting here."

After another brief hesitation, the cowboys dropped their six-shooters into their holsters and stared at her with hostility. Tension twanged in the air.

Della stepped forward. "Gentlemen, Wild Wind has been employed by my uncle to train the Morgans for the cavalry. You are to treat him as you would any other person working on the Slash L. If you cannot do that, you may get your things and collect your pay."

One of the cowboys spoke up. "You can't fire us, Mrs. Hunter. We don't work for you. Only Mr. Donovan or your uncle can fire us."

Della drew herself up to her full height and glared at him. "Mr. Donovan is well aware of my uncle's expectations regarding Wild Wind.

He will let nothing interfere with Uncle Clint's orders. At a word from me, Mr. Donovan will let you go."

The men traded resentful glances and slouched out of the dry goods store, ignoring Della and Wild Wind as they passed. Their boot heels rang on the plank flooring and thudded across the porch, then down the steps to the dirt lane fronting the emporium. Della watched through the open door until they passed from her line of vision.

She pivoted toward Wild Wind and caught his eye. Once again, his face wore the deadpan expression she was beginning to associate with his encounters with the ranch's inhabitants. As alarm drained away, anger on his behalf took its place. Her hands fisted at her sides until her fingernails pressed into her palms. "Once again, I must apologize for my people's rudeness."

Wild Wind's expression gentled. His gaze stroked her face. "My fierce defender, Lona, my heart. I thank you, but you cannot fight my battles."

She narrowed her eyes. "I may not be able to fight your battles, but in my presence, no one will treat you with disrespect."

Their stares tangled, and the moment spun out. The air between them hummed until the middle-aged clerk broke the tension when he cleared his throat. Della glanced in the direction of the long wooden counter at the back of the store. Mr. Smith and his customer still stood in rigid apprehension. Della nodded toward them. "Good afternoon, Mr. Smith, Mrs. Farmer. Don't let us interrupt your business."

Giving her attention to the commissary's merchandise, Della turned in a slow circle. The store resembled a dim cave. The only light in the building filtered through the open door and the two windows flanking the aperture. Halters, bridles, harnesses, rope, and lanterns hung from the ceiling. Bins and shelves crowded the walls. To her left, shelves filled with men's heeled leather riding boots jostled with side-button ladies' shoes and children's footwear. The new style of durable denim pants favored by the cowboys resided in a separate bin beside long-sleeved wool shirts. Bolts of colorful gingham and calico fabric rested on a counter in the middle of the room. Lamp oil, bullets, tools, wire, hammers, and nails filled other bins. To her right, needles, pins, soaps, coffee beans, dried beans, flour, and sugar stocked the shelves. A coffee mill, a glass jar filled with soda crackers, a container full of peppermint sticks, and a small scale rested on the counter top beside an ornate register.

A cast iron potbellied stove filled the space in the center of the room. Della faced Wild Wind. "What did you have in mind?"

Narrowing his eyes, he gave the mercantile a slow perusal. His attention snagged on the denim pants. "I think I would cause less fear if I dressed like the other men. I would purchase some of those trousers."

Curling her fingers around his biceps, Della turned him toward her. She studied his face. "Are you sure? Do you really want to dress as we do?"

"My heart mingles the blood of the Cheyenne with the blood of my mother's people. Now, it is time for me to be one with my mother's people."

Della squeezed his arm, noting the hard muscle beneath the smooth deerskin sleeve. "Very well. I'll help you choose what you'll need."

While Della sorted clothing items and deliberated over what to buy, Mrs. Farmer paid for her purchases and scuttled out the door. Mr. Smith braced his arms on the counter and watched with a wary expression.

Della chose four pairs of the denim pants, four wool shirts, socks, and a belt with a silver buckle. She laid the items on the counter and joined Wild Wind where he stood contemplating the boots.

"Do you want boots, as well?"

He glanced down at her and gave a slow nod. "How do I choose?"

Glancing at his moccasined feet to gauge what size he would wear, Della reached for a pair of sturdy brown leather cowboy boots. "Try these on. I think they'll fit."

When she'd added the boots to the pile of clothing on the counter, Della selected a sheepskin jacket and a black, low-crowned felt riding hat to complete Wild Wind's wardrobe. Mr. Smith continued to watch them with a frown.

"What kind of rifle do you have?" Della recalled the weapon which had hung over Wild Wind's shoulder when she'd first seen him.

"Mine is what the pony soldiers call a Henry."

Della pursed her lips. "Hmm... We can do better than that. Uncle Clint prefers the Winchester 1873 model, and all of the men who work for him carry them. We can get one for you here."

With Wild Wind trailing her, she approached the counter. Halting when she reached the rough barrier, she folded both hands on its planked surface. "Mr. Smith, please get down one of those Winchesters hanging behind you and add it to the tab. And a box of cartridges."

Mr. Smith didn't move. He stared at her with the air of a rabbit cornered by a wolf. "Mrs. Hunter, I can't do that. I can't sell weapons to an Injun."

Fury boiled through her, though she attempted to keep her voice controlled. Behind her, Wild Wind collected himself into the stillness only a tribal warrior could achieve. Della leaned over the counter, icy hauteur coloring her tone. Her stare bored into the clerk's face. "You *will* sell us that rifle and the cartridges, or you *will* be relieved of your position on this ranch. You'll be transported to Denver on the next wagon to make the trip."

Mr. Smith's mustache quivered. His lips twitched. "Mrs. Hunter, it ain't safe to sell arms to the Injuns, considerin' they're attackin' us. The army forbids it."

Della breathed deeply and snatched at her patience. "Wild Wind is my husband's blood brother. He has been hired by Uncle Clint to train remounts for the cavalry. He isn't at war with us. Now, will you get that Winchester down off the wall, or shall I?"

Mr. Smith's shaking fingers plucked at the collar of his shirt, but he didn't move.

"I promise you that if I have to go behind the counter and get the rifle myself, you will be out of a job." Della stepped to the left and the counter's open end, as if to make good on her threat.

"All right, all right." Muttering to himself, the hapless clerk turned toward the wall. Reaching up, he lifted the Winchester from the brackets that attached it to the wall and laid it on the counter beside Della's other purchases.

"A box of cartridges, too."

Mr. Smith brought a box of ammunition from a shelf beneath the counter and deposited it beside the rifle with a thump.

"Thank you. Now, please ring up everything and put it on Wild Wind's tab. He'll have an account here like every other employee. I expect you to treat him with the same consideration that you do everyone else the next time he comes here to make purchases."

When the transaction was complete and their acquisitions had been stuffed into two baskets, Wild Wind and Della stepped outside. The Winchester hung by its strap over Wild Wind's shoulder.

They paused on the porch, and Wild Wind looked over at Della with a grave expression.

She raised her eyebrows in a silent question.

"For you, I will keep my peace as long as I can, but the time will come when I must fight. When the white eyes look at me as though I am a dog to be kicked, then I must fight to take my place here as a man. A warrior never runs."

For long moments, Della stared back at him. She'd lived in the Colorado territory long enough to know that by the code of the West a man was measured by the respect he earned, a respect acquired by his actions and, if necessary, backed up by his fists or his gun. In his own culture, Wild Wind had earned the respect of all the Plains tribes. Here, in her world, he was feared. The respect he must earn.

"You must do what you must. I'll not ask you to turn your back when you should fight."

∼

That evening when Della took a dinner tray to Wild Wind, she halted just inside the barn, staring. Wild Wind waited for her by the tack room door. Instead of his buckskin shirt and trousers, he wore the jeans and a blue wool shirt they'd purchased that afternoon. The belt with the silver buckle had been threaded through his pants' loops and encircled his trim waist. New heeled leather riding boots clad his feet, adding to his height.

She admitted to herself that she was relieved he wore a new outfit instead of Shane's clothes.

He said nothing. He merely waited in silence while she looked him up and down.

"You scarcely look like the same man. You look almost like a cowboy."

Wild Wind nodded in unsmiling agreement.

"Come." Della brushed past him and stepped into the tack room where he took his meals. She laid the dinner tray on the trunk they used as a table and straightened, turning toward him when he followed her. "Eat. Then I'd like to ask a favor of you."

Wild Wind moved to the trunk and thrust out a hand. "Sit with me while I eat. Then you may ask me what it is you wish me to do."

Della perched on the stool at the other end of the trunk and watched while he ate. When he finished, he laid the cloth napkin beside his plate and pinned her with a stare. "What favor do you ask of me?"

"I would like you to tell me something about your people that would help me know them better. Perhaps some of your legends."

Wild Wind rose to his feet and with silent tread approached Della. He took her hand and laced his fingers through hers. "Come. We will walk, and I will tell you how Death came to be."

Her request stemmed from more than idle curiosity. If Wild Wind should become a God-fearing man and they married, she would accept his culture as her own.

After a slight hesitation in which she ignored the warning that vibrated in her heart telling her that she crossed a line from which she could never return, Della accompanied Wild Wind from the barn and through the compound gate. They followed the track up the knoll past the cemetery. When they'd passed the spiked iron fence surrounding the graves, he halted.

"The legend of how Death came into the world has been passed down from the Old Ones." Wild Wind kept his hand linked with hers.

He dipped his chin to look into her face. "When Mother Earth was created, there was no death. After a time, the earth became so crowded that there was no room for more people. The chiefs called a council to come up with a plan. They decided that some people should die and be put in a grass house that faced east. This way, there would be room for more people on the earth. But the chiefs didn't want the relatives of those who had gone away to be unhappy forever, so they decided that after a while, everyone would return."

Wild Wind paused and swept the prairie's billowing grassland with a glance, then returned his attention to Della. She watched his face fill with animation while he talked. A current of summer's breeze stirred his hair.

"Coyote didn't like the plan. He thought that when all the people returned from the grass hut, there wouldn't be enough food for everyone. No one else listened to him because they wanted their relatives to come back." Wild Wind stared out across the prairie and spoke as though his words came from deep inside.

"When the first person died, he was laid to rest in the grass hut. The medicine man called to the man's spirit. A strong whirlwind came and tried to enter the hut, but Coyote ran and slammed the door before the whirlwind could enter. The whirlwind was angry and swept by the hut. After that, Death came into the world."

Della shivered. The nearby cemetery gave mute testament of the reality of death. Her Bible taught that death had come into the world through sin, but the Cheyenne legend touched her, nonetheless. "That's a moving legend. You will have to teach me more of your people's stories."

"When we are one, my people's history will be your history."

Della recalled her days in his village when his aunt had been tasked with teaching her to be a good Cheyenne wife. "If we marry, Neha will have to teach me more about how to be a Cheyenne wife."

"You will learn and will please me very much." Wild Wind loosened his hand from hers and stepped away a pace. His chin lifted, and he breathed deeply, as if testing the air.

While they'd talked, dusk had settled over the grasslands.

She didn't know how to reply. He stood alone, a solitary symbol of the unification of two cultures. Nothing could express what she felt. Words seemed inadequate. Her heart swelled. She bridged the distance between them and wrapped her arms about his waist, laying her head on his chest. After a moment his arms stole around the small of her back, pressing her against him, and he rested his cheek atop her hair. They stood in a silent embrace while the sun sank below the horizon and the first star blinked in the heavens.

CHAPTER 10

On the third Sunday after Wild Wind's arrival, Della sat at the pump organ in the schoolhouse. She twitched her lavender gown's pleated lawn fabric aside so that she could work the pedals without the material getting in her way.

The organ had been transported to the ranch from Denver by wagon and had been positioned off to one side at the front of the classroom. On Sundays, the desks were shoved beneath the windows along one wall and backless benches brought in to transform the school into a makeshift church. When her Uncle Clint was at the ranch, he delivered the sermon. In his absence, Emory Dyer stood in as the preacher.

On this Lord's day, the benches were full. Women in their Sunday best calico dresses and poke bonnets sat beside their husbands, their children ranged in rows beside them. The single cowboys filled the benches at the back.

Coral sat in the front row on the organ side of the room, her two older children on either side and Jesse on her lap. Jake sat beside Flossie. He wriggled, unable to sit still, and swung his feet back and forth. Reaching behind Flossie's back, he jerked one of her braids. Retaliating, Flossie slapped him. Coral laid a restraining hand on her daughter's knee and squeezed. She gave her a look of stern disapproval.

Della caught Jake's eye and frowned at him, shaking her head. A guilty expression crossed his face. He looked down at his hands, now clasped with deceptive innocence in his lap.

A lanky cowboy with curly mink-colored hair strolled along the aisle beside the windows on the organ side of the building. At the front row, he lowered himself to the bench beside Jake, leaving enough room for Della to sit between them. Lifting his hat from his head, he leaned down and set it on the floor beneath the bench. He straightened and caught her eye, tossing her a mischievous grin.

Unsure of what to make of Grady's action, Della nodded at him.

At that moment, Toby, the ranch cook, stepped to the podium and signaled for the hymn singing to commence. Toby's checkered background included a well-defined musical talent, so he led the singing for every service. When Toby gave her the cue, Della launched into the first hymn. The old organ bellowed, filling the schoolhouse with sound. The worshippers joined in, lifting their voices to the rafters.

After the hymns had been sung, Toby turned the service over to Emory Dyer. Della scooted off the organ bench and had taken one step toward her seat when a movement at the back of the room caught her eye. On silent feet, Wild Wind slipped through the open door. He paused for a heartbeat, framed in the aperture, a dark silhouette against the sunshine's glittering dazzle. Della halted, poised beside the organ. For a brief instant, their eyes met over the heads of the worshippers. The impact jolted Della to her toes. Recovering herself, she hurried to the planked pew and took her seat between Jake and Grady.

Speculating at Wild Wind's presence distracted Della from focusing on the preaching. Grady O'Brien's lean length beside her where Shane should have been filled her with a piercing sense of loss. She struggled to keep her attention on the sermon.

While the service progressed, heat built up in the schoolhouse. Women fanned themselves with paper fans, and children squirmed. Men wiped sweat off the backs of their necks. Flies buzzed. When at last the service drew to a close and Della had accompanied the singing of the final hymn, the worshippers hurriedly filed outside.

Wild Wind had slipped out at the beginning of the hymn, though not before catching Della's eye once again when she settled herself on the organ bench. She fumbled the hymn's first notes, distracted by Wild Wind's glance.

Coral took the children with her at the end of the service, but Grady O'Brien waited beside the first-row bench until Della finished. With his cowboy hat in one hand, he grinned down at her.

"You sure make a pretty picture this mornin', Miz Della. That get-up you're wearin' becomes you in a fine way." His glance traveled in a slow perusal up the length of her slim lavender gown to the little straw hat decorated with silk violets perched on her upswept curls.

Flustered by his compliment, Della murmured a thank you. She reached to gather up her Bible from where she'd left it on the plank seat, but Grady swooped down and plucked the black book off the bench before she could reach it.

"Here you go." He held the Bible out to her. "May I accompany you as far as the gate? I'd ask if I could walk you all the way to your front door, but I'm on guard duty right after lunch."

Della hesitated. Outside of Denver, social mores in the West were more relaxed than in Boston. Had she still lived in Boston, she would have been in full mourning three months after Shane's death, and Grady's offer would have been deemed highly improper. In the West, life wasn't kind to women without a man or a family to care for them. She'd known widows to remarry brief weeks after burying their husbands. Perhaps Grady thought nothing of offering to walk her home. Still, Della wasn't ready to allow another man such privileges. And what Wild Wind would do should Grady show her attention didn't bear considering.

"I thank you for your kind offer, but I fear I'm not quite ready for another man to walk me home."

Grady spread his hands wide. "I meant no offense. I thought that since you spend so much time with Mr. Wild Wind, you might be ready to take up with another man."

Guilt that she should discuss marriage with Wild Wind while at the same time refuse an offer from another man made her defensive. Della drew herself up and squared her shoulders. "Sir, you presume too much. Wild Wind is family."

Grady shrugged. "My apologies, Miz Della, for readin' the signs wrong. I hope I can at least walk with you to the church steps."

Still feeling guilty, Della relented. "You may."

Outside, they paused on the top step while Grady settled his hat on his curls. He glanced at Della. "I thank you, Miz Della. One day, I hope you'll consider allowin' me to squire you about. And you can be sure I'll give you and your uncle my loyalty on the ranch, whatever happens between us. I ride for the brand."

Della gripped her Bible in a tight clasp. "Thank you, Grady. I make no promises regarding my personal life, but I do appreciate your loyalty."

Grady tilted the brim of his hat forward and flashed her a cocky grin. "A fella can hope, can't he?" He nodded in her direction. "Good day, Miz Della."

Della watched him clatter down the steps and turn toward the cook shack. At a much slower pace, she descended the stairs. She strolled through the main compound's arched gate and across the yard to the house. Inside, Coral was in the dining room setting the table for luncheon when Della halted in the doorway.

Coral, wearing a flattering gown of peacock blue voile with swaths of fabric gathered over a bustle, paused in the act of laying a silver fork beside a gold-rimmed flowered china plate. She raised a questioning eyebrow.

"Aunt Coral, do you ever wonder what we'd be doing now if we hadn't come West?"

Coral straightened the fork before she replied. She lifted her gaze from the silverware and looked at Della. "I suppose Clint would have taken up his lawyer's practice in Boston again after he mustered out of the army."

"Do you miss your life on the plantation?"

Coral fingered the linen tablecloth, a remnant of her former life, and sighed. She met her niece's questioning gaze. "At one time, I would have said yes, but now, this life with Clint in the Colorado territory is all I want."

Della mused on that comment a moment before she said, "If I hadn't come West with you and Uncle Clint, I'd still be in Boston, undoubtedly married to an acceptable and boring gentleman. I can't imagine such a life, after having known and loved Shane."

Coral tipped her head sideways, eying her niece with a considering stare. "You weren't meant for a life in such society."

Della shuddered. "Certainly not."

Coral stared at her a moment longer. "Sadie has fixed enough food to feed half of the ranch. It's time I made good on my offer to invite Wild Wind to dinner. Why don't you ask him to eat with us instead of taking him a tray later?"

Wondering what Grady would think if he knew, Della hurriedly dismissed the thought. "All right. I'll ask him."

Outside, she crossed the yard to the barn. The noon sun hammered the earth with heat. Pausing just inside the barn's open double doors, Della took a grateful breath of the building's cool dimness. She glanced about, hoping to spy Wild Wind. Zeus, her uncle's aging stallion, lifted his graying black head and pricked his ears at her behind the bars of his stall. In the loft, the ever-present swallows flitted among the rafters, filling the silence with their shrill cries.

Della had taken only two steps when Wild Wind appeared in the doorway of the last stall, the stall they'd made into a bedroom for Shane before his marriage to Della. Wild Wind watched while she drew near, the broad-brimmed cowboy hat he wore a symbol of his new identity. His boots, jeans, and wool shirt belied his Cheyenne blood.

In the dim light, he so resembled her dead husband a pang pierced Della's heart. When she halted before him and tipped back her head to look into his face, she couldn't speak. They stared at each other for several moments of weighty silence.

Wild Wind's blue gaze drifted over her, taking in her heeled high-buttoned shoes, her flounced and ruched long-sleeved lavender gown, and the stylish straw hat with its rolled brim, tilted at a saucy angle atop her up-swept curls. "Lona, you are very much the lady today. The memory of how you looked wearing Cheyenne dress in my village is almost gone as the smoke of a cooking fire."

Della glanced down at her outfit. "I dress up on Sundays."

"Perhaps one day you will visit the reservation and wear Cheyenne dress again."

"Perhaps."

They stood in silence once more, while the air between them thrummed. At last Della blurted, "I was surprised to see you in church this morning."

"I came because you told me you would marry a man of your own faith. I wanted to hear more of what you believe."

"That is good. And we can talk of the Bible, and of Jesus Christ, the Savior of the world."

"My mother talked of the man/God, Jesus, when she was married to my father and we lived in my village. Then, when the pony soldiers came and took us to the fort, I went with her to church until I ran away."

"Do you remember what she told you?"

"I remember the stories she told me from your black book, the Bible."

"Perhaps we can talk this afternoon, after we eat. Aunt Coral sent me to fetch you. She's inviting you to eat dinner with us."

Wild Wind nodded. "She is very kind."

"I want you to know that I'm praying for you, that the Lord will show you the truth."

"It is good."

Together, they left the barn and crossed the yard. Reaching the steps, Wild Wind took Della's elbow in a firm clasp. He didn't loosen his hold while they crossed the veranda to the wide mahogany front door. He reached around her, opening the portal and swinging it wide. When he waited for her to enter ahead of him, Della cut a surprised glance in his direction.

In reply to her unspoken comment, Wild Wind looked down at her.

"My mother taught me how a gentleman treats a lady. I didn't want to learn. I caused her no end of grief and trouble, but I watched how her white-eyes husband treated her. I know what is expected of a gentleman. I will give you the all the respect that you would expect of a white man."

His confession touched her, the admission of a man who'd been reared as a warrior, yet who now adapted to a culture that conflicted with many things he'd learned as a Cheyenne male. "When I lived in your village, I saw that you were a man of many faces. I see that's even more true today."

"A tree must be flexible in the wind, or it will break. I am that tree."

Della nodded. Flicking him one more glance, she stepped ahead of him into the foyer. Inside, Wild Wind snatched his hat from his head, then stared at it as if wondering what to do with it. Della pried the headgear from his fingers and hung it on a hook on the mahogany hall tree in the corner.

When they reached the dining room, Coral greeted them with a bright smile. "I'm so glad you could join us, Wild Wind."

He dipped his head. "I thank you for your invitation."

Standing behind her chair at the hostess's end of the table, Coral indicated the chair on her right. "You can sit there, between Della and me."

The children ranged along the other side of the table like three inquisitive birds.

Wild Wind seated first Coral, then Della, before he took his own seat. Coral sent Della an approving look.

Della saw by the anticipation on her son's face and the gleam in Flossie's eyes that they had questions bursting to be asked. At the first lull in conversation, Jake jumped into the silence.

"Uncle Wild Wind, have you stolen any horses lately? Where did you put them? Can I see where you hid them?"

Della's fork clattered to her plate. She glared across the table at her son. Before she could reprimand him, Flossie tossed her own conversational bomb into the shocked hush.

"How many people have you killed? Did you scalp them?"

Aaron, Coral's middle child, echoed his bolder sister. "Yeth, how many people have you killed?" His grin displayed a gap where his front teeth should have been.

Coral choked. Della leaned over her plate and leveled her sternest stare at Jake. "You're being rude, young man. Uncle Wild Wind isn't a horse thief. You must apologize."

Wild Wind curled his fingers about Della's forearm, where she'd rested it on the table's edge, silencing her. He directed his attention to his nephew. "When I was a young brave trying to prove myself, I stole many horses. Stealing horses is one way a Cheyenne brave proves he is a man. Now I know that stealing horses is wrong and will cause trouble. I no longer steal horses."

He slid his stare to Flossie, who quailed a little beneath his intent regard. "I admit to killing many people. I have killed more people than I can remember, but I kill no more. I will kill only to protect you and your family, and Lona."

"Who is Lona?" Flossie asked.

Wild Wind loosed his grasp on Della's arm and rested a hand on her shoulder. "Lona is Jake's mother."

A puzzled expression crossed Flossie's face. "I didn't know her name was Lona."

"My momma's name is Della," Jake insisted.

Della caught her breath, wondering how Wild Wind would explain the name he'd given her. She turned her head to stare at him, noting that Coral also had fixed a fascinated gaze on his face.

"Before you were born, your mother lived for a while in my village. I saw that she was very beautiful, so I called her *Lona,* which means beautiful. She is Lona to me."

Jake's eyes rounded, and he looked at his mother. His expression betrayed his amazement that his mother had actually had a life before his birth.

A smile tugged at Della's mouth.

Sadie's entrance into the dining room with a savory dried apple pie diverted the children's attention. The scent of apples and cinnamon drifted through the room, and the children begged for a piece of the treat.

After the meal, Della accompanied Wild Wind to the veranda. They paused at the top stair. He settled the black cowboy hat atop his dark hair, tugging the brim down to give it a cocky angle.

Della leaned against the carved white-washed column at the top of the steps. "That didn't go too badly." She curled an arm around the post and tipped her head at Wild Wind. "Except for the children's questions."

"Children are children."

"Apparently the adults are still talking, and the schoolchildren are repeating what they hear their parents say."

Wild Wind shrugged.

"What about the men? How are they treating you?"

Wild Wind's silence told her all she needed to know. Her fingers tightened on the post. "Who is it? I'll deal with them."

Wild Wind sliced a sharp glance at her. His eyes glittered. "You will not. I will fight my own battles. A Cheyenne warrior does not hide behind his woman."

Chastened, Della regretted her unruly tongue. She'd insulted him. Would she never learn to think before she spoke? She loosened her arm from the porch pillar and stepped close to Wild Wind. "I didn't think. I'm sorry."

Wild Wind hooked one hand about the back of Della's neck and pulled her to him, pressing her face into his shirt front. She breathed in his warmth while he held her in a brief, one-armed embrace. Loosening his hold, he set her away from him. He looked into her face, his fingers still curling around her neck. "I thank you and your Aunt Coral for dinner. Now, I must go."

His hand fell away from her. With his usual grace, he took the porch steps two at a time and strode across the yard to the barn. Leaning once more against the post, Della tracked his progress. With his innate Cheyenne arrogance, he now cut an imposing dash in his cowboy attire.

She understood the challenges he'd overcome to live in her world, yet he faced each one with dignity and courage. In spite of her grief for Shane, her heart couldn't help but respond to Wild Wind. His fortitude in the face of adversity chipped away at her defenses. He had begun to fill the empty spaces left by Shane's death, and he bore her along on the tide of his relentless determination despite her reservations.

Colorado Territory
Late Spring, 1876

CHAPTER 11

Della shut the front door. She crossed the veranda and looked out into the bleached whiteness of the hot afternoon. Across the yard, Wild Wind stood outside the corral which enclosed the army's four-year-old Morgans. Jake leaned on the fence beside him in a miniature copy of his uncle's stance, elbows splayed wide on the rail, one foot hooked over the bottom bar exactly like Wild Wind. They seemed to be absorbed in a serious conversation about the merits of each horse.

Della smiled. Ever since Wild Wind had eaten his first Sunday dinner with them, Jake had followed his uncle each day after school. His conversation these two weeks past had been peppered with "Uncle Wild Wind says..."

Wild Wind had shown his nephew unending patience and treated him as an equal, never looking down on him. She hoped Jake wouldn't wear out his welcome.

Della tripped down the steps and crossed the yard, coming to a standstill beside her son. "What are you men up to now?"

Jake tipped a flushed and freckled face up to her. "Uncle Wild Wind is teaching me how to pick a good horse." Jake's voice quivered with excitement.

Della looked over his head at Wild Wind. As grateful as she was for Wild Wind's interest in her son and for standing in as a father figure, illogical resentment niggled. Shane should have been the one to teach his son the things a man passes on to the next generation. Yet Shane couldn't teach Jake how to be a man, how to live honorably, or how to do all the many things expected of him. She banished her selfish thoughts and smiled at Wild Wind. "I thank you for being kind to Jake."

A smile curled Wild Wind's lips. "Your son is a fast learner. He will make a good horseman."

Jake tugged at her sleeve. "Uncle Wild Wind is teaching me how to ride. I told him Papa had started to teach me, but I still have lots to learn."

That Jake could speak of his father in so natural a way showed how much he'd healed. Della supposed she had Wild Wind to thank for her son's emotional progress. Apart from her Uncle Clint, she couldn't think of a better man to help her son than Wild Wind. Della lifted her gaze once more to her husband's brother. "Do you have time to teach him?"

With the sun behind him, his cowboy hat shadowed his face. "The Morgans need riding, so it is no problem for me to saddle a spare horse for Jake and take him along."

Della glanced down at her son again, at his hopeful and glowing countenance. He hadn't seemed so happy since Shane's death. "All right, but you must remember Uncle Wild Wind has a lot to do, so you mustn't get in his way if he's too busy."

Jake dropped his foot to the ground and bounced with excitement. "I want to learn to ride just like Uncle Wild Wind."

"You couldn't have a better teacher than Uncle Wild Wind." Even as she spoke the words aloud, her mind protested. Shane had been every bit as good a horseman as his brother and could have passed his skill along to their son. Once more, Della struggled against the injustice of Shane's untimely death. She closed her eyes, trying to keep in mind that the Lord ordained life and death, and Shane's death had been no accident to God. Her husband had been taken to Heaven at the right time decreed by her Lord, and she should accept that.

A movement more sensed than heard made Della open her eyes. Wild Wind had sidled around Jake and now stood at her side, close enough so that she could feel his warmth. His gaze bored into her, demanding her full attention. She pivoted so they faced each other.

"You must not blame your son for putting his father behind him. Little Wolf has gone down the Road of the Departed and is not here to be a father to his son. Jake needs a man to teach him the things a man must learn. I will not take Little Wolf's place in Jake's heart, but your son is young. The seasons will pass, and I am here. In time, he will look on me as a father. Do not blame him, or me, when that happens."

The restless wind plucked at the sleeves of Della's white blouse and slapped her split riding skirt against her boots while she stared into Wild Wind's unyielding face. Life lived by the Plains tribes had no room for sentimental weakness, so she shouldn't blame her brother-in-law for his pragmatic attitude. "I don't blame you, not really. I'm actually grateful for what you're doing for Jake." A tentative smile trembled on her mouth.

Bored with the adult conversation, Jake wriggled around them and headed toward the barn. His boots scuffed along the ground and sent up puffs of dust with each step.

The tack room door slammed. Grady appeared in the double doorway at the near end of the barn. Spying Della and Wild Wind standing close together, Grady halted. Della felt his accusing stare across the distance.

Guilt made her step away from Wild Wind, though they hadn't been touching. "I think... I think... I must go back to the house."

Leaving behind the men and the factions they represented, Della fled to the house. Inside the foyer, she turned into the parlor. Once through the room's wide doorway, she dropped onto the piano stool. Music had always been her refuge. Now, her fingers hovered over the piano keyboard, but no song came to mind. Instead, thoughts of Wild Wind whirled through her head.

She lowered her hands to her lap and stared at the sheet music arranged on the rack, not seeing the pages. Instead, she thought of the past three Sundays when Wild Wind had attended the church services. He'd sat in the first row with Coral and her and their assorted children. The children loved him and quarreled over who would sit beside him. Following the service, he accompanied them home and stayed for dinner. Often, the sermon was a mealtime topic, and the women answered his questions as best they could.

Also, during these past three weeks, incidents had occurred that made Della angry on Wild Wind's behalf. Except for Grady, the men who helped with the horses grumbled and balked at working with him, but Della had managed to keep them from quitting. They ignored Wild Wind or talked about him in his presence, as though he couldn't understand English. One day, a sliced girth strap gave way while he was riding, and both he and the saddle had tipped off the horse. Another time, he found that his bedding had been soiled with horse manure. A prairie rattler had been turned loose in his bedroom. No one confessed to the pranks, but the men watched Wild Wind to see how he'd respond. So far, he'd remained stoic, but Della knew that sooner or later, he'd react.

During her evening prayers that night, she brought her concerns to her Heavenly Father. Wild Wind had begun to mean too much, and he wasn't a God-fearing man. Thoughts of him often occupied her mind, and images of Shane began to dim, leaving her guilt-ridden. Fear for what Wild Wind would do when pushed too far by the other men gripped her. Della poured out her burdens to her Lord. Finding a measure of peace, she crawled beneath her blankets and fell asleep.

~

During the dark hours of that night, she woke to the sound of horses stampeding across the yard and out the compound gate. Tossing back the covers, she leaped to the window and peered out just in time to see the last of the Morgans gallop onto the prairie.

After flinging on her clothes and stomping her feet into her boots, Della hurried downstairs. She snatched her jacket from the hall tree by the front door and stepped outside, skimming down the veranda steps while she thrust her arms into the jacket's sleeves. By the time she reached the yard, Wild Wind had appeared, fully dressed. Grady and the other wranglers tumbled from the bunkhouse, Scipio in their midst.

They all converged beside the open corral gate. Della drew up beside Wild Wind, who stood with his hands on his hips, elbows akimbo, staring at the empty corral. When Della halted beside him, he turned his head toward her.

"Wasn't the gate latched properly?" she asked.

"I was the last person to shut the gate after I took one of the geldings for a ride after supper. I always latch the gate."

Wild Wind would never be careless of something so important as making sure the gate was properly secured. This had to be another prank, although this prank went beyond the others in severity. Della and Wild Wind shared a glance. The unspoken realization of what had happened simmered between them.

Scipio halted beside them. "Someone wants real bad to make it look like you didn't fasten the gate," he muttered to Wild Wind.

With his back to the other men, Wild Wind nodded his agreement.

Cocking his graying curly head at Della, Scipio murmured, "I'm not pointing fingers, mind you, but Virgil came into the bunkhouse just before the hosses cut loose. Said he'd been to the privy."

"Hmm... I'll keep that in mind. Virgil hasn't been happy about working with Wild Wind."

Della approached the knot of wranglers standing a few paces away. She heard mutterings of "that breed let the horses get out."

Halting beside the hostile men, she tackled the problem head on. "Wild Wind told me he latched the gate properly, and I believe him. That means someone let the horses out. I mean to get to the bottom of this."

"You'd take his word over ours, Miz Della?" Virgil Bledsoe, a bull of a man with a broad face, challenged. He hunched his shoulders and fisted his meaty hands. "We were all in the bunkhouse, sleeping."

"Wild Wind doesn't lie."

"We all know Injuns lie."

"Enough!" Della exclaimed, her tone sharp. "That's nonsense, and I'll hear no more of that talk!"

The men shifted and muttered. Hostility radiated from them in waves. Grady stepped away from the rest and distanced himself from the bunch. He came to a standstill beside Della.

"What we have to do now is to get the horses back," Della snapped. "Saddle up."

"I stand with you, Miz Della," Grady declared. "I'm not with those malcontents."

Della acknowledged his confession with a nod. "Thank you, Grady."

When the men had tacked up their horses, they clattered out of the compound. A full prairie moon rode the night sky and illumined their way with it silvery light. Wild Wind rode point to track the herd. Della rode beside him, with Scipio on the warrior's other side.

They located the Morgans a few miles from the ranch, heads down and grazing. When the horsemen rode up, the runaways bunched and took flight again. By the time they'd been rounded up and returned to the corral, dawn had chased the moon from the sky and pure golden light tinted the heavens.

Della swung down from her mustang. Weariness dragged at her.

Wild Wind shut the gate behind the last Morgan and secured the latch. Leading his own mount, Scipio strolled up to Della. Concern for her etched his dark face.

"Miz Della, I'll take care of your mustang. You'd best go on back to bed and get some sleep." Reaching out, he pried the reins from her fingers.

Della shook her head in protest as Wild Wind approached in time to hear Scipio's offer. He curved one palm over her shoulder and squeezed with tender concern.

"Lona, you have done enough tonight. Let us take care of your horse." Turning her about, he gave her a gentle push toward the house.

Della relented and stumbled across the yard. From the corner of her eye, she saw Grady watching. She couldn't muster the energy to fret that he'd seen Wild Wind touch her shoulder. She was too exhausted to care.

CHAPTER 12

After supper three days later, Scipio knocked on the front door. Silvie, Coral's childhood nanny, answered the summons. She returned to the dining room where Della and Coral were stacking dirty supper dishes on a tray.

Silvie halted in the doorway. "Miz Della, Scipio is at the door. Says he needs to see you right away."

Exchanging a curious look with Coral, Della added the plate she held to the tray. "Did he say what he wants?"

Silvie shook her graying head and smoothed her apron over her calico skirts. "No, just that you should come right away."

Wondering what emergency could have sent Scipio to her door during the evening hours, Della hurried outside. Scipio waited on the veranda, his back to her. When he heard the door shut, he wheeled.

"We got trouble, Miz Della. One of the Morgans has the colic."

Colic! Dread grabbed at Della's chest. One of the many conditions horsemen feared most, colic could kill a horse. "How bad?"

They left the veranda before Scipio even replied. Della trotted along beside him, trying to keep up with his long strides.

"Bad. Wild Wind and I have been walking him, but he wants to go down."

"Which one?"

"The big bay gelding."

Della halted, shaking her head in dismay. "Not the bay gelding! He's one of our best prospects for the army."

Scipio paused long enough to cast her a sideways look and reply. "We're doin' what we can to save him, Miz Della."

"I know you are."

They continued to the horse barn and passed through the open doors into the building's shadows. Della spied Wild Wind holding the lead rope of the ailing bay gelding halfway down the corridor between box stalls. He led the horse toward them, taking care to let the bay set the pace.

Della hurried to his side. Sweat drenched the bay's glossy russet coat. The gelding sank to its knees. Before the horse could go all the way down, Wild Wind tugged on the lead rope and urged the Morgan back to its feet.

Della rubbed the horse's damp neck and glanced at Wild Wind across its black mane. Beneath the brim of his hat, his expression reflected the gravity of the crisis. Grimness darkened his blue stare.

"Tell me what you've done," she said. She addressed both men when Scipio joined her and Wild Wind.

"I dosed him with some linseed oil," Scipio replied.

"That's good." Della nodded. "Has it helped?"

"Can't see any improvement."

"My people make a tea of herbs when we have horses that colic," Wild Wind said. "I am brewing some to give him."

Grateful for any help, Della agreed. "Thank you. Scipio and I will keep walking him until the tea is ready."

Della worked alongside the men all that long night to bring the gelding through the bout of colic. They lit lanterns and hung them from hooks in the posts separating each stall. The lanterns cast flickering amber light along the length of the hallway, punctuated by patches of shadow.

They dosed the horse with the linseed oil and the tea Wild Wind brewed.

Della took turns walking the gelding. She coaxed him with pats and encouraging words. His suffering wrenched at her heart. When the gelding halted and refused to move, his head hanging, she ran her hands down his neck. "Come on, beautiful boy. Don't give up. You can't stop now."

Wild Wind took the lead rope. "Let me. I will get him moving again."

Toward dawn, they began to see some small improvement in the gelding. He ceased his attempts to lay down, and his eyes brightened. The bay lifted his head and pricked his ears at the humans gathered about him.

Della smiled in relief. She gripped Wild Wind's arm. "We did it! He pulled through."

Wild Wind drew her close with one arm locked about the small of her back. He pressed her to his chest and put his mouth close to her ear, speaking in a tone so gentle it nearly broke her heart. "Lona, my own, you fought for his life like a she-bear fights for her young, and the gelding will live. Now, you are tired. Come with me. There is nothing more for you to do. Scipio will take care of the gelding."

Della didn't budge. "But I can..."

When she resisted, Wild Wind scooped her up in his arms and carried her from the barn. With a sigh, she tucked her head beneath his chin.

A rim of light glimmered above the edge of the wide expanse of dark, rolling prairie, heralding the approach of dawn. They reached the veranda steps.

Della yawned against Wild Wind's shoulder. "I didn't realize how exhausted I am. But saving the gelding was worth giving up a night's sleep."

"It is life. Illness comes to horses and children during the darkness."

Della tightened her grasp around Wild Wind's neck. "Could we stay out here a bit longer? I'm not ready to go inside."

Without replying, Wild Wind mounted the steps and turned left toward the swing hanging from the porch ceiling. With exquisite care, he settled onto the swing and positioned Della across his lap. Her legs dangled to one side. His arms tightened around her. Her head still rested beneath his chin.

"We will stay here until you are ready to go inside."

"Thank you. I'd rather be with you."

He said nothing, but one large hand stroked her back in soothing circles. She relaxed into his warmth and closed her eyes. With a sigh, she pitched into oblivion.

Sometime later, Wild Wind stirred and woke her. She pushed away from his chest and sat up. Dawn's pure light shimmered, etching the world in rosy gold. Della blinked. Looking about her, she wondered why she wasn't in her bed. An instant later memory flooded back. The bay gelding. Colic. Healing.

She glanced at Wild Wind. One of his hands curled about her forearm. "It wasn't a dream, was it? We saved the bay gelding."

"It was no dream."

"Thank you for staying here with me. I'm sorry I kept you up when you could have gone back to your room and slept."

His eyes crinkled. His lips tilted up at the corners. "I would rather have been here with you."

Unspoken yearning hung in the air between them as their gazes locked. Della studied Wild Wind's face. His tight expression reflected the longings she knew he kept in check. The atmosphere grew heavy.

Thinking it best to stifle a moment fraught with emotion, Della slid off his lap. "I must check on Jake and make sure he's getting ready for school. If I don't make him go, he'll play hooky."

As if he'd heard his name, Jake banged through the front door and erupted onto the veranda. He jerked to a standstill when he saw his mother and his uncle by the porch swing.

"Mama! I was looking for you."

"Here I am." Della moved to her son's side and knelt before him, giving him a hug.

Having found his mother, he returned her hug with desperate relief and then wriggled out of her arms. "What are you doing out here with Uncle Wild Wind?"

Out of the corner of her eye, she saw Wild Wind halt beside her. She tossed a quick glance at him over her shoulder before she turned back to her son. Placing both hands on his thin shoulders, she told him, "One of the horses colicked last night. Uncle Wild Wind and Scipio and I stayed up all night helping him."

"Oh." Jake's eyes grew round and solemn. He peered up at his uncle. "Did you help him get better, Uncle Wild Wind?"

Wild Wind went down on one knee to better see into his nephew's face. "Yes, Jake. Your mama and Scipio and I stayed up all night helping him get better. Your mama was very tired, so she fell asleep out here."

Jake's face lit with curiosity. "What will you do with him now?"

"Scipio and I will make sure that he doesn't eat or drink for a while. We must watch him to make sure he's not getting sick again. We want him to be strong."

Jake looked from Della to Wild Wind. "Can I help?"

An immediate denial sprang to Della's lips. "Certainly not, young man. You have school."

"But Mama, who cares if I miss school today? Uncle Wild Wind needs my help."

Della rose to her feet and turned her son about. "You need to go to class. Go on in, now, and eat your breakfast." She gave him a firm push toward the door.

Feet dragging, shoulders slumping in an attitude of pitiful dejection, Jake returned to the house. When the door had shut behind him, Wild Wind stared at the closed portal for a long moment.

Watching him, Della guessed he had an opinion on the matter. "What is it? I know you've got something to say."

Wild Wind slanted her a look, his eyes narrowed, his mouth a firm slash. "He is your son, and you must do with him as you think best."

"But?"

"But life is hard, and he must learn to be a man. Helping us to care for the gelding will teach him about life. You must not shelter him."

"And what about school?"

Wild Wind shrugged. "What will he learn today that he cannot learn later? Today, he can learn a lesson that will help him understand something of what it takes to become a man."

"But he's just a boy!" Della protested. "He's only five years old!"

"If he were living in our village, he would already be riding at his father's side, learning the ways of manhood. He is not too young. Let him come with me."

Curling her fingers into her palms, Della swept the yard with a glance. The ranch was coming to life. Horse wranglers spilled out of the bunkhouse on their way to the cook shack. Scipio stepped out of the barn to water the horses in the corral. A horse could nearly die, and life went on. Work went on. Jake wasn't too young to learn that lesson.

Della lifted her head and met Wild Wind's stare. "Very well. Take him with you. I know you'll teach him well."

"I will be as a father to him."

Della drew in a deep breath. Wild Wind spoke the truth. Shane's death had left a void in her son's life, a void Wild Wind had begun to fill. Jake needed a father figure, and she wouldn't deprive him of it. "Yes, I know you will. He needs you."

Wild Wind stepped closer to her, and for a moment, Della thought he would touch her. Instead, he traced her features with an intent gaze. "One day, my beautiful Lona, I will be a father to him and a husband to you."

Before she could reply, he brushed past her and jogged down the porch steps. At the bottom, he pivoted. "When Jake has eaten, send him to me." Not waiting for Della's assent, he spun again and strode across the yard to the barn.

Della couldn't help but watch him, an imposing figure wearing cowboy garb and hat. The back of her throat burned, and her insides jangled. The difficult night and the lack of sleep made coping with her reluctant attraction to her husband's brother challenging.

Della spent the morning indoors. She tried to sleep, but her nerves twanged, and she couldn't relax. Falling asleep on Wild Wind's lap made her realize that she was losing her battle against her heart. She was coming to love her husband's brother.

Finally, when she'd fidgeted about the parlor for several minutes, straightening the lace antimacassars on the backs of the upholstered sofas, Coral addressed her in exasperation.

"Della, what ails you this morning?" Coral thrust a feathered duster into Della's hands. "Here, finish the dusting. I need to go over next week's menus with Sadie."

Della clutched the duster Coral had shoved at her. "I know Wild Wind still has his Cheyenne religion, but I'm starting to have feelings for him. And Shane hasn't even been dead for a year."

Sympathy gleamed in Coral's hazel eyes. She enveloped Della in a one-armed hug. "You're lonely and hurting. And Wild Wind is very much a capable man with a loving heart to offer you. Of course, you're going to develop feelings for him."

Della returned her aunt's hug with a desperate fervor. "But what kind of faithless wife does that make me? I loved Shane. You know that I did. So, how can I have feelings for his brother?"

"A woman's heart knows no timetable for healing from grief. Having feelings for Wild Wind doesn't mean you loved Shane any less. Just keep in mind that Wild Wind isn't a God-fearing man, so be very careful."

When Coral had departed to discuss menus with their cook, Della swiped the duster over the parlor furniture in a desultory manner. Although her uncle employed Sadie as a full-time cook and laundress, and Silvie had charge of the children and did other varied tasks about the house, both Coral and Della had their own chores.

Della was dusting the piano when a ruckus in the yard caught her attention. Dropping the duster onto the piano's polished walnut surface, Della sprang to the window and swept back the lacy drapery. Peering out into the sun-glazed yard, she struggled to make sense of what she saw.

Wild Wind stood in the midst of a circle of perhaps half a dozen men. Virgil Bledsoe faced him across a space of several feet. Anger twisted Virgil's face into an ugly mask. Through the window glass Della heard him shout. The men encircling Wild Wind and Virgil shifted. An opening appeared between two of the wranglers, and she noticed Jake squirming between the men's legs to get closer to his uncle.

Virgil looked ready to start swinging. His bull-like shoulders tensed.

Della let the drapery fall back across the window. She spun and launched from the parlor.

CHAPTER 13

Della arrived in the yard just as Emory Dyer eased up to the group, and Scipio joined them from the barn. Della made a lunge for her son, grabbing him by the collar and hauling him away from the impending action.

Jake wriggled in protest. "I want to see Uncle Wild Wind."

"Not now, you don't."

At that moment, Virgil's outburst drew her attention from her son. She forgot Jake's presence, and he subsided into silence so as not to remind her that he still stood beside her.

Virgil waved a brown leather wallet in a meaty fist. "You stole my wallet, you thievin' Injun!"

Dread burned in Della's stomach. The confrontation she'd hoped they could avoid now played out before her eyes. Wild Wind had to defend his honor. He couldn't ignore the accusation, false though it was.

She swung her gaze to her husband's brother. He stood poised on the balls of both feet, his hands hanging loose at his sides, his face expressionless. An attitude of alertness radiated from him. The air about him seemed charged. He paused, letting the moment spin out before he replied in an even tone. "I did not steal your wallet. I did not even know it was missing."

"You're lyin.' You stole my wallet and hid it under your mattress."

"If I hid your wallet under my mattress, how did you know where to find it?"

Wild Wind's logic seemed to infuriate Virgil. Shucking his gun belt and tossing it to the ground, he flung the wallet into the dirt beside his six-shooter before he exploded toward Wild Wind in a wild rush. Wild Wind pivoted, and the other man encountered empty air. Virgil jerked to a halt and whirled. He lunged at Wild Wind again, lowering his head to butt his opponent in the solar plexus. Wild Wind spun once more. Virgil's head grazed the taller man's chest. Wild Wind staggered but didn't go down. His fist flashed and connected with Virgil's cheek. The impact smacked on bone with a loud thud. Virgil's head jerked from the blow, and he reeled back a pace. Regaining his balance, Virgil bellowed and charged Wild Wind. His rush took both men down. Wild Wind's black cowboy hat spun off to one side, flipping end over end in the dust.

The combatants rolled across the ground, pummeling each other with vicious blows. The circle of men watching them leaped back to give the fighters more room.

Wild Wind regained his footing and loomed over the heavier Virgil. More slowly, Virgil pushed himself off the ground. The fighters crashed together again. Wild Wind twisted aside to avoid a wicked punch. Bringing his fist up to his shoulder, he drove the point of his elbow down onto the other man's kidneys. Virgil grunted and went to his knees.

Della gasped and covered her mouth with her hand. She forgot to breathe. The violence that could erupt here in the West always took her by surprise, made doubly intense this time because of Wild Wind's involvement. As much as she decried the fighting, here, men often settled their differences with their fists, and she knew better than to interfere.

Virgil jumped up. Wild Wind moved in close, his fists hammering the other man in the chest, the face, and the stomach, wherever he could land punches. Blood streamed from Virgil's nose. One eye was swollen almost shut, and his lip had been split, but he charged again, twisting so his shoulder caught Wild Wind in the stomach. His impetus lifted Wild Wind off his feet and flung him backward.

The men crashed to the ground in a wild tangle of punching arms and thrashing legs. Wild Wind grunted when Virgil's fist connected with the side of his head. He rolled and came upright in a lithe movement. Virgil lashed out with one boot in an attempt to knock Wild Wind's feet out from beneath him, but Wild Wind danced aside. The other man regained his feet. Spinning, Wild Wind caught Virgil under the chin in a powerful uppercut that sent him skidding onto his back in the dirt. The warrior loomed over him, fists raised, waiting for Virgil to rise. The men's ragged breathing filled the air with harsh dissonance.

Instead of coming to his feet, Virgil raised his hands, palms out, in a gesture of surrender. His head fell back onto the ground, his eyes closed. His chest pumped.

Wild Wind stood over him, staring down at his fallen foe, his chest rising and falling with his labored breaths. His shirt hung in ribbons about him. Hard bronze muscles gleamed beneath the tattered fabric. His eyes glowed with fierce battle light. "I did not steal your wallet. Do not accuse me again." Lifting his head, he swept the onlookers with a furious stare. "Does anyone else care to fight me?"

Della expelled her breath in a long sigh. A fine tremor quivered through her at the savage display of manhood she'd just witnessed. Wild Wind had been the victor. He'd just established his place as a man to be respected, to leave alone and not bully. No one offered to take up his challenge.

At some point during the fight, Coral had joined them. Della glanced at her aunt, and the women shared a look of commiseration over the unfathomable ways of men. The wranglers had begun to saunter off, avoiding looking at Virgil lying vanquished in the dust.

Emory Dyer spoke for the first time. "Well, they'll leave him alone after this." With a shrug, he took one step toward his office.

Della glanced once more at the fallen man. Virgil had raised his head and was watching Wild Wind through the one narrowed eye that wasn't swollen shut. Wild Wind had turned his back on his defeated opponent and bent to retrieve his hat. A look of hatred twisted Virgil's face. His hand stole toward the six-shooter lying on the ground nearby.

Horrified, Della realized his intent. Virgil would shoot Wild Wind in the back in an act of despicable cowardice and hope the system would absolve him because of Wild Wind's Cheyenne blood. Acting on impulse, she whirled. Emory Dyer still stood only a pace away. Without thinking, she snatched his Colt from its holster and pivoted. Virgil's fingers had wrapped about the handle of his six-shooter. He was sliding the weapon from its holster when Della thumbed back the hammer of the Colt, aiming at the ground mere inches from Bledsoe's wrist. She squeezed the trigger. The revolver roared and bucked, spitting a bullet. The slug buried itself in the dirt near Virgil's hand. A skein of gun smoke curled from the weapon's muzzle.

Virgil froze, his glance darting toward Della. Wild Wind straightened and whirled, clutching his hat. Emory Dyer whipped about, his hand going down to his empty gun belt. The wranglers all turned back at the sound of gunfire. Wise to the ways of the West, each person there understood what had happened. No one needed to be told.

"If you move, the next bullet won't miss." Della addressed Virgil in a cold voice as she trained the Colt with a steady aim on the prone wrangler. "Toss away your gun."

With a careful motion, Virgil threw his revolver away. It landed with a thud and puff of dust several feet from him.

"Now, get up. You're finished here. Collect your things and leave. Mr. Dyer will give you your pay before you go. I want you off the ranch before dinner, and if anyone sees you on Slash L land after today, they'll shoot. Neither Uncle Clint nor myself will tolerate a back-shooting coward."

Virgil rolled to his feet. A sullen expression turned down his battered features. He slapped dust from his pants and scooped his six-shooter off the ground. He aimed a hostile glare at Della from his one good eye before he shambled toward the bunkhouse.

"If anyone else has a problem working with Wild Wind, you might as well leave now," Della called out to the rest of the wranglers.

With the fight over and the men returning to their chores, Della wilted inwardly, though she kept her chin in the air. She returned Emory Dyer's weapon to him, butt first. "I'm glad you hadn't walked away. I wouldn't have been able to get your weapon in time." She tossed him a smile that trembled at the edges.

Dyer dropped his Colt into its holster. "Good thing you saw what Virgil was up to, or this would have ended differently."

Beside her, Jake tugged at the sleeve of her riding blouse. "Mama, would that man really have shot Uncle Wild Wind?"

Belatedly, Della recalled her son's presence and realized he'd seen all the violence, including her own. She glared down at him. "What are you still doing here? I thought I told you to go back to the house."

Jake shook his head in emphatic denial. "No, you didn't. You just told me that I didn't want to watch Uncle Wild Wind. But I did. Want to watch him, I mean."

Della huffed an exasperated breath at her son's irrefutable logic.

"You can't win this one," Coral said with a smile.

At that moment, Wild Wind strode up to them. Della took one look at his bruised face, at the lump forming at his temple, at the battle light still glowing in his eyes, and her world fell apart. In the instant their gazes connected, all the strain and emotion of the recent days, culminating in Virgil's attempt to kill the man who was becoming very dear to her, crashed down on her with the force of a sledgehammer. Every vestige of composure crumbled. With an incoherent cry, she whirled, brushing past Jake and Coral. Her running steps took her toward the compound's gate.

Behind her, she heard Jake's frantic call.

"Mama! Where are you going?"

Della kept running. She couldn't stop. If she stopped, she'd shatter into a thousand pieces and whirl up into the sky's vast blue nothingness. She dashed beneath the arched gate, with the words "Slash L" burned into the wood.

Grady O'Brien approached from the direction of the cattle ranch headquarters. He carried a new lariat looped over one shoulder. Seeing Della, he halted. "Miz Della? Are you all right?"

She shook her head at him, but she couldn't reply. Brushing past him, she fled up the track toward the cemetery and hoped he wouldn't follow. By the time she reached the cemetery gate, her breath panted in ragged gasps. Her lungs burned. Her chest heaved. She flipped the metal ring looped over the railed iron gatepost and pushed open the spiked gate. She stumbled to Shane's grave and dropped to her knees beside the mound covering his body. Wildflowers and buffalo grass had grown over the spot, softening the finality of his resting place.

For a moment Della stared at the grave, trying to bring Shane's features into focus. Memories of their time together, brief as it had been, swam through her head. Anger that they'd been deprived of years of loving and living overtook her. And anger at Shane, however illogical, burned in her chest and clogged her throat. How could he have died and left her behind, alone? Why couldn't he have survived the storm?

All the training she'd received while growing up in Boston at the young lady's academy vanished in the tempest of her grief. She'd been taught from her earliest memories that a proper lady never gave way to bouts of emotion. A genteel lady always presented a façade of composure to the world and kept her feelings private. Della abandoned her training and let her emotions rip forth.

She screamed. She shrieked to the heavens until her voice cracked. Her fists beat at the earth, and she tore off clumps of prairie grass, flinging the shredded blades at her husband's grave.

"Shane, Shane! How could you have done this to me? How could you have left me here alone?" she cried. Her fists pounded his grave. "Why did you leave me? Why?"

She leaped to her feet and stomped. Doubling over, her hands clutching both sides of her head, she screamed again, a primal sound torn from her heart.

She railed against the harsh, unforgiving, sprawling land that was the Colorado High Plains. A land she both loved and hated, a land that had taken from her both a husband and a daughter. A land that, in spite of its harshness, had seeped into her very essence to bind her to it in ways her native New England couldn't lay claim.

In her extremity, she railed against the Lord. "Oh, God, why did you take Shane from me? Why?"

At last, her anger gave way to tears. She dropped once more to her knees. Scalding tears rained down her cheeks, dripping unchecked onto her riding skirt. She sobbed in despair and grief, gasping sobs that tore her throat and shook her body. When the last tear had been wrenched from her, she swiped at her face with a sleeve. Her breath came in gasping hitches which subsided into hiccoughing sobs. The sobs gave way to rough pants and uneven breaths.

Della stretched out beside Shane's grave and closed her eyes. She draped one wrist across her eyelids to shield her face from the sun. Blades of buffalo grass cushioned her back and poked up around her like a green wall, concealing her from any possible passersby. Pink, blue, and white wildflowers danced in the wind. The smell of sun-warmed grass scented the air. A honeybee droned from blossom to blossom over the graves.

The paroxysm of emotion left her spent, yet the episode had been cathartic. For the first time since Shane's death, she felt at peace. Now, she could put his death behind her and face the future. Something she'd forgotten in her anger and despair surfaced to give her strength.

She remembered Job, the Old Testament patriarch who'd lost all his children, yet in spite of his grief had praised God. "The Lord giveth and the Lord taketh away. Blessed be the name of the Lord," Job had said. Could she do less than Job and not recognize God's hand in Shane's death? She sent a prayer for forgiveness winging heavenward.

She embraced the reality of her husband's demise. She reminded herself that his death, and that of her dear little Fanny, had been no accident but had been ordained by God. Her all-wise Heavenly Father had known from the beginning the number of days allotted to Shane's life, and she must accept His will. She must trust the Lord to give her grace and wisdom each day to fulfill her responsibilities at the ranch. She needn't tread that path alone.

Late afternoon shadows stretched across the prairie when Della rose. She cast a final glance at Shane's resting place. Straightening her spine, she lifted her chin and walked to the cemetery gate. After passing through, she latched the gate and paused. Below her, in a large bowl formed by the encompassing swells of rangeland, lay the Slash L ranch buildings, swathed now in lavender shadows. She loved the ranch with each beat of her heart, loved it as much as her Uncle Clint loved it. He'd poured his entire fortune into developing the ranch, and she'd do whatever she could to help make his venture a success.

Della turned toward the track leading down to the ranch. She'd taken two steps when a figure ahead of her rose from a sitting position and stretched to his full height. *Wild Wind.* How long had he been there, watching over her? A mixture of gratitude and irritation warred within her.

She halted before him, tipping back her head to look into his bruised and swollen face. "I didn't know you were here."

"You did not need to know. If I had wanted you to know, you would have known."

Della thought about that for a moment, aware of the Cheyennes' ability to move about undetected. "How long have you been here?"

"As long as you have."

"You've been here a long time, then. Why did you stay?"

"You are the heart of my heart. A warrior protects what is his. I thought Virgil might take out his anger on you, should he find you here." The glimmer of a smile lifted his lips. "But I thought it best to leave you alone until you were ready to go. I would rather fight Virgil again than face a she-bear such as you when you are angry."

Della couldn't help but smile. "Coward!" she teased. Her smile faded when she remembered that Jake had witnessed the whole fight. She smacked Wild Wind in the stomach, angry all over again at the ways of men. "And you! How could you fight right in front of my son? He saw everything."

Wild Wind flinched at her blow and laid a hand over his stomach. "Take care. I have a bruise there." He grinned down at her even as he admitted the fact before his smile faded. "Lona, Jake learned another lesson today. He is not too young to learn that sometimes a man must stand up for himself. Some things are worth fighting for. For me not to have fought Virgil would have made me a coward in the eyes of everyone there. It would have made me look guilty of stealing. I had to do what I did, no matter that Jake saw the fight. He will be a better man for having seen it."

Della sighed, daunted at the prospect of rearing her son alone. "I suppose you're right."

A beat of silence followed, broken by the soughing of the wind through the grasses. Wild Wind and Della stared at each other, caught in an emotion-charged tangle.

She touched his beaten face with tender fingers. "When we get back to the ranch, Toby will get something for you to put on that bruise. A raw steak should work."

"I have remedies of my own, but I will not turn down your offer of help."

She nodded, recalling that Shane had always carried with him a leather pouch filled with an herbal salve made by the Cheyenne women. No doubt Wild Wind did the same. Lifting one of his hands, she examined his raw and swollen knuckles. She brushed her fingertips across his injuries. "It will be a while before the swelling goes down and you can use your hands."

"I will soak them in cold water." He looked at her steadily for a moment, his blue eyes thoughtful. "Lona, I am alive now because of you. If not for you, Virgil would have killed me."

"I know."

"We are bound together, you and I. Because of what you did, we are one."

She caught her breath when he curled one hand about her neck and drew her against his side. He tucked her beneath his shoulder and curved an arm about her, resting his cheek against the top of her head. She hesitated a moment before she crooked her arm about his waist. Beneath the remnants of his shirt, she felt hard muscle below warm skin. Her fingers encountered ridges of raised flesh, scars from battles past. Her mind tucked away the knowledge, to ask him about later. They leaned together until Wild Wind lifted his head to peer into her face.

"You are ready to go back now?"

Della nodded. "Yes. Yes, I can go home now."

Together, they took the first steps down the track to the ranch, each aware that now everything between them had changed.

CHAPTER 14

Wild Wind dropped his arm from Della's shoulder when they approached the ranch gate, and they strolled into the compound at a respectful distance from each other. At the bottom of the veranda steps, Della turned to him. "Wait here. I have something for you."

She skimmed up the steps and entered the house. Inside, Coral appeared from the kitchen when she heard Della enter.

Coral eyed her niece with an anxious air. "Are you all right?"

Della nodded. "I am now."

"We all were worried about you, but Wild Wind said he would watch over you. He told us to leave you alone."

"I needed to be alone."

Jake squeezed around Coral's cornflower blue skirts and rushed at his mother. "Mama!" He clutched her around the waist. "You came back!"

Della ran her fingers through her son's tousled hair. "Of course. I just visited your papa's grave for a while."

He tipped his face up to her. "Uncle Wild Wind told me he would bring you back."

"And he did. He's waiting outside."

Jake's face lit. "I want to see him." Abandoning his mother, he charged toward the door.

Della and Coral exchanged shrugs and smiles.

Della excused herself and mounted the stairs to her bedroom. Inside, she crossed the Aubusson rug to her fourposter bed. Shane's gun belt was draped over the bedpost at the head, just where he'd put it when he undressed every night of their marriage. Della had left it there as a reminder of her husband.

Now, she lifted the belt from its resting place. The bedpost looked bare without Shane's gun belt and his six-shooter.

Della caressed the oiled leather holster, running her fingers over its slick surface. The weapon's walnut handle, worn smooth from Shane's palm, felt warm to her touch, as though Shane had just held it. The Colt and his gun belt, each loop filled with a cartridge, were heavy, yet for a moment Della held them against her heart and closed her eyes. Could she part with such a personal reminder of her husband? Somehow, having his six-shooter and gun belt hanging over the bedpost had made it seem as though he might walk through the bedroom door. Taking his weapon from the post underscored the finality of his death and reminded her that he would never walk through that door again.

Della rubbed the handle of his Colt against her cheek. Who better to offer Shane's weapon to than his brother? Taking a determined breath, she left the room.

Outside, she paused on the top veranda step. Jake stood with Wild Wind, his face tilted up to his uncle. Della waited, loathe to interrupt their conversation.

"What I did today when I fought Virgil was something that you only do when you have no other choice."

"I bet you could beat up any man on the ranch!" Jake crowed.

"Perhaps I could, but a man does not fight for the fun of it."

Jake's avid expression fell. His mouth turned down.

"There are many ways a man proves himself to be a man. A man takes care of his family. Right now, you might think fighting is more fun, but taking care of a family is a man's responsibility. So, do not get into any fights at school."

"Yes, sir."

At that moment, Flossie clattered down the steps, followed by Aaron. She came to a standstill before Wild Wind and peered up at him. "What happened to your face? Did you get that in the fight?" she asked with bloodthirsty relish.

Wild Wind nodded, hiding a smile behind a bland expression. "Yes."

Della thought it time to intervene. Descending the steps, she laid a hand on her niece's shoulder. "Flossie, why don't you take Jake and Aaron back to the dining room? I think Sadie may have a treat for you."

Flossie, as if suspecting that the adults were trying to get rid of the children, cast a rebellious look at her aunt and thrust out a lower lip.

Della shook her head at the youngster. "You're the oldest, Flossie. You must be a good example to the boys."

"But I don't want to be a good example."

"Flossie..." Della warned.

As facile as quicksilver with an abrupt change of mood, dimples flashed in Flossie's cheeks. She skipped up the steps. "I'll be the first one to get a treat."

Not wanting a girl to beat them to the treat, the boys charged up the steps and raced to the front door. They shoved past Flossie. She shrieked and gave chase. The door slammed behind the children.

A moment of silence passed while Wild Wind and Della shared a smile. Recalling the reason she stood there, Della offered the Colt in its holster and the gun belt to Wild Wind. "I want you to have Shane's six-shooter. I realized today that you'll need more than a rifle, and I think Shane would be pleased if you'd take his Colt."

Wild Wind hefted the weapon. "Thank you. I will have to learn how to use it. I use only a rifle."

"Shane taught me. I can teach you, if you don't mind learning from a woman. Or Uncle Clint can teach you when he gets back from Denver."

Wild Wind frowned down at her. "A Cheyenne warrior learns to use weapons from another warrior, usually his father."

Della shrugged. "Perhaps Uncle Emory can teach you. He's not a bad shot, he's just not as good as Uncle Clint."

"I will ask your Uncle Emory."

"Try it on." Della gestured to the six-shooter.

Wild Wind strapped the gun belt around his slim waist. The Colt hung alongside of his thigh. The sight of Shane's weapon draping his brother's leg reminded her of how Shane had appeared wearing the sidearm, and Della couldn't prevent a lump from forming in her throat. The six-shooter molded to Wild Wind as if it were a part of his body. She fastened a smile on her face to cover her lapse into grief. "Now, you look like a real cowboy."

Della leaned against the top rail of the holding corral gate where the cowhands and their horses sweated in what appeared to be mad confusion. This week was the spring roundup, and the bawling cattle raised a monotonous din. The pound of hoofbeats sounded as cowponies chased down darting calves, who ducked and whirled in a frantic effort to return to their mothers.

Dust hung over the cattle yard in a hot golden haze.

Since the first year Uncle Clint had purchased the cattle, Della had manned the corral gate during the branding.

She pulled her low-crowned riding hat from her head and fanned herself with it. The afternoon sun, a molten golden orb in a brassy sky, gleamed through the dust haze. She wiped grimy sweat from the back of her neck with her blue cotton bandana and returned her hat to her head. The wind, hot and dry, blew against her and swirled the dust, giving her temporary relief from the flies.

Across the corral, Jake stood on the bottom rail and leaned over the top bar. His eyes shone with excitement. Wild Wind had prevailed upon her to allow her son to watch when she would have restricted him to the house instead. Della admitted that Wild Wind had been right. Jake quivered with the thrill of being included and learning another part of ranch life. Scipio had been appointed her son's guardian. The two of them appeared to be enjoying each other's company. Della watched while Scipio answered another of her son's never-ending questions.

Each year during the branding time, horse training was suspended until all the calves had been branded and the cattle had been trailed to the summer range. Each horse wrangler pitched in with the cowboys to help.

Wild Wind stood by the fire. Bending, he thrust the branding iron deep into the molten coals, reheating it for another use. He straightened, stretching. Beneath his dark green wool shirt, muscles rippled across his back and shoulders. As if he sensed her watching, he pivoted. His glance settled on her face, and their gazes locked across the width of the corral. He snatched off his black cowboy hat, swiping his other arm across his forehead and raking his fingers through his hair. Settling his hat on his head once more and tilting the brim low over his brow, he sauntered toward her.

Della eyed his approach, a tall, dusty figure wearing a green shirt and denim trousers. His heeled riding boots didn't hamper his graceful stride, though a layer of grit covered him.

When he reached the gate, he halted and looked at her over the bars. His blue eyes gleamed with a glittering energy through the dusty mask of his face. "This is man's work." One hand swept out in a wide arc, encompassing the cattle yard and corral. "This cattle business makes a man feel like a man."

"You're enjoying this, aren't you?"

Wild Wind nodded. "A man must work, or he is not a man. There is no work, not much hunting, on the reservation. Our men are idle. It is not good. I think we need some cattle."

"You should talk to Uncle Clint about that. Perhaps he could get you started with a small herd of cows and a bull."

"I will do that when I see him. And I will learn the cattle business, so I can help my people."

The hot wind swirled the dust. Della didn't notice. She didn't hear the cacophony of sounds filling the air. She noticed only Wild Wind, motionless on the other side of the gate. His gaze roved over her face, touching her with his eyes. When he broke the connection between them and stepped toward the water barrel beside the gate, she remembered to breathe and gulped in a quivering gasp of air.

Wild Wind snagged one of the metal dippers hanging over the barrel's rim and dipped the ladle into the water. Tipping back his head, he lifted the dipper to his mouth, drinking with thirsty gusto. Della watched his throat work as he swallowed. Liquid dripped from the sides of the dipper onto his chin and ran in a muddy rivulets down his neck. When he'd emptied the ladle, he wiped his mouth with his sleeve.

Once more, he filled the utensil and returned to the gate, offering the dipper to Della across the top rail. Without removing her gaze from his, she took the instrument from him and drank. When she'd finished the last drop, she passed the ladle back to Wild Wind, her attention still on his face. "Thank you." Unspoken yearnings simmered beneath the surface of their conversation, heating the moment.

"Gate!" The shout shattered the tableau.

Before he returned to the fire, Wild Wind vowed to Della, "Next branding season, I will be roping calves."

CHAPTER 15

Della and Coral, along with the other ranch wives, stood elbow to elbow along the length of a makeshift wooden table loaded with dried apple and lemon buttermilk pies. The women dished slices of pie onto tin plates and served them to the men.

At the end of each day during the branding, after the men had washed away the sweat and donned clean clothes, they gathered around long tables to eat the evening meal. On this night, the two ranch cooks had prepared a feast of ham, fried potatoes, and biscuits. The women served pie to the men after the meal had been devoured.

Della carried a slice of dried apple pie in each hand. She placed the pie on the table in front of two cowboys, then returned to pluck two more plates from the dessert table, where she encountered Mrs. Donovan, who had just returned for a refill.

Della nodded and smiled at Hugh's wife as both women reached for pie. "Thank you for being so patient with Jake. He's not a very diligent student."

Mrs. Donovan returned Della's smile. "He did much better during the last few weeks of school. He hit a rough patch after..." Her smile faded, and her voice faltered. A wash of embarrassed color flooded her cheeks at her inadvertent reference to Shane's death.

Della patted her shoulder and completed the older woman's sentence. "... after his papa died. You needn't tiptoe around my husband's death. It's a fact I'm learning to live with."

Mrs. Donovan ducked her head and cut a glance at Della. "Jake finished the school year on a good note. I'm sure the summer break will be helpful."

Della looked across the barn to where Wild Wind sat between Hugh Donovan and Grady O'Brien. The ranch ramrod's and Grady's approval of Wild Wind had helped to ease him into the network of cowhands. Most of the men accorded him a grudging acceptance and a respect for his hard work.

"We can thank Jake's uncle for that. Jake wants to please his uncle much more than he wants to please me," Della said.

"Whatever the reason, Jake is a different boy now. I've been very pleased with his progress."

"I fear I must accept the fact that Jake will never be a scholar. Right now, his fondest wish is to break horses like his papa."

"He's only five. Perhaps he'll change his mind and want to be a rancher like his Uncle Clint when he grows up."

The women shared a smile and returned to their task of serving pie to the weary cowmen. Without appearing to hurry, Della crossed to where Wild Wind and Grady sat. She set a slice of apple pie in front of Grady. The irrepressible cowboy tilted back his curly head. A rapscallion's grin tilted up the corners of his mouth, and his dark eyes laughed.

"I consider myself fortunate to have my pie served by your own fair hands," he teased.

Della shook her head at him and tried to hide a smile. "It would have tasted the same had someone else served it."

"I hate to disagree with a lady, but the pie will be sweeter for having been served by my favorite ranch boss."

"Stuff and nonsense." Della moved around Grady's back to Wild Wind's side, not sure how he would react to Grady's flirting.

She'd learned during the Sunday dinners when Wild Wind was a guest at the ranch house that apple pie had become his favorite dessert. Now, she served him an extra-large portion. "Your favorite."

Wild Wind shifted on the bench, twisting his shoulders to better study her face. "Lona, you know what pleases me. I thank you."

Aware of Grady at her other side, listening to their conversation while he forked bites of pie into his mouth, Della tried to prevent Wild Wind from making another personal comment. "You earned it today with all your hard work. Now, I have more pie to serve." She made her escape before he could detain her.

Later that week, with the branding and tallying of the calves finished, the ranch community celebrated with a barn dance the night before the Shorthorns would be driven to their summer pastures. Della, with Coral and their children scampering ahead, strolled along the lane to the cattle ranch barn and entered through the open double doors. The murmur of men's and women's voices, interspersed with laughter and overlaid by Toby's violin, greeted them.

In search of friends, Jake and his cousins disappeared into the press. Della and Coral paused just inside to scan the crowd. The cowboy's wives resembled a flock of songbirds in their colorful gingham dresses. The men wore clean shirts and denim trousers. In honor of the occasion, Della and Coral had donned simple lawn gowns with slim skirts gathered in the back over a bustle. The summer-white material gleamed in the lamplight. Eying the fabric, Della sighed. The bottom of her dress already sported a layer of dust along the hem. Sadie would have her work cut out for her when she tried to brush away the stain.

Lanterns hanging from each post between the stalls cast a warm golden glow over the barn's interior. Bouquets of wildflowers tied with pink ribbon hung on the stalls' half-doors. Along one side, tables draped with red and white plaid napery boasted plates of snitz, apple, and lemon buttermilk pies. Platters of pound cake, apple spice cake, walnut honey cake, and gingerbread sat alongside the pies.

Another table held pitchers of cider and tea.

Even while Della watched, Jake and his cousins sneaked up to the food tables. Before an adult could stop them, the children snatched pieces of cake in both hands and darted away. Shaking her head, Della abandoned an impulse to reprimand her son. An abundance of sugar tonight wouldn't hurt him.

"Would you care to dance?"

The masculine voice, pitched loud enough to carry over the clamor, sounded close to her ear. Della glanced at Grady, who had appeared at her side.

The cowboy flashed a grin. "This is a frolic, so I thought I'd ask if you'd care to take a whirl on the dance floor. Toby is really cranking out the music tonight. Makes my toe tap."

Della looked down at his leather riding boot. The aforementioned toe was indeed tapping in time to the violin's rhythm. Though the music pulled at her, she hesitated. Would she disrespect Shane's memory if she enjoyed a dance?

On her other side, Coral nodded her encouragement. "Dance if you want to. No one will think less of you." She paused. "And Shane would want you to enjoy yourself."

"Very well. One dance."

Grady's dimples glinted. His fingers curled about Della's elbow, and he drew her into the crowd.

The back of the building had been cleared for a make-shift dance floor. Toby and a couple of other cowboys sawed on their fiddles, providing lively accompaniment for a polka. While Grady whirled her through the steps, Della wondered what her Boston friends would think if they could see her now.

At home, only the most refined of Boston's citizens attended the soirees she had frequented. Discreet musicians accompanied waltzes in a refined style. The guests spoke in hushed tones. No one dared to show too much pleasure, for a vulgar display of emotion bespoke of a lack of breeding. Della tossed her head and smiled at Grady, determined to flaunt the rules.

When the music wound down, Grady towed her toward the refreshment table. "Dancing makes me thirsty. How about some cider?"

"Cider would be refreshing." Della dodged to avoid another couple headed to the dancing area.

At the drinks table, Grady ladled cider into two tin mugs and handed one to Della.

"Thank you." She sipped her drink, scanning the barn's interior over the rim of her mug. "I think everyone is here tonight."

"Everyone except those of us who are on guard duty. We're working in shifts, so I'll have to take my turn later."

"I hope we won't have Indian trouble."

"Your uncle isn't taking any chances. I reckon we're lucky to have your brother-in-law living with us. He's given us some tips on how to spot Injuns and how to keep from being seen."

"He should know. And Uncle Clint thinks having him here may actually prevent an attack."

Grady snagged a plate of lemon buttermilk pie from the dessert table. "Would you care for something to eat?"

Della shook her head.

"Then let's move out of the way." With a hand at the small of her back, Grady guided her away from the food tables. He forked a bite of pie into his mouth, chewed, and swallowed. "Why does Mr. Wild Wind call you Lona?"

Della paused with her mug halfway to her mouth, swinging her attention to Grady's face. "It's a long story."

He shrugged. "I have time."

She looked down at her tin mug and ran one finger around its rim, debating how much to tell him. Sighing, she began her tale, keeping her account brief and omitting Wild Wind's courtship.

Grady stared at her, his dark eyes narrowed as if speculating on the details she'd omitted. "I suppose Mr. Hunter rescued you."

"He did. And the chief of the village gave us the horses back. He didn't want trouble with my uncle over the stolen horses." While they'd been talking, a pretty, blond-haired girl had sidled close and watched them with interest. Della turned her back to the young lady and grinned. "I think you have an admirer."

A puzzled frown wrinkled Grady's brow. "Who?"

"Betty, Hugh Donovan's eldest daughter. She's just behind me."

Grady peered over her shoulder. Della glanced around at Hugh's daughter, who was blushing and casting shy glances at Grady. Della swung back to Grady again.

"Why don't you ask her to dance? I think she'd like that."

"She's a bit young for me."

"She's not too young to dance. And you're not proposing marriage." Della reached for his mug and empty pie plate. "I'll take those. Ask her." She gave the reluctant cowboy a little push toward the girl.

He cast her a disgruntled look. "I'd rather talk with you."

"Go."

Grady ambled toward Donovan's daughter and exchanged words. Another smile lit the girl's face, and she placed her hand on Grady's arm. Della watched them work their way through the revelers to the back of the barn, where the fiddlers were tuning up for another dance. With a sigh, she deposited their dirty mugs and the plate in a tin tub next to the wall provided for that purpose. Turning back to the barn's interior, she noticed Coral dancing with Emory Dyer. Hugh Donovan squired his wife about the dance floor, and Grady seemed to be enjoying Betty's company.

The warm lighting cast by the oil lamps gave the whole scene a mellow air, staining the partiers in gold. With the branding behind them and the cattle drive before them, the cowboys could kick up their heels tonight and forget hard work for a few hours.

Delighting in the revelry, Della hummed along with the music.

After a moment, she felt herself watched. She glanced over at the barn's double doors. Wild Wind stood framed in the opening, his gaze fastened on her face. When he saw that she'd noticed him, he worked his way through the crowd to her side.

"So, you decided to see what a barn dance is like." Della smiled at him.

Propping his fists on his hips, he scanned the scene around them before he returned his attention to Della. "It is different from the dances of the Cheyenne villages. Our dances have meaning, a purpose. And men do not dance with women."

"Our dances have purpose, too. A dance gives neighbors a chance to socialize, to relax and have fun. Life is hard. A dance is encouraging for everyone."

Wild Wind shrugged. For the first time, Della noticed that he hadn't smiled. She wondered if a piece of apple pie might put him in a better mood.

"Would you like some pie? I'll get you a piece."

"I am not here to eat pie."

"Why are you here, then?"

He didn't reply. Instead, he grabbed her hand and hauled her through the crowd to the door. She would have resisted, but with Wild Wind in such an odd mood she thought it better to humor him. When they passed through the open double doors into the twilight, Wild Wind towed her around to the barn's side where they could be private.

They came to a halt, her back against the wall. She pulled her hand from his and twitched her lacy shawl up over her shoulders against the evening's bite.

Wild Wind glowered down at her.

Della lifted her chin and narrowed her eyes at him. "What? What have I done?"

He answered her question with another one, his tone curt. "Why was that boy dancing with you? And he talks to you too much."

"Grady? He's not a boy."

"Why was he dancing with you and giving you a drink? I watched you with him."

"It's one of our customs for men and women to dance together. You must have noticed other men and women dancing. And we partake of refreshments together."

"I do not like it. He touched you."

Della frowned. Wild Wind must have watched Grady hold her elbow and seen him place his hand on her back after the dance. "He only touched me in a socially acceptable manner."

"Other men do not touch a Cheyenne chieftain's woman."

They'd hit the wall of cultural differences. Della suspected this might be the first of many such instances. "Wild Wind, it meant nothing. In our culture, he was simply being courteous. You'll have to get used to it."

A beat of silence followed while he glared down at her, his mouth a tight line. "I will not get used to it. Other men will not touch my woman."

"I'm not your woman. I haven't agreed to marry you."

"We will marry when your heart is ready. You are my woman."

"Remember that I will marry a man of my own faith."

He nodded. "And I am considering the things we have talked about. I have many questions."

"That is good. Uncle Clint can discuss our faith with you when he comes home."

"Is Mr. Grady courting you?"

His abrupt question took Della by surprise. "Why do you ask?"

"I see how he looks at you. And he spends time with you."

"I haven't allowed him to court me."

"He will not court you. You belong to me. I will talk to him about this."

"No, you won't talk to him. Leave it."

During their conversation, night's shadows had enveloped the land. His resolute features blurred in the darkness. Della stared up at him. The arrogance inherent in the Cheyenne male made it difficult to dissuade one from a course once his mind had been made up. Wild Wind had decided they would marry. Nothing she said deterred him from his intentions.

"I am on guard duty, so I must leave now."

Della noted Shane's gun belt encircled Wild Wind's slim hips. The six-shooter rode along his thigh, tied down with a leather thong, looking as much a part of him as his boots. Ever since Emory Dyer had given him shooting lessons, he'd worn the Colt every day.

Without giving her time to reply, he commanded, "When the dance is over, do not leave with another man. I will come for you and see you safely to the house." In an unexpected and tender gesture, he cupped her cheek with one palm before he melted into the darkness, leaving her alone in the night.

CHAPTER 16

Della shivered in the predawn darkness and pulled the collar of her sheepskin jacket up around her ears. Her breath fanned out in a silver cloud. She stood near the barn with the wives of the cowboys who were taking the cattle onto the summer range. The women waited to share a final goodbye with their husbands.

The men, mounted on their cowponies, were bunching the Shorthorns in preparation for moving out. Their yips and whistles filled the air. Cattle bawled. Horns clacked against horns while the dogies milled.

While she waited, Della thought back to last night's dance. She'd been exasperated by Wild Wind's high-handed manner, yet also touched by his protectiveness.

When she'd returned to the party after Wild Wind left her, Hugh Donovan had approached her. He'd taken her arm and drawn her to one side.

"Mrs. Hunter, if you can spare Wild Wind, I'd like for him to go with us tomorrow morning. He'd be invaluable to me scouting for Indian sign." The ramrod peered into her face, his gray eyes concerned. "It would help to know if there are hostiles in the area where we plan to summer the cattle."

"Certainly. Take him with you."

"Much obliged, Mrs. Hunter."

At the end of the dance, Wild Wind had appeared in the barn doorway, scanning the interior for her. Emory Dyer had just escorted Coral and the children to the house. Della had declined the lieutenant's offer to accompany them and had instead waited for Wild Wind. While she waited, she helped the women clean up.

She had just begun to roll a red and white checkered cloth from one of the tables when she sensed his arrival. She glanced at the door where he loomed, tall and imperious. Their gazes connected. Wild Wind strolled toward her, his boot heels thudding on the barn floor. She dropped the wadded-up napery onto the table and met him halfway. They created an island of silence in the hubbub about them. His face tipped down to hers, and her head lifted to meet his stare. Unaware of the curiosity they created in the onlookers, they stood several inches apart, yearning together as if drawn by an invisible cord.

Wild Wind murmured, "We will go now."

Della had gone, strolling beside him in the darkness. When they reached the house and the veranda steps, they halted, turning to face each other. For several heartbeats, they didn't speak.

At last Della drew a breath and said, "Thank you for seeing me home."

"I would keep you safe." Reaching out, he fingered the delicate lace of her shawl. His rough fingers snagged the fabric. "You are beautiful when you wear the fancy white eyes clothing, but you are not the same Lona who wears riding clothes or Cheyenne deerskin."

"I'm still the same person no matter what I wear." Even as she spoke the words, she recalled how different she'd felt wearing a fringed deerskin dress in his village. Clothing mattered, despite her protests.

Remembering Hugh Donovan's request, Della changed the subject. "Mr. Donovan asked me if you could go along on the cattle drive tomorrow. He'd like to use your scouting skills to let him know if there are hostiles around."

He nodded and seemed pleased. "And I can learn more of the cattle business." He paused and stared down at her. "It would make my heart sing if you would see me off in the morning."

Della had promised. Now, she waited to say good-bye to Wild Wind. Hoof beats thudded toward them, and riders materialized out of the night. The married men had come to bid their wives goodbye.

Astride one of the ranch's cow ponies, Wild Wind reined in his galloping mount and flung himself from the saddle before the horse had plunged to a halt. Leading the gelding on a loose rein, he strode toward her. He drew her away from the others with a light clasp on her elbow. "Lona, my own, my heart will be empty until I return. You will wait for me."

"Of course. I'm not going anywhere."

"It is good for a woman to wait for her man. Your thoughts will go with me."

"Yes, my thoughts will go with you. Be careful and come back safely."

A shrill whistle gave the signal for the drive to start. Hugh Donovan shouted, "Let's get these dogies movin'."

The married men snatched final kisses and mounted, wheeling their horses about and loping toward the herd. Though the Cheyenne way wasn't to indulge in public displays of affection, Wild Wind snagged Della with his free arm and pulled her close, pressing her against the muscled hardness of his chest. She hugged him back. After a brief moment, he set her away. Pivoting toward his mount, he flipped the reins over his gelding's head and leaped into the saddle without toeing for a stirrup.

Within minutes, the herd and the horsemen had vanished over a bluff. Morning lightened the sky. Another day had dawned.

~

The days after the men had taken the herd dragged. Della wandered about the house, filling her time with the endless chores that needed doing, or she hung about the corral where Wild Wind would have been had he been at the ranch. Even Jake moped. Della didn't want to admit that she missed Wild Wind, too, or that his absence caused her moodiness. To yearn after another man seemed disloyal to Shane's memory. She preferred to blame her doldrums on the weather, which had turned hot and still.

On the second day, Grady approached Della while she curried Shane's mustang, whom she'd tied to a hitching post beside the corral fence. Della glanced up when the wrangler halted at the grulla's shoulder. Draping an arm over the gelding's back, she smiled at the curly-headed cowboy.

"Don't you have enough to do?" she teased.

For once, he didn't return her smile. "I won't be askin' you to step out with me, Miz Della."

Catching his mood, her smile faded. "What do you mean?"

"Mr. Wild Wind, he warned me off you. Said you were his woman, and I was to leave you alone."

Della's lips firmed. Wild Wind had spoken to Grady, after all. "Wild Wind has asked me to marry him, but I haven't given him a reply. It's too soon after Shane's death for me to marry anyone."

"No matter. I don't plan to rile that hombre. If he says to leave you alone, I'm leavin' you alone. I'd rather poke a rattler with a stick." Grady ducked his head and stirred the dirt with the toe of one boot before he peered up at Della from beneath lowered brows. "Just wanted you to know."

"Thank you for telling me. I'm sorry Wild Wind threatened you."

Grady shrugged. "I could see the lay of the land between you two. We can all see it. I shouldn't have tried to toss my loop over you."

"Don't blame yourself."

Touching his hat brim with two fingers, Grady took his leave. "Guess I'll shove off. I've got chores to do."

Della watched him slouch toward the barn, then pivoted back to the gelding. Wild Wind had had no right to warn off Grady, without so much as a by-your-leave from her. She clamped her lips shut and swiped the curry comb angrily along the mustang's flank. The grulla swung his head around and pricked his ears at her, as if wondering at the rough treatment. Reaching out, she stroked his velvety gray nose.

"I'm sorry, boy," she told the horse. "I shouldn't take out my bad mood on you."

By the time the cowboys returned three days after they'd left, and Wild Wind loped his mount beneath the arched entrance of the ranch compound, Della had worked herself into a temper. She heard his gelding clatter into the yard. Hurrying to the mahogany front door, she watched through the oval glass window while he dismounted. She waited until he'd cared for his cow pony and disappeared into the barn before she slipped outside and marched across the yard. Her heeled riding boots kicked up spurts of dust with each stride, and her split riding skirt flared about her calves.

Wild Wind had just closed the tack room door when she entered the barn's shadowed interior and came to a halt just inside. He glanced her way. His gaze stroked her face, and his handsome countenance warmed. "Lona! You have come to greet me."

Della stalked up to him, so close they were almost touching, and thumped his chest. "I told you not to talk to Grady about us."

Astonishment chased the pleasure from his features. "Why should I not? I told you I would fight anyone over you. This way, Mr. Grady knows what will happen if he courts you. I would have done the same to any brave if we were in my village."

"But you had no right! I'm not your woman."

"You are my woman. It is time everyone knows that. I will not have other men chasing after you."

Della's knuckles rapped him again. "It's my choice to make! You took away my right to choose! Now, no other man will even ask to walk me home after church."

Wild Wind looked puzzled and snagged her hand, folding his long fingers about her smaller ones to prevent her from thumping him again. "Would you choose Mr. Grady over me? Would you choose any other cowboy over me?"

Della shook her head. "Of course not!"

"Then why are you angry? Now, you will not have to turn them away. They will not try to court you."

"I'd liked to have had the right to choose whether or not to let other men court me. Even the women in your camp can choose which suitor they marry."

Wild Wind held up both hands, palms out, seeming genuinely perplexed. "I do not understand women. You would not choose another man over me, yet you are angry that I protect you from other men."

His logic silenced Della. Having lived in the Cheyenne culture, she understood a little of why Wild Wind had done what he'd done. To him, staking his claim to her was a logical decision. She sighed. "I'll try to remember that you think like a Cheyenne, if you'll try to understand my way. Perhaps someday, if you live with us long enough, you'll start to think a little as we do. It would make things easier."

"When we marry, I will spend much time here. I will learn from the men how the white eyes think."

Deciding not to disagree with him again about the inevitability of them marrying, Della didn't challenge his statement.

"But we will also live at my village. I will be chief, and I must see to my people."

Della let that comment pass, as well. If they did marry, she expected that she and Jake would live part of the time with him on the reservation. He would carry the burden of his people's welfare on his shoulders, and to do his best for them, he must live in the village at least some of the time. His next words brought her wandering thoughts back to him.

"Now, you she-bear, will you greet your man in a proper way?" His fingers curled about her shoulders, and he tugged her toward him.

Balking, she dug in her heels and braced her palms against his muscled chest. His high-handed interference still rankled. "No. You'll not kiss me."

The pressure of his hands on her shoulders eased, while disbelief crossed his face. "You do not want me to kiss you?"

"Not at this moment, no."

"You did not miss me? Was your heart not empty because I was gone?"

Honesty compelled Della to admit she'd missed him, though she hesitated, not wanting him to guess how very much she'd missed him. At last, she spoke the truth. "Yes, I missed you."

"Are you glad I have returned home?"

"Yes..." Her voice trailed away into silence.

"They why do you refuse to let me kiss you?"

Swallows swooping in the loft shrilled to each other. A horse stamped in its stall, and the wind eddied around them along the central passage through the open double doors at either end of the barn. For a brief moment, those distractions turned Della's attention from her discussion with Wild Wind. Shaking her head, she returned her focus to his puzzled countenance. "I'm still angry with you for taking away my right to choose."

He studied her face in silence, his blue eyes narrowed. "I have displeased you, though I told you many summers ago that no other braves would court you. I had claimed you. Now, I have claimed you again. How is this different?"

"We're not in your village anymore. We're here, at the ranch, and you can't behave as though you're a chieftain."

"I am a chieftain. I cannot help who I am, but I am sorry I made you angry." Wild Wind paused. "Do you want me to tell Mr. Grady he may court you?"

His ridiculous offer chased away Della's irritation. In spite of her vexation, she smiled. She opened her mouth to reply, then shut it. The opportunity to tease him was irresistible. Her lashes swept down, veiling her eyes. She concentrated on the spot where his blue shirt met his throat. Her finger traced circles about his top button, feeling his skin warm beneath her hand. "Perhaps. You could make amends for your interference by telling Grady you've changed your mind."

A taut silence sizzled the air. When Wild Wind didn't reply, Della peeked up at him. His lips were clamped in a tight line, and the brackets on either side of his mouth had deepened. His eyes smoldered down at her. At the sight of his obvious jealousy, she giggled.

His expression relaxed. "You do not mean it."

"It would serve you right if I did."

Their gazes snagged. Heat flared between them. Her fingers tingled at the feel of his muscled chest beneath her palms. This time she didn't resist when he drew her to him.

She bumped into his chest. His arms tightened about her, holding her close. His head lowered, and his mouth took hers with an aching tenderness.

At first, Della couldn't respond. It seemed disloyal to Shane to let another man kiss her, but Wild Wind's gentleness won her. He kissed her with a tender mastery, a kiss full of promise that left no doubt of his love for her. Her bones melted, and her hands left his chest to steal about his neck. She returned his kiss until he broke away and rested his forehead on hers.

"This is one white-eyes custom I will like. Kissing is pleasurable."

Della pulled back enough to scan his face. "Cheyenne don't kiss?"

"The ancient ones never did. Kissing is something the Cheyenne have learned from your people." Wild Wind drew her back into his hold, tucking her beneath his chin. "I will not kiss you again until you are done with your grieving, and I am courting you. Then we will kiss."

Della didn't reply. She closed her eyes and leaned against him, breathing his scent. He smelled of campfire smoke, horses, and sunshine. His arms about her felt right, as if she belonged in his embrace.

That night, a high plains summer storm swept over the ranch. Della wakened to the boom of thunder. Gusts rattled the windowpanes. A sudden onslaught of hail clattered on the roof and beat against the windows.

Pushing back the covers, Della swung her feet over the edge of the mattress and toed for her slippers. She reached for the silk robe she'd left draped over the end of the bed. When she'd shrugged her arms through the sleeves and tied the sash about her waist, she drifted to the door.

Bright flashes of lightning erupted into the room, illuminating her way with a pulsing white glare. A crash of thunder shook the house. Della slipped into the upstairs hall and crept down to the foyer. Opening the front door, she stepped out onto the veranda. Rain, driven sideways by the wind, slashed at her, defying the protection of the porch roof. Within moments, her nightclothes were soaked. She shivered while the icy drops pelted her. Her flesh stung where the rain collided with unprotected skin.

The air smelled of wet earth and brimstone.

Della lifted her head and laughed into the elements. These summer storms always called to something primitive within her. She thought she might fly apart and be swirled up into the sky, caught up by the gusts and blown about into the heavens. The tempest released her from the social bonds that anchored her to the earth. For a few moments, she felt free.

A nearby presence her caught her eye. Coral had joined her. She linked her arm through Della's. The two women watched while lightning lit the earth with its iridescent glare, drenching the corrals, the barn, and the stockade wall with alabaster. Thunder crashed. The earth trembled. Darkness swallowed the glow when the lightning vanished, making the ensuing blackness absolute.

When at last the storm rolled away into the distance and thunder muttered over the far-flung bluffs, Della turned to her aunt. Sharing the storm's violence had bound them together with an intimacy unexpressed yet felt. Without preamble and taking advantage of the moment, Della said, "Now, I sometimes make it through a whole day without thinking of Shane. Is that so very wrong?"

Coral studied her niece with grave intensity before she replied. "Each of us deals with the loss of a loved one in a different way. Healing from grief has no timetable. Personally, I'm happy to see you smile again."

Della glanced out into the night. "I sometimes feel guilty because I enjoy Wild Wind's company too much."

Coral shook her head. "Don't feel guilty. Enjoying his company means you're coming back to life."

"He talks marriage, but as you told me once, I must remember he's not a God-fearing man."

"We'll keep praying for him. Prayer is a mighty weapon."

Silence fell between them, broken only by the water dripping off the veranda roof and pattering onto the soil.

At last, Coral said, "I must start packing. Clint wants us in Denver before the end of the month so we can prepare for the July 4th festivities. He wants us to have time to shop and enjoy ourselves before the celebrations begin."

A reluctant interest in the approaching festivities stirred in Della's chest. For the first time, she looked forward to the visit. A couple of weeks spent in Denver might be enjoyable, after all.

And what would Wild Wind do while she was gone? What should she do with him?

Denver, Colorado Territory
Summer, 1876

CHAPTER 17

The cavalcade wound along the faint track toward Denver. Della scanned the horizon where the long prairie and grassy swells met the sky, but she didn't see Wild Wind. The cowboys guarding them from possible attack rode in a loose circle about them, but she saw no sign of Shane's brother.

Della rode beside the wagon, keeping her mount at a walk. Jake and Flossie rode alongside her, excited to be astride and not riding in the buckboard with Silvie and the younger children. Mounted on a sorrel Morgan mare, Coral flanked the two children on the far side. Emory Dyer maintained a position at the wagon's rear.

Wild Wind had refused to stay at the ranch when she told him they were leaving for Denver. "I will go with you," he'd insisted.

"I'm not sure this is a good time for you to be in Denver, what with the tribal hostilities and all."

He flung back his head and stared down his nose at her, his jaw set. "I will not let my woman travel without my protection." Steel laced his tone. The brim of his cowboy hat framed his obdurate face.

"Uncle Clint has arranged for us to have an armed escort. I'm sure we'll be safe."

"Your uncle does not know the tribes as I do. And your cowboys do not know the ways of warriors looking for a fight."

Della laid her hand on his chest. Beneath his shirt's cotton fabric, the warm hardness of his muscles flexed with his breathing, and the steady beat of his heart thudded against her palm. "I would have you stay here, on the ranch. I'm not sure it's safe for you to be in Denver now."

He covered her hand with his own. "I have been a Dog Soldier. I can protect myself, but your concern for me warms my heart. You, my own brave woman, and Coral and the children, will be safe under my care. I will deliver you all to your Uncle Clint. I will not leave your safety to anyone else."

In spite of Della's misgivings, when they'd left the ranch that morning, Wild Wind had accompanied them. He'd ranged far ahead, scouting for Indian sign, and Della hadn't seen him since.

He appeared as they made camp for the evening, swinging down from a black Morgan gelding. She strolled toward him.

"Did you find anything?"

He nodded. "There is a band of Lakota warriors three hour's ride from here. Tomorrow morning, we will swing east to avoid them."

They ate a cold supper and drank tepid coffee.

After they ate, the women and children rolled into their blankets beneath the buckboard and fell into an exhausted slumber. Once during the night's black hours, Della roused to see Wild Wind seated beside her, his back against one of the buckboard's wheels, his Winchester across his knees. Closing her eyes again, Della snuggled her blanket around her ears, secure in his protection. When they awakened before dawn to begin the day's trek, he had already left the camp.

The travelers rode into Denver late that afternoon. As befitting proper ladies, Della and Coral donned riding habits with long skirts and exchanged their Western saddles for sidesaddles before they entered the city.

Now, Della stared about her as their cavalcade plodded along the wide main street. Drays loaded with canvas-covered supplies headed for the mining camps, Conestoga wagons pulled by teams of oxen, buckboards, buggies, and stagecoaches clogged the dusty thoroughfare. Throngs of miners, shop keepers, ranchers, cowboys, and railroad men, alongside of Easterners with their wives and families, idled on the wooden walkways. The clamor of city noises beat at Della's ears, so foreign after the quiet of the ranch. Raw energy pulsed in the air.

Glancing at the children, Della smiled to herself. Jake and Flossie gazed about them in wide-eyed wonder. For once, Flossie had nothing to say. Silvie and the younger children, seated on blankets in the buckboard's bed, gaped at the activity.

Della turned her attention to her adult companions. The phalanx of cowboys escorting them rode point ahead of the wagon. Traffic mired their progress. Their escorts cleared the way for them, sometimes shouting for a stagecoach loaded with trunks and passengers to move aside, or a mule team pulling a wagon loaded with supplies to clear the street. The cowboys' shouts added to the din.

To her left, the side facing the street, Wild Wind rode alongside her, providing a buffer from the traffic. He wore his hat pulled low over his brows so the brim shielded his eyes, but his sharp gaze missed nothing.

Despite activity along the street, their group attracted their share of attention. At her uncle's request, each rider had made the trip astride a Morgan horse to display the ranch's blooded horseflesh. The superior breeding of their splendid Morgan mounts caught the eyes of the people who watched them make their way down the avenue.

By the time they reached the Tremont House in western Denver, where Uncle Clint had reserved rooms for them, Della wished she could return to the Slash L.

They pulled up before the colonnaded white porch of the Tremont House, an imposing three-story brick structure with tall arched windows fronting the street.

Beside her, Wild Wind swung down from his black gelding and ducked around his horse's head to help her dismount. Reaching up, he caught her about the waist with both gloved hands. Della leaned down to place her palms atop his shoulders. When he lifted his face to her, his hat brim tipped up and revealed his eyes, warm and shining with a possessive blue light. Their gazes snagged for a drawn-out moment, while the city noises faded.

Wild Wind's fingers tightened about her waist. He tugged her toward him and lifted her from the saddle. Della slid to the ground and wobbled a bit when he set her on her feet. She clutched his shoulders to steady herself, their glances still snared.

She had to clear her throat before she could speak. "Thank you."

He nodded and dropped his hands, then stepped back to secure their horses' reins to the hitching post.

Uncle Clint must have been watching for them, for he emerged from the hotel's wide mahogany door just as Emory Dyer assisted Coral from her mount.

When she spied her husband, Coral darted up the steps with a glad cry and flung herself at his chest. Uncle Clint's arms closed about his wife.

Della turned away. Emory Dyer was helping Silvie from the buckboard. The cowboys who'd escorted them now swarmed about the back of their wagon. They unloaded the women's trunks and valises, setting the luggage on the ground at the wagon's tail.

Grady O'Brien kept his face averted while he pulled a tapestried valise with leather handles from the buckboard.

Della sighed. Ever since their conversation about Wild Wind, Grady had kept his distance. If Wild Wind was near, he wouldn't look at her. The cowboy had apparently taken Wild Wind's threat seriously. Now, she missed his conversation and humor.

Her uncle greeted his children after he'd turned Coral loose, hugging Flossie and Aaron, and lifting Jesse high.

Inside the Tremont House lobby, Della glanced about while she removed her riding hat. At the right, a balding hotel clerk with spectacles perched on his nose watched them from behind a long mahogany receptionist bar. To her left, a spacious area where guests could relax rivaled the Boston hotels for luxury. Cushioned chairs invited guests to sit. On the floor, a patterned Turkish carpet glowed with jeweled tones. Newspapers lay on lamp tables waiting to be read.

Potted ferns on marble pedestals provided a discreet screen to shield guests from curious eyes. A hushed atmosphere provided welcome relief from the city's bustle.

Wild Wind remained at her side while Uncle Clint signed them in at the reception desk register. With that task completed, Uncle Clint returned to their group, who stood in the lobby amid a clutter of luggage. Her uncle addressed a drooping Silvie.

"Silvie, why don't you take the children to their room? I'll have the kitchen send a snack up, and you can rest until dinner."

Silvie nodded and gathered the exhausted children about her skirts. A porter appeared to show her to the children's room, and they straggled toward the wide, carpeted stairs at the lobby's far side.

"We have time to rest before dinner," Uncle Clint said, eyeing his wife and Della. "And I'm sure you ladies would like to refresh yourselves."

"Uncle Clint, Wild Wind came along to protect us," Della said. "He scouted for us and kept us away from any hostiles."

Stepping forward, her uncle thrust out a hand to Wild Wind. "I offer you my sincerest thanks and gratitude for seeing my family safely to Denver."

Wild Wind clasped the proffered hand. "I would not allow Lona or your family to travel without my protection."

Her uncle never blinked at the other man's reference to Della as Lona. "If anyone can keep my family safe, you can, and I can't thank you enough. Why don't you join us for dinner tonight? Emory will join us, too, won't you?"

They made their plans, and the women departed for their rooms upstairs.

At the appointed time that evening, Coral and Della joined the men, who waited for them in the lobby. In deference to Denver society, Della had donned a simple lawn gown which Silvie had dyed black. Instead of her usual French braid, she wore her hair in a fashionable upswept style with a fringe of bangs hanging over her brow. The image who stared back at her from the cheval glass resembled the privileged girl she'd been in Boston, before she'd met and married Shane. The black gown gave lie to that image and proclaimed her widow's status.

Though she might look like the same girl who'd come West almost seven years ago, time had changed her. She'd been captured by the Cheyenne, married and widowed, born two children, buried a daughter and a husband, and faced down the hardships of the Colorado territory. The pampered girl who left Boston in another lifetime no longer existed.

Now, she stepped off the bottom stair tread. Coral, clad in a stylish peacock-blue frock with a slender silhouette and a flounced bustle over her hips, strolled beside her. Intent on joining their men, the women didn't notice the admiring glances other guests cast their way.

Their men watched them approach. As they neared, Uncle Clint stepped forward and took his wife's arm. He'd dressed for the evening in dark trousers and a broadcloth jacket that displayed his wide shoulders.

"You ladies are a picture tonight," he commented. He slanted an admiring look down at Coral. "I should bring you to Denver more often. It gives you an excuse to experience civilization and to dress accordingly."

"I must admit I'd almost forgotten what it feels like to mingle in society," Coral agreed. "Not that I'd trade the Slash L for Denver, but it's a treat to dress up and enjoy a fine restaurant again."

"Let me add my compliments to General Logan's." Emory Dyer bowed over their hands, giving each lady a teasing smile. "I'm sure we'll be dining tonight with the most beautiful women in Denver."

Della dimpled at him. "And I'm sure you've kissed the Blarney Stone, Uncle Emory, but you can keep on passing out compliments. We don't mind."

She took back her hand and turned to Wild Wind, who stood a pace behind the other two men. He'd changed into clean jeans and shirt and brushed the trail dust from his boots. He'd combed his hair into ruthless order. The six-shooter she'd given him rode low about his hips. His commanding air clothed the simple cowboy garb with dignity.

She smiled up at him. "You look very dashing tonight."

His solemn expression didn't change, but his eyes gleamed. "I can almost forget who I am. I feel like one of the white eyes, my mother's people."

"You should never forget that her blood runs in your veins. You have as much white blood as you do Cheyenne."

He gave a curt nod. "I am trying to remember that." He took a breath and gave Della a slow perusal. "You are looking very beautiful in your fine clothing. I can see that I will need to work hard to let other men know you are my woman."

Della shrugged. "My black costume should tell every man here that I'm in mourning. No gentleman will flirt with me."

"Lona, my heart, you do not realize your beauty. That man across the room has not taken his eyes from you since you came down the stairs."

Della cut a discreet glance to her left. The man Wild Wind referred to, a dapper gentleman with sandy hair and a mustache that curled up at the ends, was indeed staring at her. She turned her back to the ogler. "I can't help it if men stare at me."

"I can understand why men stare at you. That is why you need me at your side to protect you."

Clint interrupted their discussion with a suggestion that they proceed to the dining room. "I don't know about you, but I'm ready for a big steak. Let's go to the dining room. I've reserved a table for us."

They trooped across the lobby toward the dining room door, an arched entrance to the left of the staircase. When they passed the gentleman who stared at her, Della didn't acknowledge his presence, but Wild Wind turned a cold glare on the ogler and drew Della against his side in a show of possession. In the face of Wild Wind's unsubtle message, the man shrank back against the reception desk and turned away.

A white-jacketed maître d' met them at the dining room door. He bowed and swept their party with an experienced glance before he addressed Uncle Clint. "May I ask if you have a reservation?"

Uncle Clint nodded. "I reserved a table for a party of five."

The maître d' cast another glance at them and stepped closer, his voice pitched to a murmur. "I'm sorry, sir, but I cannot seat that redskin. Policy, you know. We don't want to distress our other diners."

Though the words had been meant for her uncle's ears, Della heard every word. Wild Wind had certainly heard them, and she burned with anger on his behalf. Sidling closer to him, she grasped his hand, threading her fingers through his. She squeezed and was relieved when he squeezed back.

Uncle Clint drew himself up to his full impressive height. For a long moment, he pinned the other man with the stare he'd used as a general commanding his troops during the War Between the States. When he spoke, his tone left no doubt that he was used to having his orders obeyed. "My good man, please do not refer to Mr. Wild Wind as a 'redskin.' He is in my employ, and I expect you to treat him with the same respect you would accord to any other guest of mine."

A wash of color flooded the maître d's face. "I'm sorry, sir. No disrespect intended, but I cannot seat him. I must uphold our policies."

Another silence ensued while Uncle Clint stared down the squirming maître d. In a show of support, Emory Dyer eased back to flank Wild Wind on his other side.

When the maître d showed no sign of relenting, Uncle Clint continued, "Very well. We will take our meal at another establishment more accommodating to my guests. You may cancel our dinner reservations. And I believe that I will also cancel our room reservations, as well. I cannot patronize an institution that shows such a lack of sensitivity to my guests."

Indecision crossed the maître d's face. The general's threat apparently caused him to reconsider his position regarding Wild Wind.

Uncle Clint pressed his advantage. "I've reserved four rooms for the next two weeks. Do you want to be the cause of the hotel losing my patronage over your lack of seating one guest?"

The loss of four rooms for the two-week period mentioned decided the maître d. "Very well. Please excuse my lapse of good manners. Let me show you to your table."

When they stepped into the dining room, conversation dwindled. Every diner watched their progress to a table near the center of the room. Della clung to Wild Wind's hand and held her head high.

When they'd been seated, she studied the dining room. White damask napery covered each square table. Snowy cloth napkins and polished silver cutlery graced each place setting. Sparkling, stemmed goblets gleamed. Overhead, gas light chandeliers with crystal prisms hissed and cast a golden glow over the diners.

When Della's glance swept the room, the other patrons either avoided her eyes and paid studious attention to their plates, or they stared with rude curiosity, as though wondering if Wild Wind might leap up and begin scalping them all with his tomahawk.

CHAPTER 18

By the time a black-jacketed waiter came to take their order, a snowy napkin draped over one forearm, they'd all agreed they wanted a steak dinner. One by one he wrote down their orders, until he came to Wild Wind. In a smooth move that excluded the warrior, the server passed him by and addressed Della.

"Madame, may I take your order?"

Della gave Wild Wind an uncertain look, then replied, "I'll have steak and a baked potato. With tea."

The man scribbled on his pad, then flipped the order book closed. "I'll bring your drinks, and your meal will be ready shortly." He bowed himself away.

The waiter had taken one step when Uncle Clint's low but implacable voice halted him. "Excuse me, but you're not finished here. You've missed one of my guests."

The waiter pivoted and looked down at Uncle Clint, his face haughty. "I believe I've taken the orders of everyone at this table."

"You most definitely have not. You've overlooked one person."

In a show of great patience, the waiter flipped open his order pad and glanced down at their order. "Four people. That is everyone."

Beside Della, Wild Wind tensed. He looked ready to surge to his feet, but Uncle Clint forestalled him. Shoving back his chair, the general rose, towering over the waiter. "You will take the order of every person at this table, or we leave this restaurant immediately. And I will have your job."

As if sensing a disaster in the making, the maître d hurried to their table. Drawing the waiter aside, he whispered in the other man's ear. A chastened waiter then stepped to Wild Wind's side. "I apologize, sir, for my misunderstanding. May I take your order?"

"I will have steak and potato with tea."

The waiter nodded and scribbled in his pad before vanishing in the kitchen.

His mouth a grim slash beneath his mustache, Uncle Clint seated himself. He looked across the table at Wild Wind. "My apologies. I never imagined this would happen when I extended my invitation this afternoon."

"Many seasons will pass before our two peoples will be able to live together in peace. There is much bad blood between us."

Uncle Clint nodded. "I hope we can achieve peace in our lifetime, but I'm afraid that much more blood will be spilled on both sides before it's over."

"It will not end well for my people."

After their meal had been served, Uncle Clint commented, "A curious thing happened the other day. I received a telegram from my solicitor back in Boston. Someone has made an offer for the Slash L."

Della lowered her fork to her plate, startled.

Coral laid a hand on her husband's arm. "But who would want the Slash L?"

He shrugged. "I don't know. The offer was extended through a third party. I directed my solicitor to make discreet inquiries to see if he can discover who wants the ranch."

"Are you going to sell?" Della asked.

Her uncle shook his head. "I have no plans to sell. I'm as curious to know *why* someone wants the ranch as I am to know *who* wants it."

Speculation about the offer filled the rest of the meal. While they talked, Della watched Wild Wind from the corner of her eye. He conducted himself as though he ate in high-class restaurants every evening, and she marveled anew at his adaptability.

Over pie at the end of the meal, Clint addressed his bookkeeper. "Emory, I'll be tied up through the rest of this week with the final details of the state constitution. Would you take the ladies to the shops? They both need to refurbish their wardrobes. Denver may be well on its way to becoming a civilized city, but it still has many elements of a frontier town. It's not safe for the ladies to go about unescorted."

Emory Dyer agreed with gallant chivalry. "Certainly. I'd be delighted to take the ladies shopping."

Della stared at the lieutenant. "Uncle Emory, you hate shopping."

"I can make an exception for you and Miss Coral."

Wild Wind spoke up. "I will come along. Lona will need me."

Della whipped her head toward Wild Wind. "You? Shop with us? Do you know what happens when women shop?"

An amused smile twitched at Uncle Clint's lips while he waited for Wild Wind's reply.

"I have never been around women who 'shop.' I do not know what this 'shopping' means, but if you are doing it, I will go with you. There are too many rough men about the city. You need my protection."

"Really, Uncle Emory will be protection enough. You can stay at the livery with the horses or do whatever it is that men do when they're not around women."

"If you are shopping, I will go with you. I will not entrust your safety to another. Other men will stare at you. This I will not allow."

Noticing the speculative gleam in her uncle's eyes and guessing an accounting for Wild Wind's possessive behavior would be forthcoming later that evening, Della attempted to halt Wild Wind's declaration. "Very well, come along. But I warn you, you won't like it. Before the morning is over, you'll wish you were back on the Slash L."

∽

Della leaned over a glass-encased jewelry display and examined the ornate items inside, laid out on dark velvet for customers' inspection.

She'd purchased a couple of black, ready-made dresses to expand her meager widow's wardrobe. The dresses had needed few adjustments, and the modiste had promised the frocks would be delivered to her room within two days. Some jewelry would complete the outfits.

She and Coral had found a jeweler's shop just down the street from the modiste. Coral, with Emory Dyer trailing at her elbow, browsed along another counter. Wild Wind stood close to Della. His expression alternated between impassivity and disbelief.

The number and variety of shops in Denver had astounded him. "Why do your people need so many things? If you have food and shelter, what more do you need?"

Della had grinned at him. "In our culture, possessions show a person's wealth or status in society. If one has money, one spends it to impress others."

Wild Wind had shaken his head. "I do not understand this."

"It's not so different from Cheyenne warriors owning many horses. It shows wealth."

"It is not the same."

She'd teased him in the modiste's shop. "What would your Dog Soldiers think if they could see you now?"

An indefinable expression had crossed his face so briefly Della thought she'd imagined it. Then he shook his head. The hint of a smile tugged at his mouth. "My Dog Soldiers would think that you have very strong magic and have bewitched me. Nothing else could explain what I am doing here."

Now, Della examined a pair of jet earrings and a matching brooch. She had no jewelry to go with her mourning gowns. At the ranch, she never bothered with jewelry, but here, in Denver, she must dress the part of wealthy rancher's niece. She pointed to the items and addressed the clerk, who hovered on the other side of the counter waiting to serve her. "I'll take that set of jet earrings and the matching brooch."

She straightened and scanned the shop's interior while the clerk lifted her purchases from the glass case and wrapped them for her.

A red-haired miss who wore a stylish white frock and straw bonnet pretended to be absorbed in the jewelry, but Della noticed the interested glances the young lady sent toward Wild Wind, who appeared oblivious. He preferred to stand watch for any males who might show an interest in accosting Della.

Della had become accustomed to how Wild Wind looked, but now, she appraised him through the eyes of a beautiful young society miss. Strong men abounded in the West, but even in a land replete with men of strength and character, Wild Wind's innate *presence* dominated. His height, the width of his shoulders, and his handsome features combined with an aura of danger made him a romantic figure for susceptible females. His cowboy hat, tilted at a dashing angle over his brow, added a flamboyant flair. Della knew he didn't realize it, but had he been so inclined, he could have left a trail of broken hearts behind him.

She ducked her head and eased away, curious to see what the red-haired miss would do.

With Della leaving the coast clear, the young lady browsed closer to Wild Wind, ostensibly giving her attention to the jewelry displayed on black velvet fabric. When she was a couple of paces from her quarry, the miss dropped her reticule at Wild Wind's feet.

Wild Wind swung his head about and stared at the young lady, who eyed him with a coy expression. He glanced down at the beaded purse puddled about his boots as if wondering how the bag had gotten there.

"I'm so very sorry," the girl exclaimed in coquettish tones while Wild Wind bent to retrieve the reticule.

When he'd straightened and offered the purse to her, she smiled and widened her eyes, the very picture of demure innocence.

"Why, thank you, sir. You're ever so kind."

"I could not leave your bag on the floor."

The young lady blinked. Apparently Wild Wind's reply wasn't the witty repartee she'd expected.

The clerk had packaged Della's jewelry, and Della counted out the bills to pay for her purchase. With the transaction complete, she took pity on Wild Wind, knowing he had no experience with games of flirtation. Breezing up to him, she took his arm and favored him with her most dazzling smile. "I'm ready to leave. Where shall we go next?"

Della nodded at the crestfallen redhead on their way to the door. Moments later, Coral and Emory Dyer joined them on the boardwalk.

Wild Wind halted two strides from the door and swung Della around to face him. "What was that about? What did that young lady want?"

"You don't know, do you?"

Wild Wind looked puzzled. "She seemed to want something from me."

"She did. She wanted to carry on a flirtation with you. She wanted your attention."

"Why would she want my attention? I do not know her."

Della laughed. "That young lady thought you were handsome and wanted you to notice her. She hoped you'd speak to her."

"I did speak to her."

"Only after she practically threw herself at your feet. And then she hoped you'd engage her in conversation." Della couldn't help but laugh again at the expression on his face. "Now you see how it is in our society. Men and women talk to each other. It doesn't always mean anything. You mustn't run off every man who looks at me or talks to me, and you'd better get used to young ladies smiling at you."

CHAPTER 19

Della craned her neck to see around a top-hatted gentleman. Beside her, Wild Wind maintained a tight grip on her elbow to prevent her from being swept away on the tide of humanity thronging the boardwalk. On her other side, Uncle Clint and Emory Dyer flanked Coral, protecting her from the jostling crowd.

An atmosphere of patriotism and exuberance infected Denver on this July 4th, 1876. Not only was the city celebrating Colorado territory's impending statehood, Denver commemorated the Centennial anniversary of the United States of America. American flags fluttered from every flagpole. Red, white, and blue bunting hung from shop and bank windows along the main street. A parade several blocks long wound its way down the thoroughfare. Marching bands, interspersed between the floats, played patriotic songs with ear-ringing enthusiasm. The throng lining both sides of the avenue cheered. Ladies waved their handkerchiefs.

Della stood on tiptoe to see around the gentleman. The Colorado militia approached, its officers mounted on white horses and riding five abreast. The officer in the center carried the militia's guidon. The silk banner snapped in the breeze. Behind the officers rode the troops, all astride black horses. Among the mounts, Della recognized many Slash L

Morgans, which the army had purchased. She squeezed Wild Wind's arm to get his attention. When he glanced down at her, she leaned close to shout into his ear.

"Many of those black horses are Morgans Uncle Clint has sold to the army. The Slash L is well represented here today."

Wild Wind nodded and straightened, giving the passing mounts a closer scrutiny.

Behind the militia the territorial governor and his wife, Mr. and Mrs. John Routt, followed in an open barouche pulled by a team of dapple grays. Next, a white wagon pulled by two white horses and swathed with red, white, and blue bunting rolled past. A woman stood in the wagon's bed, wearing a dress made of bunting. A high golden crown perched on her curls. With one hand at her waist, she held a gold scepter. With her other hand, she waved at the jubilant crowd.

Thirty-eight young women, representing each of the thirty-eight states of the Union, marched behind the wagon. Ear-splitting whistles and cheers from the bystanders greeted the ladies, who waved back.

When the parade finally ended, the noon hour approached. With one arm about Coral's waist, Uncle Clint said, "You all must be parched. Let's get something to drink." He ran a finger about the inside of his shirt collar. "The sun is scorching today."

Della cooled herself with a paper fan. She perspired in her black widow's weeds and underlying corset. She wished she could wear her riding outfit instead. Coral, clad in a white lawn frock, appeared untouched by the heat.

Food and drink vendors lined the boardwalk. The buttery scent of popcorn wafted to them over the smell of horses. Just down the street they located a booth selling iced cider. Reaching into his jacket pocket, Uncle Clint pulled out a flat leather wallet. He purchased drinks for them all. When they'd slaked their thirst, they strolled on.

The excitement of the day infected Della. She determined to let nothing spoil the festive atmosphere. When Wild Wind claimed her hand, she allowed him the liberty. If she were honest, she'd have to admit that she'd allowed him such liberties nearly since the moment he stepped onto the Slash L. Holding her hand seemed harmless after the kiss he'd taken from her in the barn.

"What do you think of our festivities?" Della hoped he could come to at least tolerate, if not enjoy, her culture's customs.

Wild Wind pondered her question. "Your parade is not so very different from some of our ceremonies, when all the Cheyenne bands gather to celebrate."

Della tugged on his hand and pulled him to a halt. He tipped his head down to look at her, his hat brim shadowing his face from the noontime sun. A question lurked about his eyes.

"Tell me about your ceremonies."

"One of the most important ceremonies is the Sun Dance."

Della glanced down at their linked hands. Somehow, the sight of their hands joined together seemed fitting for the conversation and that moment in time. She cut a look upward at him. "I've heard of the Sun Dance."

Wild Wind's features became earnest. He tugged her closer. "The Sun Dance is celebrated in the summer. All of the Cheyenne bands gather for a week. There is much feasting but also fasting by those who have committed to dance. Only those who have made a vow or who are seeking wisdom will dance. It is also a time for women to gossip and the men to show their skill with horses or weapons."

Della suspected that the Sun Dance represented more than Wild Wind confessed, but she appreciated whatever he wanted to share with her. His life with the tribes fascinated her. This year, he'd missed the ceremony because he'd been living on the Slash L. "You missed the dance this summer because you're with us."

Wild Wind shrugged. "It was not meant to be. I am here with you. I would not be any place else."

"Thank you for attending the parade with me."

"I am learning. I could not have done this when we first met, but now, I am ready to try to fit into your world."

Della searched his face. His battle-hardened features, with grooves slashing each lean cheek, squint lines fanning out from his eyes, and his firm mouth relaxed now in a tenderness at odds with his warrior's appearance, seemed different, yet somehow the same, as the man she'd known in his village so long ago. Her heart clenched. "You're fitting in so well I sometimes forget that you're half Cheyenne."

"I can never forget that I am Cheyenne, one of The People. Yet, since coming to the Slash L, I feel kinship with my mother's blood, as well."

Della nodded her understanding.

"One day, you will share my Cheyenne heritage. We will go to the reservation and will share a lodge there. You will see my people as they now live."

"If we marry."

"We will marry."

A hail from Uncle Clint drew them back from their private world. "Are you hungry for some fried chicken? Here's a booth selling chicken."

Wild Wind and Della caught up to the others, who stood before a vendor offering pieces of chicken. When they'd purchased enough chicken to satisfy their hunger, they stood in the shade of a striped canvas awning that arched over the entrance of a brick bank building and ate their meal with their fingers, laughing like children.

After they'd finished and wiped their fingers on the paper napkins that had wrapped the chicken, Coral suggested, "Do you suppose anyone is selling taffy? I have a hankering for something sweet."

Wild Wind's brow wrinkled. "Taffy? What is taffy?"

"Taffy is an American tradition. You must try it," Coral replied. "Taffy is made mostly from molasses and is 'pulled' until it's light and chewy."

"You'll like it," Della told him. "It will satisfy your sweet tooth."

They located a vendor whose booth displayed pans of braided golden taffy ropes cut in three-inch pieces. Della offered Wild Wind a piece of the candy on a paper doily. "Here, try this." She popped the morsel into his mouth and watched, smiling, while he tasted the confection.

Pleasure crossed his face. "It is good. I would have more of that," he said when he'd swallowed.

When they'd devoured their taffy, Uncle Clint suggested, "I suppose we should return to the Tremont House for some tea, and then the ladies can rest before dinner."

They made their way back to the hotel, threading through the crowds that still thronged the boardwalk. Wild Wind had snagged Della's hand again, interlacing their fingers, and Della leaned against him. The day's activities and the food she'd eaten made her feel pleasantly drowsy and content. With a surprised jolt, she realized she felt happier today than she had in several long months. Much of that happiness had to do with the man at her side, and only a twinge of guilt dimmed her pleasure.

They reached the Tremont House and trooped into the lobby's cool dimness. A lanky man with thinning chestnut hair and clad in a brown tweed suit rose from a chair when he saw them. He approached their group.

"General Logan?"

The man's apologetic air hinted to Della of the gravity of his mission. A cold foreboding shivered down her spine, spoiling her pleasure.

"Yes? What can I do for you?" Uncle Clint stepped forward.

"General Logan, I hate to interrupt your day, but the governor is requesting your immediate presence. Will you please come with me?"

Without questioning the man's mission, the general agreed. "Certainly. I'm sure Governor Routt wouldn't ask for me unless it was necessary." He took Coral's hand and squeezed, then turned her over to Emory Dyer. "Emory, will you take the ladies and Wild Wind into the dining room for tea? I'll be back as soon as I can."

With that, he and the governor's messenger vanished through the hotel's ornate door onto the sun-washed street.

The incident dampened everyone's spirits.

Coral clutched Emory's sleeve. "What do you suppose happened?"

Emory patted her hand and tried to appear encouraging. His pleasant face crinkled in a smile. "I'm sure it can't be anything too serious. We'll find out soon enough. Come along now, and let's have our tea."

Della and Wild Wind followed them into the dining room and to their table. Wild Wind had eaten his meals with them each day, and there hadn't been a repeat of the episode they'd experienced on the first evening.

When they'd ordered iced tea with wedges of lemon, they sat back in their chairs. Wild Wind stretched out his long legs to one side so as not to bump the ladies' feet.

"Say what you will, something serious must have happened for the governor to take Clint away from today's festivities," Coral fretted.

"I agree." Della's restless fingers traced patterns on the damask tablecloth. "The governor had his own agenda this afternoon. He was scheduled to give a speech in the town square. Whatever happened must be important enough to take him away from his speech."

"Ladies, we'll find out when the general returns. Now, let's drink our tea," Dyer said while the waiter put their drinks on the table.

During a bit of half-hearted conversation, they finished their tea and returned to the lobby. Emory Dyer left them and went outside on an errand of his own, and Coral trudged upstairs to the room she shared with her husband.

Wild Wind paused in the lobby. "Now, I will go to the livery stable and check on the horses. I will return for dinner." He scanned Della's face with an expression that hinted at his reluctance to leave her company.

"Will you accompany us to the concert at the opera house this evening? The orchestra will play patriotic music."

"I do not care about patriotic music or the United States government, but for you, I will attend the concert. I would be with you every waking moment." Reaching up, he touched her cheek with gentle fingers. "Lona, your heart is healing. You look at me now without shadows in your eyes."

His words rang true. She *was* healing. Her honest nature compelled her to admit the truth. "Yes. Yes, I am healing."

"That is good. Soon we will court. Then we will marry."

"Before that, I would have Uncle Clint talk to you about our God. He can explain everything so much better than I can."

"You and Coral have given me much to think about, but I have questions. I will ask them of your uncle when we return home."

Home. He'd called the Slash L home. Could he really have begun to consider the ranch his home? Della didn't draw attention to his words. He probably hadn't even realized he'd made the reference, but she tucked his unconscious admission away in her heart.

"Now, my beautiful Lona, try not to worry. I will see you at dinner." Wild Wind's thumb stroked once across her cheek before he pivoted and strode from the hotel.

Late afternoon shade banded the street with strips of shadows cast by adjacent buildings when Uncle Clint returned to the Tremont House. Della had spent a restless afternoon pacing her room. When her uncle knocked on her door, she pounced and swung the portal wide. One look at his grim face told her the reason for his meeting had been serious. Her heart plummeted.

"Uncle Clint, what's happened? I know it isn't good."

"Come into our room, and I'll tell you all about it."

Della ducked into the room her uncle shared with Coral. Her aunt stood beside the four-poster bed, her hands clenched at her waist, her face pale. Uncle Clint shut the door, and Della whirled to face him.

"Tell me! What happened?"

Her uncle's shoulders rose as he breathed deeply before beginning his tale. "On the Sunday before last, June 25, General George Custer pitted the 7th Cavalry in a battle against a large coalition of Sioux, Cheyenne, and Arapaho hostiles. They were Sitting Bull's and Crazy Horse's warriors."

Della held her breath, dreading to hear the rest of his news. She wanted to know what had happened, yet at the same time, she wanted to cover her ears with her hands to block out the tale.

"The 7th Cavalry had orders to track down the Indians and return them to their reservations."

Della knew this much. News that the cavalry had been scouting for hostiles since late spring had reached the ranch.

"Custer came upon a large encampment of men, women, and children along the Little Bighorn River and decided to attack. It seems he severely underestimated the number of hostiles he'd encounter."

Della moved to Coral's side, and the women gripped hands. They stared at Uncle Clint with unwavering attention.

"The warriors surrounded Custer's men in the valley beside the river. Within an hour, every last man had been slaughtered."

Della caught her breath, and Coral squeezed Della's fingers so hard she winced.

"All of them?" Coral breathed.

"Every man under Custer's direct command perished. Major Reno managed to retreat to a bluff overlooking the river and hold the position until reinforcements arrived the next day, so many of his men survived." Clint let out his breath in a gusty sigh and rubbed the back of his neck.

The enormity of the event took a moment to absorb. "We couldn't have envisioned this when you predicted a bloody summer," Della said.

Her uncle strode toward her and took both her hands in his. "I have more bad news. Captain Asher was with Custer that day. He was among the slain."

The news stunned Della. Captain Asher had been a former suitor and a friend. Though they'd parted ways years ago, she still felt a spot of fondness for the handsome captain. "Oh, no. I'm so sorry. His wife will be devastated."

Uncle Clint nodded. "There's no way this can be hushed up, and it will stir up more animosity toward the Indians."

Della sat down on the bed with a thump. If Wild Wind hadn't come to the Slash L and had continued warring against her people, he might have been among those Cheyenne who had attacked the 7th Cavalry. She breathed a silent prayer of thanksgiving that a sovereign Providence had shown him the futility of fighting and had brought him to the ranch.

Uncle Clint took Coral in his arms. "My dear wife, the governor has requested that I re-enlist. He wants me to report to the nearest fort to be given a command and commissioned to chase after the hostiles."

Coral gave a small cry and clutched her husband about the neck. "What did you tell him?"

"I didn't give him an answer. I told him I'd discuss it with you and pray about it."

Della returned to her room shaken by what had happened and distressed about the possibility of her uncle returning to combat. She'd thought that once the Civil War had ended and he'd resigned his commission, he'd never have to go to war again. Her thoughts then went to Wild Wind. Once the news spread through Denver, he wouldn't be safe here. Perhaps she could convince him to return to the Slash L.

Della met Wild Wind in the lobby before dinner. She drew him aside into the sitting area and broke the news of Custer's defeat. He listened with grave attention, eyes narrowed, his mouth a grim line. Della gripped his arm just above the elbow and gave him a little shake. "You should leave Denver. It won't be safe for you here."

He scanned her face with an intent stare, touching her with his eyes. At last, he spoke. "Are you staying?"

"Yes. We're not leaving until after Governor Routt's soiree on Friday night. We should be back at the Slash L by Sunday evening."

"Then I will stay. A Cheyenne warrior does not run from danger."

"You're just one man against a city. I wish you'd go."

"If you stay, I stay. If I go, I will take you with me."

"Uncle Clint will never countenance me traveling alone with you. We aren't married."

"Then I stay."

CHAPTER 20

Della took her uncle's gloved hand and stepped from the hired carriage which had conveyed them from the soiree at the governor's mansion. Her dangling jet earrings brushed against her jaw when she ducked out the carriage door. The ball gown Silvie had made up from the black satin fabric Uncle Clint had purchased whispered with rich luxuriousness as she stepped onto the street.

Hissing gas lamps on ornate pillars on either side of the hotel steps cast pools of golden light onto the pavement. A clock in the church tower on the next block chimed the ten o'clock hour.

Emory Dyer followed her down from the equipage. "These past two weeks have been enjoyable, but I'll be glad to sleep in my own bed again."

Clinging to her husband's arm, Coral agreed. "This visit has been charming, but it will be delightful to be back at the Slash L."

Silently, Della concurred. So far, Wild Wind had encountered only hostile glares and muttered imprecations from Denver's citizens, but the tension against tribal people mounted daily. She'd be relieved to leave the city in the morning.

The carriage rolled away, traces and harness riggings jingling, iron-rimmed wheels rumbling.

They'd just reached the steps of the Tremont House when footsteps pounding toward them along the footway caught their attention. Grady O'Brien appeared out of the darkness from the direction of the livery stable. He'd lost his hat, and his torn shirt hung off one shoulder. A purpling bruise stained one cheek.

"Quick," he panted, his chest heaving. "They're fixing to hang him!"

Shaking Coral's hand from his arm, Clint stepped forward. "Who?"

"Wild Wind. A vigilante committee says he stole a horse."

"Where?"

"The livery."

"Emory, come with me." The aura of leadership, the result of his years of command, dropped about the general like a cloak. He pivoted and leaped into a run.

The lieutenant followed, with Grady on their heels. The men vanished into nighttime's blackness, the sound of their footsteps fading.

With a shared glance, Della and Coral gathered up their skirts and hurried after the men.

Panic tore through Della. Her worst fears were becoming reality. What if Uncle Clint didn't reach the livery in time? What if she arrived to see Wild Wind dangling at the end of a rope? She blanked the image from her mind and increased her pace. The trailing skirt of her gown caught on a rock. She jerked it free, not caring if the fabric tore.

They reached the livery. One side of the double doors had been rolled open. Lantern light lit the interior. A mass of male bodies cast shifting shadows against the walls. Over the heads of the men, Della saw Wild Wind, hands tied behind his back and a noose about his neck, standing on a wooden barrel. A length of rope attached to the noose snaked up over a rafter and disappeared in the gloom. A stranger stood beside the barrel ready to kick it from beneath Wild Wind's feet. An involuntary cry tore from her throat, and she lunged forward as if to snatch Wild Wind to safety.

Before she took two steps, the boom of her uncle's six-shooter echoed through the barn. The rope dangling from the rafter parted and slithered to the floor. Wild Wind swayed.

The vigilante men gave a protesting roar and swarmed toward the chieftain. The Colt roared again, halting the rush toward Wild Wind.

Della and Coral came to a standstill just inside the doorway. Uncle Clint, flanked by Emory Dyer and Grady O'Brien, stood poised in the middle of the livery's aisle. Her uncle and Emory had drawn their sidearms. Grady's empty holster gave mute evidence to the fact that the vigilantes had disarmed him during his attempt to rescue Wild Wind.

The general's authoritative air momentarily stayed the violence of the mob, though danger still simmered in the atmosphere. His commanding voice rang out. "There will be no hanging here tonight. You men disperse and go home."

Mutters sounded while the men shifted.

"This thieving savage is a horse thief. We hang horse thieves." The leader of the group, a disheveled man with a scraggy dark beard and a floppy hat, swaggered forward. He spat in the direction of Wild Wind.

"How do you know he's a horse thief?"

"He was takin' that gelding out of the livery." The vigilante leader nodded toward the black Morgan Wild Wind had been riding. "That horse wears the Slash L brand."

"He rides that horse because he works for me. I own the Slash L." Uncle Clint wiggled the barrel of his six-shooter. "I won't tell you again. You men disperse."

"We aim to have a hangin'," the leader insisted. "We're goin' to rid the world of one more thievin' redskin." He took another step toward Wild Wind. "We aim to avenge Custer's death by hanging this savage."

Watching the scene, Della clamped her mouth shut. A silent scream lodged in her throat. Unable to stop herself, she edged closer. Coral kept pace with her.

The Colt barked again. A bullet lodged in the stable's dirt floor just in front of the leader's down-at-the-heels boots. Dust flew.

The vigilante leaped back and swung his head toward Uncle Clint.

"If you take one more step toward my employee, the next bullet will be for you. And Lieutenant Dyer will shoot anyone else who makes a move toward the man you want to hang." Her uncle's low voice left no doubt he meant every word.

Della viewed her uncle as the men in the crowd would see him. Uncle Clint's long-tailed black dress jacket, his silk shirt and striped gray vest, and his slim trousers all bespoke wealth and privilege. His tone gave evidence of command. Della knew none of the men doubted her uncle's ability to follow through on his threat. Not one man of the vigilante posse mistook him for a hapless dandy, despite his elegant evening ensemble.

Several tense seconds passed while bloodshed hung in the balance. At last, the men began to ease toward the door. Tension drained from the atmosphere. Della and Coral stepped aside while the vigilantes vanished into the night. Bruises marked their faces, and some had torn shirts. Della felt satisfaction that Wild Wind had left his mark on his attackers.

When the livery had been emptied, Della and Coral darted toward Wild Wind. Her uncle and Emory Dyer were easing the chieftain down off the barrel when the women reached them. The men set him on the floor and leaned him against the wall.

Della gasped when she knelt beside him, her satin skirts puddling about her. From his bruises, it was apparent he hadn't been taken without a fight. Both eyes were blackened and swollen shut, and one cheek bulged twice its normal size. His shirt hung in shreds about him. Purpling bruises colored his chest and stomach. His swollen knuckles showed the evidence of his resistance.

"They jumped him when he took his horse out," Grady said. "He gave as good as he got, but there were too many. I tried to help, but we were outnumbered. They took my six-shooter, and Wild Wind's, too, so we were without weapons."

Della glanced at the cowboy. "Thank you for helping. You took a few licks, yourself."

Grady ducked his head. "I did what I could."

"I'm so grateful you were here when Wild Wind was attacked. If he'd been alone, we couldn't have saved him."

Uncle Clint went down on one knee on the other side of the warrior. "Wild Wind. Can you hear me?"

For a moment, Wild Wind didn't respond. Then he managed to slit one eye open and nod.

"I'm sending for a doctor. You just rest easy."

Della laid gentle fingers over his heart.

He cracked one eye again and stared at her. With an effort, he gathered strength to speak through his bloodied lips. "Lona. You should not be here."

"Why shouldn't I?"

"No warrior wants his woman to see him in such a helpless state."

"What kind of woman would I be if I turned tail and ran when you needed me? I'm not that woman."

Wild Wind closed his eye and remained silent for a moment, breathing with an effort. "You are a she-bear ."

Della sat on the floor beside him and held his hand while they waited for Grady to fetch a doctor. Coral, her mulberry-colored gown gleaming with a jeweled sheen in the lantern light, perched on a wooden trunk along one wall. No one spoke.

Uncle Clint prowled the stable until he located both missing six-shooters on the floor of an empty stall.

When Grady arrived with the doctor, a gray-haired man with gold-rimmed spectacles and bristling eyebrows, Della scooted out of the way to give the doctor room. She clambered to her feet and stepped around the men to join her aunt on the trunk.

Except for the sounds of horses rustling in their stalls and munching hay, silence filled the stable. The doctor pulled Wild Wind's tattered shirt from his trousers and probed his chest and sides. He listened to Wild Wind's heart with a stethoscope. The warrior remained stoic, though Della knew he felt pain.

"I need to look at his back," the doctor said. "Roll him over."

With careful hands, Uncle Clint and Emory Dyer turned Wild Wind on his side. Della gasped when she saw the dark bruising on his back. With expert fingers, the doctor prodded Wild Wind's injuries.

With the examination completed, Clint and Emory leaned Wild Wind back against the wall. The doctor drew the others aside and murmured his diagnosis.

"He has a couple of cracked ribs. His spleen and kidneys are enlarged. Apparently, someone got in some good kicks to his back when he was down. He needs complete bed rest for at least a week. Longer would be better, but I doubt you can keep him down any longer than a week."

Uncle Clint and Emory exchanged glances. They'd been planning to leave Denver in the morning, but with Wild Wind unable to travel, their departure must be delayed.

"Do you have a place for him to rest?"

Finding a safe place for Wild Wind created another difficulty. They couldn't return him to the boarding house where Grady and the other cowboys had rooms.

The doctor rubbed his hands together. "I see your dilemma. Well, bring him to my house. I have a room in my clinic where he can stay while he mends." The physician packed his stethoscope in his black leather bag and snapped it shut.

Uncle Clint laid a hand on Coral's shoulder. "I'll accompany Wild Wind to the clinic. You go on back to the Tremont House. Don't wait up. It may be morning before I make it back."

Della stepped forward. "I'm going with you." She tilted her up chin.

Her uncle took one look at her face and didn't attempt to dissuade her. "Come along, then."

The doctor lived in a quiet residential part of town. His wife met them at the door, a lamp held high and a shawl draped about her shoulders. Her faded flannel nightdress dragged the floor.

"I'm so sorry to disrupt your evening," Uncle Clint apologized.

"I've been married to Dr. Trent for forty-five years. I've had my sleep interrupted many a time in those years, so think nothing of it. Come on in." Mrs. Trent pulled the door wide and motioned them in.

With Uncle Clint on one side and Grady on the other, his arms draped over their shoulders, they got Wild Wind inside. Della brought up the rear.

Mrs. Trent laid a hand on Della's arm while the men disappeared down the hall toward the back of the house. "Let the men care for him, honey, and then you can go back there to see him. Would you like some tea?"

Della didn't want tea, but her hostess seemed anxious to be hospitable. "Yes, thank you."

"A nice cup of tea will calm our nerves." Mrs. Trent bustled to the kitchen.

Sometime later, Dr. Trent and Grady emerged from the back of the house. Della laid her cup and saucer on a lamp table beside her chair and rose when the men appeared in the parlor door.

The doctor nodded at her. "You may go back there now, ma'am."

Della turned to her hostess. "Thank you very much for the tea. Now, if you'll excuse me, I'll see how Wild Wind is doing."

"Go all the way to the back," Dr. Trent told her. "It's the last door on the right."

Della turned into the clinic and hurried to the bedroom just off the examining room. A lamp on the bedside table had been turned down. The flame cast a dim light across the room. Uncle Clint reclined in an oversized rocking chair, one ankle across his other knee. Windows framed by lace curtains presented black faces in both outside walls.

Wild Wind lay motionless in a large brass bedstead.

Della came to a standstill beside the bed, looking down at him. A white swathe of bandage wrapped about his chest contrasted with his burnished skin. His swollen eyes made two purple pools in his face. His bruised hands lay lax on the sheet, and he breathed with the deep, steady rhythm of one drugged.

Della glanced at her uncle. "Will he be all right?"

He nodded. "The doctor treated his injuries and gave him laudanum. Sleep is the best thing for him right now."

Della's shoulders rose and fell on a deep sigh. "I thought the vigilantes would hang him before we could intervene."

"It was close."

Della dragged a rocking chair with a flowered petit point seat close to the bed and reached for Wild Wind's hand. She'd sat in silence for several minutes when her uncle spoke from the shadows.

"You've told me Wild Wind plans to marry you, and he seems set on the notion. Have you considered that he follows a pagan religion?"

She turned her head toward her uncle. "Yes. He and I have discussed this. I've told him I will marry only a God-fearing man, and we've had conversations about the Bible and salvation. He's been attending Sunday services at the ranch, and he remembers much of what his mother taught him when he was a child."

"I'm glad you've made a stand on that issue, though I'm not sure Wild Wind is really hearing you. He's made it clear he considers you his future wife."

"I hoped you could talk to him when we get back to the ranch. And Aunt Coral and I have made a pact to pray for Wild Wind's salvation every day."

"I'll talk to him, man to man. Except for his animism, he seems to be a fine man and would make you a good husband. The two of you would have to work out your cultural differences, however."

"You have no objections to me marrying a someone who is half Cheyenne?"

Uncle Clint shrugged, the movement almost indiscernible in the gloom. "You must remember that he was reared in a culture foreign to your own upbringing."

Della nodded. "I know that. I encountered the Cheyenne influence with Shane."

"Shane wasn't born Cheyenne. He was definitely influenced by the years he spent in their village, but he was essentially of our culture." Her uncle paused and drew a deep breath. "One thing you should ask yourself."

Della waited, lifting an inquiring eyebrow at her uncle. "And that would be?"

"Can you marry and live with a man who has tortured and killed white settlers?"

She bit her lip, turning over in her mind the very thing that initially had given her reservations over a relationship with Wild Wind. To marry him, she must look beyond his violent past. She hesitated. "I've thought of that. I think, given how much he's changed, I can't hold it against him. And if he becomes a God-fearing man, then I would have to forgive him. If Christ can forgive anything, then I must."

Uncle Clint smiled. "If it's not a problem for you, it's not an issue for me. I'm more concerned that he should be a godly husband to you and father for Jake and any children the two of you may have."

"He's loved me ever since I was a captive in his village."

"I remember that story."

The two fell silent. The night stretched on, deep and still. Della cradled Wild Wind's hand on her lap, her fingers curled about his. She dozed.

When she woke, morning's lemon light painted the windows and limned the furniture in the room with a golden edging. She leaned closer to Wild Wind, who still slept. She laid one palm alongside his face.

At that moment, he stirred. His swollen eyes opened a crack. "Lona, my heart. What are you doing here?"

"I couldn't leave you. I've been here beside you all night."

"Your presence must be why I slept so well."

Della smiled. "That was the laudanum Dr. Trent gave you."

Wild Wind closed his eyes and squeezed her hand. "No. I am sure it was you sitting by my bed that made my sleep so sweet."

State of Colorado
Late Summer, 1876

CHAPTER 21

The riders swept to the bluff and pulled their horses to a halt. Wild Wind stepped down from his mount and crawled to the top of the hill, keeping low. When he reached the skyline, he removed his hat and laid it beside him on the grass. Edging to the crest, he lifted the field glasses to his eyes and scoured the country below.

Della settled back in her saddle seat, watching Wild Wind. In the weeks since their return to the Slash L, he'd made a remarkable recovery from the beating he'd received in Denver. The bruises had faded, and his face had returned to its normal shape. Yet she couldn't forget how close they'd come to losing him. Her heart had opened and taken him in during his brush with death, and she wondered how she would deal with refusing to marry him if he didn't become a God-fearing man. She would lose him as surely as if he'd died.

Beside her, Coral's mount stamped at a fly. Beyond Coral, Uncle Clint sat astride a black Morgan gelding, his rifle butt propped on his knee, muzzle aimed skyward. His gloved right hand held the Winchester in readiness for use. Two other cowboys who rode with them slouched in their saddles while they waited, their rifles across their saddle bows.

Della studied her aunt's profile, shaded by her hat brim. Since Uncle Clint had declined to accept a position with the army, the strained expression had left Coral's face. She'd reverted to her usual serene self, and Della could empathize with her aunt's relief. After what had happened to General Custer, no wife would want her husband chasing after Sitting Bull's and Crazy Horse's warriors.

A movement at the top of the bluff caught Della's attention. Wild Wind had finished his study of the land and was scooting backward off the crest. When he couldn't be seen from anyone on the other side, he shoved his hat onto his head and pushed to his feet. Moving with caution, he worked his way down the slope.

"Is it safe to proceed?" Uncle Clint asked when Wild Wind had reached the bottom and caught up his mount.

"I did not see any sign of hostiles, but I am sure that warriors have been here." Wild Wind halted at his gelding's shoulder. The two men shared a long look. "There is something about half a mile to the east that we should check."

Uncle Clint nodded. "We'll follow you."

Grasping the saddle horn with one hand, Wild Wind leaped aboard his sorrel without using stirrups and turned his mount about, his rifle across his knee. He halted his horse beside Della's grulla gelding and met her questioning gaze. "Stay at my side and keep your rifle handy. I do not like this, though I saw nothing."

Della slid her Winchester from its scabbard. Coral did the same.

Avoiding the crest, Wild Wind led them along a trough between two low swells of the billowing prairie. He paused often, listening and using the field glasses, keeping an eye on their back trail as well as what lay before them.

No one spoke. The afternoon sun beat down upon them without mercy. Before they'd ridden far, buzzards appeared, coasting on the air currents, circling above something as yet unseen.

When they reached the spot below the hideous black birds, Wild Wind called a halt. Before them, the land dipped into a shallow hollow. In the lowest point, three pale, elongated objects lay scattered about on the browning grass. The loud buzzing of hundreds of flies filled the air with an obscene drone. A wisp of breeze brought with it the stench of blood and death.

The riders pulled up, six abreast, and stared in horror at the scene below. Wild Wind turned his head toward Della, his expression revealing deep pain. He shoved his rifle into its scabbard, then reached out and grasped her mustang's reins. "Lona, do not come closer. You should not see this."

"Coral, stay here with Della. This isn't a scene for a lady's eyes."

The women watched while the men urged their mounts down the slope. At the bottom, they dismounted and approached the objects. Della knew what they'd find. Three men, killed and mutilated by either Sioux, Cheyenne, or Arapahoe warriors.

Della and Coral strained to hear the men's conversation. Though they spoke in low tones, the wind carried their words across the distance.

Uncle Clint and Wild Wind squatted beside the bodies. Several arrows protruded from the men's chests, and Wild Wind flicked a finger across one of the arrow's feathers.

"Sioux," he said.

"When?"

"Early this morning. Probably while they prepared their breakfast."

What personal items the men owned that hadn't been taken lay scattered about in the grass. Uncle Clint rose and stared down at the dead for a brief moment. Then he roused and lifted his head. "Let's get these men buried."

The cowboys retrieved short-handled spades from behind their saddles and set about the business of burying the dead. Clint helped, while Wild Wind gathered up the men's personal effects.

The women dismounted and sat in the shade cast by their horses, watching. Della's stomach rolled, though she'd seen a similar sight before. She turned her face away and tucked her split riding skirt about her boots. Her fingers needed something to do to keep her mind from the scene below, though she could hear each time the shovels split the soil.

With the gruesome task finished, Uncle Clint and Wild Wind climbed the knoll to fetch the women. "I'm sorry you had to see that," Clint said.

Pushing to her feet, Coral stepped close to her husband and pressed a small hand against his chest. "Neither Della nor I are shrinking violets."

Her husband covered her hand with one of his own. "For that, I'm grateful."

Wild Wind halted before Della. Reaching down, he grasped both her hands and pulled her up.

"Who were those men?" she asked, standing close to him.

"They left behind some papers that might tell us something. Let's go down and see what we can learn." Uncle Clint turned to Wild Wind. "Is it safe for us to spend a few minutes here?"

"The warriors are gone. We have a little time."

The four of them descended into the hollow, their horses trailing behind. One of the cowboys held a leather pouch with a folded top secured by a strap. The pouch had been emptied by the attackers, and the papers were strewn about on the buffalo grass. Most of the men's other possessions had been taken. Their food, boots, clothing, weapons and ammunition, as well as their horses and rigs, had been stolen. A harmonica, a letter from one of the wives, and a pocketknife were among the few things left behind.

They all busied themselves collecting the scattered pages that belonged in the pouch. When the last paper had been gathered, everyone handed their pages to Uncle Clint. He organized them in a neat pile and spread the paper out across his horse's back. Frowning, he studied the lines drawn across the surface. Della and Coral crowded close on either side of him.

"This may shed some light on the reason I've had an offer for the Slash L. I received another letter from my solicitor last week. The offer from the unknown third party has been increased by a sizable amount."

"Your solicitor hasn't discovered who's making the offer?" Della asked.

"Not yet, but I think these papers may give him some clues."

"Tell us," Coral cried. "What is this paper?"

"This is a geological map." Her husband traced marks on the paper with a forefinger. "These are the ranch boundary markers. These lines show the government land where I have legal grazing rights. These symbols indicate elevation and topography, and these lines designate something that may be of interest to us, and definitely to our mystery buyer."

Both women stared at him with an impatient air.

He pointed to an oval marking. "This is an oil seep. Here is another." His finger stabbed at a second location. "And another. Someone has found more than one place on the Slash L where oil is seeping to the surface. Our mystery buyer must be someone in the oil business, and these men were 'bird dogs' sent to scout out the oil."

Wild Wind appeared on the Morgan's opposite side. He stared down at the map. "You are looking for the black water?"

Uncle Clint's head snapped up. Across the gelding's saddle, his stared bored into the other man's face. "You know of this?"

"The tribes use the black water for medicine, for a purge, and for war paint. We all shared the bounty. There was plenty for all."

"Will you take us to the nearest seep?"

"It is several miles toward the setting of the sun. We must ride with care. Our horses need water. We will have to find water first."

"What about the Shorthorns?" Della asked.

Her uncle glanced down at her. "We'll check out the herd after I've had a look at one or two of these seeps."

The danger from the tribes had stretched the manpower of the Slash L nearly to the breaking point. Some cowboys guarded the ranch. Others rode the range, keeping an eye out for rustlers, for hostiles, or any other danger that might threaten the stock. Coral and Della had insisted that they could do their part riding the range with the men.

They located the first seep just before the sun slid behind the distant mountains. In a shallow dip, black sludge collected in the bowl. They dismounted and strode toward the seep's edge. The dry grasses rustled about their boots.

Uncle Clint squatted beside the black tarry pool. He dipped his fingers into the viscous liquid and rubbed the stuff between his thumb and forefinger. Raising his hand to his nose, he sniffed. "This is crude, all right. Probably enough to make us very rich."

"Will you try to dig?" Coral asked.

Her husband shrugged. "I haven't had a chance to think about it, but now, I know why someone wants the Slash L."

They ate a cold supper squatting on the ground, not daring to light a fire, and drank a little water from their canteens.

"I will ride out and scout the land and will sleep when I return," Wild Wind stated. "I will keep watch in the hours just before dawn, which is a favorite time for warriors to attack."

"I would like to have at least two of us on guard all the time," Clint commented. "I just don't know if we have enough men."

"Petey and I will take the first shift," Slim, one of the cowboys, offered.

"I'll take the shift after midnight," Uncle Clint said.

"I'll stand watch with you," Coral insisted. "That will make two."

"I'd prefer for you to stay in the camp."

Coral curled her fingers about her husband's. Raising his hand to her mouth, she kissed each knuckle with tender care. "My dear husband, when we married, I promised to stand beside you in the bad times as well as the good. You didn't promise me things would always be easy, but you promised to love me. Well, you've kept that promise. And now, I would keep my promise to you. I'll stand beside you in this dangerous time and not sleep while you face the danger alone."

Uncle Clint cleared his throat. "My darling, you should be the lawyer, not I. How can I argue with that logic?" He touched her cheek with a gentle forefinger.

Feeling like an intruder on the tender scene, Della looked away. A lump clogged her throat. Sensing Wild Wind's gaze as he squatted beside her, she glanced at him and then wished she hadn't. His eyes blazed with the fire of his love, drawing her into his inferno. Caught up in their own emotional whirlpool, awareness of the people around them faded. He reached out and snagged her hand in his. From her cross-legged position on the ground, she let him take her hand and rest their linked fingers on his knee.

"I'll stand guard with you during your watch," she told him.

Tilting his head to look into her face, his gaze bored into hers. "You will stay near me, and you will do what I tell you. I will not risk your safety, my she-bear."

The stillness of the night surrounded them. From over a distant hill, a lobo wolf howled at the moon, his wails trailing off into the dark silence.

"I have been thinking," Wild Wind addressed Della's uncle across the space where they all sat in a circle.

The other man cocked an inquiring eyebrow.

"I do not need the money you have paid me. I have everything I need at the ranch, so I have no need to spend, except for ammunition. Could I use what I have saved to buy a bull and some cows? I would start a herd on the reservation."

Uncle Clint studied the ground for several thoughtful moments before he lifted his head to stare at the other man. "I could spare one of the yearling bulls and a few heifers. In fact, I can throw in a few extra to help you get a better start on a herd. We'll drive the cattle along when you return to the reservation, and I'll vouch for you with the agent. I don't want you hung for a cattle thief."

No one commented, but they all recalled Wild Wind's near hanging in Denver.

"I'll have to clear it with the Bureau of Indian Affairs to guarantee you won't have trouble. You must think of a name for your ranch so we can choose a brand and mark your cattle with it. I'll make sure everything is done up legally so no one can take your stock away from you."

Wild Wind nodded. Della squeezed his hand, and his fingers tightened about hers.

"I thank you. My people must change the way they live, or they will starve. We cannot wait for the government to feed us. Raising cattle will give the men something to do and provide food as well."

"It will be a few years before you'll have enough cattle to spare for eating. I will teach you what you need to know when you come back to the Slash L."

"I will return when Mother Earth awakens from her winter sleep. I will help you with the horses, and I will learn the business of ranching. I would learn everything so I can teach my men."

Wild Wind turned his head toward Della, and he squeezed her fingers again. "When I return, I will court Lona. Then I will take her as my wife."

Della's heart stopped. Would they really marry? Would Wild Wind understand Christ's salvation for him and become a man of God? She prayed that he would.

Wild Wind rose, pulling her up with him. "I will ride now. You need to sleep if you plan to keep watch with me. I will wake you when our turn comes."

His departure signaled the others to begin preparations for the night. Petey and Slim melted into the darkness to stand guard over the camp. Clint and Coral spread out their groundsheets and combined their blankets to make a bed. Della arranged her blankets beside theirs and laid down, her head on her saddle. Within moments she'd tumbled into a deep well of sleep. She didn't waken when Wild Wind spread his bedroll beside her and stretched out on the grass.

CHAPTER 22

Della halted at the veranda railing and pivoted. Wild Wind eased to a stop behind her, while Jake skidded to a standstill between them.

The youngster peered up at his uncle. The lowering western sun slanted beneath the veranda roof, washing his face with gold and striped their shadows across the wooden porch floor.

"Uncle Wild Wind, do you really have to leave?" Jake's lower lip trembled, though he attempted to be brave. His tousled, tawny hair fell over his brow.

Wild Wind knelt on one knee beside his nephew and laid a hand on the boy's shoulder. "I am a chieftain, and that means I must do what is best for my people. My people need me, but when Mother Earth awakens, I will return to your mother and you."

Jake stared into his uncle's face for long moments, as if gauging the truth of the man's words. "My papa didn't come back," he said in a small voice.

His words hit Della with their heart-rending truth. She glanced down at Wild Wind's bent head, wondering how he would answer her son.

"It is life. Your papa would have come back to you if he could have." Wild Wind squeezed the boy's shoulder. "I will come back to you, if I can. It is my word to you. A chieftain's word is not broken."

Della knelt, deciding it was time for her to break into the conversation. She curled a comforting arm about her son's waist. "Jake, God took your papa to heaven to be with Him. God knew your papa loved Him more than he loved you or me, so he took him to Heaven to live there. Papa is waiting for us in Heaven."

"I don't want you to leave!" Jake flung himself at Wild Wind's chest.

The man wrapped his arms about the small body and closed his eyes.

A lump choked Della's throat at the tender expression on Wild Wind's hard warrior's face. The love he felt for her boy couldn't be denied. He would make a good father for Jake, given the opportunity.

At last, she peeled her son from Wild Wind's chest. "Say good night to your uncle and go on up to bed. I'll come up in a bit and read you a story."

When Jake had departed and the door had shut behind him, Della and Wild Wind stared at each other. The day's fading light cast a lemon wash across their faces. Coral had invited Wild Wind to eat his last supper at the ranch house. They'd enjoyed a feast prepared by Sadie with leisurely conversation afterward, before Wild Wind had excused himself. Della had accompanied him to the door.

Now, the reality of his impending departure weighted the silence. The air between them hummed with unspoken emotions. Wild Wind hooked an arm about Della's waist and lifted her to her feet, then whirled her away from the railing and up against the house's white siding. His arms enclosed her. Lowering his head, he rested his forehead against hers.

"Lona, my heart." His husky voice rasped in the dusk. "You have bewitched me. I cannot bear to leave you, yet I must."

"You have no choice. Uncle Clint must get your cattle to the reservation in time for him to be home before the snow flies. It's a long way to Montana and back." Della tried to smile at him, but her mouth wobbled. Her palms rested on his broad chest.

"I will remember you here, at the Slash L. I will take your image with me in my heart."

She raised one hand and laid it alongside his cheek. "Will you promise to think of all that we've talked about? And what Uncle Clint has discussed with you?"

"I will. I think I understand about Jesus Christ, the Savior. But I am not sure that He can forgive me." Wild Wind loosened his hold on her and stepped away. He thrust out both hands, palms up. "These hands have done evil. They are covered in blood. They have killed men and women and have taken scalps. They have done things I will not talk to you about. Can Jesus Christ forgive me for those things?"

Della closed the gap between them. Curling her hands about his, she peered into his face. "Yes, there is no sin that anyone has ever committed that is too evil for Christ to forgive. He can forgive you for everything you have ever done."

He looked doubtful. "I will think on this."

"Don't think too much. Just accept the truth. And I will pray for you, every day, that you will come to Jesus."

With his palms curved about her upper arms, Wild Wind drew her into his embrace. "Lona, you have brought the sunshine to my heart once again. The cold wind no longer blows through me." He tucked her head beneath his chin. "When the snow covers the ground, I will remember holding you against my heart, warming me."

They stood in silence. With her arms wrapped about him, Della savored the feel of his strength surrounding her and the sound of his heart thudding in his chest. She gathered the fabric of his shirt in both fists and pressed the material against his muscled back.

"Will you come to say goodbye in the morning?" Wild Wind's voice rumbled beneath her ear.

She nodded against his shirt front. "I will be there."

"Now, I must go. I will see you before the dawn." His arms squeezed her before he turned her loose. His fingers trailed along her braid. Pivoting, he strode across the veranda and pounded down the steps.

Della darted to the railing and watched his long strides take him away from her. From the back, he resembled any other cowboy on the ranch, yet an indefinable quality set him apart from the others. With her fingers clutching the rail, she watched until he stepped into the horse barn and vanished into its shadows.

∼

Della shivered in her sheepskin jacket, her breath puffing out in a white vapor. She turned the collar up about her ears. The cold seeped through her split riding skirt. She wriggled her toes in her leather riding boots to warm them. The night's frigid air hinted at the approaching autumn.

Beside her, the grulla mustang shook his head and blew. The bit rings jingled with a soft, musical note.

A thin rim of light along the eastern edge of the prairie heralded the coming dawn. Toward the mountains, a sliver of moon hung low above the horizon.

The twenty-five heifers and the bull Wild Wind had purchased milled about in the holding corral, bawling. Added to the herd were the steers purchased by the army to feed the Cheyenne throughout the winter. The four cowboys who'd volunteered to accompany Wild Wind and her uncle on the cattle drive checked their rigs and prepared to mount. Toby perched on the chuck wagon's high seat waiting for the signal to begin, the reins slack in his hands. All the men rode with Winchesters tucked into their scabbards and six shooters at their sides.

Wild Wind materialized through the gloom, leading his black and white gelding on a loose rein.

Della drank in the sight of him. He hadn't reverted to his Cheyenne dress. He wore a sheepskin jacket over his wool shirt, which had been tucked into his jeans. The Colt, tied down with a leather thong, hung low at his side and molded itself to his thigh. His cowboy hat, tipped down over his brow, obscured his features.

When he halted before her, he thumbed back his hat. His gaze roved over her face, as if committing her image to memory. Both of his big hands reached up to frame her head, his long fingers spearing into her hair. "I told you I would not kiss you again until we are courting. I will keep that promise, though I wish to take a kiss to warm my thoughts during the winter months."

Della didn't trust her voice. She stared up at him in mute misery. Swallowing hard, she managed to croak, "Come back to me, Wild Wind. Stay safe."

His eyes smiled down at her, crinkling at the corners. His tender expression seemed at odds with the harsh planes of his face. "If there is breath in my body, I will return to you. Look for me when the snow melts and the grass is greening on the earth."

In a swift motion, he wrapped her in a tight embrace, his cheek resting on the top of her head. "Lona, my dearest heart, do not forget me. My days will be empty until we are together again."

"I will never forget you, Wild Wind." Her arms tightened about his neck.

A shrill whistle split the dawn. "Move 'em out!" came the call. The cowboys mounted up. One of them flipped the loop over the gatepost, and the barred entrance swung wide. After a moment's hesitation, the complaining Shorthorns lumbered out of the corral, heading for the open range. The cowponies leaped after the herd, followed by the chuck wagon and mules at a more sedate pace.

On the other side of the yard, Coral and Uncle Clint said their goodbyes. While Della watched, her uncle swung aboard his black gelding and cantered after the herd.

Wild Wind set Della away from him. "I must leave."

"Wait! I have something for you." She spun toward her mustang. Rummaging in her saddle bags, she drew out a cheesecloth-wrapped parcel. She pivoted toward Wild Wind and offered the package to him. "I wanted to send this with you. I know how you love this treat."

He peeled back the cloth to display two generous slices of apple pie. Holding the confection beneath his nose, he closed his eyes and inhaled the scent of sweetened apples and pastry. Lifting his lids, he stared down at Della. "Lona, my own, you make it hard for a man to leave."

"I wanted to give you something to take with you. And I made sure Toby packed sacks of dried provisions to help your people get through the winter."

With his free hand Wild Wind sifted his fingers through the wayward curls which had loosened from her braid. "You will make me a wise and generous wife."

Conflicting emotions tugged at Della. To remind him that unless he became a believer, she couldn't marry him seemed somehow unfeeling in this moment of emotional parting, so she held her tongue.

He turned away and tucked the pie into his saddle bags. After securing the flap, he faced her again. They stared at each other, unspeaking.

Della broke the silence. "Do you have the Bible Uncle Clint gave you?"

Wild Wind nodded. "It is in my saddle bags. I will study it during the dark nights of Mother Earth's sleep." He paused, touching her face with his eyes.

Della gave a little cry. She grasped the open edges of his jacket and tugged him close. The toes of their boots bumped. "You said you wouldn't kiss me again, but I never promised not to kiss you." Going up on her tiptoes, she placed a sweet kiss on the corner of his mouth. "Goodbye, Wild Wind."

For a long moment, their gazes devoured each other. Wild Wind cupped her cheek in a tender caress, then stepped back. With a lithe motion, he swung onto his mount and heeled the horse. The gelding flicked its tail and leaped into a gallop.

Standing at the edge of the prairie beside the empty cattle corral, Della watched him reach the bluff's rim and vanish over the other side. The sound of his mustang's hoof beats faded into silence. She pressed both fists against her lips to still their trembling. Her heart was an aching void.

Colorado State
Winter, 1876–1877

CHAPTER 23

Della stood by the veranda railing, staring out over the yard. Snowflakes swirled from a pewter sky and hissed when they hit the ground. She tugged the collar of her jacket up around her ears, but she didn't return to the warmth of the house.

Uncle Clint and the cowboys had been gone for nearly two months. The weeks had slipped past since the day they rode away from the Slash L, driving before them the cattle bound for Wild Wind's band. Della tried not to worry, but with winter coming on, her uncle and his men should be returning any day.

Behind her, the door opened and closed, and Coral appeared at her side. Her aunt leaned against the railing and stared out into the dusky afternoon.

Della cut a glance at her aunt. She knew Coral put on a brave face, but her aunt worried about her husband and his men. Della laid a gloved hand over the other woman's. "I'm worried, too, but I'm sure Uncle Clint will be home any day now."

Coral tried to smile, though her mouth wobbled. "Of course. There's no telling what they found when they reached the reservation. And Montana is a long distance to travel."

"They'll make much better time coming home than they did going up. They won't have any cattle to slow them down."

"You're right. They probably stayed longer than they intended. I'm sure Clint did everything he could to help Wild Wind's band."

Neither woman mentioned the myriad dangers that lurked between the Slash L and the reservation. Anything could have happened on the journey.

"I have to remember that Clint is in the Lord's hands." Coral gripped the railing. "I thought I'd learned that lesson when he was in the cavalry."

"Sometimes the Lord has to remind us of lessons we've already learned. At least, it's true for me." Della touched her aunt's shoulder. "Let's go inside and have a cup of tea. Sadie will brew some for us."

During the middle of the next afternoon, the sound of horses clattering into the yard drew the women to the door. Several riders, followed by the mule team and the chuck wagon, swept beneath the gate and into the ranch compound.

"Clint!" Coral shrieked. She jerked open the door and flew down the steps, flinging herself into the melee of horses and riders at the bottom of the stairs. Her husband leaped from his mount and caught up his petite wife. He lifted her off the ground and swung her about in a circle.

Della paused on the top step, watching. She tried not to let her thoughts dwell on the love she and Shane had shared. Their love had been a bright and shining flame. She'd thought they would have long years together, but it wasn't meant to be. Their years had been cut short.

Della's thoughts jumped to Wild Wind. Would they have a life together? Would it even be possible?

After supper that evening and after the children had been put to bed, the adults gathered in the parlor. Flames danced behind the stove's isinglass door, casting flickering amber light onto the carpet. Coral sat close to her husband on the medallion-backed sofa, her fingers linked through his.

Della stood with her back to the stove, soaking in its warmth. She'd waited all through dinner to ask the questions burning on her tongue, and now, she couldn't restrain herself. "Uncle Clint, what did you find when you reached the reservation? Was it as bad as Wild Wind said?"

Her uncle squeezed Coral's hand and patted her knee before he replied. A heavy sigh lifted his shoulders. "The conditions are deplorable. There's hunger, and lack of sanitation, and illness. The men languish. It's obvious that corruption in the Bureau of Indian Affairs has affected the welfare of the tribe."

Della's heart sank. "It's no wonder that Wild Wind came to us. He must have been desperate."

Uncle Clint nodded. "I shook things up a bit. The agent in charge of the reservation has been replaced. I hope the new agent will be honest. He has an incentive not to cheat the tribe, for I made it clear that Yellow Wolf's band enjoys my patronage. I established Wild Wind as a legitimate rancher and made it plain to the authorities that the cattle are his. The brand he chose has been registered, and they all know that I'll personally check up on them. I promised to return next summer to inspect the conditions there."

"Thank you, Uncle Clint." Della crossed the room and knelt at her uncle's knee. She squeezed his hand. "I knew you'd help."

"I couldn't let things stand the way I found them. Wild Wind knows that the tribe must adapt, and he has enough foresight to realize that new ways of living are necessary. The tribesmen seemed a bit reluctant at first to consider ranching, but Wild Wind rallied them around to his way of thinking."

Della smiled. She knew firsthand how persuasive Wild Wind could be. "Did you meet his father, the chief? Yellow Wolf?"

Uncle Clint nodded. "I did. He gave a formal ceremony welcoming me to the tribe. He must have been a formidable chieftain in his day."

"He was. And he was a good father to Shane. He taught Shane everything he knew."

Her uncle's mouth firmed. "He must have loved Shane very much. When Wild Wind told him of Shane's death, he took the news very hard."

Della dropped her gaze to the floor, then looked up at her uncle.

"Yellow Wolf considered Shane to be his own flesh and blood. I'm sorry that at his age he has this new burden to bear."

"He may be old, but he's as tough as boot leather. Don't underestimate that old warrior."

In spite of herself, Della smiled. "I think we can all be glad that Yellow Wolf has put down his rifle and stayed on the reservation. He could still fight with the young men."

Uncle Clint chuckled. "Agreed. I wouldn't want to face that wily old fox on the battlefield."

The days slid past into weeks. Temperatures dropped, and at night, the wind howled about the eves. Snow piled up around the corners of the buildings.

As Christmas approached, Della moped about the house. One afternoon when she and Aunt Coral struggled to decorate the parlor mantel with red ribbon and glass balls, she plopped down into a rocking chair and leaned her head against the back.

At the mantel's far end, clutching a curl of red ribbon, Aunt Coral paused and cast her niece a quizzical look. "Are you ailing?"

Della sighed. "I'm sorry, but I seem to be overtaken by a fit of melancholia. Facing this first Christmas without Shane is more difficult than I expected. And I'm missing Fanny. She loved Christmas." Memories of her little girl's excitement during the only two Christmases she'd experienced clenched Della's heart. She could almost hear Fanny's delighted cries on the last Christmas morning she'd been alive. She pressed her fingers against her eyes and breathed deeply to stop tears that threatened. When she opened her eyes, she encountered her aunt's sympathetic gaze. "I'm sorry to be such a dismal watering pot when I should be full of joy this holiday season."

Coral shook her head. "No one expects you to be joyful all the time. You've experienced the loss of two people whom you loved very much. That's a devastating blow."

Della changed the subject to prevent further maudlin emotional displays. She waggled her fingers at the mantel. "And how are we supposed to show Christmas cheer without a tree? Or evergreens to decorate the mantel? There are no evergreen trees on the plains. Jake will never know what it's like to decorate a Christmas tree."

"We'll just have to do the best with what we have."

Della remained silent for a moment. "I know you're right. But being the only parent at Christmas is rather daunting."

The front door banged open and closed on a gust of cold air. Jake's voice cut through the late afternoon.

"Mama! Mama!"

"In here, Jake." Della hurried to the parlor door. Her son stood in the foyer, his boots covered in muck from the horse barn. "Jake, you didn't stomp off your boots. You're going to get horse all over Aunt Coral's nice carpet."

Jake looked down at his feet and shrugged. "Mama, I wanted to show you this." He held up a small wooden object for her inspection.

Della knelt beside her son and took the object from his mittened hand. A small carved horse, roughly hewn but unmistakably a horse, rested in her palm. "A horse! Did you make this all by yourself?"

Jake nodded. Pride glowed on his face. "Scipio taught me. Scipio can carve any animal he wants, and he's been teaching me."

Della examined the horse from every angle. "It was very kind of Scipio to show you how to carve this horse."

A grin curved Jake's mouth. "I made it for Wild Wind. This is his war horse. I want to give it to him for Christmas. Do you think Uncle Wild Wind will visit us at Christmas?"

Della shook her head. "Uncle Wild Wind won't come until after the snow melts. He's in Montana with his people, and that's too far to come just for a visit. Besides, the Cheyenne don't celebrate Christmas."

Jakes eyes rounded. "They don't have Christmas?"

"No, Jake. They don't know about baby Jesus or why we celebrate Christmas."

"We'll tell Uncle Wild Wind, so he can celebrate Christmas with us."

Della ruffled her son's curls. "That's an excellent idea. You can tell him when he comes back to us."

When Jake had scampered outside, Della returned to the parlor and stood by a window, staring across the snowy yard. This first Christmas without Shane would be difficult. At this time last year, they'd shared secrets and gifts, together making sure Jake had a good Christmas. She'd never guessed, then, that Shane had less than two months to live.

Tears burned at the back of her eyes. She dashed them away with an impatient hand. It had been months since she'd wept over Shane's death, and she'd thought she'd gotten past shedding tears for his loss. Somehow, the approach of Christmas had made her emotionally vulnerable. Memories of their last Christmas together stole into her thoughts, and a sob caught at the back of her throat. Tangled into the mix of emotions were her feelings for Wild Wind.

She conjured up his image. A smile tugged at her mouth as memories of the months Wild Wind had spent at the Slash L chased away the images of Shane. Wild Wind standing proud and erect, his long hair with its eagle feathers blowing in the wind. Wild Wind smiling down at her. Wild Wind's eyes glowing with battle light after he'd defeated Virgil Bledsoe in a fistfight. Wild Wind dressed as a cowboy, tall in his heeled riding boots and black cowboy hat, Shane's six-shooter riding low on his thigh. And Wild Wind standing in the branding corral, his face covered with sweat and dust, staring at her from the other side of the corral gate. Much of the emotional healing she experienced could be directly linked to Wild Wind.

What of their future? Did they have a future? Would he become a believer? If he did, could she take that step to join her life to his? She knew what censure she'd face from society if she married a tribesman. After a moment's consideration, she decided what society thought didn't matter to her. Here on the Slash L, people had accepted Wild Wind, and no one would care if she married him. Besides, she'd thumbed her nose at society for most of her life, so she wouldn't let what the society tabbies might think influence her decision now. She would live her life on her own terms.

Christmas blew in with frigid temperatures and a whirl of snow.

Della wanted this first Christmas without Shane to be a good one for Jake. She did her best with a few gifts and an orange.

On Christmas morning, the family gathered in the parlor after breakfast. A small pile of festively-wrapped packages rested on the carpet before the wood stove.

Flossie squealed and dove for the gifts, her curls bobbing and her pinafore swirling about her knees. "Presents! For me!"

"Flossie! Those aren't all for you. Only the ones with your name are for you," her father admonished her.

Flossie's mouth turned down. "Why should the boys get presents? They've been naughty."

"Flossie, come here," Uncle Clint said in his sternest voice, the one he reserved for recalcitrant troopers who'd been under his leadership in the cavalry.

With downcast eyes and dragging steps, Flossie approached her father. Rising from his chair, he took her by the hand. "Ladies, please excuse us. It's time for a father/daughter talk. If the boys can wait, I'd prefer for them to open their gifts after we come back."

When Uncle Clint and Flossie had left the room, Della and Coral exchanged a look. Della didn't envy Flossie. She'd experienced her uncle's displeasure and reprimands many times during her own growing-up years, but invariably, he had been right. Flossie would learn a lesson and be the better for it, uncomfortable though the experience would be.

Minutes later, when Flossie and Uncle Clint returned hand in hand, the little girl's red-rimmed eyes testified to her father's measures, but she smiled and bounced into the room. Dropping her father's hand, she skipped over to the stove and rummaged among the packages until she found one tied with a red ribbon.

"Jake, this one's for you." Flossie held the parcel out to her cousin.

Jake glanced at his mother before he took the gift. Della nodded her permission. He snatched the package from Flossie's hand and tore at the wrapping. The paper fell away to reveal a small pocketknife.

Jake ran to his mother's side and leaned against her shoulder. "Mama, is this for me? A real knife?"

"Yes, Jake. It's for you. You're big enough now to learn how to handle a knife."

Jake's face glowed as he opened the hasp. "When Wild Wind comes back, I'll show it to him. He can teach me how to use it."

Della hid the pang his words caused. It had actually been Shane's idea to give Jake a knife this Christmas, but Jake didn't know that. Wild Wind's name had been the one on her son's lips. She smiled and stroked his hair. "That's a good idea. Uncle Wild Wind will be happy to teach you how to use this knife."

Jake's earnest face lifted to hers. "I wish Uncle Wild Wind could be here today. I miss him."

"I miss him, too, son. But spring will be here soon. Then he'll come back to us."

After a moment's silence, Jake said in a small voice, "Papa wouldn't mind that Uncle Wild Wind will teach me how to use the knife. Would he?"

Della gripped her son's shoulder and swallowed the lump in her throat. "No, Jake. Papa wouldn't mind. He'd be happy that Uncle Wild Wind can teach you."

Winter dragged on. The first anniversary of Shane's death arrived near the end of February. That afternoon, Della saddled Shane's grulla gelding and rode to the cemetery. She dismounted and let the reins trail to ground-hitch the horse. Wading through the drifts, she worked open the gate and floundered through the snow to Shane's grave. Dropping to her knees, she stared at her husband's resting place, her thoughts bringing his face into focus.

Della leaned forward and brushed snow from the wooden marker at the grave's head. The words burned into the wood read, *Shane Hunter, Beloved Husband and Father. Gone Home. Born January 18, 1838. Died February 20, 1876.*

The words blurred while tears filled Della's eyes. So few years they'd had together, so little time. The future stretched before her, a future she must live alone. Yet now, she knew she could manage. This past year had taught her that with the help of Almighty Providence, she could live without a husband. Her life might not be the life she'd chosen when she and Shane had wed, but it was the life God had ordained for her.

And what of Wild Wind? Honesty compelled her to admit that he'd become very dear to her. Did she love him with the kind of love a wife should bring to a husband? And what if he never became a believer? She must be strong enough to deny him the life he sought with her. Refusing to marry him a second time would bring as much pain to her as it would to him, but her resolve remained firm. She could marry only another believer.

Colorado
Spring, 1877

CHAPTER 24

Della leaned against the corral's top rail and watched as Grady O'Brien moved among the horses. The Morgans from this year's crop had been brought in from the range to the ranch headquarters. They bunched against the far railing, half-wild and wary of the human walking among them. Their shaggy winter coats still hung in patches, giving them a mottled look.

"What do you think of this year's crop?" Della called to Grady.

The spring wind gusted across the yard, lifting the tails of Della's neckerchief and tugging at her hat. She turned the collar of her sheepskin jacket up about her ears. Spring might have come to Colorado, and the snow might have melted, but the wind blustering down off the Rockies still carried with it the winter's bite.

Grady studied the horses milling in the corral before he sauntered toward her. He halted on the other side of the bars. Thumbing back the brim of his hat, he propped one booted foot on the bottom rail and draped his arms over the top. "As always, your uncle's broodmares drop superior foals, which the army can't get enough of for their cavalry horses."

"Black Jack's bloodlines breed true."

"They do. The cavalry mounted on your uncle's Morgans always out-perform other cavalry horses."

"At least this year, we didn't lose any horses to the weather."

Grady flashed her a grin. "Not a one. It should be a good year for the Slash L."

"The army will need every cavalry horse it can get."

Grady's grin faded as they both recalled that, with spring's advent, hostilities between the army and the tribes would recommence.

A comfortable silence fell between them while they observed the horses. With Wild Wind's return to the reservation, Grady had warmed toward her until they could laugh and tease as before. Della had even begun to occasionally solicit his advice. The cowboy, however, remained careful not to let his attentions appear to be romantic.

"You men will have your work cut out for you with this bunch. They seem especially wild."

A movement off to the left caught Della's attention. She turned her head to watch a lone rider appear beneath the compound gate, a dark-haired rider sitting tall and easy in the saddle atop a black-and-white piebald mustang. The rider turned his horse in their direction, and Della looked full in the man's face.

Her breath caught, and her heart clenched. *Wild Wind.* He'd returned, as he'd promised. She pushed away from the corral bars and started toward him, her heart soaring. She could scarcely contain her joy. Her steps increased their pace until she was almost running, her split riding skirt flaring about her boot tops.

At his gelding's shoulder, she halted and looked up at him. His shaggy hair hung beneath the brim of his cowboy hat and draped over his shoulders. His eyes, as blue as the Colorado sky that framed his face, stared down at her. For a long moment, neither of them spoke.

Della broke the silence first. "Wild Wind. You're back."

He nodded and swung down from the saddle to stand before her, his eyes blazing but his face somehow closed. "Lona. I could stay away no longer. I have much to tell you."

"Good things, I hope."

His gaze roamed over her face. "I have become a Jesus follower. My heart was opened to the words of the Bible. My mother's God, and your God, the one true God, has forgiven all the hatred of my heart. My hands are clean, as clean as the new snow. They have no blood on them."

Della gripped his sleeve. "That's wonderful news, Wild Wind. The best news that you could have told me."

"But we must talk. I have many more things to tell you."

A little fearful now, Della dropped her hand to her side and nodded. This reunion wasn't going as she'd expected. Somehow, Wild Wind seemed distant, as though the ties that had bound them together all during the years had somehow frayed. Uneasy at his odd attitude, she stepped away. "Perhaps we can talk after supper. I'm sure Aunt Coral will invite you to dinner."

Grady O'Brien strolled up and extended his hand to Wild Wind. "Welcome back, Wild Wind. We have a good crop of horses to work with this spring. It will keep us busy until the branding."

Wild Wind gripped Grady's hand and shook it. Della watched, marveling again at how easily Wild Wind adapted to white customs.

"It is good to be back. We will start on the horses tomorrow."

Just then, Jake and his cousins rounded the gate, coming from the schoolhouse at the end of the school day. At the sight of his uncle standing in the courtyard, Jake halted and dropped his books. "Uncle Wild Wind!" He pelted toward them.

Wild Wind turned as his nephew launched himself at him. The boy's arms closed about Wild Wind's waist.

"You're back! I missed you, Uncle Wild Wind."

With both hands gripping Jake's middle, the warrior hoisted his nephew into his arms. "I missed you, too. I could stay away no longer."

Della's throat closed. Whatever was wrong between her and Wild Wind, Shane's brother still loved his nephew. He couldn't hide the fact.

Jake wrapped both skinny arms about his uncle's neck and squeezed. "I have a present for you. I made it myself. I wanted to give it to you for

Christmas, but Mama said you couldn't come visit us at Christmas. I'll give it to you now."

Jake wriggled down and ran to the house, launching himself up the steps and across the veranda. He jerked open the door and banged it closed behind him.

Flossie and Aaron gathered about Wild Wind, clamoring for his attention. Della tossed a smile at Wild Wind, who tried to answer the children's questions. She peeled Flossie away from the chieftain. "Flossie, you can ask your questions later. Give Wild Wind a chance to put his horse away."

The door banged again, and Jake charged across the yard, a small object clutched in one hand. He skidded to a stop before his uncle and thrust out the wooden horse. "This is for you. It's your war horse. Scipio taught me how to whittle."

Wild Wind went down on one knee and took the proffered toy. He examined it with exquisite attention, turning it over in his hand. "Thank you, my small warrior. You have done a fine job. I will keep it in my saddle bag so my horse will know he must live up to this gift you have given me."

Jake beamed. "I got a pocketknife for Christmas. Mama told me you'd teach me how to use it."

Wild Wind slanted a glance up at Della and returned his attention to his nephew. "Of course, I will teach you how to use a knife. It is time you learned the ways of a man."

Wild Wind rose to his full height, and Della shooed the children toward the house. "Go on, now. Silvie will give you a treat if you go to the kitchen. You can see Wild Wind at supper."

When the children had scampered away, she turned to Wild Wind. "You will come to supper tonight, won't you?"

He nodded.

"Come to the house in time for dinner."

He nodded again.

After a brief consultation with Wild Wind, Grady drifted back to the corral, leaving Della alone with the warrior.

The air between them crackled like lightning during a summer thunderstorm as they stared at each other. Della sensed emotion roiling beneath Wild Wind's unrevealing expression, but she couldn't fathom the cause. She'd expected a much warmer reunion, with him renewing his vow to make her his wife, but he hadn't mentioned marriage. At last, she spoke. "I'm glad you're back, Wild Wind. I missed you."

For a long moment, he didn't reply, though some emotion flared behind his eyes. "I could not stay away from you any longer. Lona, you are the heart of my heart, and without you, my heart was empty all during Mother Earth's sleep, but we must talk."

"All right. As I mentioned, perhaps after supper."

Wild Wind lifted a hand toward her face, and Della thought he would caress her cheek, but his hand dropped to his side without touching her. "I must put away my horse. I will see you later."

Without another word, he brushed past her, leading his piebald toward the barn. Della watched his back as he walked away, feeling rebuffed and not knowing why.

Supper that night was a festive affair. The children peppered Wild Wind with questions, which he answered with indulgent patience. After the meal, the men retired to the parlor to discuss cattle and horses, while the women cleaned up the kitchen. Della was sure Wild Wind's salvation would also be a topic of conversation.

When the work was done, they joined the men.

Della endured the evening, impatient for the opportunity for some private conversation with Wild Wind. A feminine instinct warned her that whatever he wanted to share with her wouldn't be good, so in spite of her eagerness to spend some time alone with him, she dreaded the encounter. Darkness had fallen when Uncle Clint rose.

"My wife and I will retire. Wild Wind, it's good to have you back. Now, I think you'd like some private time with my niece."

Wild Wind also rose when Clint came to his feet, and he bade the couple a good night. When they were alone, Della took a step toward him. "Where would you like to talk? In here or outside?"

"I would go outside."

Together, they left the parlor. When they reached the front door, Wild Wind reached around her to open the portal. He motioned for her to precede him, all polished manners. If she hadn't known better, Della would have thought he'd grown up in polite society. She stepped onto the veranda and moved to the railing, waiting for him to shut the door and join her.

A moment later, he halted beside her. His gaze roamed her face.

Della felt as though he'd touched her. Her fingers clenched the railing. She stared at him, his face a pale blur in the dim lamplight that spilled through the parlor windows.

When he spoke, his rasping tones betrayed the emotion he concealed. "Lona, my heart. While I was on the reservation, I had many thoughts." He paused and glanced out over the dark yard. A heartbeat of silence hung on the night air, broken when a distant coyote yapped at the moon. Wild Wind swung his attention back to her. "My thoughts were hard. They brought me no sunshine. The path I must take is difficult, but I must walk that path."

Della caught her breath. What was he trying to tell her? "Wild Wind, what are you saying?"

He lifted a hand, and this time, he touched her. His fingers strayed over her face, tracing an eyebrow, the line of her cheek, her lips. She shivered at his touch and curled her hand about his wrist. He lowered his head so that his forehead touched hers and speared the fingers of both hands into her hair. "Lona, what you told me last summer is true. I have never given you a choice about marrying me. From the time I brought you to our village, I told you that we would marry. You would be mine. I did not consider what you might want. I fought Little Wolf for you, and if I had won, we would have married long ago. I would have taken you from him without asking what you wanted. I would have married you without giving you a choice."

Della sucked in a gasp of air. "I didn't want Shane to fight you, his brother. I told him I would go with you and marry you. He wouldn't listen."

"You could not have stopped that fight."

"But what does that have to do with us now?"

"Now, I am not the same man I was before I became a Christ follower." Wild Wind paused, as though the words he was about to say were too difficult to speak. His chest rose as he breathed deeply. "Last summer, I told you that you were my woman. I did not ask if you wanted to be my woman. You were right to be angry. I took away your right to choose another man when I claimed you as my own. Now, I give you a choice. I release you from my claim. You may choose any man you wish to marry. I will tell Grady that he may court you."

Della reared back. His hands fell from her face. "Wild Wind, I don't wish for Grady to court me. I want only you to court me. I no longer mourn Little Wolf. My heart belongs to you, only you."

He shook his head. "You must have time to choose. I will give you time. You are free from my claim on you."

"But I don't need time! I don't want to be free. I know what I want, and I choose you." Della stepped close to him and laid both hands on his chest.

His lips firmed. "I have decided. I will not court you. When you have had time to consider, we will talk again."

"Don't you see? By telling me you won't court me, you're taking away my right to choose *you*."

Wild Wind covered her hands with his. "My mind is made up. We will not court."

Della's lips puffed as she blew out a frustrated breath. "You're a most stubborn man!"

"The path I walk is one that I must walk alone. There is no room for you on that path."

Della spun away and crossed her arms. She stared into the darkness. What could she say to change his mind? As much as she appreciated his offer, she felt the steps he planned to take were unnecessary. Once again, his upbringing made it next to impossible for her to convince him to change his mind once he'd come to a decision. Della hoped that he'd learn to be more flexible once they married. And they would marry, she resolved. She slanted a glance up at him over her shoulder. "Very well. I accept your decision, but it's wasted time. My mind is made up. You're the only man I wish to marry."

Wild Wind stepped close and curved his hands about her shoulders, turning her toward him. He touched her face again. Tender fingers journeyed across her brow, curved along the line of her cheek, and ran down her throat to where her red bandana encircled her neck.

Della closed her eyes, reveling in his caress. Her eyes flew open when one of his thumbs stroked across her lower lip. She looked into his face, and their gazes collided. His love for her tightened his features, and for a moment, she thought he might change his mind. Just as a spurt of hope filled her, he dropped his hand and stepped away.

"I will speak to Grady in the morning. You are free." He pivoted and thudded down the steps.

Della followed him to the top stair. When he reached the yard, she spoke to his back. "We will marry, you know. I, too, have made up my mind."

Her words checked him for a heartbeat before he resumed his stride. In moments, darkness swallowed him and hid him from her sight.

For a long while, Della remained alone on the veranda, leaning against a pillar. This wasn't how Wild Wind's return should have played out. Her heart's dearest prayer for his salvation had been answered, but as a result, she'd lost the one man she could love after Shane. She hoped the separation would be temporary. One way or another, she determined to win him back.

~

The week after Wild Wind's return, Grady O'Brien hailed Della after she'd watched him and Wild Wind work with the Morgans. Wild Wind had left the corral without speaking to her. Grady called her name as she trudged toward the house.

Della halted and turned, waiting for the cowboy to catch up.

He jogged toward her. "Miss Della," he said as he stopped beside her. He swiped his hat from his head and held it against his chest. "I'd be most pleased if you'd take a ride with me after supper."

Della sighed. "Wild Wind talked to you, didn't he?"

Grady nodded. "Yes. He told me you weren't his woman any longer and that I was free to step out with you."

Della's gaze roved over Grady's engaging countenance. She noticed the dimples in his cheeks, his smiling eyes, and his handsome features. The wind feathered through his curly mink-colored hair. For a moment, she was tempted to take Grady up on his offer. It would serve Wild Wind right if she let other men court her. The temptation to make him jealous almost overcame her better sense. "Thank you, Grady, but I must decline your kind offer. If I were free to accept your invitation, I'd certainly do so, but my heart is already pledged to Wild Wind."

Grady ducked his head, then glanced up at her from beneath lowered brows. "I thought you might say that. You can't blame a fella for tryin'."

"No, one certainly can't. I'm flattered by your offer."

He raked his fingers through his hair and settled his cowboy hat on his head. "Well, Miss Della, you may say your heart belongs to Mr. Wild Wind, but I'm a determined fella. You're not married yet. I'll keep tryin' to change your mind."

She smiled at his audacity. "You can try, but Wild Wind is the man I'll marry."

He grinned back at her, deepening the dimples in his cheeks. "Like I said, you're not married yet."

Della shook her head. "You'd do better to spend your time stepping out with Betty."

"Betty's a nice girl, but I prefer a woman."

"Grady, don't waste your time on me when I know I can never give you what you're looking for. Please, take Betty riding. Sit with her in church. Spend your time with her."

He shook his head. "I have my mind set on you, Miss Della, now that you don't belong to Mr. Wild Wind."

"My heart belongs to him."

"That can change. I'm persistent, and I have a way with the ladies."

Della couldn't help herself. Laughter bubbled up at his brass. She clamped a hand over her mouth to stifle the sound.

Grady chuckled. "I'll leave you alone for now, but you'll see. We'll be steppin' out before the summer's over."

"Go on with you, now. I know you have work to do."

Grady flashed her a cocky smile and tipped his hat to her. "So long, Miss Della. I'll be seein' you soon."

Della watched him swagger toward the bunkhouse, indecision nagging her thoughts. It might be a relief to spend some time with a man less complicated than Wild Wind. She almost changed her mind about his invitation and called him back, but prudence restrained her. It wouldn't be fair to Grady to allow him to court her when she had no intention of marrying him, so she swallowed her words.

A feeling of being watched stole over her. She turned her head in the direction of the horse barn. Wild Wind stood motionless just inside the open doors. Their gazes collided. Emotion arced between them, heating the air and stealing the breath from her lungs. He'd seen her whole encounter with Grady, and Della wondered what he thought. Did he suspect that Grady had tried to initiate a courtship? Did he regret his decision to free her from his claim?

Della shivered, thankful that she'd declined Grady's offer to ride. No matter how tempting it might be to spend time with the irrepressible cowboy, even appearing amenable to his overtures would damage her relationship with Wild Wind. She took one step toward the barn, toward him.

Wild Wind wheeled and stalked deeper into the shadows, leaving her alone in the yard. At that moment, it seemed to her that she was the only living creature in a world filled with wind and sunshine, loneliness and pain.

CHAPTER 25

That afternoon, Uncle Clint called Della into Emory Dyer's office. When her uncle had shut the door behind her, she glanced in puzzlement at first him, then across the room at the lieutenant, who stood behind his desk. Her scrutiny stopped when she noticed Aunt Coral sitting in one of the two wooden chairs before the desk.

Uncle Clint motioned toward the second chair. "Della, why don't you have a seat? I think we'll be more comfortable having this discussion when you've joined my wife."

Della crossed the room and sat. "It must be something very important if you've arranged for all of us to be here." She tipped back her head to look into her uncle's face.

"I've called this meeting to inform you that I've had a letter from my solicitor in Boston. As you know, he's been trying to learn who's behind the offer to purchase the Slash L." Uncle Clint paused and raked his audience with an intent stare. "He's following the lead we discovered of the men who had been killed by the Sioux last summer. He thinks he has the name of an oil consortium who could possibly be behind the offer."

Della exchanged a glance with her aunt.

"My solicitor hasn't mentioned a name," Uncle Clint continued. "He wants to make a positive identification before he gives me that information. However, the most interesting item is the fact that someone is trying to get my lease for grazing rights revoked. It's no stretch to link the offer to purchase the ranch with the attempt to revoke my grazing rights to land I've leased from the government. Whoever is behind this has friends in Congress."

Emory Dyer gave a low whistle. "Without the right to graze on government land, you won't have enough property to maintain all your cattle. You'll have to downsize your herd."

Uncle Clint nodded. "I doubt I could maintain enough cattle to meet my contract with the army." He squared his shoulders, and his face assumed a militant expression. "Well, the members of the oil consortium aren't the only ones with friends in high places. I've contacted a couple of senators whom I know to support my effort to block the consortium's attempt to revoke my grazing rights."

"If it really is an oil consortium, the group must be convinced that there's oil on our land. They're going to such lengths to get it," Coral said.

Her husband agreed. "They appear to want the land rather badly. I think we should be prepared for them to go to more drastic measures. I've already put guards on the range due to the Indian trouble. They'll have to keep watch for anything else that looks suspicious, as well."

After the evening meal, which Wild Wind now shared with the family, he and Uncle Clint departed for her uncle's office opposite the parlor. Uncle Clint had been conducting a daily Bible study with Wild Wind each night after supper. The fact that Wild Wind thirsted for scriptural knowledge thrilled Della, but now, she never had an opportunity for private conversation with him.

She watched the office door shut behind the men and gritted her teeth. Wild Wind wasn't making it easy for her. How long would he insist on shutting her out? Even Jake spent more time with him than she did.

The next afternoon when Jake burst into the house after school, Della met him at the kitchen door. Her son brushed past her and slung his schoolbooks, bound together by a leather strap, onto the table. Almost vibrating with excitement, he whipped about and headed out of the kitchen.

Della grabbed him by his shirt collar. "What's your hurry? Don't you want some cookies and milk before you go outside?"

Jake squirmed and shook his head. "I'm not hungry."

"Not hungry?" Della felt her son's brow for a fever. "Are you sickening?"

He swatted her hand away. "I'm not sick. Uncle Wild Wind is waiting for me. He's going to show me how to clean a horse's hoof."

"Oh." Della loosened her hold on Jake's shirt. "All right, then. Just don't get in Uncle Wild Wind's way."

"I won't." Jake tossed the words over his shoulder as he darted away. His footsteps pattered down the hall to the front door.

Della's shoulders drooped. Her son preferred Wild Wind's company to hers. Though she couldn't blame him, she still felt abandoned.

Flossie's and Aaron's squabbling as they approached the kitchen grated on Della's nerves. She left the kitchen and wandered down the hall as the children scooted past her. Except for the children's voices sounding from the kitchen and Silvie's soothing tones in response, the house was silent. She paused at the parlor door and peered in. Perhaps playing a challenging piano piece would soothe her nerves.

She eyed the piano. Sitting at the keyboard held no appeal. The only thing she wanted was to be with Wild Wind. His presence pulled at her. After a moment's indecision, Della turned her back on the piano. Lifting her chin, she hurried to the door and let herself outside. She crossed the yard to the open-air blacksmith shop where her son and Wild Wind busied themselves with the horse.

Reaching the shade cast by the shop's roof, Della halted at one side, out of the men's way. Wild Wind's mustang was cross tied between two posts at the building's back wall. Her son and the man she loved faced her, both bent over the gelding's left front leg. Jake had lifted the horse's leg and clutched its hoof between his knees, a hoof pick in one hand.

Wild Wind shot her a brief glance when she entered the shed but otherwise gave no sign that he noticed her. With his hand wrapped around Jake's small one, he demonstrated how to scrape dirt from the hoof's crevices. "Dirt, it will pack around the frog. And a horse can pick up a stone. If you don't get it out, the horse will go lame. Always pay attention to your horse's feet." With deft flicks of the hoof pick, Wild Wind cleaned the hoof of any foreign matter. Then he showed Jake how to lower the horse's leg by grasping the piebald's fetlock. "When the hoof is clean, lower your horse's leg to the ground. Do not let him jerk away."

Man and boy straightened and moved to the mustang's hind leg.

"I can do this one by myself, Uncle Wild Wind." Jake tipped an eager face up to his uncle.

"I will watch, then."

Jake's features screwed up in concentration as he bent to the task. Della observed while Wild Wind murmured encouragement and an occasional instruction. Jake seemed completely absorbed and eager to please his uncle. When they started on the off hind leg, Della turned her back to them and leaned against one of the shed's front corner posts. She stared out over the yard, only half listening to the conversation behind her.

A spring breeze played about the compound, swirling around Della's riding skirt and ruffling the sleeves of her blouse. She shivered, wishing she'd taken time to don her jacket.

Though Wild Wind had scarcely acknowledged her presence, being near him both soothed and thrilled her. She vowed she wouldn't let him shut her out when the task was done. Even if she had to plant herself in front of him, she would initiate a conversation.

Minutes later, Jake finished the final hoof. Della pivoted to see Wild Wind and her son stretching the kinks out of their backs and grinning at each other. They ambled around the horse's rump toward her. Wild Wind gave Jake's shoulder a rough shake, as one man to another.

"You are a fast learner. With more practice, you can clean the hooves of the Morgans we are training."

Jake glowed. "Can I really, Uncle Wild Wind?"

Della closed her mouth on the protest she'd been about to utter. She saw how Wild Wind's praise made Jake's chest swell, and she didn't want her fears to depress her son's desire to please his uncle. She could discuss her reservations with Wild Wind later.

"When you have cleaned the hooves of many more horses, you can try out a Morgan." Wild Wind strode to his mustang's head and loosed the lead rope. Turning the horse about, he handed the line to Jake. "You can put him in the small corral."

Jake's eyes rounded, and he bounced on his toes. "You would let me lead your horse?"

Wild Wind nodded. "I do not trust my mount to just anyone, but you are a good horseman."

Grinning at his uncle's tribute, Jake stepped forward and took the rope. With careful steps, he led the gelding toward the small paddock beyond the barn. Della watched him for a moment, her heart swelling. Her son was thriving beneath Wild Wind's tutelage.

Behind her, Wild Wind spoke. "You have a fine son. He wants to learn."

Della turned. She wanted to move closer, to put her hands on his chest or clasp him about the neck, but she stood rooted to the ground. "Jake is trying hard to please you."

"If he were the son of my own body, I could not love him more."

She swallowed the words she wanted to say, that Jake could be a real son if only they would marry, and commented instead, "He thrives on the attention you're giving him. He's learning things I can't teach him." She shrugged. "I'm just his mother. You're the one he wants to please."

"I will do my best for him."

Silence fell between them while they eyed each other, heating the air with unacknowledged yearnings until Della thought the very soil on which she stood must melt. She took a rough breath and blurted out her fears for Jake. "Do you really mean to let Jake clean hooves on the Morgans?"

"He must learn how to deal with a horse that doesn't stand still for him."

"But the Morgans aren't used to being handled. He might get kicked."

"Then he will learn to be more careful."

"I don't want him to get hurt!"

"Lona, you cannot protect him from getting hurt. Do not baby him. Let him learn to handle himself and discover what it takes to be a man."

"He won't be a man for a long time. I don't want him to take on something that's too hard for him."

"He will never become a man if you baby him. He must learn that life is not easy, and he should work hard to earn the respect of others."

"But..."

Wild Wind took one stride toward her but checked himself before he got close enough to touch her. His hard stare silenced her. The brackets on either side of his mouth tightened before he spoke. "Do you trust me?"

She gave a jerky nod and clasped her arms about her middle, gripping her elbows.

"If you trust me, you must let me deal with Jake as I think best. Women have soft hearts, but in this, Jake does not need a soft heart. He needs a man to teach him a man's ways. He must learn to be tough, or he will not survive here."

Della glanced away from Wild Wind, her vision lingering for a moment on the bunk house before looking into his face again. "All right. I must trust you in this. I just hope he doesn't get hurt."

"I will take care with him, but every boy gets hurt before he becomes a man. It is life."

She considered his words. "Of course. It's just hard for a mother to watch her children get hurt."

Wild Wind's eyes crinkled at the corners, and his expression softened. "You are a good mother."

Once again, the words he hadn't spoken hung in the air between them. Della thought of the many times he'd told her she would give him strong sons, and now, she wished he'd tell her again she would be a mother to his children. The seconds ticked past while they yearned toward each other, oblivious of the ranch activity about them.

Wild Wind broke the impasse when he shoved the hoof pick into the back pocket of his jeans and shifted his weight to his other leg. "I would ask a favor."

Della's heart leaped. "Of course. Whatever you need, you have only to ask."

"While I was at the reservation, I tore one of my shirts. Would you mend it for me? I know I have no right to ask this of you, but I have no one else to do it."

"Certainly. Where is your shirt?"

"It is in my room in the barn."

"I can get your shirt now, if you'll give it to me." She turned away and took a step toward the barn.

"Lona."

Wild Wind's voice checked her. She glanced at him over her shoulder.

"Put on your jacket. You are cold."

The fact that he'd noticed her discomfort and commented warmed her heart. Despite the barriers he'd erected between them, he still thought of her welfare. She nodded and hurried to the house.

After shrugging into her sheepskin jacket, Della met Wild Wind at the barn's open double doors. Together, they paced toward the stall at the back of the barn where he slept. At the stall door, she came to a stop and waited while he entered and rummaged in a dresser drawer. He plucked out a faded wool shirt and carried it into the barn's center aisle where Della waited.

She held out her hand, and he dropped the shirt onto her palm.

Their gazes snagged again. Frustrated at the barriers he'd erected between them, Della couldn't contain her impatience. Hasty words tripped off her tongue before she could halt them. "How long will you keep us apart?"

He stepped so close to her that his chest nearly brushed against her, but she refused to back away. He stared down into her face, his expression impassive, though Della knew him well enough to sense the emotion roiling beneath his calm mask. She gave him back a feisty glare.

"You have not had enough time to decide. You have not spent time with another man to know if you would rather marry someone else."

"Grady asked me to go riding with him. I turned him down."

Wild Wind's nostrils flared, and his lids hooded his eyes, but he gave no other sign that her words provoked him. "You should go with him."

"Why? I don't want to give him false hope."

"The women of my tribe have many suitors. They choose the one they want to marry. Let Grady be your suitor, and then you can choose."

Frustrated, Della clenched her hands. "I don't need another suitor. I have already chosen. I choose you."

"You need another suitor to make a wise choice. Take many suitors."

"I don't want many suitors! I had many beaux to choose from before I married your brother. I don't need more now."

Wild Wind stared at her through the barn's dimness. "I have not changed my mind. We will not court until you have spent time with other men."

Della narrowed her eyes at him. "Very well. I'll do what you demand, if that's what it takes to make you see reason." She stifled the impulse to shake him and decided that honey would serve her purpose better than vinegar. Going up on her tiptoes and gripping his upper arms, she kissed him on the mouth.

He stiffened and remained unresponsive. Della kissed him again and feathered little pecks on the corners of his lips. She went down on her heels and stepped away. "There. Just think about that while I'm spending time with Grady."

CHAPTER 26

Della stood outside the corral fence and watched the men work the Morgans. The morning sun warmed her back and cast her shadow into the paddock. When Wild Wind and Grady had finished giving a sorrel gelding a lesson in being saddled, she waited while they turned the horse loose and approached her from the other side of the bars.

Wild Wind nodded at her but didn't speak. His closed expression and tight mouth discouraged her from engaging him in conversation. Last night's discussion had defined the behavior he expected from each of them until they resolved their situation. After flicking a glance at him, she turned to Grady. She rested both hands on the corral's top bar and curled her fingers about the rail. As much as she loathed the idea of stepping out with another man, she determined to do whatever it took to break the impasse between herself and Wild Wind. She smiled up at the cowboy. "Good morning, Grady."

At her greeting, Grady grinned at her and thumbed his hat back on his head. A dark curl fell over his forehead, giving him a roguish look. "Good mornin' to you, Miss Della."

Della took a breath. "I wonder if I might speak privately with you?"

Surprise crossed his face, to be replaced by a grin. He leaned his elbows on the fence rail. "Sure thing, Miss Della. Do you mean now?"

Conscious of Wild Wind catching up another Morgan in the middle of the corral, Della decided to have her discussion with Grady later. No doubt Wild Wind could hear every word she and the cowboy spoke. "Not now. Later. Perhaps after supper?"

A speculative gleam shone in his eyes, and his gaze perused her face before he replied. "We can meet after supper. I'll come for you. Then we can talk."

Della nodded. "Thank you. I'll see you then." Pivoting on her heel, she crossed the yard to the house, conscious of Wild Wind watching her. Although she didn't turn to look, she felt his stare until she closed the door behind her.

At the end of the meal that evening, Della waited until Uncle Clint and Wild Wind had left the dining room for their nightly Bible study in her uncle's office. When they'd disappeared down the hall, she made an appeal to her aunt. "Aunt Coral, if you don't mind, I'd like to be excused now. I have to meet with someone."

Aunt Coral added the plate she held to the stack of dirty china in the middle of the table. "I see that things aren't going well between you and Wild Wind."

Della sighed. "He's decided that I should have a choice about whether or not I should marry him. After all those years of telling me we were going to marry, now he's got it into his head that I should choose. He wants me to step out with other men so I can make up my mind about whom I want to marry."

A smile curved Aunt Coral's lips. "Isn't that what you told him last summer?"

"Yes, but... "

"Well, indulge him. I'm sure one of your cowboy pals will be willing to help you out."

"That's what I'm going to discuss with Grady."

Coral made a shooing motion. "Go along now. Meet with Grady. Sadie and I can manage in the kitchen."

Della hurried outside. She crossed the veranda and leaned against one of the pillars that bracketed the steps. Wrapping her arms about the column, she leaned her head against the fluted post and waited.

She didn't wait long. Grady sauntered toward her from the direction of the bunkhouse. He paused with one booted foot on the bottom step.

"Well, Miss Della? Shall we have our discussion here, in the porch swing?"

Della straightened away from the pillar and cast a brief glance at the swing. Memories assailed her. She and Shane had sat on that swing during their courting days. Wild Wind had sat there and held her on his lap while she slept after a night spent with the colicking Morgan gelding. Still, she supposed it didn't matter if she and Grady shared the seat. "Yes, come on up. The swing will do nicely."

With a grin, Grady sprinted up the steps and came to a halt beside her. "What has changed your mind about us keepin' company, I wonder?" He smiled down at her. "I've been puzzlin' over it all day."

"It's probably not what you're hoping for." She wondered how she could do what she was about to do to a decent man like Grady.

"That's for me to decide." He gestured toward the swing. "Let's sit, shall we?"

They settled themselves on either end of the swing and sat staring at each other. Grady had changed into a clean red shirt and neckerchief and had donned fresh jeans. The damp ends of his hair showed that he'd washed up at the pump before joining her. He'd obviously made an effort to be more presentable.

Della glanced down at her clasped hands before she took a breath and swung her gaze to his face. "Grady, I must apologize to you before I even begin. I'm afraid I'm going to use you shamelessly."

He gave her a lopsided grin. "I'll be the judge of that. Why don't you tell me how you plan to use me?"

She plunged into the ultimatum Wild Wind had given her and finished by saying, "I thought if you knew the score right up front, and if you still want to keep company with me, I'd be happy to oblige."

Grady's features showed no reaction while he listened to her tale.

When she'd finished, he studied her face intently before he replied. "You're right. It isn't exactly what I'd hoped to hear, but from where I sit, it's a start."

Della tipped her head to one side. "How do you see it that way?"

Grady smiled, a sweet smile unlike his usual flirtatious grins. He leaned closer. "I get to spend all the time I want with the most beautiful woman this side of Denver. Not only are you beautiful, you're brave and strong and kind." He paused. "I've been hankerin' to tell you that for months, but when Wild Wind claimed you, I thought it best to keep my distance."

"It was definitely safer for you." His unexpected tribute moved her. "Thank you for your compliment. I feel undeserving of such praise."

He shook his head. "No, Miss Della, you deserve every word." He reached for her hand and wrapped his own about it. "I hope you don't mind me takin' a few liberties. I want to make the most of whatever time I have with you."

Della turned her hand beneath his and linked their fingers. "I don't mind. Being a widow gives me more freedom than if I were a debutante. Besides, it's the least I can do when I'm using you in such a shameless manner." She smiled. "And after all, this is Colorado, not Boston."

Grady tightened his fingers about hers. "You may consider what we're doin' as a means to get back together with Wild Wind, but I consider this a real courtship. For me, keepin' company with you isn't an act. For however long we have together, I'll do my best to win your heart. If, whenever this ends, you still love Wild Wind and want to marry him, I'll step away and let you go." He squeezed her hand again. "But, if by some good fortune I've won your love, then Wild Wind will be the loser."

His kindness wrung Della's heart. "Why are you being so nice about this? You should hate me for what I'm doing."

Grady glanced over the veranda railing at the shadows beginning to pool about the yard, then looked back at her face. "You still don't understand, do you? I'd do anythin' for the chance to win your heart." He spoke in the gentlest voice she'd ever heard him use.

His words failed to make her feel better. "I don't want to hurt you."

He smiled again and shook his head. "You won't. Remember, I know the score. Bein' willin' to wager on gainin' your affections, I know I might lose."

"Thank you, Grady. You're too kind."

"Kindness has nothin' to do with it. My whole future is ridin' on this gamble." He paused. "I have feelin's for you, Miss Della. I'd marry you tonight if you'd say the word."

Della struggled to control the panic his words caused. "Don't say that! Don't mention love or marriage. Let's just enjoy being together."

"If you say so. I won't mention either one. At least, not for a while. But I wanted you to know how it is with me."

She nodded and thought it time to change the subject. "Well, what shall we do now?" She slid her hand from his.

"For tonight, let's just sit here and talk. Tomorrow night, we'll take that ride I asked you for earlier."

After a moment when neither of them spoke, Della said, "Tell me about yourself. I know you're from Texas, but I don't know many details of your life."

Grady leaned forward and braced his elbows on his thighs, his dangling hands clasped loosely between his knees. He canted his head and peered at her over his shoulder. "My folks had a small spread in northern Texas. My pa ran some cattle and had a few horses. I was the oldest of eight brothers and sisters. My ma nearly worked herself to the bone, keeping us all fed and clothed. So, when I turned fifteen, I lit out. Been on my own ever since. Never went back. For years, I was like a tumbleweed, blowin' from one place to another, until your husband hired me. I've never had a hankerin' to leave."

"I'm glad you like it here."

"It's a good place to earn a livin'. I have everythin' I could ask for, except perhaps the affections of a certain lady." He cocked a dark eyebrow at her and tossed her a flirty grin, though his serious tone belied his levity.

"You have my respect and my friendship. I'm afraid that's all I can offer you."

He straightened and leaned against the swing's back, tucking himself into the corner. "That's a good start. It's more than some marriages ever have."

"Since we're being honest with each other, you should know that I won't settle for just respect and friendship when I marry again. I had love in my first marriage, and I won't marry for anything less the next time." Della leaned closer to him, her voice earnest.

"Wouldn't expect you to. When I marry, it will be for love, nothin' else." Grady brought his face closer to hers. "That's why I hope I can win your heart."

"And I have a son. Whomever I marry must love him, too, and be a good father."

"Jake is a fine boy. I'll love him as I do you."

Their gazes tangled, and Della whispered, "Maybe this isn't such a good idea. I'm a terrible wretch, agreeing to this when I know how you feel. It's not fair to you."

"Don't say that. You've given me a chance for a future with you, somethin' I've hankered for ever since your husband died."

Della studied his eyes. He looked back at her with steady regard. "Very well, as long as you don't mind."

They sat in companionable silence for a time, while twilight leeched the color from the land and darkness crept in among the shadows. Overhead, in the far-flung heavens, stars dotted the fading sky. The occasional call of a bird as it settled for the night sounded in the hush.

Grady kept the swing in motion with one booted foot on the floorboards. Finally, he spoke, his gaze intent on her face. "Della—may I call you Della?"

She nodded. "Certainly. You've earned the right."

"Della."

His tone warned her that his next words might be something she wouldn't care to hear. She tensed.

"Don't you think it's about time you told me the whole story of why

Wild Wind calls you Lona? I know you left out some of the important details when you gave me the bare bones of the story last spring."

Della relaxed and met his gaze. "I suppose you should know, considering that we're stepping out together." She made an effort to make her hands lay lax in her lap, when she wanted to wring them instead. "I told you that I was captured by Wild Wind's Dog Soldiers when they attacked the thieves who were stealing Uncle Clint's horses."

Grady nodded but didn't speak.

"Wild Wind had seen me once before, when Shane and I were out riding. Wild Wind seemed very interested in me at that time. He even asked Shane if I was his woman." Della paused, lost in the memory of that first encounter with Wild Wind. After a moment, she roused. "I didn't know it then, but Wild Wind had already decided that he wanted me, so when the Dog Soldiers killed the thieves and took the stolen horses, he claimed me as his woman. When we got to his village, he placed me in the care of his aunt and set about courting me. Wild Wind wanted to erase any trace of my white heritage, so he gave me a Cheyenne name. *Lona*. If Shane hadn't rescued me before the wedding, I would have been married to Wild Wind all these years and living with his tribe on the reservation now."

For several moments, Grady stared at her in thoughtful silence. "I can see why he feels he can lay claim to you."

"Yes. Long ago, we almost married."

"No matter. You and I, we have a fresh beginnin'."

The minutes flew by while they talked. Della was laughing at something Grady had said when Wild Wind stepped through the door onto the veranda, apparently having finished his Bible study with her uncle. He halted at the sound of her laughter and turned his head in their direction, his face expressionless.

Della froze when Wild Wind's stare bored into her. She lifted her chin and nodded at him, refusing to let him make her feel guilty for being in Grady's company. After a moment, he returned her nod, then strode across the porch. His long strides carried him down the steps and into the yard. His footsteps crunched on the gravel as he stalked to the barn.

Della swung her head in Grady's direction to find him watching her.

"He'll have to get used to seein' us together," Grady said.

Della shrugged. "If he doesn't like it, he has only himself to blame."

Darkness had enveloped the range. A lopsided moon hung from an indigo sky. Nighttime's chill bit through the sleeves of Della's blouse, and she hugged herself to ward off the cold.

Grady touched her shoulder. "You're cold. You'd better go inside."

He accompanied her to the door. "Good night, Della. I'll see you tomorrow."

"Good night, Grady." Della smiled at him before she slipped inside and shut the portal.

When she passed the parlor, she saw her uncle and aunt still sitting on the medallion-backed sofa, holding hands. She stepped into the cozy room.

"How did your meeting with Grady go?" Aunt Coral asked. "I've told your Uncle Clint all about it, so he knows what's going on."

Della moved closer to them and sighed, relating her agreement with Grady.

"Well, I think Wild Wind is doing you a real favor by insisting on some time apart to consider your next step," Aunt Coral said. "Spending time with Grady can help you decide if you really love Wild Wind."

"I don't think I'll change my mind. I know what love is."

Uncle Clint rose. Stooping, he kissed his niece on the forehead. "Wild Wind was right to insist on some time for reflection. Enjoy stepping out with Grady. You might surprise yourself."

CHAPTER 27

Grady called her name the next morning when Della hugged Jake goodbye at the door and sent her son to school. As Jake thumped down the steps and ran toward the gate to catch up with Flossie and Aaron, Grady left the corral and sauntered toward her, moving with a horseman's unconscious grace.

Della stepped onto the ground and met him halfway across the yard. Grady halted close to her and smiled down at her, his dark eyes soft and glinting with a possessive gleam. A twinge of misgiving filled her, but she tamped it down and smiled back.

"Mornin'," he said in a husky voice.

"Good morning to you."

"Did you sleep well?"

Della hesitated. "Not really. I had a lot on my mind."

The dimples in his cheeks deepened when his mouth turned up. "Me, neither. I couldn't stop thinkin' about the fact that we're keepin' company."

"It's a lot to take in." Della glanced beyond Grady's shoulder to see Wild Wind in the corral, currying a bay gelding tied to the bars. Though he gave no indication that he knew she stood nearby talking to the cowboy, she sensed the warrior was aware of her presence.

"I can't believe that you're my girl. Shall we meet after supper for that ride?"

"Yes, after supper."

After the evening meal, Della met Grady at the corral. He'd already tacked up her grulla gelding, and the mustang stood at the hitching rail, one hind leg cocked. Grady was tightening the cinch on his own saddle when she came to a stop on the other side of the rail. He looked up at her, his hands busy with the leather straps. A grin lit his face.

"I'll be ready as soon as I tighten the girth on this cayuse." A moment later, he flipped the stirrup off the saddle seat and stepped around her horse's rump. "Come here, Della, and I'll give you a hand up."

Grady loosened her mount's reins as Della skirted the hitching rail and stopped beside the grulla. "There's no need. I can mount by myself."

He rested one hand on the mustang's neck. "I know you can. I want to be a gentleman, is all." Stooping, he laced his fingers together and waited for her to mount.

Della placed her left boot in his cupped hands and braced herself by gripping his shoulder. He straightened and tossed her into the saddle. When she'd toed both feet into the stirrups, he flipped the reins over the horse's head. She took the reins from him and backed the mustang away from the rail.

They rode beneath the arched gate and out of the compound, away from the ranch and over the grassy swells. She enjoyed Grady's company more than she'd thought possible. By the time they returned to the ranch after dark, he'd completely melted any reserve she'd felt at their relationship.

On Sunday, while Della played hymns on the pump organ as a prelude to the morning church service, Grady sauntered down the outside aisle of the schoolhouse on the organ side of the building. Della watched him make his way to the front, where he settled himself on the first bench. He caught her eye as he removed his hat and placed it on the floor beneath his seat. He winked at her and patted the space beside him.

She nodded in acknowledgment just as an imposing figure appeared in the door, creating a dark silhouette against the outside glare. *Wild Wind.* His stare held her captive across the room before he turned aside and claimed a spot on the back row, instead of seating himself with the family as had become his habit. Della's fingers fumbled on the keyboard, causing her to hit a wrong note.

When they'd sung the last hymn before the sermon, and Uncle Clint rose to take his place behind a make-shift pulpit, Della scooted off the organ's stool. She met Grady's glance as she settled herself between him and Jake, and his possessive smile caused a tiny flutter in her stomach. She remained aware of him throughout the preaching, though she felt Wild Wind's gaze boring into the back of her head. Being the focus of attention between two males made her quiver with nerves.

Grady waited for her after the service, while Della played a final hymn to accompany the congregation's exit. When she'd climbed down from the organ's stool, he met her at the end of the row.

"May I walk you to the house?" he asked, his expression hopeful.

"Actually, Aunt Coral has invited you to dinner." Della smiled up at him, her Bible held against her waist.

"Will Wild Wind be there, too?"

"He always eats with the family."

"Won't it be awkward, having the two of us at the table with you?"

"I'm sure it will be, but you're adults. You both can handle any awkwardness."

Grady shrugged and grasped Della's elbow, turning her toward the door. "It's fine by me. Wild Wind and I don't have a problem when you're not around."

With his palm cupping her elbow, Grady set a slow pace to the house. The spring sun beat down upon them, warming the earth.

While they strolled, he gave her a long, thorough perusal from the top of her silk-flowered bonnet to the toes of her high-button shoes. "You're as pretty as a picture this mornin', Della. I don't feel fit to be seen in your company."

Della blushed, not wanting to admit, even to herself, that she'd taken extra care with her toilet this morning. She'd hoped to gain Grady's approval, as well as to make Wild Wind notice her and perhaps even to regret letting Grady court her.

She glanced down at her Sunday dress. The gown she'd chosen was a daring shade of poppy red lawn, fitted at the bodice and waist, falling straight down to her toes and caught up in the back in a waterfall of white lace over a bustle. Pearl buttons marched down the front of her bodice, set off by tucks and ruching. She'd enticed Silvie to style her hair in a cluster of ringlets at the crown of her head and falling over one shoulder, with a fringe of bangs fluffed above her eyebrows.

Overcome by unexpected shyness at his compliment, Della hesitated a moment before she replied. "Thank you, Grady. That was very sweet, but I'm sure you have no cause to feel cast in the shade by me."

He shook his head, his expression mournful. "Aw, I'm just a clumsy cowpoke who breaks horses."

Della chuckled. "You're anything but clumsy. And you're not just a cowpoke."

They crossed the ranch compound and climbed the steps. Uncle Clint and Wild Wind reclined in rockers on the veranda, waiting for the summons to the noon meal. The children played a game of marbles at their feet. Uncle Clint held his youngest son on his knees.

When they halted beside the group, Grady dropped his hand from Della's elbow. She leaned closer to her uncle and laid her palm on his shoulder. "Aunt Coral has invited Grady to eat with us. I'll leave him out here with you men while I go inside to help with dinner."

From his chair beyond Uncle Clint, Wild Wind tipped his head in her direction in casual acknowledgment, his face impassive. She flashed him a brief smile. Sprawled in the rocker, he looked as relaxed and lazy as a big cat, but beneath the brim of his cowboy hat, his watchful eyes scanned the bluffs beyond the compound wall, alert for any danger. Shane's six-shooter rested against his thigh like an extension of his body.

With a nod in Grady's direction, she vanished inside, leaving the men to pick up their discussion on the progress of the Morgans' training.

When the table had been set and Sadie had deposited large platters of antelope steaks, mashed potatoes, pickled beets, and biscuits on the linen cloth, Della returned to the porch to call the men. She stepped outside. "Sadie says to come in for dinner. You men look starved."

They jumped to their feet, not needing a second invitation. The children dropped their marbles and scampered into the house ahead of everyone, ducking beneath Della's arm as she held open the door for them. Uncle Clint took the door from her and motioned for her to precede him. She slipped into the hallway and waited for Grady while Wild Wind and her uncle filed past.

Everyone was standing by their places at the table when she and Grady entered the dining room. Uncle Clint and Aunt Coral stood behind their chairs at either end of the table at the host and hostess's places. Aunt Coral had moved Wild Wind from his usual position beside Della to a seat across the table between Flossie and Aaron. Grady had been placed in Wild Wind's former chair on Della's left, between her and Jake.

As Grady reached for her chair to seat her, Della risked a quick glance across the table at Wild Wind. He met her look with an inscrutable expression, hiding whatever he might be feeling at being displaced from her side.

During the meal, in which Wild Wind conducted himself as a gentleman without showing a trace of jealousy, Della breathed a sigh of relief. She couldn't fault his behavior. He chatted with Flossie and bent his head to listen to Aaron's prattle. When the conversation turned to the possibility of Indian trouble that summer, he added his comments. If Della hadn't known that he'd been determined to marry her just months previously, she wouldn't have guessed he'd ever declared his love for her. A niggle of doubt wormed its way into her thoughts. Had he changed his mind about wanting to marry her? What would she do with Grady then?

Grady entertained them with tales of his adventures while working his way North from Texas. He charmed Aunt Coral with his wit and even had Flossie in giggles. Just before the dessert was served, he leaned toward Jake and peered behind the boy's ear. "What's this I see?"

Jake put a self-conscious hand to his ear. "What? What's there?"

Grady bent closer. "Why, you have a nickel behind your ear." He snagged a silver coin from behind Jake's ear and flourished the money beneath the boy's nose. He reached for a second one. "I do believe you'll make us all rich." He plucked a third nickel from Jake's other ear. "All I have to do is to keep pullin' silver coins from your ears, and we'll be rich in no time."

"Is it magic?" Flossie cried, clapping her hands.

The adults smiled at her question and glanced at Grady, as if curious about his reply.

"Why, Miss Flossie, you do me an honor if you think my humble trick is magic," Grady said and spread one hand over his heart. His eyes crinkled at the corners.

"My turn!" Flossie begged. "I want you to take money from my ears now."

At that moment, Sadie entered the dining room bearing two kinds of pie on a tray.

"Well, now," Grady remarked in a thick Texas accent, drawling out the words. "Ya'll have to wait until after we eat our pie. I'm so tired from pullin' all that money out of Jake's ears that I'll have to eat pie to get my strength back."

Flossie giggled. "Eat a big piece so you can get very strong. I want you to pull lots of money from my ears."

Aunt Coral aimed an indulgent smile at Grady. Della caught his eye and flashed him a grateful look for his regard for her son.

Jake turned his attention across the table. "Uncle Wild Wind, can you do magic? Can you make money come out my ears?"

Wild Wind stared at his nephew as if giving his reply serious consideration. "No, Jake, I cannot do magic. Any magic in our tribe is done by the shaman, and he will not make coins come out of your ears. But I can track wild game, or man, and I can keep you alive anywhere on Mother Earth."

A brief silence enveloped the dining room. After a moment, Della leaned around Grady to address her son. "Actually, Jake, what Uncle Wild Wind does with his tracking and hunting skills is a special kind of magic. Not everyone can do what he does."

Jake's eyes rounded. "Will you teach me, Uncle Wild Wind? I want to learn to track, too."

Wild Wind nodded at his nephew. "We can start this summer."

Aunt Coral shooed Della and Grady outside after dinner. "You two go on, now. I can manage with Sadie and Silvie's help."

Outside, Della and Grady seated themselves on the swing. The afternoon sun warmed the air, bringing the promise of summer's heat. Della had removed her hat before lunch, and now, the mellow breeze teased her curls and ruffled her bangs. She leaned her head back and closed her eyes, enjoying the late spring weather and the lazy afternoon.

When Grady said nothing and silence had stretched out, Della turned her head to look at him. He leaned back into the corner of the swing, sitting at an angle, his attention on her face.

"What? Why are you staring at me?"

"You're so beautiful, I can't believe you're sittin' here with me."

"I can't believe you're sitting here with me, when I'm using you so selfishly."

"Don't fret about that. I told you, this is my chance to change your mind, and I know it's a gamble." Grady shifted, stretching out his legs. He slid one arm along the back of the swing, and his fingertips brushed her shoulder with feather-light circles on her gown's poppy-red fabric. "Della, maybe I shouldn't ask, but I need to know…"

His uncharacteristic hesitancy aroused her curiosity. The cocky assurance that usually defined him had been replaced by an unfamiliar doubtfulness.

"What do you need to know?" She tipped her head and leaned toward him in subtle encouragement.

He breathed deeply, and his fingers halted their circling caress. His hand, resting now on the point of her shoulder, felt warm through her dress's lawn material. "If Wild Wind hadn't come here, would you have kept company with me?"

Della scrutinized his face. He'd removed his cowboy hat when they sat down, and now, a lock of curly dark hair flopped forward across his brow. His chocolate eyes held an uncertain look, and a troubled expression overlaid his handsome features. Her conscious smote her again. "Perhaps. Now that I know you so much better, I very well may have stepped out with you."

"Last year when you wouldn't let me walk you home from church, I wondered if you thought..."

Della interrupted him, not wishing to hear what he'd thought, lest she hear something she'd rather not. "Last year was too soon, Grady. I was still grieving for Shane. I wasn't ready to think about another man, even Wild Wind." She paused. "Now, I'm ready to look ahead and put the past behind me. I'll always love Shane, and he'll always be a part of me, but now, I can move on."

His gaze searched her face before he replied. "I can only hope that you'll find it in your heart to move on with me."

CHAPTER 28

Leaning back on her braced arms, Della tipped up her face and stretched her legs out on the red and white checkered tablecloth spread out on the grass. Puffy white clouds piled up in the sky, casting their scattered shadows across the rambling prairie. Sunshine kissed her cheeks, while the wind tugged curls from her braid.

Grady lifted the picnic basket from the buckboard's bed and sauntered toward her, his brown cowboy hat framing his face. When he reached the tablecloth, he knelt and deposited the hamper beside Della. A grin creased his cheeks.

She rolled her head toward him and smiled. Three weeks had passed since they'd begun their courtship, and she now regarded him with true affection. He proved to be a gallant suitor, a good-humored companion, and an understanding friend. When they'd begun keeping company, she hadn't expected to find herself warming toward him in such a manner.

"Are you hungry? I think Sadie has prepared a feast for us." Grady flipped open the lid of the hamper and rummaged inside.

Della leaned forward to peer into the basket and curled her legs beneath her. "Fried chicken and biscuits, pickles and tea. And gingerbread. We certainly won't go hungry."

Grady fished out two plates and passed one to Della, then distributed the food. As they ate, their conversation turned to the approaching summer.

"The calvin' season is almost done," Grady said after swallowing a bite of chicken. "Then we'll have the brandin', and the cattle will be moved to the summer range. That will interrupt our trainin' the Morgans."

Della sipped her tea before replying. She balanced her glass on a level spot near her knee and looked up at him. She shrugged. "The army will have to wait for its cavalry horses until after the branding season."

"We have a good crop of calves this spring, what with us losin' only a few cows this winter and the wolves not gettin' many."

"We had a good year. Now if only Uncle Clint's contacts in Congress can prevent the oil consortium from shutting down our grazing rights, we'll have a good summer. The cattle should fatten up well."

Grady nodded. "We'll need all of those acres for grazing."

They discussed the looming crisis the oil consortium presented. Then their conversation turned to the continuing Indian war.

"So far, we haven't had any Indian trouble this spring, either, so perhaps we won't have to guard the cattle as carefully as we did last summer," Della commented.

Grady laid his empty plate down and pushed back his hat. "I thought my spine would wear down to a nub with all the ridin' I did last summer." He grinned at her. "I must be inches shorter now than I used to be."

Della laughed and began to collect their dirty plates and glasses. Grady watched her repack the hamper. When she'd finished loading the basket, he reached for her hand.

"I think I'll catch forty winks. You don't mind?" He cocked an eyebrow at her.

She shook her head. "Go ahead and take a nap. I know you've been working hard to get the Morgans ready for the army, so rest while you can."

He stretched out on the tablecloth beside her, and with his free hand, he tipped his hat over his face. With their fingers still entwined, he drifted into sleep.

While Grady napped, Della, unable to move without pulling her hand from his, sat immobile and let her thoughts roam to Wild Wind. Although he remained civil to her, he took pains never to be alone in her company or to engage her in personal conversation. His manner toward her was that of a casual acquaintance. She wondered how long he'd continue to keep his distance before he decided that she could make an informed decision about marrying him. The sudden notion that perhaps Wild Wind had concocted the scheme as a means of freeing himself from his promise to marry her chilled her. Could he have been so devious?

Her knowledge of Wild Wind made her reject the notion. In all his dealings for as long as she'd known him, Wild Wind had been direct. He'd never resorted to subterfuge. Surely, if he'd changed his mind about wanting to marry her, he would have told her himself. She glanced down at Grady, still sleeping. She hoped he wouldn't be too hurt when their courtship ended. Although he'd assured her he understood the risks, she knew he wouldn't remain unscathed when Wild Wind demanded a decision from her.

She sighed. Life wasn't simple, with options divided into boxes that never spilled over onto each other. Life was a jumble of choices, some of them not even right or wrong, but a matter of what was better or best.

Della looked deep into her heart. Though she felt a deep fondness for the cowboy, what she felt for him wasn't the love that a wife should bring to her husband. That deep, consuming emotion and desire to spend her remaining years with one man belonged only to Wild Wind. Sitting there, with the wind-swept prairie's bluffs and creases billowing around her, she prayed for wisdom to make the decision that would be best for everyone.

After a time, she realized she no longer felt the sun's warmth. A chill had crept over the plain. Glancing upward, she saw the tumbled clouds that had sailed the sky earlier had massed into a dark, boiling cauldron, casting a murky shadow over the range. A cool gust flipped the tablecloth's far edge over the picnic hamper. Buffalo grass and wildflowers rippled in the wind. The patient horses, still hitched between the buckboard's traces, tossed their heads and snorted. A thunderstorm seemed imminent.

She leaned toward Grady and pulled her hand from his. "Grady!" She shook his shoulder. "Wake up!"

He swept his hat from his face and sat up. "What's wrong?"

"We'd better get back. It's going to rain." Even as she spoke, a splatter of cold drops pattered onto the tablecloth and smacked her face.

Grady rolled to his feet, snatching up the basket by its handles. "Get the tablecloth!"

Della snatched up the checkered napery. Grady grabbed her hand and hauled her along beside him as they dashed toward the buckboard. He pitched the picnic hamper and the tablecloth into the wagon bed, then grabbed Della about the waist. After flinging her up onto the seat, he clambered over the wheel and slid onto the bench beside her. He loosened the reins and released the brake, then turned the team about and slapped the leathers against their rumps. The horses broke into a gallop.

Boiling clouds scudded through the sky. Wind gusted across the prairie, snatching Della's riding hat from her head so that it jounced by its strings between her shoulder blades. She grabbed for her hat and jammed it back on her head, holding it there with one hand while she clung to Grady's arm with the other. The buckboard pitched and swayed as it rumbled over the grass. If it hadn't been for her grip on Grady's arm, Della might have been hurled to the ground. She braced both feet against the footrest to steady herself.

The smattering drops erupted into a cold downpour. The scent of damp earth and rain filled the air.

Grady slowed the horses to a walk as the shifting drapery of rain obscured their vision, letting the team pick its own way over the range. By the time they'd followed the track down the hill past the cemetery and trotted beneath the arched entrance gate, Della and Grady were drenched and shivering.

The team swept in a curving arc through the yard toward the barn. Grady hauled on the reins to halt the horses just before the stable's open doors. He wrapped the leathers about the brake handle and leaped to the ground. Twisting, he reached up for Della. She leaned down toward him and placed both hands on his shoulders. He gripped her waist and swung her from the wagon seat. Shielding her with his body, one arm wrapped about her shoulders and the other curving around her middle to turn her into him, his head bent over hers, they ran in an awkward embrace toward the barn. Laughing and leaning together, with one of Della's arms about his back and her other hand clutching the front of his jacket, they stumbled into the shelter of the barn.

Inside, they halted and regarded each other, laughter still bubbling. Water streamed from their clothes.

Della swept off her hat. Bending forward, she wrung moisture from her matted braid.

Straightening, she flipped her plait over her shoulder and eyed Grady. She giggled as she watched him shake raindrops from his jacket. "We look like we just swam the Mississippi River."

"I'm wet enough to have swum it."

Della shivered in her sodden clothing. "We'll be lucky if we don't catch pneumonia."

Before Grady could reply, Wild Wind appeared from the back of the barn, a gray woolen blanket folded over one arm. He halted beside Della and offered her the blanket. "Lona. You are cold and wet. Wrap this about you."

Before Della could reach out, Grady snatched the blanket from Wild Wind. "Thank you, Wild Wind. I'll take care of Della now." He shook out the bedding and stepped closer to her.

Acutely aware of Wild Wind's looming presence, Della allowed Grady to flip the coverlet about her shoulders. Though its rough texture scratched her jaw's tender skin when Grady snuggled the bedclothes about her ears, the woolen fabric cocooned her in its warmth. He wrapped it about her and held it together at her front so the material enveloped her from neck to toes. His hands fisted at the edges just below her chin, holding the blanket closed.

She tried to ignore Wild Wind, who towered at her right. Though his face remained inscrutable, his disapproval knifed through her. Della felt his jealousy simmering beneath his calm demeanor as surely as if he'd shouted it from the roof top.

Closing her mind to the warrior, she turned her attention to Grady, who stood a breath away from her. His hand still held the blanket closed beneath her chin. His dark eyes twinkled down at her, and his dimples flashed when his mouth quirked up in a smile.

"Thank you for a bang-up afternoon."

"You didn't mind that we got caught in a rainstorm?"

"How could I mind, when I was with you?"

Della searched his face, noting the affection he felt for her. She smiled. He slipped an arm about her shoulders and turned her away from Wild Wind. She leaned against him. Together, they stood staring at the yard through the slanting rain at the dripping horses still harnessed to the buckboard, at the corral and the house, until the storm blew out and the sun shimmered through the shredded clouds.

CHAPTER 29

The next morning, while Della flicked a feather duster over the mahogany china cabinet in the dining room, Silvie appeared in the doorway.

"Miss Della, Mr. Wild Wind is waitin' in the parlor. Says he wants to talk to you."

In an instant, Della's fingers turned icy. Her heart began a heavy pounding against her ribs. The moment of reckoning had come. Wild Wind had decided she'd had long enough to make up her mind about which man she should marry and had come to demand her answer. She agonized over the pain she'd cause Grady when she chose Wild Wind, for her heart had remained steadfast toward Shane's brother in spite of her pleasure in the cowboy's company. She squared her shoulders. "Thank you, Silvie."

She laid the duster on the sideboard and moved toward the hall. Silvie stood aside to let her pass.

At the parlor door, she paused a moment before she stepped over the threshold. Dressed in his cowboy gear, Wild Wind stood before the empty wood stove, his back toward the wall. He held his black hat down along one thigh. Their gazes met and clung. Forgetting her qualms, Della sped across the parlor, coming to a halt before him.

An air of stillness enveloped him. He stared at her, his face stony. He could have been one of the sculpted wax figures she'd seen in a wax museum when she'd visited London one summer. Only the rise and fall of his chest betrayed the fact that he was a flesh and blood, breathing man. Della guessed he wasn't as impassive as he appeared. Several heartbeats passed while neither spoke.

Wild Wind lifted his head in an imperious gesture, his nostrils flaring. Looking down at her, he finally broke the silence. "Lona, I have given you time to court with another man. What does your heart say now?"

The temptation to make him pay for the wasted weeks and to draw out the suspense before she gave him his answer tantalized her, but a rush of joy checked the impulse. "My heart says it loves you, only you." She snatched a quick breath. "If you still want to marry me, that is."

For a moment he showed no reaction, as though her words hadn't registered. Then one hand lifted. His fingers stroked her cheek in a feather-light caress.

Della launched herself at him. She thumped against his chest, and his arms closed about her. His hat dropped unnoticed to the carpet. She returned his tight embrace. Her arms stole about his back. Her cheek pressed against his muscled chest, warm beneath his wool shirt. Under her ear, his heart thudded with a frenzied rhythm. No, she thought, smiling to herself. He wasn't as composed as he appeared. His heartbeat betrayed him.

One of his hands stole up her back and clenched in her hair. With his fingers tangled in her braid, he pulled her head away from his chest and tipped her face up to his. His gaze scorched over her features. Della read his intent in his eyes, and she welcomed his kiss. The next moment, his mouth swooped down on hers, claiming, cajoling, and proclaiming his love.

Della exulted in his fierceness. She reveled in the strong band his arm made around her back, cradling her close to him. She gloried in the touch of his fingers thrust into her hair. Her own arms clutched him tight, feeling the strength of his back beneath her palms. Her love overflowed, and she gave back to him what he offered her. She accepted his claim on her and in turn stamped her own proprietorship on him.

When at last he lifted his head, Della dragged in great gulps of air. Her gaze roamed over his countenance, touching on each beloved feature. His heavy-lidded eyes glittered. The slashes that grooved his cheeks bracketed his firm mouth. His patrician nose and the square jaw that framed his lean face stamped his mother's lineage upon him. She traced her fingertips over his cheekbone, down the side of his face and the firm line of jaw. When the pads of her fingers rested on his mouth, he covered her hand with his and held it there, while his lips puckered beneath her fingers in a kiss.

Wild Wind framed her face with his big hands. "Lona, you stole my heart when I captured you and brought you to my village seven summers ago." He made an attempt to control his ragged breathing. "No other woman has touched my heart. Now, you are mine. It is almost more than I can bear, to hold you in my arms and know you are truly my woman."

Della smiled at him and brought her hands up to clasp his strong forearms. "I am your woman, as you are my man." The words sounded strange to her, that after all the years they'd spent apart they should now be together as a couple. Yet the truth of her declaration seemed right.

He took one of her hands and placed her palm over his heart. "Feel my heart beating. It beats for you. Our hearts are now one. Our lives will be joined until death parts us."

Della shivered. She thought of Shane who rested alone beneath the sod on a windswept hillside. "Don't speak of death. Let's talk of love, and our life together."

"Our love will cross the divide of our two cultures. Together, we will walk in the white eyes world and also the way of The People. Our children will grow up knowing both worlds."

"I will learn to be a good Cheyenne wife and stand by your side when you lead your people."

Wild Wind stroked the back of her hand, which still lay over his heart. "You will be a wife to make me proud and will guide me when I need your council."

His heart still thumped beneath her palm. Her hand stole up to the spot where his shirt's top button rested at the hollow of his throat. Her fingers traced a circle on the warm burnished skin there, then moved upward across the red bandana knotted about his neck. With a light caress, she trailed her finger along the edge of his jaw and up to his cheek. At last, she laid her hand against the side of his face.

His eyes blazed at her touch. "You are the heart of my heart and the breath of my body. You are my sunshine, and the dreams that fill my visions in the night." An aching tenderness laced the velvet huskiness in his voice.

His love words, so foreign to her upbringing, touched her as no others had. Though he hadn't used the word *love,* he bespoke the depth of that emotion in his earthy declaration. "That was beautiful, Wild Wind."

"It is what I feel." With reverence shining in his eyes, he grasped her shoulders and drew her to him. "I would hold you again. I have had enough of watching Mr. Grady touch you."

Mention of Grady reminded Della that she now must end her relationship with the cowboy. She braced her palms against Wild Wind's chest and resisted when he pulled her toward him. "I forgot about Grady! He might come looking for me."

"He will not. I sent him, and the other wranglers, on a long ride. The Morgans needed some trail time."

Della punched him playfully on the arm. "You schemer, you."

"I did not want him to find us together. We need time, just the two of us." Wild Wind's eyes glittered down at her. "And if you had told me that your heart now belonged to Mr. Grady, I wanted to make you wait before he claimed you."

Della allowed him to pull her close. She wrapped her arms about his neck, tipping back her head so she could look into his face. "Did you think my love so shallow a thing that another man could steal it from you?"

"Mr. Grady wanted you. I could see that he tried to take your love from me."

"No man could take the love that belongs to you."

An expression of a conqueror's pride flashed across his face. "I will tell him that you are mine. No more courtship. No more touching you."

Della studied her beloved's features. She shook her head. "No, Wild Wind, I'll tell him. I've used Grady shamelessly. He willingly let me use him to satisfy your demand. He knew, and yet he still allowed me to use him. He hoped that perhaps I would come to love him. I owe it to him to tell him personally." She dropped her forehead against his chest. "I'm ashamed of what I did."

They stood in a close embrace, her face tucked into his shirt. After a moment, she felt his hand in her hair, then stroke down her back. "I would do this for you, take your burden and spare you from dealing with Mr. Grady. I was the reason he courted you."

"Thank you, but the burden is mine. I'll talk to Grady."

A long finger beneath her chin tipped her face up to his view. Wild Wind's head dipped, and his mouth claimed hers once again.

CHAPTER 30

Della crossed her arms on the corral's top rail and leaned against the bars. She watched while Grady stripped the gear from his Morgan mount and turned the horse loose. He carried the saddle in one hand and the blanket and bridle in the other, approaching her with a horseman's rolling stride, spurs jingling. His face creased into a grin as he drew near.

Della dreaded the coming conversation. Grady was a decent man who didn't deserve what she was about to do to him.

He halted before her with the corral rails between them and smiled down at her. "It does my heart good to see you waiting for me. Let me wash off the horse sweat. Then we'll sit on the porch swing. A glass of Sadie's lemonade sure would get rid of the trail dust."

Della hesitated, wondering what Wild Wind would do if he saw her sitting with Grady. Still, a conversation on the veranda would be more private than here in the open yard. She owed Grady at least a measure of privacy when she broke the news.

He swung the saddle onto the top rail, then hung the bridle over the saddle horn and draped the blanket atop the saddle. He slipped through the corral gate and secured the latch, then halted beside Della. "I won't take long."

She nodded and turned toward the house.

When Grady joined her on the veranda minutes later, Della was waiting in the swing, her fingers clenched about a glass of lemonade. He lowered himself into the swing and took the glass from her. He drained the lemonade in a few swallows, then balanced the glass on one knee, holding it steady with his hand. He looked at Della and smiled. "I just want to sit here with you for a few minutes and enjoy the afternoon."

Della's face seemed frozen. She couldn't make her mouth smile. All she could do was stare at Grady.

When she didn't respond, his smile faltered and died. His eyes narrowed. "What is it?"

Her mind blanked. How could she make this easier for him? No matter how she couched her words, she would hurt him. "Grady, Wild Wind came to me this morning."

Comprehension dawned in his eyes. "He made you choose, didn't he?"

She nodded, mute.

For a moment, Grady searched her face as if he could read her answer there. "And you chose him."

She nodded again, unable to speak. They stared at each other.

"Well, I knew where your heart was when we began," he said. "I'd hoped I could change how you felt, but since I couldn't... I guess I should thank you for givin' me the best weeks of my life. It's been a pure pleasure, Della, bein' your fella for a while."

Desperation loosened her tongue. "No, it's I who should thank you. I feel like a wretch for using you as I did."

He shrugged. "Don't fret over it." He touched the side of her face with a gentle hand. "I was your man for a while, and you gave me the honor of lovin' you. I won't ever forget it."

An unexpected tear formed along Della's lower lid and spilled onto her cheek. "I won't forget our time together, either. If I already hadn't loved Wild Wind, I might well have come to love you."

Grady's thumb brushed the tear from her cheek. "I can't promise that I can stay here now. It will be hard, watchin' you with him, but I won't leave until after the horses are finished and the army has collected them."

"Thank you. I appreciate that."

"I told you once that I ride for the brand, and I meant it. I've enjoyed workin' for you and Mr. Hunter while he was alive, but I'm not sure I can stay now."

"I hope you will consider this your home, Grady. It's my fault that I've ruined it for you, and I don't want you to leave. You've been good with the horses, and a fine man to have around the place." She tried to smile.

"I'd like to stay. I just don't know if I can." He pushed the lemonade glass into her hand and shoved to his feet. Glancing down at her, he said, "I'd better get back to work."

When he'd clattered down the steps and she was alone, Della leaned back in the swing and closed her eyes, feeling drained.

The front door opened and closed, and soft footsteps padded to the swing. Della opened her eyes and sat up. Her Aunt Coral, clad in a simple apple-green cotton frock, stopped before her.

"From the way you look, I must conclude that you just had your conversation with Grady."

Della nodded. At lunch, she and Wild Wind had informed her uncle and aunt of their new status as a couple. "Yes. He took the news as a gentleman. I do admire him very much, now that I know him so much better."

"He'll make some young lady a fine husband. It just won't be you."

"I wish there'd been some other way to do this without hurting him."

"It couldn't be helped, and he knew what he was getting into." Aunt Coral laid a sympathetic hand on Della's shoulder. "Your decision is made. Now, we'll plan your wedding to Wild Wind."

"Wild Wind and I haven't had a chance to discuss the wedding. I don't think he'll want to wait very long. He's waited long enough."

That evening after supper, Wild Wind followed Della outside onto the veranda. He halted when she turned toward the swing. "How do the white eyes court? I know only the Cheyenne way of courting."

Della stopped and swung about. "Well, a courting couple will talk."

A grave expression crossed his face. "Cheyenne couples talk, also."

She recalled her days in his village seven years before, when he'd brought his courting blanket to the lodge where she'd lived with Neha, his aunt. He'd wrapped them both in his blanket, and they'd stood before the lodge talking until darkness enveloped the camp, and Neha shooed him back to his own tepee. Her gaze flew to his face, and she saw that he also remembered. The memory entwined about them in invisible skeins, pulling them together.

When he spoke, his low tone took them both back to those days in his Cheyenne encampment. "This time, Lona, no one will tear us apart. This time, we will marry."

"Yes. Nothing stands between us now. Our God has brought us together." She hesitated, wondering how to tell him what was in her heart. Would he understand? She brushed a loose tendril of hair out of her face and prepared to share her painful memories. "Wild Wind, there's something that you must understand. I love you. You fill my heart, but there's a part of me that belongs to Shane and always will."

Della studied his face. His expression was grave and his mouth unsmiling, but he seemed attentive. "Shane and I were married for six years. He was my life, and I loved him." Della realized that she'd never told Wild Wind about Fanny's loss. It was time to share that heartache with him. She glanced away from him and took a breath, then brought her attention back to his face.

"Wild Wind, you aren't the only one who has lost a child. I, too, have buried a child. Shane and I had a daughter after we had Jake. She died when she was two. Shane and I suffered through that loss. It bound us closer together. Part of me will always love him, even though now, I love you and want to be your wife, but I can't undo the past. Can you live with that?"

For a moment, he remained unmoving before he brushed the backs of his fingers across her cheek in a tender caress. "You say you still love

Little Wolf. It is his memory that you love." Dropping his hands, he hung his thumbs from his jeans back pockets and stared down at her. "If I could have turned Yellow Wolf's will toward me that day in our village, he would have let us marry. You would have had no other husband but me. Mine would have been the only children you would have birthed. That was my wish, but it wasn't meant to be. You married Little Wolf. Now that he is gone, we will marry. Our hearts will be one, and we will make our own path. As the seasons pass, we will weave our lives together as one would braid a rawhide rope. We will weave the strands together to build a strong life full of love." He smiled. "You belong to me now. Little Wolf is in the past."

She would have to be satisfied with that, Della thought. Though Wild Wind seemed to have accepted her declaration, he was confident in his ability to bind her to him with the force of his love and his will.

His next words brought her back to their previous conversation. "Now, tell me. What other things do your people do while courting?"

"Courting couples do the things we did in Denver last summer. They attend the theater, and band concerts, and go for rides in a carriage."

"Doing those things with you was the only reason I could stay in the city."

Della nodded. "Yes, doing things with someone you love makes ordinary events special. Also, being seen together in public lets other people know that the two of you are courting."

"Such as when a warrior throws his courting blanket around the woman of his choice, he tells the village of his interest in her."

"Exactly." Her eyes twinkled at the memory of Wild Wind accompanying her to the shops the summer before. "And the gentleman accompanies his lady when she shops."

Wild Wind grimaced. "I hope you do not want to shop again."

Della grinned and continued her recital of courting customs in white society. "A couple goes to social events, such as a dance, or a picnic, or they go walking. They sit together in church. And flowers... the gentleman brings his sweetheart flowers."

"Flowers!" Wild Wind looked incredulous. "Why would a man bring his woman flowers?"

Della giggled. "Flowers show a man's love for his sweetheart. In our society, flowers speak a whole language. If a man thinks a lady is beautiful, he gives her a calla lily. A red chrysanthemum declares a man's love for the woman he bestows it upon. Ivy shows fidelity."

Wild Wind shook his head. "Of what use are flowers? Can you eat them?"

"Flowers are a thing of beauty. They express the emotions of the giver, and they're to be enjoyed."

Wild Wind made a dismissive gesture with his hand, chopping through the air with the edge of his palm. "I would bring you an antelope. You can eat antelope."

"Our culture sets value on appreciating things for their beauty and meaning. They don't have to be useful." She laid both hands on his chest. "But I would appreciate anything you might give me, Wild Wind. I was most grateful for the antelope you brought me in your village."

"I remember the antelope you prepared for me. I was very proud of how well you learned our ways." His hands covered hers.

"I wasn't in your village long enough to learn very much. I hope Neha can teach me more about being a good Cheyenne wife. I may not be much of a cook, but I can sew and embroider. I can make you a deerskin shirt decorated with beading and porcupine quills."

"I would be proud to wear a shirt you made for me." Wild Wind stroked one hand down her French braid. "When we go to my village, Neha will teach you our women's ways. You will make my heart sing, both because of who you are and of what we will be together."

Moved by his declaration, Della rose to her tiptoes and kissed him. "Your people were kind to me when I didn't know anyone in the village except for Neha and you." She kissed the corner of his mouth. "I remember the beautiful horses you gave me. You were a generous suitor."

"I would have given you anything you wished."

Della remembered how much more Wild Wind had given her than

gifts. He'd showered her with his love and protection. "Now, what would you like to do tonight?"

He hesitated. "Did Little Wolf sit with you on the swing when you were courting?"

"Yes."

"I will not walk in my brother's footsteps. Wait here."

CHAPTER 31

Wild Wind released her hands and jogged down the veranda steps, crossing the yard to the barn. When he returned, he carried the same courting blanket he'd used in his village seven years before. He mounted the steps and crossed the porch to where Della waited beside the swing. "I will also court you in the custom of my mother's people, but tonight belongs to the Cheyenne way."

Della fingered the woven blanket. Symbols of the Cheyenne courtship ritual interlaced the fabric. "You brought your courting blanket."

He flipped the blanket about them both and drew her into his body, his hands clasped about the small of her back. Her arms encircled him. His warmth, and the strength of his body, made her realize how much she'd missed the affections of a man she loved.

"Now, we talk." He looked down at her. "You have told Mr. Grady that he is no longer courting you." His words were a statement, not a question.

Her gaze dropped to the hollow of his neck. She nodded. "It was a hard thing for me to do. Grady is a very decent man, and he loves me. I hurt him badly."

"I could see that he loves you, so I thought it best to stop it. And I did not like him touching you. Lona, no other man will touch you now that you are mine."

Della lifted her glance to his face. "Grady and I were keeping company. He had every right to hold my hand."

"He will not touch you again." Wild Wind's arms tightened about her in a possessive gesture.

"No, he won't. He'll honor the decision I made." Della searched Wild Wind's face. "I thought you might like to discuss our wedding."

"I would have us marry soon. I have waited seven years to make you my wife. I will not wait much longer."

"I don't want to wait, either, but we have to consider the ranch. We should choose a time that won't interfere with the branding season or the Morgans' training. We have to meet the deadline that the army set for picking up their horses."

"The branding time is soon. Let us marry after the branding. I will go with the herd to their summer range, and when I return, we will marry. The Morgans training is almost finished. I can finish them after we marry."

"Having the wedding after the branding will give me time to plan. Aunt Coral wants to help."

"It is also the Cheyenne way. The woman's family helps."

"I hope we can find common ground with both of our cultures in our marriage."

"Yes, that would make our marriage strong." Wild Wind loosened the courting blanket and tossed it across the swing. "Now, here is another Cheyenne custom that I would use for courting you." He pulled a cedar wood flute from his jean's back pocket and flourished it before her. Lifting the instrument to his lips, he began to play. Breathy, mellow notes filled the air with a haunting melody.

Della clasped her hands together beneath her chin and stood transfixed. Remembering the courting flute's origins in the Plains Indian lore, the music moved her and brought tears to her eyes. The music told her of Wild Wind's love in ways that words couldn't express. His gaze held hers while he played, snaring her in a web of emotion that left her shaking by the time he finished.

He lowered the flute and stood immobile, both of them held prisoner by the moment's sentiment. The air crackled between them. Tears blurred her vision. When she spoke, her voice trembled. "I have no words to tell you what I feel."

"Nor do I. I cannot tell you how you fill my heart to overflowing."

The moment spun out. Neither of them moved. The past, when Wild Wind had played his flute for her in his village so long ago, and the present in which he stood before her now, collided in a tempest of emotion. Neither of them was the same person each had been seven years ago. Since that time both of them had married, had lost a spouse and a child, and had lived separate lives. Yet, despite all the things that should have prevented any possibility of a life together, the Lord had reunited them.

The front door crashing open shattered the moment. The children tumbled out onto the veranda. Jake charged toward them, with Flossie and Aaron on his heels. They skidded to a stop in front of the adults.

"Did you make that music, Uncle Wild Wind?" Jake asked. He motioned toward the flute without giving his uncle a chance to reply. "Can you play it again?"

"I want to play the flute!" Flossie cried. She clapped her hands. "Can I play it?"

Wild Wind and Della exchanged a glance before he squatted before the children. He held out the cedar wood flute so they could examine it. "This is a courting flute, Jake. Among my people, it is only played when a man wants to tell a woman of his love."

Jake eyed his uncle as if processing what his words meant. "Does that mean that you love my mama?" He peered over Wild Wind's shoulder at Della.

"Yes, Jake. That's what it means. Your mama is the heart of my heart."

Della knelt beside Wild Wind and rested her hand on his back.

"Jake, your Uncle Wild Wind has asked me to marry him. Would you mind very much if we got married?"

All three of the children goggled at her. Even the irrepressible Flossie remained silent. Jake swung his glance from his mother to Wild Wind and back again to her. A variety of emotions chased across his face. Della held her breath, wondering if her son would resent Wild Wind taking Shane's place as her husband.

At last, in a solemn tone, Jake said, "Papa won't ever come back, will he?"

With her other hand, Della squeezed Jake's shoulder. "No, Jake, he won't. He's in heaven with Jesus."

"He'd want you to be happy, wouldn't he, Mama?"

Della nodded. "He would."

"I don't think Papa would want you to be alone for the rest of your life."

"No, I don't think he would. If he knew that I'd be happy with Uncle Wild Wind, he'd want me to marry him. Your papa always wanted what was best for me."

Jake's head gave a jerky nod. A lock of sandy hair flopped over his forehead. "Then I want you to marry Uncle Wild Wind. He'll be my papa, and we'll be a family."

Wild Wind spoke in a grave tone. "I cannot take Little Wolf's place as your real papa, but I will be as a father to you, as much as you will let me. We will be a family."

Jake hesitated, then launched himself at Wild Wind. The boy clutched his uncle about the neck. "I want you to be my papa. I love you, Uncle Wild Wind. I'm glad my mama is marrying you."

For the third time that day, tears clogged Della's throat. When had she turned into such a watering pot? She flung her arms about her son. "Thank you, Jake. You've made your mama very happy."

The door opened again, and Uncle Clint and Aunt Coral stepped outside. Both took in the scene at the other end of the porch. Aunt Coral frowned at the children. "It's time for bed, all of you. Inside, now."

When Flossie and Aaron hesitated, obviously reluctant to leave, Uncle Clint added his own stern admonition. "You heard your mother. Upstairs, on the double."

With a final hug for her son, Della rose and turned Jake toward the door. "You, too. It's bedtime for you. I'll be up in a while to tuck you in."

"Aww, Mama. You don't have to do that. I'm not a baby."

"Maybe not, but your mama needs to say good-night to her son."

Feet dragging, the children returned to the house. With smiles aimed at Della and Wild Wind, Uncle Clint and Aunt Coral vanished into the house behind the youngsters.

Della and Wild Wind stood. She drew a deep breath. "That went better than I thought it might. I wasn't sure if Jake would accept our marriage."

"He wants a father. And I have begun to fill Little Wolf's place in his heart."

In the next moment, Wild Wind stepped close to her. Wrapping her in a tight embrace, he whirled her about so that her back pressed against the white clapboard siding.

One hand fisted in her hair. The other spanned her throat. He leaned into her, his forehead touching hers. His rasping voice was a mere breath, so low she strained to hear him.

"Lona, my own, what have you done to me? My Dog Soldiers would tell me that you have very powerful medicine and have bewitched me." His hand stroked down her braid again. His fingers worked at the plait until he'd loosened one strand at a time and her tresses sprang free. He lifted his head to watch as he sifted her hair. "Your hair is like the rain that waters the earth, soft and cool." He clenched his hand in the curling chocolate filaments. With light touches, the fingertips of his other hand caressed her throat. His thumb pressed beneath the point of her jaw, easing her chin up so her face lifted for his kiss. His mouth took hers.

Darkness had fallen and cloaked them in its folds. The cool night breeze eddied about them, but Della didn't notice. Lost in Wild Wind's kiss, she held him tight and returned his fervor.

At last, he lifted his head and stared down at her with narrowed eyes. "It is not the Cheyenne way to show affection such as I am showing you. Love between a husband and wife is an accepted thing and is not often demonstrated outside of the marriage bed. But with you, I am helpless." His thumb left her chin, and his palm cupped her cheek. "It must be my mother's blood that makes me feel so."

Della turned her face into his hand and kissed his palm. "I'm glad of it. You make me feel loved."

Wild Wind gathered her close. Dipping his head, he murmured into her ear. "I must leave you now. Tomorrow night, we will sit on the swing when we court."

Later, after bidding Jake good night, Della went to her room and closed the door. She leaned against the portal, trying to still her racing heart and bring order to her whirling emotions. Everything that had happened to her that day caught up with her. When she'd wakened that morning, she'd had no notion that Wild Wind would demand an answer of her, or that she'd be catapulted into marriage plans. The wild seesawing of emotions that had assaulted her during the day left her feeling both euphoric and drained.

She stepped away from the door and glanced down at her left hand. Shane's simple gold wedding band still graced her ring finger. Lifting her hand, she stared at the ring, lost in the memory of the moment Shane had placed it on her hand during their wedding ceremony. The time had come to remove the token of his love. At the thought, her other hand curled about the ring, as if to protect it. Could she take it off, even now that she and Wild Wind had pledged their hearts and lives to each other?

She was plighted to another man. Shane's ring had no place on her finger. Della squared her shoulders and paced across the room. At the marble-topped vanity, she halted. She glanced at the ring one final time, then worked it off her finger and rested it on her palm. The gold gleamed dully in the lantern light. After a moment she lifted the ring to her mouth and kissed it, then laid it in her silver jewelry box. When the lid shut the ring from her sight, a brief spurt of panic gripped her.

She'd just removed the last symbol of her life with Shane, severing her final tie to him. She closed her eyes. Now, she was irrevocably committed to Wild Wind.

CHAPTER 32

"Did Wild Wind tell you he'd be late for dinner?" Aunt Coral asked. The family was gathered in the parlor two evenings later, waiting for Wild Wind. Aunt Coral had instructed Sadie to hold dinner until the chieftain had joined them.

Della stood in the parlor doorway, keeping an eye cocked for her beaux. She shook her head. "No, he didn't mention it to me."

"I'm sure he has a good reason." From where he reclined in a padded rocking chair by the stove, Uncle Clint commented. "He'll be along soon, I'm sure."

"But you're hungry." Aunt Coral laid a hand on her husband's shoulder. "Should I tell Sadie to bring the food to the dining room? We can start without him."

He shook his head. "I won't starve in the next few minutes."

A quick rap sounded at the door. Della sped down the hall to answer the knock. Wild Wind's tall form showed through the door's oval glass window. At the sight of him, relief mingled with pleasure. Reaching for the crystal knob, she swung the portal wide. Wild Wind stepped into the hall.

"Are you all right? I was getting worried."

He bent his head to murmur in her ear. "I did not mean to worry you.

I had something to do before I came to the house." He swept his black cowboy hat from his head.

Della snatched the headgear from him and hung it from a peg on the hall tree beside the door, as her aunt and uncle appeared in the parlor door.

"I'm glad you're here," Aunt Coral said with a smile. "Della was convinced you'd been hurt."

Wild Wind spread his arms wide. "I am not hurt. As you can see, I have both arms and legs."

Della snagged his hand and linked their fingers, curling her other hand about his muscled biceps, needing the contact to reassure herself that he was unharmed. He cocked his head at her and halted their progress toward the dining room.

"I am a Dog Soldier of many battles. What did you think would happen to me here on the ranch?"

She hesitated. "I don't know, but you're never late. I thought perhaps you'd been thrown from a horse."

Wild Wind squeezed her hand. "Your concern for me warms my heart."

After the meal, Wild Wind detained her on his way to the parlor, where he would join her uncle. "When you have finished here, I have something to show you."

Curiosity spurred Della to hurry through her chores. When the women had finished cleaning up after the meal, she sped down the hall and paused in the parlor door. The men were discussing the upcoming branding. She listened without interrupting them until Wild Wind caught her eye and excused himself. He snagged his hat from the hall tree and settled it on his head as they left the house.

"What do you want to show me?" Della took his arm and skipped a little along beside him as they crossed the yard.

He slowed his stride to match hers and smiled down at her. "You will see."

Inside the barn, dim and cool, and fragrant with the scent of hay and horses, he turned them toward the tack room. Reaching around her, he opened the door and ushered her inside. Della halted on the threshold, transfixed.

Several wooden buckets had been set in a row along the far wall. A spray of spring wildflowers sprouted from each bucket. A froth of pink wild roses foamed over the buckets' rims. Stalks of lavender penstermon's trumpet-shaped flowers arched tall above the roses. White flowers sprinkled among the pink and lavender added a charming touch.

Della spun toward Wild Wind. Disbelief at the vision of flowers almost overrode the evidence of her eyes. "You picked all these flowers for me?"

His eyes crinkled and his lips twitched. "You said that giving flowers is a white eyes courting custom. Giving flowers shows a man's heart toward his woman. I wanted to show you my heart."

She flung her arms about his neck, and his arms closed about her waist. "Well, you most certainly have done that." She leaned back against the band of his arms. "Is this why you were late for supper?"

He nodded. "I wanted to have them ready to show you. I filled all the buckets with water, so the flowers would be fresh for you."

Della rose on her tiptoes and kissed him. "Thank you, Wild Wind. What a sweet gesture!" She grinned. "Your Dog Soldiers would think that I've bewitched you."

"I could never hold up my head again if my Dog Soldiers should learn that I picked flowers for my woman. I would be the object of their jokes."

Della kissed him again. "I won't tell them." Freeing herself from his embrace, she drifted across the tack room toward the blooms. She stooped to touch the wildflowers' delicate petals and inhale the roses' sweet scent. Straightening, she turned toward Wild Wind and gestured toward the blossoms. "No one has ever done anything so extravagant for me. It must have taken you a long time to pick all these."

He shrugged and replied in a voice so gentle that she melted. "I did it for you."

CHAPTER 33

Della pulled on Wild Wind's arm and turned him aside, out of the path of other party goers coming behind them. He bent his head to listen, one dark eyebrow quirked in quizzical inquiry.

"Remember, our customs at a dance are different from yours. Our men and women dance together, and it's perfectly acceptable. You mustn't take offense if a man asks me to dance, and you should offer to dance with other women."

His face set in the obdurate lines she'd come to recognize as resistance to something he didn't want to do. "I do not want to dance with other women."

Della sighed. They'd been over this topic before, when she'd coached Wild Wind in some of the dances they'd be doing tonight. Being athletic, he'd picked up the steps with little effort, but he balked at the notion of dancing with someone other than her.

"You are the only woman I will dance with." His tone brooked no disagreement.

The branding had been completed, and in the morning the cowboys would trail the cattle to the summer range. Wild Wind would accompany them, looking for Indian sign, then would return with the men after the cattle had been settled on their grazing lands.

Since last summer, Sitting Bull had taken his people up into Canada rather than surrender. The army had skirmished with Crazy Horse and other bands of Sioux and Cheyenne, raiding their camps and meeting in battle. Now that they stood on the summer's threshold everyone expected hostilities to commence again, but the area around the ranch had been quiet.

Della brought her thoughts back to the situation with Wild Wind. "You told me you would try to adopt our ways."

He nodded, unsmiling.

"You remember from last year that a barn dance at the end of the branding season is a tradition on the Slash L. It would please me very much if you would join the rest of us in celebrating. You even learned our dances so you could participate."

He stared down at her, his eyes flinty. "I will dance, but only with you."

She laid a palm on his chest, ignoring the people who passed by them. "Wild Wind, please."

He remained stiff as a marble statue, staring down into her face. Her gaze clashed with his, and just when she'd given up hope he'd relent, he sighed and covered her hand with his. "For you, I will dance with other women." The lowering sun, sitting on the rim of the far-flung bluffs, bathed one side of his face in amber.

"Thank you. This means a lot to me, and I think you'll find that the ranch people will accept you even more if you make an effort to join in our traditions."

"This is a hard thing you ask of me."

"I know, and I appreciate your willingness to try. What I'm asking you to do goes against everything you've learned in your culture." Her hand still lay over his heart, and she patted his chest. "If you ask Aunt Coral to dance, and perhaps Mrs. Donovan, that might be enough. If you really don't want to dance with other women, you can stand at the sidelines and sip iced tea."

"I will dance with you, every dance that I am not dancing with your Aunt Coral."

"Well, I may be dancing with other men. You must not make a scene if other men dance with me. Promise me." She gave him a pleading look.

He gave a grudging nod, his gaze traveling up and down her form. "I will try to behave as a white man when I see other men dancing with you. I will try to remember that white men do not fight other men who dance with their women." His eyes burned. "You are very beautiful."

Della glanced down at the square-necked frock of daffodil yellow lawn that she wore. She knew the gown set her off to advantage, and she'd donned it with Wild Wind in mind. "Thank you for the compliment, but the men will treat me with great respect." She tried to lighten the moment with a little humor. "You won't have to challenge anyone to a fight."

They turned toward the barn's open double doors. Inside, lamp light from lanterns hanging from posts between the stalls warmed the interior corridor with a golden glow. Tables loaded with food and drink lined one side. The revelers mingled along the open space between the tables and box stalls along the other wall. Toby and another cowboy fiddled at the far end while couples twirled. A cacophony of sound filled the barn.

Aunt Coral and Uncle Clint worked their way toward them through the crowd. When they stopped nearby, Aunt Coral pitched her voice to be heard over the din. "I hope you don't mind if Jake fills up on pie and cake." She nodded toward the refreshment table, where Jake and his cousins loaded their plates with sweets.

Della shook her head. "One night of sweets won't hurt him. I can't ride herd on him every minute."

"You and Wild Wind enjoy yourselves," Aunt Coral said. "Clint and I will keep an eye on the children."

When the dance ended and music began for a reel, Della tugged on Wild Wind's arm. "Come, let's dance."

Fingers linked, Wild Wind allowed her to tow him toward the back of the barn to the dancing area. With that dance, they plunged into the revelries.

About halfway through the evening, Della stood on the sidelines to catch her breath and fan herself. The press of bodies had heated the barn's interior, and she removed her shawl, draping the lacy garment over one arm. Her adoring gaze followed Wild Wind as he danced a polka with Hugh Donovan's wife. For such a big man, he was light on his feet, and Della had discovered that he possessed an innate sense of rhythm. He'd been a delightful dance partner, and she'd noticed the envious glances the single young ladies had cast in their direction. She smiled to herself. *He's my man*, she thought, marveling. *My man*. Sometimes she had to pinch herself at the wonder of their love.

A touch at her elbow roused her from her musing. She turned her head. Grady stood at her side, a crooked smile lifting one corner of his mouth.

"Evenin', Della."

She hadn't seen much of him in the days since she'd ended their courtship. He'd taken care to stay out of her way, especially if she and Wild Wind were together. "Hello, Grady. It's good to see you."

His lips compressed, and his eyes darkened. "It's good to see you, too. I've been missin' your company."

"And I've missed yours, as well."

A beat of silence fell between them in the midst of the music and hum of voices. Grady shifted his weight to one hip and thumbed back his hat. "I still haven't made up my mind about stayin' here."

"Please stay. The Slash L needs you." Della shifted so she faced him. "And I need you." She thrust out a hand when he seemed about to speak. "Not in the way you wish, but I need your support and experience. I value your friendship, and I would hate to lose that."

Grady's steady gaze met hers. She read the pain there, and she regretted all over again her role in hurting him. He glanced beyond her over her shoulder. She knew from the change in his expression he'd seen Wild Wind. He brought his attention back to her. "I hate to admit it, but you made the right choice. You light up like the sun when you're with him. You never did that with me. Anyone can see where your heart is, so I can't begrudge him your decision."

Unable to speak, she could only nod.

"I wish you happiness with him."

She nodded again, and her lips quivered. "Thank you, Grady." The whispered words trembled. "I wish you the same."

He shrugged one shoulder and pulled his hat forward over his brow. "I'd ask you to dance, but that would be pushin' my limits. I think I'll call it a night instead." He wheeled and worked his way through the crowd to the door.

Della stared after him until she felt herself watched. She pivoted toward the dance floor. The music had stopped, and Wild Wind had returned Mrs. Donovan to her husband. Now he stood motionless on the edge dancing area where partners were gathering, oblivious of the men and women jostling around him. He was watching her over the heads of the other revelers. When he saw that she'd noticed him, his eyes smiled at her.

His innate regal air impressed her once again, as if she was seeing him with new eyes. His muscular form gave the simple green cotton shirt and neckerchief a distinction other men didn't possess. Her heart lurched with the knowledge that soon they would be joined in wedlock and become one.

He took a step toward her but was intercepted by one of the bolder young misses, who engaged him in conversation and smiled up at him with a coquettish air. Della had coached him in the art of flirtation, so he'd know how to react when a young lady tried her wiles on him. With an apologetic glance in her direction and a slight shrug of one shoulder, Wild Wind offered his arm to the young woman and turned her toward the dancing area.

The night sped by. As the evening wound down, Della had just completed a reel with Emory Dyer when she turned to find Wild Wind at her elbow. He bent his head to speak into her ear.

"I would like to leave, if you are ready to go."

She nodded. With one hand at the small of her back, he guided her through the throng. Outside, nighttime's chill enveloped them. With tender solicitude, Wild Wind draped her shawl about her shoulder's and drew her against him. His arm about her waist held her close along his side, and Della snuggled into his warm embrace.

Their ambling steps took them down the track past the corrals, the commissary, school and married staff houses to the main compound's gate. Overhead, diamond-bright stars glittered down at them from a black velvet sky. They strolled in companionable silence, and Della was content to enjoy Wild Wind's closeness.

When they reached the house, they mounted the veranda steps and turned with unspoken consent toward the swing. They settled down, and Wild Wind pulled Della's head onto his shoulder. With one arm about her and a booted foot braced on the floor, he kept the swing going with a lazy rhythm.

After a moment, Della lifted her head to peer through the darkness into his face. "That wasn't so bad, was it?"

His chest rumbled, and he gave a low chuckle. "I am glad you have a dance only at the end of the branding season. Dancing with other women, and watching other men dance with you, was harder than I thought. I do not think I could do it again soon."

Della patted his cheek. "Well, I thank you. You were a great success. The ladies adored you, and you were a perfect gentleman."

He grimaced. "I do not want ladies to adore me."

"They can't help but adore you. You're handsome, and strong, and very mysterious. The single young ladies will dream of you tonight."

He shook his head at her words and changed the subject, cupping the side of her face with a big hand. "Will you see me off in the morning?"

"Of course."

"When I return, we will be married."

Della pushed herself upright and twisted so that she faced him. "Wild Wind, what kind of wedding do you want? Do you want a Cheyenne wedding, or a Christian wedding? Aunt Coral and I are making some plans, but I wondered if there's anything in particular you want us to include."

"A Cheyenne wedding is an agreement between the two families. We have no ceremony such as what you consider a wedding. We have a feast, a dance, and the husband gives the bride's family horses." His mouth curled in a lopsided smile, and his eyes laughed down at her. "Although I do not think your uncle needs any more horses. I will offer him horses, though, to prove to him that you are worth many horses."

Wild Wind continued his recital of Cheyenne wedding customs. "The women paint the bride's face with designs. Do you want your face painted?"

Della shook her head.

"The ceremony takes place under a full moon. The drums beat all night."

"Our wedding will take place in the morning, if you don't mind. And I think we'll do without the drums."

Wild Wind's expression turned serious. "I know nothing about Christian weddings, but now that I am a believer, I would have a wedding that will proclaim my faith."

"Of course, we'll be married by a preacher to make it legal."

He nodded. "A Cheyenne marriage would not be recognized in your society. I do not want your people to look down on you because you married me according to Cheyenne tradition. So, we will be married by a preacher. Where do you find a preacher?"

"Uncle Clint will ride over to Fort Bridger and bring back the army chaplain to perform the ceremony." She hesitated at her next question. "Will we exchange rings?" Knowing that the Cheyenne didn't wear wedding rings, she wondered what Wild Wind thought about the custom.

"Sweet Water, my mother, wore a wedding ring," Wild Wind said. "It was the wedding ring of her white eyes husband. Yellow Wolf allowed her to keep it when he could have taken it from her. My mother brought much sunshine to my father's heart, and he did not want to cause her pain by taking the ring from her." He paused. "What does a wedding ring signify?"

"For one thing, it shows the world that a person wearing a wedding ring is married."

"Ah. Men will know you are married to me."

"I'm sure that if any man should wonder if I'm married to you, you'll disabuse him of the notion immediately." Della smiled. "The ring is a circle. It symbolizes the eternal love that the married couple bears for each other."

Wild Wind seemed to consider the thought before he spoke. "The Cheyenne have many things that are symbolic. The ring will be another that will add meaning to our marriage. As the ring shows unending love, our love for each other will last beyond the grave." He tugged her back down against him, her head once more nestled on his shoulder. "Lona, when I take my last breath, my thoughts will be of you, of the love we share." His head dipped, and he sealed his words with a kiss.

State of Colorado
Summer, 1877

CHAPTER 34

Four days after the cattle had been trailed to the summer grazing grounds, some of the men returned to the Slash L, leaving enough line riders to keep a loose eye on the herd.

One night around the middle of June, Della woke to the sound of pounding on the door and footsteps thudding down the stairs. In the yard beneath her window, male voices shouted. She sat up and glanced outside. A strange, pulsating orange glow glimmered beyond the lacy drape. Thrusting back the covers, she tumbled from the bed and hurried to the window, sweeping aside the curtain.

Flames consumed the barn on the cattle side of the compound wall. Silhouetted against the inferno, blackened roof rafters stood out like charred skeletal ribs.

She darted to the wardrobe and wrenched open the door. Dragging a blouse and a riding skirt from its depths, she wriggled out of her nightrail and flung on her clothes. She stomped her feet into her riding boots and ran to the door.

In the upstairs hall, she encountered Aunt Coral, for once looking less than elegant, her clothes fastened haphazardly and her mussed hair still in its nighttime braid. The women exchanged glances, then bolted down the stairs and outside.

They halted on the top veranda step. The conflagration's roar resembled the low growl of a giant beast, intermingled with popping sounds.

Della gasped at the sight. With Aunt Coral at her heels, she gathered up her skirts and sped down the stairs. The women dashed across the yard and through the gate, turning right toward the burning barn at the edge of the ranch buildings.

A crowd had already gathered before the flaming structure. The blaze tinted their faces with an apricot hue.

Della stumbled to a halt. Glancing about, she saw Uncle Clint, Wild Wind, and Hugh Donovan at the front of the throng, flanked by Grady and Emory Dyer. With Aunt Coral at her side, they wormed their way through the press to the front. Here, the heat from the inferno was a living thing, searing their skin. A draft from the blaze lifted Della's hair away from her face. Black smoke billowed and drifted toward them, fouling the air with its acrid scent. She covered her nose with one hand.

Flames snapped and reached for the sky, devouring the building. Beams and stall partitions showed through the flickering fire.

Della glanced again at the men who ranged in a semicircle at the front of the mass. Several of the cowboys carried buckets, testimony to their futile efforts to extinguish the blaze. Soot blackened their faces. All of them wore expressions of grim disbelief.

A sudden explosion brought Della's attention back to the barn. With a whoosh, a massive shower of sparks shot skyward, like orange fireworks spiraling toward the heavens. Almost at the same moment, the remains of the roof collapsed downward with a mighty roar. The earth trembled with the impact. Flames leaped.

To Della, the scene had the macabre beauty of a maniacal nightmare, yet this was no dream. This was all too real. She knew what the loss of the barn would mean to the ranch. She hoped that the horses inside been removed to safety rather than being lost in the disaster.

No one slept again that night. When dawn cast its pearlescent glow over the prairie, the barn's remains lay in a smoldering, smoking pile of charred beams and rubble. The wooden corral rails next to the barn had also caught fire, and the fencing that hadn't gone up in flames had been torn down to remove the fuel from the hungry conflagration.

People stood about in clusters, discussing the fire in disbelieving tones.

Della approached her uncle. He stood with Hugh Donovan and Wild Wind before the remains of the barn, their heads close together. She came to a halt just behind Wild Wind's shoulder in time to hear Uncle Clint's words.

"This wasn't an accident. The fire was deliberately set."

Wild Wind corroborated the statement. "I found the boot prints of three men behind the barn. I tracked them to where they left their horses just over the ridge."

"It appears that they entered the barn through the back door and set the fire at more than one location," Uncle Clint said.

Della couldn't remain silent. "Did anyone rescue the horses?"

The men glanced her way, then exchanged a bleak look.

"No, not the horses!"

Her uncle laid a comforting hand on her shoulder. "The cowboys saved most of them, but the fire moved so quickly they couldn't get the last two out."

A mixture of sorrow and anger swept through Della at the thought of the helpless cow ponies trapped in the burning barn. Her hands clenched. "You'll find them, won't you?"

"Wild Wind will track them as soon as it's light enough. Hugh and I will go with him. We intend to bring back the cowards who did this and turn them over to the army at Fort Bridger."

Della turned to her future husband. "I know you'll find them."

He nodded and crossed his arms. "They did not even try to hide their tracks. I will find them."

With Wild Wind and Della accompanying him, Uncle Clint eased closer to the rubble, his mouth a grim slash. "I'll have to put in an order for lumber from Denver to rebuild the barn. Rebuilding the barn will mean I'll have to pull men from other jobs."

In spite of the grim situation, Della couldn't prevent a tiny smile from tipping up the corners of her lips. "They'll hate that. I've never met a cowboy yet who could stand to do any work that wasn't done from the back of a horse."

Her uncle managed a smile in return. "We'll have a barn raising, with a dance afterward. Maybe we can roast a whole hog and make a shindig of it."

"I think a dance and a hog roasting might make up for the fact that the cowboys will have to pound nails instead of saddle leather."

The men then moved toward the commissary. Della trailed along beside Wild Wind.

They halted before the store. Whoever had set fire to the barn had also vandalized the shop. Glass had been smashed from the windows. Inside, merchandise had been tossed haphazardly from the shelves. Women's shoes lay strewn among farming tools, and a jar of pickles had been upended over bolts of fabric. Chaos reigned among the once-orderly shop.

His hands fisted on his hips, Uncle Clint stood in the center aisle and surveyed the damage. Beside him, Aunt Coral stared at the disorder.

"We won't be able to tell what's been stolen until we take inventory and get this place back in order. Although I can see that a Winchester is missing off the back wall." He nodded toward the empty spot behind the counter. "And I suspect some cartridges were taken, as well."

"It is getting light enough for me to read sign," Wild Wind said. "We should leave soon." Taking Della's elbow, he steered her outside of the commissary and off to one side of the porch. "When we find the men who did this, we will take them to the army fort. We will marry when I return."

"Our wedding is scheduled for the first week of July. You will be back by then?"

"I cannot promise. I do not think these men will be hard to find, but it will take us some time to reach the fort. If I do not return by our wedding date, we will marry as soon as I get back."

"Will you buy rings for us at the sutler's store? I think you can find rings there. If not, we'll send to Denver for them."

Wild Wind nodded. "I will look for rings. I have money from my wages."

"I'll give you the ring Shane gave me. That way you'll know what size I wear."

He nodded again, thumbs hooked in his back pockets.

"And don't forget to bring the army chaplain with you."

A smile flickered around his mouth. "I will not forget the chaplain. Without him, I will not have a wedding."

Della tossed a handful of bread scraps left over from supper into the yard. The squawking chickens came running from every direction, waddling from side to side with their wings spread wide for balance. Serrated combs flashing, the red hens and the rooster descended on the feed as if they were starving.

The sound of hoof beats coming from the direction of the compound gate caught her attention. She turned, hope bursting in her chest. It had been ten days since the barn had burned and the men had left to hunt down the perpetrators, ten long days since she'd seen her love.

Her Uncle Clint, with Hugh Donovan and a stranger whom Della guessed must be the army chaplain, rode beneath the arched entrance. She glanced behind them, wondering if Wild Wind might be following, but she saw no sign of her fiancé. Hope faded, to be replaced by concern. Where was Wild Wind?

She tossed the last of the crumbs at the foraging chickens and brushed her hands together. By the time the men had halted their mounts at the corral, she'd intercepted them. With a hand on the off shoulder of her uncle's black Morgan, Della addressed him before he could dismount. "Where's Wild Wind?"

Uncle Clint grinned at her and swung his leg over his gelding's rump before he replied. Facing her from the other side of the horse, he rested one hand on the saddle's pommel. "And good evening to you, too. I'm very well, in case you're wondering."

Della sighed. "I'm sorry. I should have greeted you before I inquired about Wild Wind. I see that you came to no harm while you were gone." She gazed at her uncle from across the saddle. "Did you find the men who burned the barn?"

He pushed back his hat. "We did. We caught up with them on the afternoon of the second day out." A grim expression darkened his features. "The ringleader was Virgil Bledsoe."

"Virgil Bledsoe!"

"Yes. It seems he carries quite a grudge against us for firing him."

"He deserved to be fired, many times over. He would have shot Wild Wind in the back."

"He doesn't see it that way."

The old anger at the many things Virgil had done to Wild Wind stirred again. "Still, to shoot a man in the back is cowardly and not to be tolerated. He should know that."

"Wild Wind is half Cheyenne. To men like Virgil, that makes him fair game for anything."

Della shook her head and clenched her fists. "Well, Wild Wind gave him the beating he deserved."

Uncle Clint led his mount to the hitching rail and tossed the reins over the bar, while Della trailed along behind. He flipped the stirrup over the saddle seat and worked at the leather girth strap to loosen it while he talked. "There's more to this than simple revenge. Virgil eventually showed up in Denver and began hanging around in the saloons. Whenever he could get someone to listen to him, he complained of the unjust treatment he'd received here."

Della's eyes flashed. "I could have done a lot worse than fire him for what he did. He got off too easily, I think."

"Well, he's worked up quite a grudge. After several days, while he made the rounds of all the saloons, a couple of men approached him. They were well dressed and apparently had a lot of money. Easterners, Virgil said."

"Easterners?" Della lifted her head and narrowed her eyes at her uncle. "What did they want?"

"They offered Virgil, and the other men with him, a hefty amount of money to burn us out. Half before and the rest after they'd done the job."

"Do you think the Easterners were connected to the oil consortium?"

Uncle Clint pulled the saddle from his gelding and tossed it over the corral's top bar. Turning toward her again, he stood with his hands on his hips, elbows jutting. "That's my guess. The oil consortium must really want to force me out."

"So, you took Virgil and the other outlaws to Fort Bridger?"

He nodded. "They're in the stockade until the army deals with them. I brought back the chaplain so you can get married." He grinned at her again.

While they'd talked, Hugh Donovan and the chaplain had untacked their horses and turned them into the corral. Uncle Clint motioned to the preacher. He laid an affectionate hand on Della's shoulder when the chaplain joined them. "Della, I'd like you to meet Chaplain Major William Smith. Chaplain Smith has kindly consented to perform your wedding ceremony."

Della smiled at the major. She acknowledged the introduction by offering him her hand. "Thank you for coming, Chaplain Smith. Wild Wind and I appreciate you riding all this way to marry us."

The major, a tall, rangy man with ginger hair and a mustache, smiled back at her and took her proffered hand, giving it a firm shake. "It was a good excuse to get away from the fort and enjoy some civilization for a few days."

Della took back her hand. "I'm sure you're tired and would like to freshen up. In just a moment, I'll take you to the house and show you to your room. Then, we can have tea and something to eat."

"That would be pleasant. I welcome your hospitality."

Della turned her attention to her uncle and planted her hands on her hips. "Now may I ask where Wild Wind is?"

"Wild Wind had some personal business to attend to before he could come back. He should be along in a couple of days."

"He knows the date of our wedding. I hope he can finish whatever business he has before then."

Uncle Clint smiled, a gleam in his eyes. "He won't miss the wedding. You can count on that."

CHAPTER 35

Della stared at her image in the pier glass. To demonstrate that her marriage was more than the joining of a man and a woman but was also the merging of two cultures, she'd donned the deerskin dress she'd worn when she'd been a captive in Wild Wind's village. The dress had hung in the back of her wardrobe ever since Shane had rescued her.

After bathing this morning, Della had pulled the garment from her wardrobe and shimmied it over her head. Its musky, smoky scent had enveloped her as the leather draped her body. The soft deerskin felt more comfortable than her own clothes, and its tribal style had its own kind of savage beauty.

The fringe hanging from the hem dangled about her calves. The exquisite Cheyenne beadwork and dyed porcupine quills made a blue, red, and yellow starburst pattern on the bodice. More fringe swung from the elbow-length sleeves and dangled about her wrists. Supple deerskin moccasins decorated with delicate beading encased her feet. Della had plaited her hair in two long braids wrapped in strips of beaded leather.

The outfit took her back to her days in the Cheyenne encampment, when she hadn't been sure she'd ever see her family again. Today, she'd come full circle and would joyously join her life to the fierce warrior who'd once taken her captive.

The woman staring back at her from the glass looked Cheyenne, *felt* Cheyenne.

Aunt Coral's face appeared over her shoulder in the mirror. "We should leave now. You don't want to be late for your own wedding."

Della turned toward her aunt and smiled. "No, I don't want to be late. I'm ready to go."

Aunt Coral laid both hands on her niece's shoulders. "You look radiant. You're glowing."

"I'm delirious. I can't believe that Wild Wind and I are actually getting married."

"The Lord gave you another love."

"One I certainly didn't expect."

Aunt Coral linked her arm through Della's and turned them toward the bedroom door. "Your Uncle Clint is downstairs waiting to escort us to the school."

Together, they left the room and descended the stairs. Deerskin garbed one woman. A long-sleeved cream silk gown with a swath of fabric gathered over a bustle at the back draped the other. A tiny straw hat with a curled brim perched at a jaunty angle atop Coral's head.

In the downstairs hall, Uncle Clint waited, dressed in a dark broadcloth suit that displayed his wide shoulders. He strolled toward the women as they stepped off the last tread. "Here are my two beautiful ladies." Bending, he bussed Della on the cheek. "What? No flowers? What bride doesn't have flowers?"

"I'm going as a Cheyenne bride. Cheyenne brides don't carry flowers."

He offered her one arm and his wife the other. They left the house and crossed the compound, passing beneath the arched gate at a measured walk. As they turned toward the schoolhouse, Della's pulse thrummed through her veins, echoing the hurried beat of her heart. In moments she'd see Wild Wind, the man with whom she would join her future. Impatient to unite with him in the bonds of matrimony, she chafed at the slow pace her uncle set.

Wild Wind had returned to the ranch just before supper last night. When she'd questioned him about his mysterious errand, he'd smiled and kissed her but remained enigmatic.

"You will see," he'd said and refused to satisfy her curiosity.

Now, late morning sunshine spilled golden rays through the clear air, promising baking heat later in the day. Cottony clouds sailed across the sky. It was a glorious Western summer's day with weather perfect for a wedding.

They neared the schoolhouse. A tall figure stood beside the steps, watching the approaching group. *Wild Wind.* Della's gaze lifted to his face, which was shaded by the brim of his black cowboy hat. Their glances snared, and she felt his power jolt her in the chest. *This man will be my husband,* she thought, *my husband through all the remaining days of our lives.*

He wore new jeans and a new blue cotton shirt for the occasion. The tails of the dark blue neckerchief tied about his throat fluttered in the wind. His face remained expressionless until she halted before him. His perusal of her form warmed her while his eyes spoke to her of his love.

On either side of her, Uncle Clint and Aunt Coral remained silent.

At last, he said, "Lona, our day has come. We will wed."

"Yes, we'll be married this day."

He held out the lead rope of a shimmering golden palomino mare who stood patiently at his shoulder. "It is the Cheyenne custom for the husband to give horses to the bride's family. Your uncle did not take me up on my offer. He does not need more horses, but I would give a bride gift to you, my wife. This mare is yours as a token of the sunshine you have brought to my heart."

Della turned her attention to the mare. Superior breeding showed in her sleek lines, her large dark eyes and wide forehead. "Wild Wind, what can I say? She's gorgeous." She stretched out a hand toward the mare, who sniffed and blew at her fingers. "Thank you."

Della stroked the mare's glossy neck. The horse shook her head and stamped at a fly. She glanced across the palomino's back at Wild Wind. "What is her name?"

"Morning Star."

"Morning Star," Della repeated, sliding her hand along the horse's withers. "It fits her."

Uncle Clint cleared his throat and addressed his niece. "It's time for the wedding to begin. I'll seat your aunt, then come back for you."

Proffering his elbow to his wife, he led her up the steps and into the schoolhouse while the notes of Toby's violin drifted through the open door.

Wild Wind looped the mare's lead rope about the bar of a hitching rail beside the steps and moved closer to Della. He studied her face with a grave expression. His glance roved over her, taking in each detail of her costume. "You look like a Cheyenne bride. Thank you for honoring my people."

"It's a symbol that we're joining two cultures."

Wild Wind touched her with his gaze. "You are very beautiful."

Della smiled up at him. "And you're as handsome a groom as any bride could wish for."

"This is not the wedding we would have had in my village seven summers ago, but it will join our hearts as surely as a wedding of The People would have done."

She curled her fingers about his arm. "It wasn't the right time for us seven years ago, but today is our time. Today, and every day for the rest of our lives."

Uncle Clint appeared in the door. He smiled down at his niece. "Are you ready? Everyone is waiting."

Della and Wild Wind had decided that they would walk the aisle together, with her uncle escorting her on her other side. She linked her arm through Wild Wind's. He pressed her elbow against his side in a possessive gesture. She cast him a quick glance, and the look in his eyes made her catch her breath. His love for her burned with a vivid blue flame. His gaze scorched her before he dipped his head and took her mouth in a snatched kiss. When he lifted his head, Della couldn't speak. He turned her toward the schoolhouse door and led her up the steps.

At the top step, Uncle Clint took her other arm. For a moment, the three of them stood poised in the open door, staring into the building's dim interior. Benches had been arranged in rows on either side, leaving an aisle down the middle of the room. Bouquets of wild roses tied with white ribbon had been attached to the inner edges of each row. At the front of the room, Chaplain Smith waited in full dress uniform, a Bible in his hands. Since no one on the ranch besides Della played the organ, Toby provided the music with his violin.

Della's pulse throbbed, and she took a deep breath. She stood on the threshold of a new phase of her life. Once again, she'd be a wife. The gravity of the covenant she was about to enter tempered the joy that filled her. Her life with Wild Wind wouldn't be easy, but they both had the Lord to help them through the trying times.

Toby ran his bow across the violin strings, and the clear, pure notes of Mendelssohn's *Wedding March* soared to the rafters. With Uncle Clint on her left and Wild Wind on her right, Della took her first step down the aisle.

CHAPTER 36

Della kept her palomino mare close beside Wild Wind's piebald war horse. Their mounts strode through the buffalo grass at an easy walk, the foliage swishing about their legs. Wild Wind ponied along a packhorse laden with supplies.

After the ceremony, they'd stayed long enough to partake of a wedding feast prepared by Toby and Sadie. When they'd eaten, Della had changed from her Cheyenne dress to a split riding skirt and long-sleeved blouse, and they'd departed for their wedding trip amidst a hail of rice tossed by the ranch's well-wishers. Now, several miles from the ranch headquarters, Della couldn't contain her curiosity a moment longer.

"Where are we going?" She brushed a loose tendril of hair, plastered to her cheek by the wind, off her face and tucked it behind her ear. She glanced at her husband. *Husband.* Wild Wind and she were finally married.

Alert for danger, he scanned the prairie's grassy knolls and ridges before he replied. "I have prepared a wedding lodge for us. We will stay there until we return to the ranch."

"A wedding lodge? What is that?"

Wild Wind's eyes crinkled, and the grooves on either side of his mouth deepened. "You will see." He halted his gelding. Reaching out, he grabbed the reins of Della's mare and pulled her to a stop. His expression heated. Wrapping a large hand about the back of Della's neck, he tugged her toward him.

Pulled off balance, she braced herself with a hand on his leg. His face loomed above her, framed by his cowboy hat. Blue eyes stared down at her.

"I would kiss you, wife."

Before she could respond, his mouth swooped down and covered hers. Under the limitless Colorado sky, with the range billowing around them and a red-tailed hawk riding the air currents above them as the only witness, Della received her first private kiss as a married woman. She closed her eyes and gave herself up to her husband's love.

When he lifted his head, he covered her face with tender pecks, her eyelids, her nose, and her cheeks. Dazed, Della opened her eyes and laid her free hand alongside his cheek.

"*Wife.* You have been the wife of my heart since those first days in my village, but now, you are my wife in truth."

"As you are my husband."

He stroked her face and ran a hand down her arm, then let her go. "We have miles to travel before we can stop. It is time to ride."

They reached the camp Wild Wind had prepared late in the afternoon. A single buffalo-hide teepee located in a hollow thrust up from the prairie grasses. Billowing knolls spread out around them as far as Della could see. On one side, the ground sloped down to a burbling creek. When their horses halted before the lodge, Della turned to her husband.

"Where did you get this teepee?"

"I traded it from some tame Arapaho Indians who were camped outside of Fort Bridger. I made a travois with the lodge poles and brought it here. This is our wedding lodge."

"*You* put up this teepee? But that's woman's work."

Wild Wind shrugged, stacking his hands on his saddle horn and relaxing against the cantle. "My Dog Soldiers are not here to see. They will not know I did woman's work. I will not be the butt of their jokes."

Her time in his village had taught her that setting up a teepee required at least two women working as a team. She could only imagine how he'd struggled to erect the poles without another person to help and to drape the hide about the poles once he had them in place. Reaching out, she covered his hands with one of hers. "You're full of surprises, my husband."

"I did it for us."

"I'm glad you did, even though you almost missed our wedding."

Wild Wind turned his hand beneath hers and linked their fingers, then brought her hand to his mouth and kissed her knuckles. "Nothing would have made me miss our wedding." He placed her hand in her lap and swung a leg over his horse's rump. "Come. We have much to do."

Della scrambled off her mare and dropped the reins to ground hitch her mount. She stroked the palomino's creamy mane, crooning soft words before she loosened the girth and dragged off the saddle and blanket.

Together, she and Wild Wind unloaded the supplies from the packhorse and hauled everything to the teepee. Brushing aside the privacy flap, Della ducked through the opening and stepped inside. She straightened and swept the interior with a glance. In the center, a ring of rocks encircled a shallow pit where the cooking fire would be built. Beyond the fire pit, a pile of blankets had been stacked on several fur buffalo robes, where she and Wild Wind would sleep.

Behind her, Wild Wind stooped to enter the lodge, blocking the sunlight that spilled through the entrance. He straightened, standing so close behind her that Della felt his body heat along her back. His presence surrounded her and filled the teepee, making the tent feel crowded. She moved away, overcome with shyness, and glanced at him over her shoulder. He flicked a look beyond her to the bedding, but he didn't comment. Instead, he pivoted to the left and laid the supplies he carried on the floor.

She laid her parcels beside his, then turned toward him. He stood with booted feet spread wide, his shoulders thrust back, eyes slitted in an expressionless face. She couldn't begin to guess what he was thinking.

At last, he reached for her hand. "We have much to do. Come." He towed her outside. Reaching down, he snagged a tin bucket that lay on its side at their feet and thrust it at her. "We need water. Will you fill this from the creek? I will care for the horses."

Working together to finish the chores, Della carried water into the teepee and rummaged in the supplies for something to eat while Wild Wind hobbled the horses and stowed his weapons and their rigs in the lodge. With his usual fluid grace, he sank to a cross-legged position beside the fire pit and watched while Della laid out the food.

"Tonight, we'll have leftovers from our wedding feast." She knelt beside him and offered him a chunk of roasted venison and a biscuit on a tin plate. "I don't know what we'll eat tomorrow. I can manage porridge for breakfast, but I warned you that I can't cook."

He took the plate and laid it beside his knee on the buffalo fur rug. "Do not fret, Lona. A warrior traveling without women knows how to feed himself. I can manage for us."

Della's shoulders slumped. "Cooking is women's work. You shouldn't have to fix our meals. I'm not much good to you."

Wild Wind stroked her face, his touch gentle. "Do not fret. We will work it out. At the ranch, you have no need to cook. When we are on the reservation, Neha can teach you what a Cheyenne wife needs to know." His fingers curled beneath her chin, and his thumb rasped across her lower lip. "Now, eat."

When they'd finished, Della gathered up the plates and forks. "I'll wash these in the stream."

She stooped through the entrance and hurried down the slope to the brook. A stand of cottonwoods and brush that grew along the creek bed whispered in the evening breeze. Their shadows stretched toward her, staining the prairie grass with a bluish tint. She knelt at the stream's edge and scrubbed their utensils with sand, then rinsed them in the water.

Rocking back on her heels, she stacked the dishes on a flat rock and stared at the brook eddying between its banks. Her stomach quivered at the thought of Wild Wind waiting for her. Their wedding night loomed. As much as she loved her new husband, her nerves twanged at the thought of their first night together. Her fingers were icy.

At last, she could procrastinate no longer. She gathered up the tin ware and stood.

Wild Wind met her outside the teepee. "We will have rabbit tomorrow. I have made a snare to catch a rabbit."

"You'll have to show me how to cook it."

"We will do it together." He motioned for her to enter the lodge.

She ducked inside ahead of him. While she'd lingered at the stream, he'd lit a fire from wood the packhorse had carried. Since the herds of buffalo had been decimated by white hunters, buffalo chips were no longer readily available, so they'd provided their own fuel.

Della stowed the dishes in a leather pouch. She straightened and turned. Wild Wind stood beside the fire. The flames lit one side of his face, burnishing his strong features and casting the other half in shadow. The firelight played along his hair, lending copper gleams to the dark strands.

Outside, a distant wolf yipped at the darkening sky. The sound grated against Della's taut nerves.

Wild Wind held her prisoner with his gaze. When he beckoned, her feet carried her, unresisting, to his side. She placed her hand in his, and he drew her close. His other arm wrapped about her waist, pulling her against him.

He stared down at her, a husband's love and desire tightening his features.

"Lona, you are my heart's whole being. Tonight, we begin our journey as husband and wife, and we will walk together all our days. Your happiness will be my happiness, and your sorrows, my sorrows. We will share our burdens." Freeing her hand, he laid his fingers over her chest where her heart thudded wildly beneath his palm. "Our hearts beat as one. Our hearts will be one until we take our last breath."

Della caught her breath. She thought his vows to be as moving as the most sentimental poetry she'd ever read. "That was beautiful, Wild Wind." She paused. "You are my life."

His eyes gleamed with blue heat. Dipping his head, he took her mouth.

CHAPTER 37

Della stepped into the crystalline morning air. She shivered and drew her jacket more closely about her. Though she'd slept later than usual, the sun hadn't yet burned away night's chill. She tucked her hands into the jacket's pockets.

She hadn't bothered to braid her hair. Instead, she'd gathered its spiraling curls at the nape of her neck and tied the mass with a rawhide thong. The tresses sprang out below the band and tumbled to her waist.

She wondered where Wild Wind could be. The horses grazed a few dozen yards from the teepee, but she didn't see her husband. Pivoting, she searched along the creek bed for sight of him. A movement beside the stream caught her attention. Wild Wind was kneeling alongside the water, his back to her.

She picked her way down the slope toward him, a little shy and wondering how to greet him this morning. Before she'd covered half the distance, he rose and turned toward her, his face expressionless. A skinning knife dangled from one hand. He thumbed back his hat with his other hand and waited for her to draw near.

Della caught her breath at his physical impact. He stood so tall and splendid, and she could only marvel at the miracle that had brought them together. *This man is my husband,* she thought. *Mine, when he could have chosen any other woman.* Her heart skittered.

He watched her approach. When she halted before him, he leaned down and kissed her. "It is a good morning, my wife."

"Yes. Yes, it is a good morning."

"Today is ours, to do as we choose." He motioned toward a skinned rabbit that he'd laid on the flat rock at the water's edge. "I caught a rabbit in my snare. We will eat rabbit today." He turned toward the water and stooped to wash the blood from the knife and his hands, then laid the weapon beside the rabbit. He wiped his hands on his jeans.

Wild Wind stepped close to Della and linked his hands behind the small of her back, pulling her close. His long legs bumped against hers, and the insides of his boots brushed against the outside of her shoes. She clasped her hands about his neck, feeling his skin smooth and warm beneath her palms. Not quite daring to meet his eyes, she leaned her head against his muscled chest.

After a moment, he put a finger beneath her chin and tipped up her head, forcing her to meet his gaze. Love and tenderness filled his eyes. Her reservations melted, leaving only love behind.

"Lona, now, we are one in truth." His thumb stroked her cheek. "Your welfare is my concern. Do not fear. A Cheyenne warrior guards what is his. I will protect you with my life and love you with all of my being."

"I am fortunate to have such a strong and loving husband." A final confession tripped off her tongue. "I can scarcely believe that you love me, when you could have chosen any girl from The People."

A grave expression crossed his face. "When I was a young man, you came to me in a vision quest. I saw you standing before me, with the sun shining on your hair. Your hands reached out to me. I knew then that you would be the woman of my heart." He kissed her neck just below her ear, then tucked her head beneath his chin and held her close. One hand removed the leather thong that confined her hair. His calloused fingers snagged on her curls as he fisted her tresses in his palm. "You were meant to be mine. How could I love another?"

They stood entwined while the sun poured golden rays earthward, and the wind tossed Della's hair about them. Flying chocolate strands wrapped about Wild Wind's shoulders, binding them together.

CHAPTER 38

Della woke. She lay motionless on the buffalo robes with the blankets pulled up to her chin. An empty silence filled the darkened teepee. She couldn't hear Wild Wind's even breathing, and she reached across the bedding, feeling for him. The spot beside her where he should have lain was empty, though his body heat still warmed the blankets. She was alone in the lodge.

She scrambled out from beneath the covers. Fumbling in the dark for her riding boots, she found them beside their pallet and pulled them on. Then, snatching a blanket from the pile on their bedroll, she flung it about her shoulders and hurried across the lodge. Sweeping aside the privacy flap, she ducked outside.

An obsidian darkness enveloped the range. No moon spilled silver light onto the plains. Seeming almost close enough to touch, thousands of diamond stars glittered with icy light in a black velvet sky.

Della paused outside the teepee's opening, scanning the area around her, searching for her husband. At last, she spied him off to her right, a dark shape against the sky. Gathering her cotton night rail in one hand to prevent it from trailing through the damp grass, she tramped toward Wild Wind. His right hand held his rifle hooked through his elbow, muzzle down, as if the weapon were an extension of his arm. When she halted beside him, he leaned the Winchester against his thigh and wrapped an arm about her. He pulled her toward him and settled her in front of him. Her shoulder blades pressed against his chest. His arms bracketed her on either side, and his hands crossed over her stomach.

She leaned back against him. He rested his chin on her hair.

"What is it?" she whispered. "Why are you out here?"

"I heard horses and cattle over the ridge. I came out to check."

"Who do you think it is?"

"Men moving cattle at night can only mean rustlers."

Della turned her head and tipped her face up to better converse with her husband. The back of her head rubbed against his chest muscles. "Could you tell how many?"

He shook his head. "There are many, but I cannot separate the cattle from the riders just by sound."

They stood in silence while Wild Wind listened. At last, he stirred. "They are gone."

"I don't know how you do that. I couldn't hear anything."

"Warriors are trained from an early age to hear everything. If it had just been horses, I could have told you how many riders there were." With an arm about her shoulders and the rifle in his other hand, he turned her toward their lodge. "Come, wife. Let us return to our buffalo robes. I will track them in the morning."

Wild Wind left at first light. He kissed Della good-bye and rode over the ridge to trail the cattle and rustlers. She puttered about the camp, straightening their things in the lodge, tidying up the bedding, washing the dishes, and brushing her palomino mare with a fistful of grass. When she ran out of chores, she wandered to the creek and settled down on the bank. She hooked her arms about her updrawn legs and rested her chin on her knees.

The brook swirled and eddied between its shallow banks. Della stared at the water and contemplated her married state. She and Wild Wind had spent five days alone on the prairie. They'd talked, lazed about the camp, and ridden the range. Wild Wind had promised Uncle Clint that he'd check on the cattle and keep an eye out for anything that looked suspicious. Her uncle suspected that the oil consortium would send men back onto the property for their own nefarious purposes and wanted Wild Wind to check out the land.

The Slash L line riders were out there somewhere, but there were too many acres for the men to patrol all the grazing grounds. Another couple of riders would be an invaluable asset.

Della picked up a pebble and tossed it into the water. Droplets splashed, and ripples spread out from where the stone had entered the brook. She curled her hands about her knees and leaned back, tipping her face up to the sky.

She blushed as she thought of her nights with her husband. Wild Wind was a most loving groom. She knew he wanted a son, and she hoped that soon she'd be able to tell him she carried their child.

An abrupt cessation of birdsong warned her that something was amiss. Something had caused the birds to hush their music. She straightened and looked over her shoulder toward the teepee. Four riders sat their horses in a semicircle between her and the lodge.

Fear gripped her. Her heart began a rhythmic hammering against her ribs, and her mouth went dry. She'd forgotten to bring the six-shooter Wild Wind had left her. How could she have been so careless? Now, she had no means to defend herself.

Della climbed to her feet and pivoted to face the men, tipping up her chin. She refused to let them see how they terrified her.

As if by an invisible signal, the intruders walked their mounts toward her. By their clothing, three of them appeared to be Easterners. They wore Derby hats with rolled brims, brown tweed jackets, and flat-heeled riding boots.

The fourth man frightened Della more than the others. His craggy face was sun-browned and weathered. Pale, cold eyes ogled her, and his thin mouth had a cruel slant. He wore a brown leather vest over a stained white shirt and denim pants tucked into worn heeled riding boots. A battered flat-crowned hat rode low over his brow.

The men halted their horses in front of her.

Della swallowed hard as four pairs of eyes studied her. It took every bit of her Beacon Hill upbringing to address them with her most haughty society air. She straightened her shoulders and stared down her nose at them. "May I help you gentlemen?" she asked her most refined Boston voice.

The down-at-the-heels saddle tramp whistled. "Gents, we've got ourselves a real la-de-dah lady."

The other three men continued to study her. One of them dismounted and strode toward her. He came to a standstill before her and perused her from head to toe. Della felt like a butterfly impaled on a pin.

She kept her head high, staring back at him with her best lady-of-the manor air.

The man was handsome in a thin-faced, urbane way. A chestnut mustache covered his upper lip. "Who are you, and what are you doing here?" He gripped Della's upper arm and pulled her closer.

She glared up at him. "I might ask the same of you."

His fingers tightened about her arm. "Ma'am, you're in a precarious position. We didn't count on running into anyone, and now that you've seen us, we can't let you go."

One of the other men who still sat astride, spoke. "She has to be Clint Logan's niece. The reports we received from the agency gave a detailed description of everyone in his family."

The man's expression turned speculative. "Perhaps she can be of use to us. Clint Logan might be more willing to give up his grazing rights if he knows we have his niece."

Easterners. Their accent betrayed them.

Della kept her face impassive, though her mind whirled. These intruders had to be on the oil consortium's payroll. From the quality of their clothing and their speech, they most likely would be comfortable in the drawing rooms of her Boston acquaintances. They'd be high up in the consortium's leadership structure. She guessed the saddle tramp had been hired as a guide.

The gentleman holding her jerked her about and hauled her up the slope. On the way, he passed his ground-hitched gelding and snatched up the trailing reins. She struggled to keep up.

The others followed. When they reached the teepee, he shoved her onto the ground beside the entrance. "Don't move." He turned toward the saddle tramp. "Jed, watch her. See that she doesn't go anywhere."

Jed scrambled off his gelding and loomed over her, leering down at her. "You can't be such a real la-di-dah lady if you took up with a redskin." He spat a globule of tobacco juice in the direction of her feet. His lips twisted in a sneer and displayed long, yellowed teeth.

Della tucked her toes closer to her body and turned her face away. She didn't dignify his comment with a reply.

The other two men dismounted and joined the first man. They ducked into the lodge.

Della heard them moving about inside, ransacking hers and Wild Wind's belongings. She wondered what they hoped to find. Finally, with exclamations of disgust, they squeezed back through the oval entrance.

The leader stood over her, hands on his hips, his brown eyes narrowed. "Ma'am, you'll have to come with us. You're a valuable bargaining chip." Bending down, he grabbed her arm and pulled her to her feet.

She jerked away and glared at him. "You'd be wise not to abduct me. When my husband returns, he will hunt you down."

Her captor shrugged and narrowed his eyes at her. "Husband? I doubt that he's your husband. Redskins don't understand love as we know it. He'll find himself another woman. You're coming with us."

"You're wrong. My husband loves me. He is a Dog Soldier and a Cheyenne chieftain. He will avenge me."

Jed sneered. "We ain't had no Injun trouble here this summer. You're just tryin' to scare us into leavin' you here."

Della gambled that Jed had lived in the West long enough to have heard stories of the feared Dog Soldier, Wild Wind. Perhaps invoking her husband's name would help. She addressed the saddle tramp with more confidence than she felt. "Have you heard of the Dog Soldier, Wild Wind?"

Jed's startled expression told her that he'd heard of her husband's reputation.

"My husband is Wild Wind."

Fear replaced the startled look on Jed's face before he covered his lapse with bravado. "Ain't true. That Dog Soldier is dead."

"I assure you, Wild Wind is very much alive, and you don't want to cross him by taking me."

Jed licked his lips. "He ain't been seen in two years. He's dead, I tell you."

"If you take me with you, you'll find out that he's very much alive."

The russet-haired gentleman who appeared to be the leader grabbed Della's arm again. "Come on. We're wasting time. What has a redskin who hasn't been seen in two years have to do with us?"

Within minutes, one of the men had tacked up the palomino mare and tossed Della into the saddle. Being ponied along on a lead line, her mare accompanied the men's horses.

Della struggled to keep her fear at bay. Wild Wind would find her. He would come for her. She tried to find comfort in the thought.

CHAPTER 39

Della's bound hands rested on the saddle horn. The mid-afternoon sun bleached color from the sky and baked the range. Droplets of perspiration ran down her neck into the collar of her riding blouse. With her tied hands, she dabbed her face with her bandana as best she could.

They'd ridden all day yesterday and camped at evening. Early in the morning, they'd broken camp and mounted up. With only a short break for a nooning, they'd been riding since sunup.

As much as she resented the Easterners, she feared their guide and his ogling eyes more. The leader kept her close to him, away from the uncouth Jed. She felt marginally safer with him, and she didn't resist when he kept her at his side.

She listened to the men's conversation, hoping to learn as much about them as possible. They made no effort to keep secrets from her. They were indeed associated with the oil consortium and apparently had plans to meet up with a drilling crew.

Della straightened her shoulders and lifted her head. Wild Wind would rescue her soon. Their trail would be child's play for him to follow. Jed was either lazy or incompetent, for he made little effort to conceal their passing and had done nothing to erase the signs of their night camp. The Easterners were such tenderfeet that they didn't recognize his ineptness.

The pound of hooves sounded behind them, and a blood-curdling Cheyenne war cry shattered the afternoon's silence. *Wild Wind!* He'd come for her. Della twisted in her saddle to look over her shoulder.

Silhouetted for a brief instant against the sky, a black and white piebald horse mounted by an Indian brave riding bareback wearing nothing but a breechcloth and moccasins crested the knoll. The horse and rider hurtled down the near side at a ground-devouring run. Black and red war paint masked Wild Wind's face. Her husband brandished a rifle over his head. A second war cry split the air. Even as Della watched, he slipped to one side of his mount and fired from beneath the gelding's neck.

Wild Wind's galloping war horse closed the distance between him and the panicked oil men. Their mounts whirled in a melee of flashing manes, bunching muscles, and tossing heads.

While his face contorted with terror, Jed clawed for his six-shooter and tried to control his bucking horse. He managed to get his weapon out and aimed a shot at the warrior before a blast from Wild Wind's Winchester knocked him from the saddle. Jed cartwheeled onto the grass and lay still.

Another bullet from Wild Wind's rifle felled one of the oil men. Then he was upon them. His war horse, ears flattened against its head, mane and tail streaming behind him, smashed its shoulder into the group leader's mount at a full gallop. The other horse staggered to its knees, and the rider somersaulted over his gelding's neck onto the ground.

Della's palomino mare shied sideways, out of range of the fallen horse.

Wild Wind snapped off a final shot at the last oil man, who was disappearing over a ridge, his spooked mount bolting from the terrifying creature who'd descended upon them in vengeful wrath.

Wild Wind pulled his mount to a halt just beyond his fallen foe. The piebald sank to its haunches, muscles flexing and front legs bracing as it plunged to a stop. Before the horse had halted, Wild Wind leaped from its back and launched himself at Della's captor. The man was just rising to his knees when Wild Wind knocked him backward. His eyes glowed with battle light, and his mouth grimaced. One knee pressed against the Easterner's chest, pinning him to the earth. Wild Wind's strong brown hands gripped the other's wrists, immobilizing him against the ground. His chest pumped.

The oil man's Derby hat had gone spinning off into the buffalo grass when he fell. Now, his stylish chestnut hair fell in disarray about his head. His tweed jacket sported grass stains and a rip along one seam. His eyes, filled with the expectation of certain death, fixed on Wild Wind's painted face. Droplets of perspiration dripped from his temple down into his hair.

An abrupt silence hung in the air while the two men stared at each other.

Della watched her husband struggle with his decision. His inclination, honed by years of combat, was to slay his fallen opponent. His new-found faith contradicted that action.

At last, Wild Wind spoke, his voice ragged with anger. A thread of steel overlaid his words. "I should kill you for taking my wife. He who takes the wife of a Cheyenne chieftain does not live."

Her terrified captor didn't respond. Della spared a moment's pity for him, knowing that he was out of his element, faced with an enemy he couldn't begin to understand or combat. He belonged behind a desk in a city where civilization ruled, but his greed had taken him from his natural habitat to an untamed frontier. He'd chosen to operate outside of the law, so he'd suffer by the code of the West.

"If you have harmed my wife in any way, I will kill you." Wild Wind's soft, lethal tone left no doubt that he meant what he said.

"I-I didn't hurt her. I d-didn't touch her in any way except to tie her up." The man's voice shook. "You can ask her. She'll tell you."

Wild Wind canted his head to look up at Della. "Does he speak truth?"

"Yes, he's telling you the truth. I'm fine." She managed a weak smile to reassure her husband.

After a long moment, Wild Wind relented. He released his captive and stood, legs braced wide apart, staring down at the other man. He reached for the knife at his waist. The weapon slid from its sheath with a deadly hiss. Its wicked blade gleamed in the slanting afternoon rays. He bent and brandished the weapon beneath the Easterner's nose. "Do not move. If you move, first I will take your hair. Then, I will slit you open and leave you to bleed out on the grass."

His face blanched white, the frightened man nodded.

Wild Wind turned his back on his captive in a dismissive gesture and strode toward Della. He halted beside her mare. "Give me your hands."

Della held out her bound hands. With a single slicing motion, her husband cut the rope that entwined her wrists. The bonds fell to the earth. Leaning down, she tumbled from the saddle into Wild Wind's arms. He caught her up and wrapped her close. Breathing in his scent, she snuggled against him. His strength and warmth surrounded her. She was safe.

∽

"Now Uncle Clint should be able to stop the oil consortium from drilling on his range. With the confession of the man you captured, he has the proof in writing."

Della and Wild Wind rode their mounts at an easy walk across the prairie. They'd delivered their demoralized captive to her uncle, and Clint had extracted the whole story from him. After the prisoner had made a full confession, Uncle Clint and Wild Wind had taken him to Fort Bridger and turned him over to the military. Then, they'd returned to the Slash L, gathered up the men who remained on the ranch during the summer, and ridden to where the drilling crew had begun building the first derrick. A battle with the drillers had ended in defeat for the oil company, and the cowboys had torn down the derrick and escorted the oil men to the fort.

At the moment, Uncle Clint was on his way to Denver, where he'd take a train to Washington to sort out the situation.

"We don't know for sure how many cattle were rustled," Della said.

"We will get a tally when we bring the cattle in from the summer range." Wild Wind, once more wearing cowboy garb, scanned the horizon, alert for danger.

"And to think that the oil consortium thought they could hire men to rustle enough cattle to hurt Uncle Clint financially. Enough so that he'd have to sell the Slash L."

"We will survive this. Your uncle knows what he is about."

Della caught Wild Wind's use of the pronoun "we". Warmth spread through her. "Do you know what you just said?"

He turned his head toward her. "What?"

"You just said 'we'. As if you're part of the ranch."

Beneath his hat brim a slow smile warmed his face. "Lona, I am part of the ranch. I am the heart of your heart, brother to your uncle. We are all one. As you are one with The People. My people are your people."

Della brought her mare closer to his mount. Reaching out, she covered his hand with hers. "I like the sound of that. I'm so very glad I married you."

His hand turned beneath hers, and he squeezed her fingers. "I am very glad, too."

They reached the teepee they'd abandoned when they'd taken their prisoner to the ranch. Now, they'd returned to finish their honeymoon before moving to the Slash L.

They halted their horses and dismounted. Wild Wind stripped off the tack and hobbled their mounts. Then, with an arm about Della's shoulders, they approached the lodge entrance, hips bumping. Just outside the opening, Wild Wind tugged her to a stop.

"Wife, I need you. Now." His husky voice mirrored his need. "My heart overflows, and I must show you my love."

Della curved her arms about her husband's neck and lifted her face to his. "Yes, show me your love."

EPILOGUE

Della lifted the teepee's privacy flap and stepped out into Montana's afternoon sunshine. Using a long-handled metal stirring spoon, she dug at the packed dirt that mounded above the beef haunch roasting over hot coals. She uncovered the meat, and the savory scent of baking beef wafted upward. The roast should be ready to eat by the time Wild Wind and Jake returned from their hunt.

She straightened and ran her hand over her belly's burgeoning mound where she carried Wild Wind's child. Their baby would be born in the early autumn.

She and Wild Wind had been married for a year. They'd been living in his village ever since they'd traveled to the reservation last fall with the cattle provided by the Slash L. Because of her pregnancy, they'd elected not to make the risky trip back to the Slash L for the spring and summer months but had stayed on with his people. Their child would be born here, in their lodge.

Della laid the spoon on a flat rock beside the coals and straightened. The fringe hanging from the sleeves of her deerskin dress jiggled. She wriggled her toes in her moccasins and sighed with pleasure. Moccasins were more comfortable than riding boots.

Around her, the teepees of Wild Wind's band thrust up from the soil.

Children ran between the lodges. Yapping dogs chased after the children. Women chatted outside their lodges.

A clatter of hooves caught Della's attention. Wild Wind and Jake trotted into the camp, an antelope draped over the withers of her husband's mount. The hunt had been successful.

They halted their horses in front of the lodge. Wild Wind slid from his bare-backed gelding and strode toward her, leaving his mount's reins dangling. A deerskin shirt decorated with beading and dyed porcupine quills molded his muscular form.

As he strode toward her, Della eyed her husband's shirt. With Neha's help, she'd cut out the leather and sewn the shirt together, then decorated the front with beads and porcupine quills to make an intricate pattern. She'd taken every stitch with love, and now, Wild Wind wore the shirt with pride.

"I see you brought home more meat." She tipped her head toward the antelope that draped her husband's horse. "We'll have plenty to share with Yellow Wolf and Neha."

"There will be no hunger in our lodges for many days. We will not have to eat beef." Wild Wind came to a stop before her and laid one hand over the soft deerskin dress at the place where their child grew. His blue eyes heated. "My son grows large in your womb."

Della covered his hand with her own. "He's certainly getting big."

The child kicked hard against the pressure of Wild Wind's palm, and her husband laughed. "He will be a strong warrior."

Jake slid from his horse and trotted toward them. Della watched her son approach. He'd shot up several inches since that spring day over two years ago when Wild Wind had first come to the Slash L. His face had thinned and lost its little-boy look. Now, a golden tan colored his features, and he carried himself with a confidence he'd acquired since Wild Wind had become a father to him.

Jake stopped before her. Excitement gleamed in his eyes. "Papa Wild Wind let me shoot his rifle. He said that one day soon, I should be able to kill my first antelope."

Della laid a hand on her son's buckskin-clad shoulder. "That will be a proud day when you bring home meat for the family."

Jake nodded and grinned. He'd taken to life in the Cheyenne camp with gusto and had made many friends among the other boys.

Della's glance slid up to her husband's face. His eyes crinkled in a smile when he caught her look. His love for her warmed his hard countenance. His hand slid from the spot where their child grew and circled around her back. He pulled her close and snuggled her against his side. She laid her head on his chest.

Though they hadn't married years ago when they'd first met, their union now was all the sweeter for the time they'd been apart. Each day was a precious gift from the Lord. Della leaned into Wild Wind's embrace, secure in the knowledge that although their future might be difficult as they navigated two cultures, together, they could face whatever lay ahead.

∽

Like what you read?
Don't miss these other books in the
FRONTIER HEARTS SAGA:

Her Traitor's Heart
Wounded Heart

Keep reading for a sneak peek at
RACHEL'S VALLEY
By Alice Patron

RACHEL'S VALLEY

BY ALICE PATRON

Chapter 1

RACHEL CLOSED HER EYES AND let her exhausted body fall onto her much-too-thin mattress on the floor. Well, not actually *her* mattress, but the mattress she had slept on for the last twenty-three months.

She was in a town of dreamers. Daily, men came into town, believing their fortune lay just beneath the soil. And daily, she saw other men leaving town; men whose burnt-out dreams had matured them in only a few weeks' time, men who realized that dreams couldn't make a living. At least not in this town.

She turned onto her stomach and reached to the other side of the bed. She pulled up the edge of the mattress enough to uncover the loose floorboard. A hiding place was necessary since a boarding house was just the sort of place that valuable belongings could easily disappear in, even inside her locked room. Especially in an ever-changing mining town in the West where the faces were different from week to week.

She reached in and took out the two things hidden there: five dollars and some change, and the clipping from yesterday's newspaper. She gently unfolded the clipping she had taken out of the Denver newspaper that circulated in Givens Grove and read it again, although she knew the contents well. *Wanted: caretaker/tutor for 2 girls. Room and board. $2 per month. Send application to Breckenridge, Colorado Post Office, c.o. Clint Harvey.*

The bell tinkling above her head brought a deep sigh from Rachel.

She quickly stood, rubbing her temples as she did so.

"Coming!" she called out as she neared the front door. Whoever it was at the door was knocking loudly. She didn't want him to rouse the whole house.

She whipped the door open and ushered the man inside. "Are you staying the night, Sir?" she asked.

"Yes, Ma'am."

Rachel grabbed a fresh pillow and blanket from the stack inside the entry closet, then stepped into Mr. Barker's office for an oil lamp. She didn't need the light to find her way in the dark, but she knew the new boarder would need it. She turned toward the man, the lit lamp in one hand and the pillow and blanket in the other. As the man looked down into Rachel's face, his eyebrows rose and a smirk made one side of his mouth come up. Now that she could see him properly, she saw what she saw in so many of the boarders that came through Givens Grove—his hair was long and disheveled, he had a beard that still bore remnants from his supper, and the state of his clothes would not pass the approval of any mother she knew.

Rachel took a small step away from him and tried to keep her tone formal. "You'll be in room three. This way, Mister." She said it with a little more disdain in her voice than she meant to use. She walked quickly up the stairs, assuming the man would follow.

"Wait, honey, slow down."

Rachel clenched her teeth and closed her eyes momentarily. She swung around. "Listen…"

The man interrupted her by grabbing her hand roughly as she faced him. She could smell his rancid breath even before he spoke. "Hang on, Princess, I ain't going to do nothing." The smirky grin returned to his face. "I just was wondering, what are you doing tonight? I ain't feeling too sleepy."

She could tell the man was drunk. Usually, they were when they showed up to rent a room after midnight. "Here is your room, Sir," she whispered, setting the lamp on the candleholder by the door and not giving him the satisfaction of an answer to his question.

"Why don't you tuck me in?" he said as he pulled on her free arm to try to get her into the bedroom. She could hear a few of the boarders stir inside the shared room.

She yanked her arm firmly from his grasp, tossed the bedding from her other arm on his bedroom floor and ran down the stairs as fast as the darkness and her skirt would allow, listening to the awful man laugh at her from his open bedroom door. She shut her door and bolted it. At least she hadn't had to wake the whole house by calling for Mr. Barker. That was always an embarrassing ordeal.

Rachel dropped onto her bed again and grabbed the crinkled newspaper clipping next to her. She couldn't live this way anymore. That boarder tonight had certainly not been the worst she had encountered, but he was the pile of manure to tip the wheelbarrow of stink that seemed to make up her life. She pulled a clean sheet of paper from the top of her small stack of borrowed books at the foot of the bed.

Two years was just a little too long to wait for Roger. Besides, like so many in this town, her dreams were really starting to burn out.

~

Rachel rose early the next morning, her excitement overcoming her exhaustion from the day before. It took her mind a few moments to remember why she felt so antsy.

"The letter!" she remarked to herself. She scrambled to the other side of the mattress and again lifted the floorboard.

"I hope this works," she said to no one in particular in a half-whisper as she lifted out her letter. "Please," she said, directing her thoughts heavenward, "I need this job so badly. I can't take one more day of this!"

As if on cue, Mr. Barker rapped his usual three staccato knocks on her door.

"I won't miss that wake-up call," she said quietly, her eyes lighting up at the thought.

"I won't miss this mattress," she muttered to herself as she sat up and massaged a kink in her shoulder. She looked around the small "room" she had lived in for almost two years. "And I won't miss this room, either."

Mr. Barker had justified giving her the tiniest room, which was probably originally meant as a closet in the large house. It didn't even have a window. But since she was so petite, he concluded that she had better stay there rather than take up valuable customer living space.

For the first time in a long time, Rachel sighed out of contentment. She wouldn't miss much of anything at the boarding house. Not the long work hours, nor the lack of women to befriend in town, but she especially wouldn't miss the miners that constantly came and went through Givens Grove that were taken by her beauty. Their unfiltered comments were always unwelcome, no matter how handsome the man may be. She was a married woman. And whether they knew that or not, she resented all those men for any hint of flirtation, no matter whether their words were kind or unkind. It was just ironic to her that, in her youth, she had flaunted her beauty and exulted in the fact that she could win over almost any man's attention. Now her looks had become a burden.

With that sobering truth in mind, Rachel changed into her plain, brown work dress, brushed and tied up her thick, auburn hair, and hurried out of the boarding house with her letter.

"Hello, Rachel," old Mrs. Givens cheerfully greeted her as she unlocked the post office door for her friend. Her eyebrows came together in concern. "Another letter for Roger?"

Rachel managed a half-hearted smile. "Not this time." She held out the letter to Mrs. Givens.

"Breckenridge," Mrs. Givens murmured, "who do you know there? I'm not even sure where that is."

Rachel took a deep breath and smiled. "I'm hoping to get taken on as a governess for a family there." Though the advertisement asked for a caretaker and tutor, Rachel thought governess wasn't too far stretching the truth. It sounded more sophisticated.

"Oh!" Mrs. Givens looked up from the letter in surprise. "I'm not going to lie, that would be a fair bit better than what you've got at the boarding house—I know how Mr. Barker works you to the bone. But what about Roger? What if he comes back?"

"I was actually hoping you could help me, Mrs. Givens." Rachel said. "If Roger comes back, or sends a letter, could you pass the word along to me at the address on that envelope?" she asked gesturing with her head to the letter Mrs. Givens now held.

"Oh, I see," Mrs. Givens said, a look of relief on her face. "I was hoping you weren't giving up on him."

"He's my husband," Rachel said. "I can't give up that easily." *No matter how much I wish I could.*

Mrs. Givens reached across the small counter and gave her a motherly pat on the shoulder. "Well, don't you worry none, Rachel. You have my word; I will send a letter if I hear anything about your husband."

"Well, Mr. Barker has probably noticed my absence by now." Rachel turned and opened the post office door as she thanked Mrs. Givens.

"You poor dear," Mrs. Givens said, as if Rachel couldn't hear her.

∼

Thoughts of the hoped-for governess job had faded for Rachel. For the first week, she told herself the post must be slow to get to Breckenridge. She wasn't even sure how far away it was. But at the end of the second week, she had started looking in the paper for other positions—mainly in Denver where there was a better chance of finding respectable work. She knew she needed to leave Givens Grove. Her job at the boarding house wasn't always so terrible, she admitted to herself, but now she felt a sliver of excitement when she thought of living somewhere where the people would not know her only for her disappointing marriage. She was almost as tired of the looks of pity from the women and married men as she was of the looks of lust from the single men.

Rachel was in the middle of making up the beds with fresh sheets when old Mrs. Givens came hobbling and huffing up the stairs. Rachel dropped the sheets on the nearest bed and hurried to the head of the stairs.

Mrs. Givens was trying to catch her breath as she grabbed the banister and hauled herself up to the top stair. She held out a thin letter to Rachel and caught her breath, fixing her shawl as she did so. Rachel smiled as she realized her friend must have been in a rush to reach her. Her usually tidy bun was somewhat disheveled.

Rachel took the letter in one hand and Mrs. Givens's arm with the other hand. "Come sit down for a moment, Mrs. Givens."

"Thank you, Rachel." Mrs. Givens wobbled over to the bed and sat next to Rachel's clean stack of sheets. "Now," Mrs. Givens said between breaths, "what does the letter say?"

Rachel unceremoniously tore open the thin envelope and took out the note from inside. She nervously read aloud: "Miss Wood, I'm pleased to offer you the position as caretaker for my daughters. The pass is clear. Please come as soon as transportation can be arranged. Send word of your plans so that I can meet you at the post office at Breckenridge when you come. If I don't receive any word from you within two weeks, I will assume that you have made other plans, and I will continue looking to fill the position. Sincerely, Clint Harvey."

Rachel sat down by Mrs. Givens, unsure of what to do or say. *She was going to leave Givens Grove!*

Mrs. Givens patted Rachel's leg. "Well, I'm going to miss having you around. This town could use more respectable women like you." Then she stood up and looked down at her. "But I'm happy for you, Rachel."

As Rachel stood and hugged her plump friend, she realized it was the first time she had done so. Now that she would be leaving Givens Grove, she felt that Mrs. Givens was the one person she might actually miss.

"There, there," Mrs. Givens said, pulling Rachel back from her. "You just make sure you stay the same good person as always." Mrs. Givens raised one finger at Rachel, reminding her of one of her mother's lectures. "Don't go falling for another man. You hold out for your Roger, and I'll let you know the moment I get word about him."

Rachel laughed lightly. She had a habit of laughing whenever she felt nervous or uncomfortable. "I promise I won't do anything a respectable woman wouldn't do." She tried to put on a more serious look to reassure Mrs. Givens. "I promise I won't 'go after another man'. I can't. As long as there is a chance that Roger is alive, I'll wait for him." Not that Rachel was at all worried about falling for another man. She had lived and worked alongside men, by herself, for twenty-three months and not once had she felt tempted by any one of them.

"Good." Mrs. Givens seemed satisfied. "Well, I left the post office unattended. I'd better get back."

"Thank you for bringing the letter."

"You are welcome, my dear." Mrs. Givens turned and walked out of the room. Rachel faintly heard her say, "The poor dear," as she hobbled downstairs.

Once Mrs. Givens was out the door, Rachel raced down the stairs herself. Mr. Barker might not notice her absence for a few minutes, so this was as good a time as ever to find a ride to Breckenridge. Mr. Givens was usually at the corral, at this time anyway, hiring out horses to miners for the day.

RACHEL'S VALLEY

As Rachel dried the last of the supper dishes that night, she felt she was ready to break the news to Mr. Barker. She'd had time while cooking and serving the food to rehearse what she would say, and her boss was always in his happiest mood after mealtime. She had prepared his favorite—fried ham and cheese sandwiches—to help his mood as best she could.

She walked into his front office where he was taking a monthly payment from one of their regular boarders. Even better. A full stomach *and* a payment.

"Rachel, what can I do for you?" he said rather amiably as the boarder shuffled past her out the doorway.

Rachel bit her top lip, took a deep breath, then began. "Sir, I just want to say that I am so grateful for this job that has allowed me to stay in Givens Grove for these past two years."

She noticed his eyebrows rise as if questioning what she would say next. She knew it would be better to make it short. That way his anger wouldn't have a chance to build.

"I've applied for a job as a governess in Breckenridge, and I just received a letter back that I've been accepted for the position."

Rachel instinctively took a step back as Mr. Barker slowly got up from his desk.

After a couple of muttered curses from Mr. Barker, he said, "Well, being a governess will suit you, I suppose." He shrugged, then added, "You know, if you last more than three days at it."

Well, that went rather well, Rachel thought. "Are you going to be able to find a replacement?"

"Yeah, I suppose I will be able to," he said. "There's always a disaffected miner that's looking for work. Not that any of them would do half as good as you." He stood and ran a hand over his nearly bald head. "I hope you know what kind of a situation you're leaving me in, though. My boarders are going to be upset when they don't see a pretty face around here anymore."

"Oh." Rachel couldn't think of a reply to that.

"When do you leave?" Mr. Barker asked calmly.

"A week from today. Mr. Givens will be taking me up."

Mr. Barker sighed. "Fine."

Rachel hadn't expected for this conversation to go so well. She figured she'd better take advantage of his momentary good nature. "I just need to send a letter to the family, so they know when to expect me. I'd better go now before the post office closes. It shouldn't take more than ten minutes."

"Just make sure you are back and starting on your nightly cleaning within ten minutes, or I'll have to turn you out today!" Mr. Barker sat down at his desk again and waved Rachel away with his hand.

As she hurried out the door for the post office, Rachel suddenly felt a weight lift off her shoulders and was filled with a sense of hope she hadn't known in almost two years.

Want more?
Get your copy now!

Made in the USA
Middletown, DE
06 October 2024